COMFREY, WYOMING

BIRDS OF A FEATHER

COMFREY, WYOMING

BIRDS OF A FEATHER

DAPHNE BIRKMYER

atmosphere press

PART ONE:
HEIDI AND NARA

CHAPTER ONE

LAYING LOW IN PENNSYLVANIA: 1988

Even at 3:30 in the morning, with detours and wrong turns, it took Heidi Vogel almost an hour to get from Lower Manhattan to the George Washington Bridge. It took her less time to cross the entire state of New Jersey. The heavy black Mercedes insulated her from the sounds of the road and the other cars also hurtling west. Billboards, gas stations and off ramps whipped by like props in a silent movie. She tried to keep an eye on the speedometer. Her husband, Claus, often accused her of driving too fast. The speedometer registered ninety; she swore to herself and slowed to seventy-five.

By the time she reached Pennsylvania, early morning commuters were spewing onto the freeway, jockeying for position at speeds that made Heidi recall the Autobahn. She slowed down as a car on the right and another on the left tried to enter the lane directly in front of her. They veered back into their lanes with a blaring of horns.

"Gottverdammte Idioten!" she shouted, her words bouncing off the car's interior. And they were 'goddamn idiots' to tempt fate so, as if life was something to throw away. She gave a dry sob. Didn't they realize their families would never heal if they died? Never.

Numb with fatigue and afraid she was no longer safe to drive, Heidi exited onto a small road heading north and

3

stopped in the first town with an open diner. She turned off the engine and pressed her palms to her face, taking comfort in the fact that her eyes, her cheekbones and lips still felt familiar. She leaned over and removed a small bundle of ashes from its carved wooden box in the glove compartment. With the bundle in her pocket, she opened the car door into an early morning that was already warming.

It was too early for families, and other than two workmen sitting at the counter chatting to the waitress, the diner was empty. The waitress called to Heidi to sit anywhere, so she slid into a booth by the window and held onto the edge of the table until the world righted itself. When a glance at her reflection in the window showed a shockingly haggard and vulnerable face, she straightened her shoulders, ran a tongue over her lips and looked again. Better.

She politely rebuffed the waitress's attempt get her to order the breakfast special and refused the menu, insisting she wanted just coffee and toast.

"And where's that accent from?" asked the waitress, tucking the menu back under her arm.

"Germany."

"I always thought of German women as heavier. Cream with that coffee?"

"We come in all sizes, and yes please, to the cream."

When her toast arrived, Heidi examined the chrome-plated rack that held stacks of jelly, grape on one side and mixed fruit on the other. They would taste much the same. She could hear Karl Engel, her second cousin and closest friend, railing against yet another example of convenience over quality. How much more it would it cost to serve strawberry preserves in an individual white china pot? Five cents? Ten?

She watched a small group of men pause on their way into the diner to examine the diesel Mercedes parked close enough to the lights of the entrance that its red leather interior glowed. She and Claus had told his father a car in New York City would be a nuisance, so of course he'd sent something large and ostentatious. For most of the last five years, it had remained parked in an exorbitantly priced, subterranean garage.

When the men entered, they cast their eyes around for the owner of the expensive foreign car and of course it would be her, a young woman with almost platinum blonde hair, sitting alone. She gave a brief nod but didn't return their smiles. From a young age she had learned to use indifference as a shield against unwanted attention.

A second cup of coffee did little to lift her fatigue. She hadn't slept in over twenty-four hours; she had no idea where she was going. Chicago, Toronto, San Francisco? Big cities with big jobs for an executive chef, or perhaps she would become absorbed into the midden of a small town somewhere and spend her days greeting customers with descriptions of the breakfast special. She felt almost ill with exhaustion.

The word '*SORRY*' written in neon script flashed from the window of the inn across the road. In Germany, a simple '*Kein*' would light up in front of '*Zimmer Frei,*' for 'No Room Free.' '*SORRY,*' such an American affectation, but kind. Sorry, no room in the inn, sorry, be on your way, but there were few cars parked next to the cabins over there and she might be in luck. When the waitress came to top off her coffee, Heidi asked when the inn's office opened.

"Around nine but I can phone over and get Ivan to open up earlier. He's not full so he won't object." The woman gave Heidi an assessing look. "You on the run?"

Heidi shook her head. "There is no one chasing me," she said, knowing it to be true. Claus, his father, and their perfectly groomed business manager, Anke Mueller, would think three days' cash from the safe and the Mercedes a small price to pay for her leaving.

Her father-in-law, Emmett Vogel, had flown in from

Hamburg and since Anke now oversaw several of his businesses in New York, it made sense that she, and not Heidi, would accompany Claus to his suite at The Plaza. Did Emmett hire someone to look for cystic fibrosis in the Mueller family background before introducing Anke to his son?

"Of course, he did," Heidi murmured, closing her eyes and fading into the sounds she knew so well—the swing of a kitchen door, the scrape of fork, the babble.

A gentle hand on her shoulder woke her with a start. Disoriented, she sat up and shook her head, her mouth as dry as cotton.

"I said, Ivan's waiting for you. You can go on over," the waitress whispered.

"Ivan? I am sorry . . . ?"

"Ivan, the innkeeper, he's waiting for you. If you make a fuss over his cat, he'll give you a cabin with a kitchenette, useful if you have to lay low for a while."

A bell jangled over the door as Heidi entered the office. A tall, cadaverous-looking man carrying a large white Persian cat materialized behind the reception counter and gave her a thin-lipped smile. The cat's luxurious tail gave a flutter as it examined Heidi with interest through copper-colored eyes.

"What is your name?" she asked the cat.

"Tabitha Mandova Bonnet," said the man, coming out from behind the counter so she could get a better look at the Persian's snub-nosed magnificence. "I'm Ivan Sinsky, her companion animal."

"My parents owned a lovely Siamese cat," offered Heidi, smiling at them both.

Ivan's mouth pinched in distaste. "One cannot actually *own* a sentient being."

"No, of course not, I speak before I think." Heidi silently vowed to look up 'sentient' in her pocket dictionary later. "May I just call her Tabitha?"

"Indeed, you may, but never Tabby."

"I can see how Tabby would not suit." Heidi reached out to touch the cat's long, silky hair. "You must have to brush her every day to keep her coat so beautiful."

"Every day." Ivan ran a long hand down the length of Tabitha's back. "We sit on a bench by the river out back and have ourselves a brush. Both Queen Victoria and Florence Nightingale lived with Persian cats."

"I am not surprised." Heidi stifled a yawn.

"I assume a cabin for yourself and . . . ?" Ivan looked over her shoulder.

"Myself and no one," said Heidi, "and I will please pay in cash."

"Ah." Ivan gave a slow nod and went back behind the counter. "A cabin with a kitchenette at the end then, where the birches will hide your car. You'll be perfectly safe. One night? Two? We do have a weekly rate."

"Today, perhaps tomorrow. I do not . . ." Heidi faltered, so unlike her not to have a plan.

"Never mind, we're not overly booked. I'll need to look at your license and if you like, you may hold Tabitha while I take down your information. She is partial to a foreign accent."

When the cat's languid form was transferred into her arms, Heidi released an audible sigh. She bent her head and whispered, "Your coat makes you appear so much heavier than you are."

"Twelve pounds," said Ivan, proudly.

Twelve pounds. Heidi placed her lips on that kissable spot between a cat's ears to inhale Tabitha's warmth. Peter had weighed just over twelve pounds when she had held him for the very last time. Silent on their crepe-soled shoes, the nurses came in to check on her as his body cooled. An hour passed before she had been able to let them take her baby from her.

The cabin smelled faintly of mildew, but was otherwise

7

clean. It had a stovetop, a little refrigerator, a cabinet with minimal but sufficient kitchenware, and a surprisingly comfortable bed. Heidi returned to the Mercedes to plumb the depths of its trunk. She found the hiking boots she had bought for the one trip she and Claus took to Maine, with socks still stuffed inside, and a pair of sandals. There was also a sweatshirt and a T-shirt belonging to Claus—much too big, but welcome nonetheless—a rain poncho and a skimpy halter-top she couldn't recall ever wearing. She brought her meager supplies inside, then went back to retrieve the road atlas and Peter's carved wooden box. A telephone and radio-alarm clock crowded the nightstand's surface but there was room for the box if she put it over a laminated sign that read 'Local Calls Only. Use Office for Long Distance.'

Heidi looked longingly at the bed, but she dared not lie down until she had made her overseas call. People couldn't just take off and disappear into the ether, leaving those dearest to them in the dark. If her cousin phoned on Sunday as usual, she didn't want him finding out from Claus that she had left New York a week ago. With her parents dead, Karl and his Italian lover, Beppe Biro, were her only family now. Munich was six hours ahead, Karl would be teaching at Kleine Kartoffeln, his culinary academy, which suited her. She didn't want to actually talk to him, just leave a message. She had no answers to the questions he would ask.

On her way to the office, she practiced what she would say. She needed to sound in reasonably good spirits. Good spirits, she mocked herself; she felt nothing. She entered the office and rang a bell on the counter.

"Coming," Ivan's dry voice called from the back.

After listening to Heidi's request, he lifted a telephone onto the counter and placed a small, black book next to it. "Record the number and the time in here," he said, tapping the book's cover with a long bony finger. "We'll add it to your bill at the end of your stay, but I should warn you, if you call overseas

8

now it'll cost you an arm and a leg. Much cheaper if you wait until evening."

Heidi cast him a half smile and said, "I think it will cost only the arm. I do not plan a long talk."

The innkeeper made a hoarse sound that might have been a chuckle and said he'd leave her to her business. Heidi cleared her throat and picked up the receiver. She paused, envisioning Karl's answering machine in the alcove that overlooked his garden. His Mirabelle plum would be setting its fruit, the purple bearded irises and red valerians would be in full bloom against the garden wall. The gray feral cat he professed to have no feelings for, but lured onto the patio twice a day with fish, might be sleeping in a patch of sunshine. The receiver made a loud protest at her delay and she returned it to its cradle.

"Problem?" Ivan poked his head around the corner.

She shook her head and tapped a finger to her temple. "I gather the wool."

Ivan's mouth gave a twitch before he disappeared with a waggle of his fingers. Heidi picked up the receiver again, dialed zero and asked for a long-distance operator.

"I have taken the Mercedes and left Claus," she said in response to Karl's light, tenor voice on his answering machine. "You and Beppe are not to worry about me. I have money. I am booked into a little cabin somewhere in Pennsylvania and I have no immediate plans. I love you both, I will call again later in the week."

She hung up, recorded her time in the little black book and closed the office door quietly behind her. On the way back to her cabin, she caught the shimmer of light on water and descended a grassy slope for a closer look at the river Ivan had mentioned. Except for the white tufts of cat hair that hovered at its feet, the green wooden bench that faced a stretch of quiet water would have been at home along any pedestrian path in Central Park.

Leaves danced to a barely perceptible breeze and Heidi sat

down to watch the interplay of light and shadow as the sun pierced the canopy of the broad-leafed copse across the water. She tipped her head back and inhaled deeply; the air smelled of cut grass and mud and, she imagined, things that flew or swam or slithered.

***

When Beppe Biro finally picked up his phone that night, Karl Engel said coolly, "When I can't reach you for hours, I imagine you collapsed among the vines with only your grandfather's ghost for company."

Beppe chuckled and explained he had been in the wine cellar with two young Americans who wanted to apprentice themselves to an Italian winemaker for several weeks.

"Male or female?" Karl asked, not concerned, just wondering.

"Males, Adonises both of them, but I have you, so I am immune. Your message said you heard from Heidi. Tell me." Beppe listened intently, then demanded, "What does she mean, 'somewhere in Pennsylvania?' Doesn't she know where she is?"

"I repeated her message verbatim, Beppe, do listen," said Karl, arranging six sardines artfully on a porcelain plate for the gray cat. "I said she sounded exhausted so I'm assuming the name of wherever has escaped her. A cabin makes me think a small town, so she's not holed up in some great American slum. She has escaped, left Claus and that dreadful woman Emmett insisted they take on, so we must applaud her for that. Now she can explore options worthy of her."

"I still haven't found a suitable person to run my tasting room. Imagine how good she'd be," said Beppe, wistfully.

"I am closing Kleine Kartoffeln next week for the entire summer," Karl reminded him. "I'm coming to you to bask in the Italian sun of course, but I'll run your tasting room until we find you someone worthy."

"Unless Heidi comes back."

"She won't, at least not yet. Peter's death changed everything for her. You know what she's like now, she's waiting for a sign, something to tell her what to do, or where to go."

"A ticket home from us would be a sign, " Beppe pointed out.

"Too prosaic." Karl tapped on the window to let the cat know supper was on the way. "I know my cousin; she is looking for something divine."

***

Over the next few days, Heidi found herself floating in a netherworld where unassociated memories coalesced and dissipated, plans formed and fragmented. In New York, she had survived the two years following Peter's death by having too much to do, working twelve to fourteen hours a day, seven days a week, returning to the apartment near the Hudson at midnight to fall into an exhausted sleep. Anke Mueller would be comforting Claus there now. Anke was not one to waste time, and Claus was not one to protest. They had probably already cleared her clothes from the closet.

Sunny skies alternated with frequent cloudbursts, which stopped almost as soon as they started, leaving the sultry summer air heavy with moisture. In the afternoons, Heidi forced herself outside. She didn't phone Karl again; what was there to say? She wandered to the river. She walked to the office to hold Tabitha. Twice she crossed the road to the diner for somewhere else to sit. In her cabin, by the river, in the diner, she waited for a sign.

CHAPTER TWO

LIMBO

The poncho had done little to protect her from the knees down and Heidi squelched her way up the grassy incline from the river. She halted in surprise at the sight of a shiny red truck parked at the cabin next to hers. For the first time since she had arrived six days ago, she had a neighbor. The truck had what she thought were called 'monster wheels,' and it dwarfed the Mercedes, now plastered with leaves. The license plate had an image of a cowboy astride a bucking bronco, hat held high in one hand, the other hand clinging to a rein. Wyoming.

Beppe had been forced to spend his adolescence in Wyoming when an American coal company offered his father, a mining engineer, twice what he'd been paid in Tuscany. Wyoming was the state where Beppe had lost his right hand. Salvation had come when, after healing from his amputation, his parents had allowed him to return to his grandfather's vineyard in Italy.

"Big dirty trucks hauling coal, the wind howls all day." Beppe's description of Wyoming's midlands sprang to her mind. "The landscape is miserable, bleak and unspeakably dreary." But the cowboy on the license plate argued for something more—freedom, strength, a kind of wild independence.

"Jetzt kannst du sehen," she said as she started to remove leaves from the Mercedes's windshield. *"Jetzt hast du einen Freund."*

She didn't hear the cabin door open behind her and jumped when a raspy voice said, "Speaking German to a German car, makes sense."

She turned to see a tall, lean elderly man grinning at her. He had a crew cut and his face was pink and white, scrupulously clean. Military, she thought.

"I knew it was German," he said, "but I couldn't tell what you were saying. I was stationed in Germany after the War."

His smile was sweet, his blue eyes twinkled behind wire-rimmed glasses, and not wishing to appear unfriendly, Heidi said, "I tell my car now he can see. Now he has a friend."

The man laughed. "My truck's a girl, so they may get along. Conrad Kearney," he said, extending a hand.

Heidi introduced herself by her married name. She was Vogel on her passport, social security card and driver's license. For now she had better stick with it.

"This truck is very tall," she said, frowning upward. "How do you get in?"

"Very carefully at my age. Stole it from my great-grandson at my granddaughter's behest. Figured I might as well take a toodle around until the boy gets his grades up."

"It is quite a toodle you are on," observed Heidi.

"Oh, I'll be toodling for a while. Sixteen hundred plus miles under my belt now, and I have the truck through the fall." He grinned at her. "If you're thinking of eating in an hour or so, I wouldn't mind sharing a bite at that diner across the road. Talk about Germany a bit."

"I would rather talk about Wyoming," she said.

Over bowls of chili, Heidi learned Conrad Kearney had been born in Wyoming and returned there after his army days. He now lived in Kaycee, a mining area. She said she had a friend who had lived in that part of the state as a youth.

Conrad looked amused. "He have anything good to say?"

Heidi shook her head and Conrad chuckled. Better leave the midlands to the miners, he advised. He'd married a miner's widow, who refused to leave her family, or he wouldn't be there now. He described Yellowstone National Park and the Grand Tetons—well worth a visit, but if she went there in the summer, she'd spend more time looking at the bumper of the vehicle in front of her than seeing wildlife or geysers.

She offered him her unopened packages of oyster crackers before the waitress came to clear their table. He put them in his shirt pocket and gave them a gentle pat, a gesture she thought she'd always remember.

"They'll be good for the road," he said. "I'm leaving at dawn so I can get to Maine for my father's birthday."

"Your father?" Heidi wasn't sure she'd heard correctly.

"Sure." Conrad gave a youthful grin. "I'm eighty. Daddy's turning a hundred and one. He can still mend a fence and catch a salmon."

"This is so wonderful," said Heidi, smiling at the thought of such an old man getting on with the business of living.

"You can see my family is blessed," Conrad said. "Our mom dies of cancer, but it's quick and we're already grown, my father meets a good woman and follows her to Maine. My stepdaughter claims me as her own, gives me a granddaughter who gives me a great grandson."

"And your granddaughter gives you her son's truck to make your toodle," Heidi added.

They both laughed, but then Conrad's eyes turned serious and he asked, "You staying here, trying to get that car of yours completely covered with leaves, or what?"

Heidi shrugged and gave the only answer she had and it would have to be enough. "I get tired of my life in New York City and now I am on holiday to decide what is next."

When it became apparent she wasn't about to say more, Conrad picked up the dessert menu and offered to treat her to a piece of pie. Since there was no peach left, and neither of them wanted banana-cream, they settled on apple. When their pie arrived, Conrad tucked in right away but Heidi first used her fork to tilt her slice and examine the bottom. She raised her eyebrows at Conrad, took a bite and chewed thoughtfully.

"The lemon peel complements the apple's sweetness very well," she said, putting down her fork. "I doubt they have cardamom so a touch of clove will bring out more apple flavor. A flaky top crust, the bottom is too soggy. The fix is not difficult—brush with egg white before filling, place on a hot baking sheet . . ." she caught herself when Conrad's eyes crinkled in amusement.

"Sounds like you know your way around a pie," he said, prodding the bottom crust of his slice with his fork. "I'd have said damn fine pie if you hadn't dissected it like that, but now I'm thinking underdone and lacking some flavor."

She was about to apologize when he added, "Underdone or not, I'll be having another slice, a la mode, this time."

They ambled back across the road. A soft breeze had arisen and crickets chirped in the boxwood hedge near the ice machine. He leaned against his truck, she leaned against her car and the likelihood they'd never see each other again hung in the air between them.

"Are you going to be okay?" he asked.

"Yes, of course," she said, swallowing at the concern she heard in his voice. "And you will be okay too on your visit to your father. We will both be as right as the rain."

"Right as the rain," he repeated, with a nod.

Heidi pushed herself off her car and smiled up at him. "Well, you have your early morning and I thank you for the company. We say our good nights and we hit the sack."

There was Conrad's sweet smile again. "Before we do," he

said, fishing a card out of his wallet and handing it over, "why not find your way to Wyoming and look my little sister up? She lives in Riverton, in the same house we were born in. She runs Saint Gemma's Kitchen, a charity for those in need. Riverton is a lot cheaper than up Jackson way, where the affluent and the mountains come together, but close enough to the Rockies that you know you're onto something."

"Who is this Saint Gemma?" asked Heidi, examining the card.

"The patron saint of the poor and unemployed. Bathsheba runs the kitchen for the McKee sisters, friends of mine. I was ten years ahead of Edith, the older girl, in school, but in those days, everybody knew everybody."

Heidi looked up. "Bathsheba Kearney, your sister's name is lovely."

"Lovely?" Conrad gave a chuckle. "I'm not sure which version of the Bible our mother was reading; I think she just liked the sound of the name. I'm lucky to be Conrad, tenth century saint and all-around good guy from what I can determine. Bathsheba is anxious to take off with her new beau, and the McKees are having a devil of a time finding a replacement. Hand the card back a sec and I'll write their number on the back. I'll give them a jingle and you follow up."

Heidi looked at the number, thanked him and put the card in her pocket.

"Heidi Vogel, you phone them," he said, as she turned away. "They'll be expecting your call."

Once in her cabin, Heidi collapsed spread-eagled on the bed. She stared at the knotty pine ceiling. Dinner had been very nice; Conrad Kearney had been a dear, but for him to say his friends would be *expecting* her call? She heaved a sigh. Pushy Americans.

She rolled on her side and scowled at the still life of fruit hanging next to the bed. By now, she knew it by heart: a partially peeled orange exposing six sections, a pear with a leaf attached—the blush on the skin of one side argued it was a Comice—and a cluster of dark purple grapes; she hadn't bothered to count them. Mercifully, no dead hare or fowl hung its head over the edge of the table.

Should she phone the McKees?

Heidi thought back to the dinner she had shared with Beppe and Karl just before her move to New York. She and Beppe had been sitting in the dining room, waiting for Karl to put the finishing touches on dinner, and full of excitement about going to America, she asked Beppe if he had seen part of the Oregon Trail. Again, she saw the candlelight reflecting off his stainless-steel hook as he crossed his muscular arms and leaned back in his seat.

"We went on a field trip to the Trail during high school," he said. "All we saw was a dirt track near the highway with grooves, cigarette butts and gum wrappers. Most of us thought it a waste of time to get on a school bus and drive more than an hour to take a look."

"But it is the remnant of a very difficult journey. That must make it worth a visit," she had argued, envisioning the illustrations from her American History schoolbook of pioneers, covered wagons and women walking in long skirts.

"We were teenagers. We were more interested in food and sex. Of course, I had to hide who I wanted to have sex with." Beppe's dark eyes became uncharacteristically hard. "For most of my time in Wyoming, I wanted to die. It's been more than twenty years, but nothing will have changed. Wyoming is a very insular place."

Karl came out of the kitchen bearing a platter of pear and pomegranate lamb tagine. He placed it on the brass trivet she had given him for his birthday and took a seat.

"You know you never have to return to Wyoming, Beppe," he said, shaking out his napkin, "and Heidi promises to avoid the place like the plague."

"I promise to avoid Wyoming like the plague," she remembered echoing in solidarity—an easy promise to make when Wyoming had been nowhere and nothing. How long ago had that conversation taken place, six years? Six years ago, when she still thought she could control happenstance. Six years ago, before she had given birth to a son and lost him.

The air in the cabin pressed close. Unable to take a deep breath, Heidi got up and stepped outside into the light of a waxing moon. From Tabitha's bench, she watched the moonlight reflect off the river's surface and heard the hollow, mournful hoot of an owl. Across the water, a deer stepped delicately out of the woods, freezing when it saw her, the outline of its ears almost comically large. Biting her lips, barely taking a breath, Heidi sat motionless. After a long moment, the deer took hesitant steps to the water, lowered its head, and she thought she could hear it lapping. Leaves rustled, wood snapped, the sounds of the night continued around her. She watched the hooting owl, or a different one, swoop low along the water. When she looked for the deer, it was gone.

A world away, Beppe would be out in the Italian sun with his vineyard workers. She could hear the rich Italian voices. Karl would be standing at his kitchen window drinking a cup of coffee as he waited for the garden cat to finish its breakfast so he could retrieve and wash the plate before leaving for work.

And what for her? Had an elderly man offered her a path forward?

A first step perhaps. Peter had taught her the foolishness of predicting the future.

CHAPTER THREE

TUMBLING TUMBLEWEED

"*Ach, mein Lieber,*" Heidi whispered to the little bundle of ashes that had been basking in a patch of sun on the passenger seat since Thermopolis. "It is our tumbleweed."

She turned off the engine and narrowed her eyes at the tumbleweed nestled against the tall chain-link fence that separated Riverton's Saint Gemma's Kitchen from the gas station next door. Somewhere on its seed-dispersing journey, or perhaps before it had even broken off from its roots, the rounded tangle of dry, prickly branches had picked up a long piece of silver flashing tape. Had others of the hundreds of thousands of tumbleweeds also bouncing their way across Wyoming's high prairie picked up silver flashing too? Probably, Heidi admitted to herself, but she chose to believe the afternoon winds had selected this particularly large specimen with its showy, light-reflecting appendage to escort her to her new job, another sign something or someone was looking out for her.

The tumbleweed had bounced onto the road ahead of the car a few miles back, dancing to the left, dancing to the right, sometimes being tossed quite some distance ahead by an overzealous gust of wind. She had lost sight of it as she entered town, yet here it was again, identifiable by its silver tail, stuck for now against a fence in a gravel parking lot.

Heidi returned the ashes to their box in the glove

compartment and fished around in her purse for hairpins. She twisted her silky blonde tresses around her fingers and pinned them into a neat bun at her nape.

Before entering Saint Gemma's, Heidi went to inspect the tumbleweed. A smattering of seeds littered the ground around the plant and she noted the tiny spikes on its branches. If the tumbleweed was still there when she returned to the car, she would pull it away from the fence so it could be picked up and sent on its way again when the prairie wind changed direction.

Heidi skirted the side of the large, white wooden building, entered an open set of arched doors and found herself in a wide, shallow anteroom. On the wall facing her, a painting of a smiling Jesus, hair perfectly parted down the middle and hand raised in blessing, greeted her. A banner above the painting held the words, "*The Holy Trinity Offers You Hope, Comfort and Healing.*"

Heidi looked more closely at the picture and saw sitting in what had first appeared to be an unoccupied cloud, a bald, grandfatherly-looking gentleman with a long white beard. A dove surrounded by a burst of light hovered in the background. Father, Son and Holy Ghost—to the artist, the Son had certainly been the main attraction.

A mason jar holding a bouquet of white daisies sat on a table beneath the painting. One of the daisies had wilted and Heidi walked over to see its stem did not extend into the water. She pulled it out, pinched off the end and tucked the flower more deeply into the jar.

"*Bitteschön,*" she murmured, 'you're welcome.'

"Talking to Jesus?"

Heidi looked around to see a disheveled man exiting what was presumably the dining hall, limping as he dragged one leg behind him.

"Sometimes, yes," she admitted.

"You the German lady taking over for Bathsheba?" he asked, his speech somewhat muffled by the half of his face that remained slack when he moved his mouth. "Gonna be part of the so-called Trinity?"

Heidi smiled and nodded, guessing the rest of the Trinity in this case would be Edith and Patsy McKee.

He pointed to the banner above the painting and demanded, "Read that, loud enough so as I kin hear you."

When Heidi did as asked, he said with a snuffle of laughter, "Okay, just checking you could read English. Lunch is over. Bathsheba's in the kitchen waiting for you."

He raised his hand in benediction and shambled off.

The windswept Wyoming sky cast its light through banks of arched windows placed high up on the walls of the dining hall. If there had been pews instead of tables, she might have been in church. Heidi followed the smell of institutional cooking toward the kitchen, her footsteps echoing in the high-ceilinged room. Wrinkling her nose, she guessed lunch had been overcooked poultry and cream of mushroom soup, probably canned—the brutal thermal processing of a canned, creamy soup gave it an unmistakable musty odor.

Pushing through a swinging door into the kitchen she called a greeting to the short, plump woman with greying red hair, who was peeling her way through a mountain of potatoes. The woman looked over and gave a broad grin.

"Ah, you must be Heidi Vogel. You're just as my brother described, pretty as a picture," she said in a hoarse, smoker's voice. She wiped her hands on a towel hanging from her apron and advanced, hand extended. "Bathsheba Kearney, so very pleased to meet you."

Her grip was strong and welcoming, but except for the twinkle in her eyes, this dumpling of a woman bore little resemblance to the tall, lean man Heidi had shared a meal with. Heidi looked around. The food may have smelled dreary, but the large, well-equipped kitchen appeared spotlessly clean.

"I understand you left Pennsylvania two weeks ago. You

stop to see the sights along the way?" asked Bathsheba, folding her arms across her ample chest and leaning against the counter for a brief chat.

Heidi said she had driven through North Dakota to see bison and stopped at a wolf sanctuary in Montana. When she entered Wyoming from the north, a man at a gas station suggested she go to see Devil's Tower.

"I've always wanted to go to Devil's Tower," said Bathsheba, wistfully. "I've seen it from the distance, rising out of the earth like that, but I'm always on my way to somewhere else. Lots of Indian prayer cloths, am I right?"

Heidi nodded . . . there had been so many of them.

She had heard them fluttering before she had seen them—colorful strips of cloth tied to the trees along the path that surrounded the immense rock protrusion. The guidebook she had bought at the park office said the four colors traditionally used represented the four winds—east (yellow), south (red), west (black) and north (white). But she also saw a few in green and blue. Some were tied into small bundles, which she read had a pinch of tobacco inside, offerings to the Spirits of the Plains Indian tribes.

She had circled the tower seeking a *Shepherdia argentea,* or silver buffaloberry, and near a pine festooned with prayer cloths she spied a large shrub matching the description and photo in the guidebook. Rounded, loosely branched, small, oval leaves arranged in opposite pairs and covered in fine silvery hairs on both surfaces, tiny berries, beginning to turn red; the shrub provided nestling habitat for songbirds, Native people had used the thorns as needles and collected the berries for food. *'Argentea'* she knew was the Latin for 'silver,' and surely *'shepherdia'* must mean 'shepherd.' This was a place where Peter would be safe.

Hidden from the path by the shrub, she had perched on a rock and taken the precious bundle from her pocket. After opening Peter's yellow infant cap and untying the white linen handkerchief tucked inside, she placed a pinch of his grey ashes in the center of her palm. She held her hand high and allowed the same wind that lifted prayers from the colorful cloths into the sky, to carry a tiny remnant of her child to safety.

"I am sorry?" Heidi said, suddenly cognizant of Bathsheba's voice in the background.

"Poor lamb, you must be exhausted, staring into space like that," said Bathsheba. "I asked if I could get you anything. I said Edith and Patsy are running late."

Heidi accepted a glass of water and asked where the kitchen crew was. Shouldn't dinner prep be starting?

"They're on a prolonged break," said Bathsheba. "Several months ago, I had twelve, then by the beginning of this month, I was down to seven, working double shifts. Yesterday, two didn't show, and apparently they won't be coming back, so now we're at five."

"These two people quit you with no notice?" asked Heidi, still trying to absorb the fact a crew of twelve had been reduced to seven and then five.

"Notice?" Bathsheba chuckled. "Kitchen work is hard; most people drop it the moment something else comes along. We've got four who have family in the area, so they have a reason to stick around. But not to worry, we trust in the Lord and always manage to put food out somehow. And now you've arrived, so if you'd like to start on the carrots, aprons are hanging in the hall."

As Heidi tied a clean apron tightly around her waist, she could hear her cousin saying from the rarefied world of his elite culinary academy in Munich, "Industrial strength cooking with a skeleton crew, what did you expect in a in the middle of nowhere? Trusting this woman's Lord won't help you."

Returning to the kitchen, she felt her spirits lift when she picked up a carrot from the fifty-pound box. It broke with a snap, releasing a crisp, sweet, slightly earthy scent. Even Karl couldn't find fault in the quality of these carrots.

"Fix them however you wish, but I suggest sticks," said Bathsheba, almost through her potato mountain now. "Think two hundred plates, a few sticks per plate, most people won't eat them anyway."

Sticks? No, decided Heidi, these carrots were so fresh, she would julienne them and toss them in a lightly sweetened vinaigrette with a touch of dill. She asked Bathsheba where the kitchen knives were, and the woman handed her a key, explaining if they weren't locked up, they tended to disappear.

Heidi unlocked the drawer and whispered, "*Danke*," when she saw the quality of the knives inside. They were good, in fact, *very* good knives—high-carbon steel and German made.

She removed an eight-inch chef's knife, tested the blade and frowned. She took out a ten-inch knife and found it equally dull. Another, with a twelve-inch blade, still had a decent edge, but it was too large for her small hands to use efficiently. She tested the edges of the boning knives, the cleaver and the paring knives. Most were nowhere close to sharp. She asked for a whetstone and Bathsheba directed her to a neighboring drawer.

"You'll have time to sharpen *and* prepare the carrots?" asked Bathsheba dubiously, as she watched Heidi put the sharpening stone in water to soak.

"I am good with the stone, I will just sharpen a few. It will go quickly and the others I will do tomorrow."

"Good with the stone," Bathsheba repeated. "Guess all that fancy European training the McKees told me about has a practical side to it."

Heidi had prepared her vinaigrette, washed and peeled the carrots, and was about to cut them into whisper-thin strips when Edith and Patsy McKee blew in through the kitchen's back door, wavy grey hair pointing every which way. Their long wait in line at the pharmacy had disgruntled them. The brakes on their almost new Lincoln Town Car were grabbing, so they stopped by the garage, and Riverton appeared to be having a tumbleweed invasion. Apologizing to Heidi for their delay, they asked if she would like to join them in a cup of tea while they got acquainted.

The three women carried their cups to a spacious office, furnished with the expected chairs, desk and file cabinets. Once seated, Edith in the swivel chair behind the desk, Patsy and Heidi opposite her, the sisters launched into a history of Saint Gemma's, interrupting each other frequently. Had Heidi seen the Statue of Liberty poem on the wall of the dining room? It was a tribute to their stepmother who had brought a vast amount of money into the family. They had hardly gotten to know the woman before she and their father were killed in a car accident, victims of the treachery of a Wyoming winter.

"We do remember her claiming to be a relative of Emma Lazarus, the woman who wrote the Statue of Liberty poem," said Patsy.

"In truth, we've been unable to find evidence our stepmother had any kind of relationship to Emma Lazarus," Edith confessed. "But we used her fortune to establish Saint Gemma's, and we do serve the tired, the poor, the huddled masses," Edith fixed her eyes on her sister, "and 'wretched refuse,' which is only a pejorative term when taken out of context."

"I did want to leave 'wretched refuse' out when we had the words painted on the wall," admitted Patsy. "Go straight to homeless and tempest-tost, not so harsh, but Edith refused. She said you couldn't edit a poem to . . ."

". . . appease your own sensibilities," Edith interrupted. "We must own the fact poverty *is* harsh, not to mention a person's written work is inviolate."

"My sister has always been a warrior. I gave up fighting her when we were very young," said Patsy, smiling contentedly at Heidi. "Do you have siblings?"

"No," answered Heidi. "I am the single child."

"Never mind," said Patsy. "Some siblings may be more of a bane than a blessing. I give you Cane and Abel, Joseph and his brothers, Olivia de Havilland and Joan Fontaine—"

"However, we digress," said Edith, when the list of sibling rivals threatened to lengthen. "Let's close the door for some privacy and share our concerns."

Lowering their voices, the sisters confided that Saint Gemma's menu had been on the decline for some time. Although still nutritious, it had gone from dull to dismal.

"It's the new man," said Patsy. "Bathsheba is so eager to take off with him in his Winnebago, she's no longer putting effort into food preparation."

"She's just going for convenience, pure and simple," agreed Edith. "Now, it's canned this, canned that and not for lack of money; we're happy to plow our inheritance into the place."

"Our Lord has asked us to share our fortune with those in need," intoned Patsy.

They told Heidi there had been an herb garden behind the building, dill, parsley, oregano, the lot, but Bathsheba had let it go, saying fresh herbs were a waste of time, and the spices in the pantry were gathering dust. They hoped Heidi, with her professional training, would add some pizzazz to the menu.

Heidi assured them she had plenty of pizzazz to give, she preferred fresh herbs when possible and spices made the difference between a nutritionally adequate meal and something truly delicious.

The sisters beamed—just the response they had been hoping for.

"Now to practical matters," said Edith. "Saint Gemma's does not provide hot meals on the weekends. Instead, my sister and I assist two women from the school district in making bag lunches to be picked up at the backdoor between noon and three, so you will have every Saturday and Sunday off."

Heidi quelled a stab of alarm at the thought of having forty-eight hours in a row off, week after week. When she wasn't physically occupied, her longing for Peter threatened to engulf her. She glanced at the clock and imagined the hands going around and around as her emptiness grew. She had agreed to stay at Saint Gemma's a year. Would she be able to bear it?

"We're almost done here," said Edith. "I can tell you are anxious to get back to help Bathsheba but first a short list of questions. Don't answer any you find too intrusive."

When the sisters finished their inquisition, Heidi tamped down her exasperation. The sisters were zealots with their Holy Trinity banner and their words of serving and mission. They wanted to recruit her into their army. They couldn't be blamed because that was what zealots did and no doubt, they had more tricks up their sleeves.

Heidi looked at the clock and Edith said quickly they still needed to discuss where she would be staying. Her living arrangements were all taken care of, Heidi assured them. The owner of the motel where she had stayed last night booked her into his brother's place, called The Trail's End. She could rent by the month.

"But we have arranged for our friend, Raymond Dolan, to show you his nice little rental house this evening," protested Edith. "It's only six blocks away and comes with a miniature dachshund, a garage big enough for that magnificent car we saw outside, and it's partially furnished."

Heidi looked at the women in disbelief. "A real dog? You tell me a dog comes with this house?"

"A miniature dachshund," said Patsy, pressing what the sisters apparently thought was a selling point.

"But when this man moves away, why does he not take his dog?" asked Heidi.

"Because the dog had undescended testes and couldn't be used for stud," said Edith.

The sisters relayed how Ray had found out the news. He had gone to check the house after the tenant left and found broken glass on the floor and the dog with a badly cut foot. Ray took the dog to the vet and she said the previous week, she had diagnosed him with undescended testes. They had not only rendered the dachshund sterile, but should be removed, lest they become cancerous. The tenant declined the operation and left with the dog, saying any animal that couldn't earn its keep was useless.

"Ray has grown fond of the dog," said Patsy. "He already got him his surgery. He installed a dog door so the dog can get outside to do his business. Ray goes by once a day to leave food and water and says the poor little boy is always pathetically happy to see him."

Pathetically happy, abandoned dog with a bleeding foot— guilt, a zealot trick if ever there was one. Heidi restrained herself from rolling her eyes and asked why Ray or the McKees didn't give the dog a home.

"We live with a wolf hybrid," said Edith. "Neither our dog nor Ray's wife's cat would find a miniature dachshund the least bit amusing."

Heidi bit the inside of her lip and tried to imagine a *miniature* dachshund. It would be a small version of the dachshund that had lived next door when she was growing up. That dog had barked and growled every time someone walked by. It had once gone after Ingo, the German short-haired pointer she had received for her fifth birthday. It had grabbed Ingo by the leg and refused to let go until its owner had hit it with a rake. Ingo had required stitches and had to wear a cone so he wouldn't pull them out. He had been her constant companion and she had been so bereft when he died, she vowed never to have another dog. But that had been a lifetime ago, now the thought of a dog was not so objectionable. Still, she would not allow the sisters to determine if she had a dog or where she would live.

"Okay," she said. "I have a place to stay tonight but I will look at your friend's house tomorrow and this dog and I will check out at each other."

"Check out at each other?" Patsy asked, looking at her sister in puzzlement.

"Check each other out, Patsy, for goodness sake, a small change in an idiom and you fall apart. Look at the context, it's perfectly obvious what she meant," said Edith irritably.

Heidi looked at the sisters in amusement and said precisely, "Yes, the dog and I will check each other out, and if we do not suit, I will continue at The Trail's End."

Loud voices and laughter filled the hall, apparently the kitchen crew had returned.

"Before I go into the kitchen to julienne the carrots," she said, "I must tell you that hiring more staff is our top priority."

"I understand we may be down a couple of people," Edith said cautiously.

"Many people," said Heidi. "Two people leave yesterday and give no notice. Now there are only five people and they work double shifts. A double shift in a kitchen is exhausting."

"Well, I must say I'm astonished," said Edith, turning to her sister for a nod of agreement. "We've been asleep at the wheel. Occasionally, Bathsheba has asked us to come in to help, but not recently, so we have been devoting most of our time to a group advocating for the restoration of Bighorn sheep habitat. Our accountant does the payroll. He didn't say he was writing so few checks, and I suppose because Bathsheba's on her way out, she didn't want to train more people. I promise you, we will get on this hiring business right away, and of course we will come in to assist you however we can."

"Thank you," said Heidi, "and I would like to participate in the interviews."

Patsy raised an aggrieved voice, "I think you'll find we're a revolving door and we'll be lucky to get more than a handful of applicants although we pay above minimum wage."

"We will beat the bushes, flush out whom we can," promised Edith.

Heidi hastened back to the kitchen to save her carrots from the banality of becoming sticks. Because of its reputation, Café Claus always had a long list of applicants wanting to work in the kitchen. Now, Edith was talking about beating a bush to flush people out. Working at Saint Gemma's was going to be very different.

The moment Heidi left for the kitchen, Edith picked up the phone and dictated an ad to put in the newspaper. She increased the starting wage by a dollar an hour, then phoned the unemployment department with the same information.

"Once they meet Heidi Vogel, they will want to work for her," Edith assured her sister. "I think Bathsheba might have lost her touch with people and gotten a little crabby."

"We shouldn't have let the Bighorn sheep take so much of our time," said Patsy.

"Indeed, but as soon as Heidi is launched, she won't need us holding her hand."

"Yes, she does seem very independent. I wish she had committed to staying more than a year."

"That is enough time to rope her in," said Edith, "and the dog was fortuitous. A dachshund, that will make her feel right at home. Anything else?"

"I would say she's too pretty by half. I doubt we'll keep her even a year," said Patsy gloomily.

Edith harrumphed. "You have a habit of assuming a beautiful face and a lovely figure mask a shallow character."

"It's not a habit," Patsy protested. "It's the voice of experience and her way of looking straight at you with those startling blue eyes is unnerving, surely you'll admit that."

"Well, where else is she going to look, Patsy? You talk, she looks."

"Do you think they are contact lenses? If so, she might consider a more natural color."

"Heidi Vogel is foreign; their blue eyes may be different. I found her sensible, practical and intelligent. Anyone who has owned and toiled in a New York restaurant is not a lightweight. She's seen a slice of life, believe me."

"She did note a pending divorce," admitted Patsy.

"Oh, I sense she's been handed more of a blow than that," mused Edith, thinking Heidi would get along well with Saint Gemma's patrons. "Her drinking appears moderate."

"After father, I would have preferred her to not drink at all and as I said, I wish she had committed to service for more than a year. We had Bathsheba for twenty."

"Let me remind you, she's a classically trained chef and still a young woman while we're a soup kitchen in Wyoming," said Edith, sounding very much the older sister. "She's going to *julienne* the carrots. Did you get that, Patsy? She'll probably toss them in a dressing of some kind—they'll surely be a step up from those sticks Bathsheba is so fond of. We've been handed a gift with Heidi Vogel coming to town, and we'll be grateful for however long she stays."

CHAPTER FOUR

RAY DOLAN'S PLACE

Ray Dolan opened the door with a small brown dog under his arm and started talking before Heidi could even say hello. "Who leaves a dog? To rent this house, you take the dog. There's a park four blocks away. A dog needs a walk every day." The old man stood back to let her enter, adding, as if it made a difference, "He's a purebred, you know."

"Yes, I see this." Heidi stepped inside, held out her hand to the dog and received a cautious sniff. "What is his name?"

"My wife says don't name an animal that you can't keep," Ray said, putting the dog back on the floor. "The naming business is yours."

The little dog looked up at Heidi and cocked his head winsomely. She bit back a smile. She followed the old man and the dog through the house, peering into its two bedrooms, twin beds in one, a double bed in the other.

"The mattresses are new," Ray assured her. "You never know what has happened in a bed."

The bathroom had a deep, claw-foot tub, the living room was small and dark, the kitchen had a dinette, the garage was roomy. The Trail's End didn't offer a garage and she hadn't thought about the Mercedes weathering the winter.

"Real big garden too," said Ray, as the dog escorted them to the backdoor.

Heidi stepped outside with some trepidation; she definitely did not want to be tending plants. She relaxed when she found a garden in Wyoming meant something entirely different from a garden in Germany. A long scrubby tract sloped gently down a hill. She could pick up the dog waste that littered the cement slab Ray referred to as the patio, buy a few colorful plants to put in the two empty planters, and allow Wyoming to continue to have its way with the rest of the yard.

"That is a cemetery?" she asked, pointing to the unkempt expanse beyond the back fence. Several stone monuments peered above the long scraggly grass and a large tree had fallen, its dead crown bridging the fence between the backyard and what appeared to be a graveyard.

"A cemetery, no longer used," said Ray cheerfully. "The new one is on the other side of town. When that tree fell several years ago, the city offered to remove it, but I told them no, leave it be. My first wife admired that tree the day we moved in here and said she wanted to be buried under it someday. She's been lying under it over thirty years, and she deserves to keep lying under it. Doesn't matter to her if the tree's living or dead, vertical or horizontal."

Thirty years, Ray's first wife must have died young. Heidi looked away from the old man, who kept rattling on with no sorrow in his voice. A passel of children chased a ball on a long patch of green on the other side of the cemetery where the land flattened out. She thought she could make out their excited cries, unless the sounds were just her imagination.

"You look like you're sensible enough not to be bothered by a bone yard," said Ray. "It didn't bother the school board when they built the elementary school over there." He pointed and Heidi saw long, low buildings on the far side of the playing field.

"No, the cemetery does not bother me," Heidi said. It was the sound of children playing in the schoolyard she would have to make her peace with.

Ray nodded, pleased. He enthused about the yard's possibilities and Heidi smiled patiently. He pointed to a raised bed surrounded by rocks so it looked like a pioneer grave and assured her it had once been a vegetable patch. She must like vegetables, being a cook, he said. Two tenants ago, the vegetable garden had carrots, cabbages, turnips and potatoes. The rose bushes had roses.

"The roses were . . . " the old man hesitated, looking around in some confusion. "The shite musta taken the rose bushes with him," he exclaimed. "A dozen bleedin' roses."

Muttering to himself, he walked partway down the slope, the dog at his heels. Heidi watched them examine some depressions in the ground and tried not to feel guilty at her relief at not having to tend a dozen rose bushes. She knew she would have been constantly checking them for cankers and mildew.

Ray returned out of breath and wheezed, "I can't believe it, the Gobshite, pardon my Irish, leaves the dog and takes the roses." He shook his head in disgust. "I'm going to have to be more careful checking references from now on."

"I am sorry for loss of the roses," said Heidi. "I would never . . ."

"Oh, you're okay," he interrupted gloomily, mopping his forehead with a reasonably clean-looking hanky. "If Conrad told you to come out here and take his sister's job, if you're a friend of the McKee girls, that's good enough for me. The dog likes you; you can't fool a dog."

Heidi looked down at the dachshund, who blinked limpid brown eyes up at her. So very small and not the breed she would have chosen, but sometimes . . . sometimes life chooses a dog for you.

"Did you help dig up the roses, Gering?" she asked, bending down to pick him up. He craned his neck to lick her face.

"Gering? What's that?" asked the old man.

"It is the name I give to him. It is the German word for low," said Heidi, holding up one of the dachshund's curved, dwarfed front legs and waving it at her new landlord.

As they moved back into the house, Ray warned her the dog would be disappointed if she didn't move in right away. Heidi explained she would not have time to prepare for moving into the house until the weekend because Bathsheba had surprised both her and the McKees by announcing she would be leaving at the end of the day, instead of next week as planned.

"I am thrown into the deep end of the pool," she said to Gering apologetically as she put him back on the floor.

"Bathsheba is leaving you in the lurch? Surprising," said Ray. "Must be the boyfriend."

Heidi refrained from saying no boyfriend was worth letting people down and settled on giving the old man a sour look, which he returned with a shrug.

"I have a solution to you thinking you can't move in and give this poor little dog comfort right away," Ray said. "Last month my sister passed and we're cleaning out her house. She had all the sheets, blankets, pillows, towels you could want, if you don't object to orange. Somebody at church told her it was the least popular color, so she decided to claim it as her own. Kitty was always looking for a cause."

"Your sister was sorry for the color?"

"Oh sure, she always felt sorry for the little guy."

"The color is the little guy?" asked Heidi, truly mystified now.

"The little guy of the color world, so to speak. But you're making our Kitty sound nutty when you ask it like that," said Ray defensively.

"No, I . . ."

Ray held up a hand. "No, you're right, Kitty was different, especially in her later years. She could feel sorry for a chipped mug; she was that soft-hearted."

"She sounds like a lovely, kind lady," Heidi offered.

"The kindest," Ray affirmed. "And she would have liked to help you out while you're swimming in the deep end."

"And I am of course very grateful," Heidi said in turn.

"Well, you're welcome." Ray nodded his head graciously. "This afternoon, I'll get my daughter and her husband to bring over some of Kitty's things, sheets, blankets, towels. There's also throw rugs, a sofa and an easy chair. To be honest, the kids will be relieved. My wife has been on at them to take Kitty's things. Everything's in great shape, nothing worn or stained, but my daughter's set on more traditional colors."

Heidi tentatively asked if the rugs and sofa were orange, too. Everything, Ray assured her; his sister didn't do anything by halves. Heidi looked at Gering and tried to imagine the two of them surrounded by orange. How ridiculous, she bit back a grin. She solemnly thanked Ray for the furniture, and for asking his daughter and her husband to deliver it today.

"And don't forget they're also bringing rugs, blankets, sheets and towels," Ray reminded her.

She hadn't forgotten and she expressed her gratitude again. She asked if she could sign the rental agreement so she could get back to Saint Gemma's.

"And you'll be back here tonight?" asked Ray.

"Yes."

Ray looked at the dog. "You hear that, Gr . . .? Gar . . .?"

"Gering," Heidi supplied.

"Gering. You hear that, Gering? Heidi Vogel here has made you a promise. She'll be coming home tonight."

Ray placed Gering on the counter so they could both witness Heidi signing her name to the rental agreement.

CHAPTER FIVE

IN THE DEEP END

Heidi discovered summer nights in a poorly insulated house in Wyoming could be very cold; however, she and Gering kept warm enough between orange flannel sheets, topped with an   orange comforter. She could just imagine what Claus would say about sharing a bed with a dog.

She put Gering's breakfast in a bag. Saint Gemma's office was large enough to accommodate a small dog and he'd spent too much time alone. The early morning high prairie wind blew icy, and they walked the six blocks to work as quickly as they could. Under her arm, she carried an afghan, orange of course. It would make a comfortable bed in the office for Gering and she could see he would need a warm jacket for the winter.

A dozen stray cats, most of them gray with generous patches of white, made their appearance from the bushes as Heidi and Gering approached the kitchen's backdoor. They gathered in a loose circle a few yards away and regarded the little dog with interest. To Heidi's amusement, Gering studiously ignored them. Live and let live? Bathsheba had said some of the kitchen crew put out scraps for the cats although she'd warned them if they did, they'd soon have an army of hungry felines begging for food. This wasn't an army, not even a small platoon. Heidi bet Wyoming winters would keep their numbers small. She had heard of people gathering feral cats for neutering, then having the vet mark them by cutting off the tip of an ear. She would talk to the McKee sisters about having their foundation extend its largess to the feline population.

She unlocked the door and prayed all five people who had worked with her yesterday would show up. Edith McKee had phoned last night to say there had been no nibbles to the employment ads she had placed, but she and Patsy could cancel their meeting with the Bighorn Conservation Committee to come in again and help if need be. Since the recipes today were simple and she had arrived an hour earlier than Bathsheba usually did, Heidi said if five people showed up today, she would be able to manage without the McKee's help.

Gering remained quiet in his orange nest as long as Heidi stayed in the office, but as soon as she left, he pawed at the door and voiced his dismay. She trotted back and forth from the kitchen to the office, reprimanding him, until she decided to just let him bark his way quiet. He soon fell silent and she felt immensely proud of him, but also a little worried. He was so very quiet.

"Stop, you silly woman," she scolded herself. She prevented herself from going down to check on him by putting ten dozen eggs on to hard boil and opening a score of the largest tuna cans she had ever seen. Bathsheba had placed the orders for the week, so she was limited to using what was on hand. She lined up jars of mayonnaise, thank God there was celery, and resigned herself to using dried parsley.

At nine thirty, she unlocked the kitchen door and three men and a woman trailed through. They stood before Heidi, grinning sleepily, waiting for instructions from their new boss. She had worked nonstop the previous day and even cleaned the bathrooms after lunch and at the end of the day. They had taken bets on if she would be able to keep it up.

Heidi frowned at them, looked at the ceiling and asked in frustration, "*Gott hilf mir,* are there only four of you?"

Massimo and Inez nodded. Heidi tried to remember the names of the other two. Yesterday had been such a blur.

"Yup, Alfonso's gone, like the two dudes who took off the day before. Rats abandoning ship. We're the four who always show up," said Massimo, a burly young man who towered over Heidi. "We're the golden ones, the Fantastic Four. I would be Mr. Fantastic," he pointed to himself. He pointed to each of the others, "The Human Torch and the Thing and the Invisible Woman." They burst out laughing as Inez, who was almost as large as Massimo, but looked to have more Native blood, took a bow.

From down the hall, Gering set up a furious barking.

"Holy shit, you got a dog?" A broad grin split Massimo's face. "Do it know how to cook, or we eatin' it?"

"I will introduce each one of you to Gering after we decide how to work with only the four of you fantastic golden people and me," said Heidi tersely. "Why do these rats jump off the ship?"

"Don't take it personally," said Inez. "Rats are rats, they just do their ratty-assed thing. No loyalty in a rat."

"Then I will have to phone the McKees to come and help us like they did yesterday," said Heidi.

The Fantastic Four released a collective groan. Not the sisters again. Edith had the evil eye, and Patsy got all hissy if anyone cussed, even one 'goddamn' set her off, they complained. Massimo said he'd phone his mother to see if she would come to help and Inez said she would phone her two cousins.

"Okay, we phone them now," said Heidi. "Human Torch and Mr. Thing, please put out some tuna for the cats, then wash up and start the egg and tuna salads. You must know Bathsheba's recipes by heart, but I would like to add a quarter cup of vinegar for each can of tuna to cut the fat and add more flavor."

When Massimo and Inez followed her to the office to make their calls, Heidi asked them to wait at the door so she could pick up Gering first. "He is so small and you are so big," she explained, wanting the introduction to go well.

"An itty-bitty wiener dog," Inez crowed when Heidi presented Gering. "Dog, you got the pointiest face I ever seen, like it's weird." She looked at Heidi with a grin and added, "Cute weird."

"This it? He your eight pounds of muscle?" asked Massimo, with a chuckle.

From the protection of Heidi's arms, Gering lifted a lip and gave a low growl.

"A dachshund is very protective of its owner," said Heidi. She had wanted to refer to herself as Gering's 'companion animal' but she thought it would be counter-productive to her mission to have the crew view her as one of them. "He will get used to you but you must not tease," she admonished and they promised they would treat the wiener dog with nothing but respect.

Massimo picked up the phone first and he nodded at Heidi as he listened to his mother. When he hung up, he said, not only would his mom come, she was bringing his brother, Raffi, who got released from the State Penn in Rawlins a few days ago. Their mom didn't want Raffi just hanging around. Plus, his brother had skills; he had worked in the kitchen and people in the Big House were not happy if they had to wait for their food.

Heidi had hired two ex-cons for the kitchen at Café Claus, and one of them had worked out well. She thanked Massimo and said she looked forward to meeting his family. He returned to the kitchen and Inez made her call.

The young woman covered the receiver and told Heidi only one cousin could come but she would bring her dad if Heidi wanted. "Just warning you," Inez said, "my uncle's a good guy but kinda prickly."

Heidi asked if he was a hard worker and Inez nodded vigorously.

"Just talk to him real respectfully," the young woman cautioned. "He has exceptional skills with a knife." She paused, before adding, "Come to think of it, best to keep him away from knives and save him for putting the food out, serving and bussing. He'll be good with the janitorial stuff too."

By ten thirty, Heidi had a crew of eight. The Fantastic Four showed the others what to do. They were following Bathsheba's recipes, using the ingredients Bathsheba ordered week after week, nothing ever changed. Heidi brought the new people into the office one at a time to introduce them to the highly suspicious Gering and fill out their paperwork.

Since the crew was working a double shift, she insisted they take regular breaks. She put chairs out in the old herb garden and encouraged them to go outside. She worked on the food line with them, greeted the patrons, bussed tables and filled in where needed. At the end of the lunch and dinner shifts, she cleaned the toilets, restocked the restrooms and left the floors to Inez's uncle.

She called a meeting at the end of the evening. Gering attended and allowed Massimo's mother to hold him. Tomorrow, Heidi said, it would be someone else's turn to do the restrooms, unless someone wanted to claim the job. Inez's uncle raised his hand. He could do all that and the floors.

"Thank you, Mr. Tolentino. Then you will promise to come back tomorrow?"

"It's Leo, and yeah, I'll come back."

"I have so much relief. You are invaluable," she said, casting him a smile of such magnitude, he looked away.

She said in two days the yeast and bread flour she had ordered would arrive and she would show them how to proof the yeast, and how to knead bread.

"Shit, we ain't buyin' bread no more?" asked Massimo.

Heidi said they would bake some bread every day because it smelled so good, but they would continue to buy loaves for sandwiches.

"What else we gotta learn?" he demanded.

"I will teach something every day. How to make a shortcrust pastry, a simple white sauce, gravy and a classic vinaigrette. We will not overcook vegetables and we will learn to season. And we practice and we practice and we will become real chefs. All of us."

"What if I don't want to be a real chef?" asked Massimo.

"Of course you do, you are one of the golden fantastic ones," Heidi reminded him.

"I didn't say I didn't want to be a chef, I just said, 'What if?'" he pointed out.

Inez burst out laughing and said, "Massimo, you an idiot and Heidi, ma'am, you a whole different kind of white lady. I got some white in me, Bathsheba was all white, but you . . . it's not just the accent and those eyes, it's like the way you're so pale blonde, and you move all fast and busy, and you're kinda extra clean, like you could be in a soap commercial or something. And you think you can teach us all this stuff."

"I know I can teach you all the stuff that you want to learn," Heidi said, rather liking Inez's description of her. "We are now *nine* fantastic golden ones. We have been brought together and you see, we make a good team. Will you promise to all come back tomorrow?"

They gave their assurances and she thought there was a good chance they'd all return. There had been more laughter in the kitchen today than yesterday, and when they transitioned to using her recipes next week, they would understand the joy of really well-prepared food, and they would find the smell of fresh baked bread addictive.

Heidi refused the offer of a ride home, saying she and Gering needed the fresh night air. There were few streetlights,

She was not afraid, but alert. She had carried pepper spray in New York, and although she'd never had to use it, it might be prudent to carry it here also.

When the McKee sisters came by Saint Gemma's at end of the week, they expressed their pleasure at seeing Heidi serving on the food line, instead of sheltering in the office during mealtimes as Bathsheba had done. Heidi told them serving was the best part of her day. She didn't say that after just a few days, she realized she needed the patrons as much as they needed her. She didn't say that before bed, as the bath water cooled around her, she used their images to populate the land outside the walls of her desolation. By talking to the hungry, she got most of them to look up and meet her eyes. Sometimes they returned her smile. Hunted, resigned, content, tired, on the decline, ascending, each person different, each person eating at a soup kitchen for a reason, each one taking comfort until the next visit of pain.

CHAPTER SIX

THE THERAPY OF DISTRACTION

On her first Saturday off, Heidi dropped by Saint Gemma's, ostensibly to become acquainted with the bag lunch operation. The McKee sisters allowed her to watch for a short while before shooing her away, telling her to stop hovering, get settled in her house or go and explore Riverton.

She returned home to collect Gering. They walked to the park, stopping along the way to talk to an elderly man about his crabapple tree that overhung the sidewalk. He said his wife used to make jelly, but neither of them felt up to climbing a ladder these days. Heidi offered to pick the sour little apples for him when they were ripe, if she could have half the harvest.

"Little thing like you up a ladder?" asked the man, but Heidi assured him she was very strong and had an excellent sense of balance, so they shook on the deal.

At the park, Heidi and Gering circled a large pond, the little dog's tail wagging frantically as he barked at the ducks, who paid him no mind. The springy, thudding pop of rackets hitting tennis balls attracted Heidi to a bench by the tennis courts, and with Gering on her lap for better vantage, they watched two young women volley a ball back and forth. The women were certainly better than she and Karl had been on the occasions they had played. If Beppe were visiting, he would shout his encouragement in his beautiful Italian accented

English when he could bring himself to look up from his mystery novel.

She hadn't noticed the baby carriage parked against the fence with a blanket carefully arranged over it, and when a baby's high-pitched wail cut the air like a knife, she startled.

"It is all right; it is a healthy cry," she assured Gering, getting up hurriedly to go.

Peter's cry had often been no more than a harsh gasping as he struggled to fill his lungs with air.

On Sunday morning, Karl phoned as usual, and at his urging, Heidi went to a hardware store and bought a radio. The clerk couldn't promise it would be able to pick up classical music.

"Problem is, you'll be wanting an FM station and unless your honey rigs you up a serious outdoor antenna," the man shrugged, "you may be limited to mostly AM. It's got a much better range." He added gloomily, "It's Sunday so no matter what your bandwidth is, you'll get mostly church music anyway."

When she got home, Heidi managed to tune in a public radio station and the maligned 'church music,' turned out to be Bach, so she couldn't complain. According to the host, during Bach's 'fertile period,' he 'birthed' three years' worth of Sunday cantatas. Heidi made a concerted effort to get over the image. If she kept the volume down, the station's minor static was tolerable but she vowed to look into a "serious outdoor antennae" at some point so she would be able to hear music throughout the house.

In the afternoon, Heidi waxed the floors and took Gering for a walk through the neighborhood. Many of the houses looked similar to hers, a small porch, two windows in front. She could imagine the layout inside. She came home tired enough to sit and read for an hour. Dinner, a bath, she picked up her book and read another chapter in bed, but her concentration began to wander. She looked at the clock, too early for sleep.

A cloud of hopelessness began to build. The doubts and questions that haunted her when she let her guard down crowded the room. What was she doing in a small town in Wyoming when her years of training would make her welcome in the kitchens of fine restaurants anywhere? Peter had died. Should she abandon the country of his birth and simply return home to Karl and Beppe? She could teach with Karl at his academy in Munich, training young chefs to blend the art and science of cooking or she could work with Beppe at his winery in the Piedmont hills. Had she given up her soul to the mediocrity of a cafeteria kitchen in a cold, windy place that offered nothing for warmth except a small abandoned dog?

She needed to do something. She should have bought an iron. Walmart was open until ten. To the abandoned dog's consternation, she got dressed and left him.

With relief, she returned to work the next day. Forty-eight unstructured hours and she had gotten through them. Another one hundred and forty-one weekends to go.

The following Friday, Heidi sat in the office on a short break before the dinner prep and cast around for what she would do on her second weekend off. She glanced out the office window, no view to speak of, a nice tree, a glimpse of windswept sky. She looked at the small calendar on her desk, Yellowstone National Park, too expensive, too far. Conrad Kearney had said too many cars. She spun around in her chair one direction, then reversed, scanning the walls. She stopped when her eyes lit on a large picture partially hidden by one of the file cabinets. She could see greens, greys and a fuzzy white diagonal line. With effort she shifted the cabinet, removed the picture and brought it back to her desk. She picked up Gering so he could take a look too.

It was a photograph, an aerial view of a town nestled against the base of what appeared to be the snow-capped Wind River Range. On the back was written, *Comfrey, Sublette County, 1983*.

"Comfrey, this was the town Beppe phoned to tell us about last week," she said to Gering. "It is where he helped the woman take stiches out of her cat."

The dog licked the picture frame with interest and Heidi frowned at something sticky that had collected dust. It would have to be cleaned before she hung it back up.

"Beppe said Comfrey is the one tolerable place in Wyoming. Do you remember that Gering? The one tolerable place, that was his hurt and anger showing."

Inez poked her head in the door. "What's the one tolerable place?"

"Comfrey, the town in this picture."

"Who says?" Inez came over to take a look. "The hurt and anger guy?"

"Yes, my friend, Beppe," said Heidi, handing Gering over so Inez could take him on a walk. He always came back smelling faintly of cigarette smoke.

"Beppe? You don't have friends here 'cept us. Doesn't sound like a local so how's he know what's tolerable? But hey, everybody gotta have an opinion. That's right, huh, Pointy-face?" Inez nuzzled Gering. "No law against people bein' narrow-minded. One tolerable place," she chuckled on her way out the door.

Heidi watched them go with amusement and returned to the picture. Beppe said he had stumbled upon Comfrey after driving for hours on one of his solitary wanderings during the first summer he'd had his license. A young woman named Ruth had found him sitting in his car outside her house and asked him to come inside and hold her cat while she took its stitches out.

"A stranger asks you inside her house?" To Heidi, that had

47

sounded very bold.

"Why not? She needed help with her cat."

"You have the dangerous look."

"Do you think so?" Beppe had sounded pleased.

"Oh, yes. The broad shoulders and muscles."

"I was a boy of sixteen. My muscles and shoulders were not so big and besides, nothing scares Ruth. *Lei vede nel cuore di tutti.*"

"In English."

"I said, she sees into everybody's heart," Beppe translated.

"And did you drive to Comfrey all summer?"

"Of course. I'd found the one decent person and one tolerable place in all of Wyoming. Where else would I go? My parents were pleased. They thought at last I had a girlfriend."

"Was Ruth disappointed you do not like girls in that way?"

"No, of course not. She was at least five years older than me, maybe more. She knew right away who I was, what I was. I told you she sees into the heart. We were friends for that one summer. In the fall I lost my hand and when I healed, I returned to my grandfather."

Heidi had held her breath, hoping Beppe would say more about the loss of his hand—even Karl claimed not to know the story—but their conversation ended abruptly when a woman hoping to manage Beppe's tasting room showed up for her interview.

Heidi cleaned the frame and examined the photograph of the Comfrey more closely. A road ran along the edge of town and directly into a narrow maw of green, emerging at a higher elevation into a parking area. She could make out tiny cars and a small building. A short trail zigzagged up a hill into a sparse cluster of trees, the silvery surface of a lake beyond. The picture had been taken only five years ago, so little would have changed. And just like that, she knew where they would go tomorrow. She and Gering would take a picnic to the alpine lake near Comfrey.

When she returned to the kitchen, she asked if anyone had been to the lake in the mountains near Comfrey. Massimo and Raffi had. Lake Cheynook, they called it, the Main Street in Comfrey becomes Wild Horse Valley Road as it enters the mountains. They said the road would climb for maybe fifteen minutes, come to a parking lot, there was a rest room and water fountain near a short trail up to the lake. Even on the weekends there wouldn't be many people, Comfrey was on the way to nowhere. Most people went to Pinedale and the bigger lakes up there, like Fremont, where you could fish, waterski, really have some fun. Cheynook was just for swimming, not much of a beach, although there were some decent trails up and around Toot's Peak and some primitive campsites. Part of the area was protected habitat for a small, very rare rattlesnake that wasn't even supposed to be there.

"Who decides this snake should not be there?" Heidi asked.

Nobody decided it, they said; it was just that the snake was out of its range. It was supposed to be mostly in eastern Utah and western Colorado. In Wyoming, it should be more down toward the Lower Green River Basin, definitely not further north, in the Wind River Range.

When Heidi asked how long it had taken them to get to Lake Cheynook from Riverton, they couldn't agree.

"Three and a half hours," said Raffi.

"Closer to four," said Massimo.

The next morning, Heidi put Peter's bundle of ashes into the zippered outside pocket of her jacket. In the one hundred and eighty-two days Peter had been alive, Heidi had told him about the adventures they would have when he was older and stronger. They would walk in forests and paddle in lakes. They would stretch out in the warmth of the sun with a picnic basket and talk and talk and talk. Had she truly believed any of it?

She put two bottles of water, some dog biscuits and a sandwich in a small backpack, and with Gering under her arm, went to the car. She placed him on a cushion next to her for his first ride in the Mercedes and he looked around, his moist black nose twitching and flaring. After driving a block, they had to pull over to come to an understanding that the passenger was to stay on his cushion on the passenger seat and not to try to sit on the driver's lap. The same conversation had to be repeated twice more before they left the town limits.

Barred from perching on Heidi's lap and without much to look at but sky, Gering curled up on his cushion to snooze. There was no direct route through the mountains to Comfrey so they drove southwest to skirt the Wind River Range and come up on the other side. They descended into the Green River Basin at South Pass and just before the highway crossed the Sweetwater River, she spied the sign for Comfrey. A small country road took them through gently rolling foothills, each one slightly higher than the one before, until the terrain flattened as they approached the town. They passed an airstrip and a low rectangular building dwarfed by a large tree. A sign warned them to reduce speed and as the car slowed, Gering woke up and looked around expectantly. Heidi powered his window most of the way down and the little dog stood up, stretched and managed to prop his front legs on the door to stick his nose out into the dry herbaceous air, the muscles in his rump and short hind legs contracting to maintain his balance.

A large billboard announced their arrival in Comfrey with the words:

Welcome to Comfrey, elevation 7272 Ft.
The little town with a big heart
Population 999, join us and make it 1000

The buildings, aligned on one side of Main Street only, faced an expanse of meadow. On the far side of the meadow stood a line of trees, probably bordering a stream or a river, and beyond, towered the Wind River Range. Heidi nodded approvingly as they drove by the long plate glass window of a restaurant; the diners would have a magnificent view. They passed a lawyer's office, several shops and a market with two gas pumps. From what she remembered of the photo at Saint Gemma's, the residential neighborhoods, other businesses, schools and churches would be down those roads sloping to the south. As they left town, a cluster of well-tended white cabins came into view. Toot's Lucky Thirteen—Heidi chuckled at the name.

"And they say there is a Toot's Peak," she said to Gering. "Do you like the name 'Toot'? Like a train I think."

Gering gave his tail a wag but didn't turn look at her, the new smells proving far too interesting. He ignored Heidi when she reached over and gave his little haunch a poke. At the bottom of Wild Horse Valley Road a sign with a wiggly arrow pointing upward warned of a steep winding climb and another sign, peppered with what looked to be rusted bullet holes, announced 'No Outlet.'

They arrived in the parking area to a scattering of vehicles, most of them pickups. Heidi opened the car door into a light breeze carrying the scent of conifers and sage. Gering ran in excited circles, stopping momentarily to visit a bush as she rummaged in the trunk for a light flannel shirt to put on under her jacket. In her experience, alpine temperatures could cool rapidly.

She grabbed the small knapsack with their lunch and water, clipped on Gering's leash and walked over to read an information board. A map showed the trails around the lake, marked with their distance and rigor. Next to it hung a poster with a photo of a coiled snake with a triangular head, tail tipped up in a jaunty fashion. The poster warned visitors to respect the privacy of *Crotalus oreganus concolor,* the Midget Faded Rattlesnake, a small subspecies known for its drab color pattern. It was described as an endangered, highly venomous, shy creature occasionally found basking on rocks near the lake from May to September. Hiking boots were recommended. Heidi looked at her sandals and Gering's four naked paws and vowed to be watchful.

They emerged at the top of a short, steep trail into a sparse stand of trees that sloped gently downward to patches of sand interspersed with broader expanses of pebbles. As they walked toward the water, they passed a sign indicating the narrow trail that disappeared around a tumble of boulders on the right led to Toot's Peak. Reeds stood in a marshy-looking area a short distance to the left. Ripples on the surface of the water caught the light and Heidi stood still, inhaling deeply, drawing in the beauty of it all.

She heard shouts from the other side of the lake and could just make out figures on a rocky ledge. One jumped and rose to the surface with a great deal of splashing. Laughter came from others bobbing in the water. She grinned at the sounds of their high spirits and marveled at how well their voices carried over the water. "There are no secrets by a lakeside," her father used to say.

Ten years ago, she would have chosen that side of the lake but now she was content to be the only visible human on this side. Ahead, a low, flat slab of granite extended into the water and she carefully checked around the rock's base for snakes before removing Gering's leash. She walked out onto the slab. It must be massive; the water at its far end looked deep. She removed her jacket and sandals and placed them with her backpack on the rock, arranging her jacket so the pocket with Peter's ashes faced the sun. Gering looked dubiously over the side of the rock into the water. Heidi rolled up her pants, walked back onto the shore and prepared to wade.

"Oh, cold, cold, cold," she gasped, laughing with the pure

joy of feeling the soft muck under her feet. She entered the water to mid-calf and called, "Gering come on. It's cold, cold, cold."

Gering gave a sharp bark and sat on the shore looking at her stubbornly, his brow furrowed in consternation. She waded back out of the water and returned to the rock, the dog at her heels. She took off her watch, and looked around before stripping down to her blue bra and underpants—they could pass for a bathing suit. She walked to the end of the granite slab and dove off into the water's darkness.

The temperature dropped precipitously with every foot and she emerged, gasping, to Gering's frantic barks as he pranced around the surface of the rock. She dove deep again and emerged to find his anxiety had reached a fever pitch. She returned with a few powerful strokes and hoisted herself out of the water with chattering teeth, chastising the dog for being so silly. He circled her feet and paused intermittently to attempt to lick her dry.

Heidi twisted her hair into a rope, squeezed it to shed the water and dried herself with her flannel shirt. She donned her jacket. It came to mid-thigh, so she removed her underpants, then managed to remove her bra. She spread her underwear and her damp shirt out on the rock to dry in the sun and walked back to the shore to stand ankle deep in the water, a breeze raising goose bumps on her bare legs. She called to Gering to come and get his feet wet. He joined her tentatively, lifting his paws and shaking them delicately until he got used to the cold, snapping at the water a few times before taking a drink. He shook his head and released a flurry of sneezes as water entered his nose. Their feet disturbed tiny flecks of black, gold and orange as they dabbled. A dragonfly hovered just off shore with an audible buzz, its abdomen bright red, its two pairs of membranous wings large and transparent.

They returned to the rock to eat their lunch. "When we come back, we bring a swim suit and towel and more food for you," she assured Gering, who had wolfed down his biscuits and was looking at her expectantly. "I love to swim," she said as she handed over a small piece of her sandwich. "Next time we do a better job. We will bring a piece of sausage for you and a little wine and chocolate for me."

Gering stretched out in the sun, ignoring the raw cry of a bird as it swept down from a rocky crag and disappeared. A breeze quaked the leaves of a tree near the tumble of rocks. Heidi listened to the happy shrieks of the people jumping into the water on the other side of the lake.

"So many miles, so many years ago," she whispered, throwing a stick into the lake. Picnics with her parents had included a table cloth, cheeses, sausage, bread, cucumber and tomato, several kinds of fruit, torte, a little wine for her mother, who would be driving them home, more for her father. After lunch, she left her parents to read or doze and walked around the lake with Ingo, hoping to find a school friend also escaping the boredom of picnicking with parents. If Ingo was lucky, another dog would join them, the dogs exploring the shore as she and her friend sat and talked about the adventures to come. Only her best friend wanted marriage, children, a home right away. The rest of them promised each other they wouldn't settle for their parents' lives, not ever.

Putting on her dry underpants was an easy job compared the gyrations required to put her bra back on under her jacket. She wiggled this way and that, laughing when one of her arms got stuck in its sleeve. With bra in place, she removed her jacket and once more arranged it on the rock so the pocket with Peter's ashes faced the sun. She stood surveying the lake with her arms stretched wide, basking in the warmth of the sun on her bare shoulders, midriff and thighs. Gering slept curled like a prawn on her flannel shirt. Although the breeze had dropped, she shivered, so she crouched down to move him.

At an explosive release of air behind them, Gering was up and barking. Heidi stood and turned, her breath catching at the sight of a man in a black cowboy hat sitting motionless on a horse at the edge of the trees. She bent over, grabbed her shirt and clutched it to her. The man remained motionless; she couldn't see his eyes, but she felt them. The horse gave another loud snort, shook its head and nickered. The man put his hand to his hat, nodded briefly and pulled the horse's head to the right. He made a clicking sound, leaned forward slightly, and the horse gave a delicate prance before taking off on the trail that led to Toot's Peak.

"You should have made the growl sooner," she admonished Gering as he slunk toward her, his tail low. She put on her pants, shirt and jacket, reminding herself that her blue underwear would look like a swimsuit to anyone who wasn't looking too closely.

"Anyway, what does it matter?" she asked Gering. "I was covered, there was nothing to see." She sat down and gathered the dog into her lap. She felt foolish for being so unaware. How long had they been watched?

"Next time I, too, will pay more attention, but it is okay," she assured Gering. "We will not let a man on a horse embarrass us. And a man on a horse is better than a man standing there watching us without a horse."

She took her watch out of her backpack and checked the time. They had another hour at least. The rock's warmth was seductive, and she determinably pushed her discomfiture away. She lay back and tucked Gering's unresisting body next to her. "Twenty-three days ago, I leave New York and now look," she said softly, "I have the job at Saint Gemma's, I have you and we have our first picnic by a lake. I am glad I went swimming. Next time, I will bring the proper suit and I will swim longer and you will have to stop being the worry wart."

She closed her eyes and willed her muscles to relax. Slowly

her tension eased and she murmured to Gering, "Shall I tell you why I had to leave New York? You are a nervous boy and if I do this, I will have to tell you about Anke Mueller and I do not think you will like her one bit."

Gering yawned, which Heidi took as his lack of concern, so she continued, "The first time I see Anke I think '*Raubtier.*' It means predator. If you see her, the hair on your neck will stand up." She scratched her fingers in the hair at his withers and the little dog stretched his neck in pleasure. "Anke graduated at the top of her class from Munich University's School of Business. She says this a lot. I first hear her say it in the car when we drive away from the airport. I tell her to sit in the front seat, so she can see more of New York, but also I want to watch her. Then she says to Claus, not to me, but to Claus, 'I am so happy to be here and to help you with your restaurant. The business of food is my passion.' Claus looks at me in the mirror. He is embarrassed, but only a little."

Something in Heidi's voice made Gering press closer and she stroked him absently.

"One day I enter the office and I find Claus and Anke standing too close, his hand on her bottom, right here," she patted Gering's behind to illustrate, "and they separate so fast I know, I know they have been having sex. Not in the office, but somewhere. I know one other thing also. I know Emmett Vogel sends her to be my replacement, and a week later, I leave."

She fell silent as she remembered standing in the darkened restaurant—the pristine white tablecloths, the rose-colored napkins folded just so—and bidding goodbye to the years of heartache and happiness, exhilaration and exhaustion. After taking the money, she had left a note in the safe, *I want nothing more.* It hadn't been true. She also took the Mercedes.

In the underground garage, the car was parked near enough to a safety light that it appeared to beckon. She slid into the seat and sat for a moment, resting her forehead on the steering wheel. What had she whispered? *"Dies ist, wie es werden soll."* This is how it shall be. *"Es tut mir nicht leid."* I am not sorry. Yes, that is what she had said to the car, the garage, the concrete pillars, the sultry night air of that proud American city.

She had taken Peter's ashes from her pocket and placed them in the carved wooden box in the glove compartment. The box was from Karl and Beppe, so of course Claus hadn't liked it. It was inscribed with the words, *Peter, Sohn meines Herzens.* Peter Son of my Heart. Claus said the inscription was maudlin, that life continues, they would have another child.

The heavy black car had rolled smoothly toward the entrance of the garage. She leaned out the window to press a button and the garage door had labored upward with a screech and a moan. She paused before turning right onto the deserted street and looked in the opposite direction, toward Café Claus.

The *door.* She had given a gasp, a great shuddering catch of air. The hand-carved door from Black Forest oak hanging between the atrium and the dining room—it was *Peter's* door.

She had parked in the alley behind Café Claus and let herself in through the back entrance to make her call. Sebastian's father answered the phone and she understood the mixture of relief and irritation in his voice. When a household includes impetuous young men, a late-night call never goes unanswered. He went to rouse his son and shortly Heidi heard male voices speaking in Spanish approaching the phone, a woman's plaintive voice joining in.

Silence as someone covered the mouthpiece, then Sebastian had come on the line. He interrupted her request with, "Heidi, it's your door. Fucking Claus doesn't get to keep the door." He said he and his cousin would get his uncle's truck and meet her in half an hour.

The restaurant no longer felt like hers and she returned to the car to wait. Two hours had already eaten into Monday's twenty-four and after leaving the city, she would drive just far enough to commit to her journey. A rap on the window and she opened her eyes to Sebastian's grin and his cousin's nervous energy. The strong young men had the door off its hinges and in the back of their truck in less than twenty minutes.

"We'll store it for you as long as you want," Sebastian promised before getting in the truck. "Go find a life, woman. It's about time. If it wasn't for my family, I'd go with you, but we're New Yorkers, born and bred. There's nowhere else for us, but you . . ." he had placed his hands on her shoulders, shaking her gently, "you find a place with a strong doorframe and we'll bring you the door."

And Sebastian's family would have to store the door for a good while yet, thought Heidi, unable to imagine it hanging in Riverton. The temperature dropped, the rock became uncomfortably hard and she looked at her watch. If they left now, there would be enough light to guide them home.

"A good day, a *wonderful* day," she said, smiling at Gering as she gathered their things. Before descending into the parking lot, she stopped to look back at the lake. She imagined a scattering of Peter's ashes fanning across the water's surface, bobbing on ripples that reflected the sun's light like diamonds.

Sunday did not go well. Heidi had finished her book the night before and the library was closed. She bought a paperback at a market and read the first few chapters before putting it down, the characters dull and the plot predictable. She and Gering went on a walk, Wyoming public radio repeated programs she had already heard, she cleaned, they went on another walk, she came home and cleaned some more. She went to bed too early and longed for Monday as her mind hovered over a nest occupied by the deaths of her baby and her parents and the dog, who had been her childhood companion.

Was it any kind of progress that her broken marriage no longer resided there?

CHAPTER SEVEN

NOT EVERYONE WANTS A FOUNTAIN

Walking home from work at the end of the week, Heidi realized with a stab of alarm that she hadn't put enough thought into planning her third weekend off. The car's engine had developed a ping during their drive back from Comfrey and she had taken it to a garage recommended by Ray Dolan. The mechanic was still waiting for a part, hers being the only foreign car he worked on. Tomorrow she could spend time at the library, she could clean while listening to the Saturday opera on the radio, she could . . . what? She didn't want to drift aimlessly in and out of shops. How many walks could she take with Gering? If she wasn't physically tired, she wouldn't be able to concentrate on a book for long; there would be gaps in the day, too much time to think, and then there would be Sunday to face.

They halted so Gering could explore a damp patch near a gatepost. Another dog had claimed this as his territory and Gering did not agree. As the little dog took his time considering how much urine this gatepost warranted when there were other places that needed to be marked before he got home, she pondered the two days looming ahead. She needed more to do, more to distract her from the emptiness that threatened to consume her if she couldn't fill it with activity. She raised her eyes to the sky and pleaded for a sign.

She closed her eyes and drew in the dry scent of sage and prairie grasses as she listened to the sound of the wind stirring the leaves of the cottonwood trees across the road.

Suddenly, Gering tugged at his leash and she heard a voice. "Hello, sweet boy," it said softly, in a tone any animal lover would use to address a small, purposeful dog. Heidi turned to see a middle-aged woman had come onto the sidewalk behind them, holding a pair of secateurs and a bunch of deep pink roses.

"I know this little dachshund," the woman said. She asked if Heidi had rented Ray Dolan's place, a block over.

"Yes," Heidi said. "Gering comes with the house."

"Gering?" The woman chuckled. "That's different, very Germanish. He didn't have a name when Ray started knocking on doors trying to find him a home. I would have taken him, but my husband's looking for a hunting dog, like the guys at his work." She looked wistfully at Gering. "Looks like you're getting plenty of love now, little fella, new leash, new collar, bounce in your step, wiggle in your wag."

Gering responded by exaggerating the wiggle in his wag and the woman handed Heidi the roses so she could pick him up.

Heidi learned the roses were a variety called *Winnipeg Parks*. Romeo's nursery purchased them from a Canadian supplier and they were the perfect, cold-hardy rose for a Riverton winter. Disease resistant, tough, and they would bloom for months if they were deadheaded routinely.

"It's not a flower with a big smell, but it's there if you concentrate," the woman said, returning Gering to the ground. "We each get half," she continued, taking the roses back and dividing the bunch. "Welcome to Riverton."

As they neared home, Heidi gave a sigh of pure pleasure, a sigh so light and comforting, she gave it again. In New York, she had bought roses from a young Armenian who had a stand near the restaurant. Often the flowers had romantic names, *April Moon, Carol Cordelia, Hayley Rose,* lovely, tender, lush and fragrant.

A *Winnipeg Parks,* a practical name for a hardy rose, yet . . . she buried her nose in the bouquet again . . . yet, with petals as soft as a baby's cheek.

"Thank you," she whispered, turning her face to the sky.

Tomorrow they would plant a rose. There was a wagon in the garage. She would pull it down to the nursery, less than half a mile away, and they would pick out their rose. If need be, she would make a second trip for potting soil and a perhaps third for some rosemary to plant under the bedroom window. Back and forth she would go, pulling her wagon. It would take up much of the day.

"A small bite, *one* rose bush, a few little rosemary plants; we do not take the bite that is too big to chew," she said to Gering.

After years of watching her father's obsessive ministrations to his large, lush German garden, she knew the incessant demands made by plants and if you let them, they laid claim to every minute of your spare time. But she could nurture a winter-hardy rose, some rosemary and perhaps she'd buy some plants for the two empty containers on the patio.

A flapping white thing greeted them as they approached the front door. Gering halted, dipped his head and gave a low growl.

"Just paper, you silly boy," said Heidi removing the note.

She turned on the kitchen light, put the roses in sink and unfolded her landlord's message. She read the words slowly, then again with mounting alarm.

"*Sie hätten uns wirklich konsultieren sollen,*" she moaned to Gering, 'they really should have consulted us!'

Tomorrow morning, four workmen would be arriving with a load of garden soil, fertilizer, plants (Ray had listed them all), and a fountain. She had been in Riverton thirteen days, her landlord was a friend of her employers. A trap was being set to keep her here and she was sure all three were involved.

"Oh yes, I know they are the dear people, but they smother me," she said to Gering bitterly as she put his dinner into his bowl. "They think a garden makes the person put down the roots."

She phoned Ray Dolan, no answer, no answering machine. She phoned the nursery. They were closed. She muttered under her breath as she arranged the roses in a vase she found on a shelf in the garage. The lightness she had felt such a short time ago had condensed into something lowering, heavy and oppressive.

She walked outside to the edge of the patio and stood staring at the scrubby expanse before her. In the gathering dark, she couldn't see much further than the end of the property, barely into the graveyard, nothing of the playing field and school beyond. In Wyoming, she would never need a school, or a fountain, or a garden filled with plants that would need tending until they became another tenant's responsibility, living things that might die for lack of care.

She had planned to buy one rose bush tomorrow. *One.* Her landlord had ordered a dozen, plus lavender, rosemary, an elderberry and a quince, flats of vegetables and a fountain. A *fountain,* everybody wanted a fountain until they had to take care of one. On days he was well enough, she had pushed Peter in his carriage to the small, gated garden near their apartment. It had a fountain in the middle and often the gardener complained to her about having to remove the algae or tinker with the motor.

When the truck arrived tomorrow morning, she would refuse to let the men take the fountain off, refuse most of the plants, certainly all of the vegetables. She worked with vegetables all day long; she didn't want to grow them at home.

She tried her landlord's phone one more time, no answer.

If the men arrived before she could halt the delivery, she would allow them to enrich a small area near the patio for two roses. Yes, she nodded to herself, she would accept *two* of the twelve roses. Life was a compromise and that would be hers. And she might accept some of the rosemary and lavender. They were tough. She would have to remain outside the whole time to make sure the men stayed by the house so the little killdeer that had attempted to hide her eggs in plain sight by laying them in an area of gravel and small rocks half way down the slope would not be disturbed.

Summer was the worst time to introduce so many new plants into a garden; the nursery and her landlord should have known better. The plants would be in shock. They would require extra water. She didn't even have a hose. Each day she would have to check them; leaves would yellow or furl, black spots or white spots might appear, she wouldn't be able to leave them on their own to fight for nutrients, combat molds and insects. Caring for Peter had awoken a vigilance within her and now all life demanded her attention in its balancing act.

"Gering," she called sharply. He had approached too close to the killdeer nest and now the little mother was feigning injury by dragging her wing along the ground to lead him away from her eggs.

"You know better," she reprimanded the dachshund and he looked at her boldly. "Gering," she said sharply, and he had the good grace to lower his eyes.

A large truck filled with dirt and pulling a trailer with wheelbarrows, shovels, hoes and a pickaxe arrived early the next morning and Heidi was waiting.

"I try to telephone to tell you not to come," she said, standing on her toes to talk to the driver. The man looked down at her, smiled, turned off the engine and climbed down.

"Office doesn't open 'til eight. I'm Aaron," he said, extending a hand.

"Heidi Vogel," she replied, giving his hand a perfunctory shake. "Please do not unload the trucks until I speak to my landlord. I do not rent this house to plant a large garden."

"Your landlord is Ray Dolan, right? He told us not to bother you and just get to work," said Aaron. "We're doing all the planting. You can just . . ."

"I only need a small part of the dirt," Heidi broke in.

As if she had not spoken, he continued, "You're going to need all of the dirt. There's a lotta plants coming and Riverton's soil is not the best."

"Riverton soil is good for Riverton plants, and I have Riverton plants in the backyard already," she said firmly.

She asked Aaron to wait and hurried over to another truck that had just drawn up. "My landlord orders all this but he does not ask me," she explained to driver, who stepped down.

"I'm Corey," he said. "Ray Dolan says you're German."

He smiled at the pretty frowning lady. He had thought of German women being squared-jawed and stocky, not looking like this.

"Yes, and in Germany, the landlord does not make up the mind for the tenant," Heidi said. She listed the plants she would accept, those she would not and concluded with, "I also refuse the fountain."

Two more men arrived in a small pickup and Heidi paused to glare at them as they got out to lean against the side of their truck, arms folded. She turned her attention back to Corey, who was sounding apologetic, and asked him to please repeat what he said.

"I said sorry but the fountain's a sale item and can't be returned."

"This is nonsense," she said in disbelief. "You cannot make a person who has rented a house without a fountain take a fountain."

She looked from Corey to the men by the pickup, inviting them to agree with her, when Aaron walked up. "Problem?" he asked.

"She's saying no vegetables, only wants two of the roses, will take the lavender and rosemary, no to the quince and elderberry," said Corey patiently. "She only wants half the soil. She likes her tough little Riverton plants."

Heidi glared at Corey. "Do not talk about me like you pretend I am not here. I do not want to take care of so many plants. I do not want a fountain; to make a person take a fountain is ridiculous."

"Got a point," muttered one of the men leaning against the pickup. As Heidi's voice rose, the other man grinned and whispered in admiration, "A looker and she's tough."

"Real sorry about the sale item rule, but Corey's right, it's out of our hands," said Aaron, shaking his head ruefully. "Let's you and me take a look at the backyard. I know these little houses have big yards. You won't even have to put water in the damn fountain, how's that? Use it to store stuff, maybe make it a planter."

"Next you will say make it a great big ashtray," said Heidi, marching toward the side of the house. "Or you tell me to have the party and cook the pig in it."

"C'mon," Aaron said, with a chuckle. He turned his head to grin and wink at the other men before following her.

He suggested a spot for the fountain just off the patio, near enough to the outside electrical outlet for an extension cord. When Heidi insisted she wasn't going to turn the fountain on, he pointed out the next tenant might and to move it later would be an unnecessary hassle for everyone. They returned to the front of the house to find all the plants off the truck and the three men now in the process of filling the wheelbarrows with dirt.

"It does not make the sense that you take all these plants off the truck before you move the dirt," Heidi said, exasperated. "Now you need to put most of them back on, and remember I say I need only a little of the dirt. We keep the garden small."

"Oh, damn, what were we thinking?" Corey asked men, who had helped him rapidly unload the plants the moment Heidi and Aaron had disappeared.

"Damn it, guys, we all heard her say it," Aaron joined in. "Now we've got a contamination problem."

"What is this?" Heidi demanded.

"The thing is, once a plant's off the truck and on the ground, it can't be reloaded and brought back to the nursery," Aaron explained. "Wyoming Department of Agriculture's real strict about it. They're concerned about contamination with, you know, stuff that could be brought back to the nursery."

"Well, I do not believe this rule from the Department of Agriculture. You or you," she pointed at Aaron and Corey, "will come inside and we will telephone them."

Corey winced and said, "Department's closed on weekends."

Heidi's stared at the four men as it dawned on her just what was going on. "You men planned this," she said slowly, evenly. "I wonder when I see the looks you give each other," her accent became stronger, her voice rose and her eyes flashed as her words picked up speed, "and now I know you make the plan to distract me. You distract me with this man," she stabbed her finger at Aaron, "and the rest of you, so fast you put the plants on the ground to contaminate them."

"Aw, Heidi," said Corey, as if they were old friends, "it's not like that and no one's saying you *have* to take all the plants, just that they can't go back to the nursery. We'll phone Ray, see if he wants them at his place. He might take the vegetables but he's got that trick knee, no way can he do a lot of gardening. He'll probably tell us to take them to the dump, and the nursery may split the loss with him."

Heidi stood, eyes narrowed, hands on her hips, trying to

control her breathing.

Aaron said soothingly, "If you let us, we'll set you up in your garden and the four of us will be out of here in five or six hours."

Heidi took a step toward him and he backed up, biting back a grin, holding his hands up as if warding her off.

Corey stepped in, "Your call, Heidi. We get it and it's not your fault if these plants die at the dump. But we do all the work planting back there and all you'll have to do is water every now and then. My wife would be happy with a big garden to putter around in, show it off when she has the ladies to lunch."

"The maintenance is more than water and it is every day, forever," Heidi snapped. "You think I am the idiot?"

The men shook their heads solemnly and stared at the ground for a good half minute until Heidi released a long, frustrated sigh and threw up her hands. "I give up. You win, and what do you win?" She shrugged, her mouth a hard, tight line. "When I move away, you will all still be here, thinking you understand women and what is good for them. If the new tenant comes and lets the plants die, I will be gone and I will not have to see it."

Six hours later, after all the dirt had been moved, the fountain assembled, the two trees, twelve roses, lavender and rosemary planted and the men had driven away, Ray found Heidi sitting on a kitchen chair on the patio.

"Thank you for the fountain on sale that cannot be returned," she said, her voice without intonation, her arms folded. "And thank you for all the plants that touch the ground so they cannot be returned. Your telephone machine does not work?"

He ignored the question. "Patsy, Edith and my wife chose the fountain," he said. "They said it would make you feel at home because there's so many fountains in Germany."

"In Germany we are busy people; we do not have more fountains than the people in other countries."

"Well, sure you do. The girls took a trip to Europe with our pastor a few years ago. They saw lots of fountains." Ray knew better than to add he hadn't felt the need to waste money on going himself. What did Europe have to offer that couldn't be found better and cheaper at home?

When she didn't respond, Ray limped over to examine the cast-stone fountain, Gering following. The old man reached out a hand to test the stability of the upper tier, and when he turned to look at her, Heidi saw his age and felt a stab of something akin to sorrow.

"Not gonna fall down, bigger than I thought it would be. You like the birds?" Ray asked.

On the upper tier, two doves perched on the handle of a stone basket with their wings partially open. They faced each other, one slightly higher than the other, necks craning toward each other, beaks almost touching as if one was about to feed the other. Heidi did like the birds. She thought she had never seen a more beautiful garden fountain.

The shame she felt at her lack of gratitude was tempered with still enough anger at being manipulated to allow her to say, "I decide to leave the fountain without water. I may cook the pig in it."

Ray chuckled and said, "Sounds like a plan but I have a hose and outdoor cord in the truck. Let's just put some water in and try it out. If you still don't like it, we'll drain the blasted thing and you can cook your pig in it."

As Ray filled the fountain, Heidi brought a second kitchen chair onto the patio, returning to the kitchen to prepare iced tea. The sound of water, dripping hesitantly at first and then settling into an even flow drew her to the kitchen window. The old man held Gering under his arm as they stood watching the water bubble up between the doves and rain down two tiers into much wider, shallower basin that rested directly on the ground.

"Peter, listen," she said softly, her throat tight.

They had both loved the sound of the water falling from the outstretched hands of three stone angels in the fountain in the little neighborhood park near their apartment in New York. She would pat the water with her hands and sprinkle the baby with drops as he gave his whispery laugh, his pale blue eyes dancing in pleasure, his little hands opening and closing.

CHAPTER EIGHT

A NEW LIFE IN NEW YORK CITY: 1985

Café Claus was well into its third year when Claus Vogel phoned to give his father a business report and inadvertently announced that Heidi was pregnant. Heidi had asked him to wait until she reached her third month but Claus said that good news had a mind of its own. It just slipped out before he could seal his lips against it, and of course, his father was elated. To celebrate, Emmett Vogel insisted that his clever, fecund daughter-in-law should have a gift of her choosing from Germany. Whatever she wished, a gift to bring some of their homeland to New York City.

Frustrated, disappointed in Claus, smothered by her distant father-in-law's relentless presence in their lives, Heidi thought for only a day before announcing she wanted a door. A door hand-carved from Black Forest oak, with arcs of glass imbedded at eye level, Heidi's eye level. And three swallows carrying a garland of Edelweiss as they flew above a German-shorthaired hunting dog. The dog on point, tail straight out, nose forward toward a pheasant escaping into the sky. The craftsman would need a very pale wood for the Edelweiss. The flowers must not be painted but embedded and feathered to denote their characteristic hairy appearance. Yes, she understood that to represent the flower's texture would be very difficult if the pieces were inlaid and not merely painted, and she knew no one else but her clever father-in-law would be able to find such a craftsman.

Heidi lay on her side on their bed, nausea temporarily at bay, and watched the heads of the geraniums on the fire escape across the narrow alleyway bounce as the rain assaulted them, brave splashes of dancing scarlet relieving the monotony of the grey concrete wall.

She listened with satisfaction as Claus, pacing back and forth in the sitting room, repeated once more into the phone, "She says she does not want anything else."

A pause then, "*Nein, Vater*. She does not find a clock necessary. She doesn't think a clock in a restaurant is a good thing. It is the door she wants or she says thank you, but she wants nothing. She says you are too kind to even offer."

Heidi received no pleasure imagining Emmett Vogel's cold grey eyes seeking his wife or daughter to receive the brunt of his indignation after he hung up. He had offered an early glimpse into his cruelty the first time they'd met. Over a laden dinner table at his house outside the North Sea port city of Cuxhaven, Emmett had ignored his wife, daughter and son and spoken exclusively to her. He heard reports that her determination and talent exceeded even her looks, he had said, fixing her with his steely eyes. For reasons he would never understand, he confided, offering a disingenuous smile, he had somehow managed to produce a handsome son, who jumped at his own shadow and everyone else's.

"Such a pity, but perhaps our dear boy will find a wife with your looks and ambition who can infuse some mettle into this family," Herr Vogel had added, raising his wine glass to her.

Her shock at the man's audacity and rudeness robbed her of comment, but she had gripped her wine glass by the stem, met his eyes and refused to raise her glass. When her lack of response threatened to lengthen, Emmett laughed, looked to his wife and asked her to pass the potatoes. That had been the moment, Heidi realized now, she and Emmett Vogel had made the same mistake; each of them had underestimated the other.

And once again poor dear Claus, "*Nein,* it has to be a door just as she described. She says only a father-in-law such as you would be able to get someone to make a door like this. But if what she asks is too difficult, even for you, she understands."

Peter was born just before noon on the third Wednesday of hot, humid August. Although full term, he had skin so translucent it barely masked the webs of purple vessels that valiantly attempted to distribute oxygen up and down his emaciated limbs. Ashen and struggling to breathe, he fixed his pale blue eyes on his mother's face and his lips twitched in a grimace. Heidi held him close and rested her lips on his damp forehead, tasting the extra saltiness characteristic of the sweat of a cystic fibrosis baby.

On the other side of his family, Karl had a second cousin, Alice Lykke, who had cystic fibrosis. But that was the *other* side of Karl's family, not Heidi's side. No one on her side had the disease, except her father was adopted and her mother a single child, so they didn't really have much data to go on.

The gene's expression was variable, the doctor said. Some children were born sicker than others, but even for milder cases, treatments would be multiple times a day for life. But Heidi knew this already. She and Alice had become friends because Alice worked for Karl. Heidi was familiar with the digestive enzymes to aid in food absorption, the nebulizers, the chest pounding to break up the thick mucus that gathered. Treatment would become habitual, a part of the routine of living. Alice was in her twenties. She was a hardworking employee, so good at her job and she enjoyed life. She lived. Peter would be like Alice.

Eight weeks after Peter's birth, stevedores carried Heidi's magnificent door from the cargo hold of the *Axel Fuchs* docked at the Port of New York. Sebastian Tellez, the newly hired sous chef, and his brother waited with a borrowed truck to transport the door to Café Claus, where it would hang between the atrium and the dining room.

"Sweet Jesus be praised," said his brother as Sebastian expertly slashed tape on one side of the heavy cardboard that fronted the door and peeled it back so they could take a glimpse. The dark, heavy oak door was magnificent. The wood carver had formed the garland of Edelweiss flowers from a silvery, almost white wood. The flowers' centers were inlaid with gold leaf. He had also applied gold to the hunting dog's eyes and the wing feathers of the escaping pheasant.

"We will hang it after work tonight so Heidi can bring the baby to see it. She calls it Peter's door," said Sebastian. "Those flowers, they're a special German thing." The young men craned their necks to see the full garland. "Looks like Heidi got what she wanted from her *imbécil* father-in-law."

"You have met him?"

"No, but Claus is scared of him. You should see his face when he has to talk to his dad on the phone. 'Course he's scared of everything, so he's *un imbécil* too."

The following month, Heidi took Peter to the restaurant to see his door hanging between the atrium and the dining room. She traced the garland with his cool little hand, as pale as the linden wood flowers, and said, "The Edelweiss flower. It is the symbol of nobility, loyalty and strength, like you, *Liebling*." The baby's colorless lips gave a tentative smile as he blinked his pale blue eyes.

But Peter was not to be like Alice. He was not to be among the majority of cystic fibrosis babies who nowadays survive beyond early childhood. She and Claus were to be excluded from families like Alice's, who looked forward to research and new treatments that offer hope, comfort, quality of life and quantity . . . years, many years of good life.

Peter died of pneumonia two days before his paternal grandfather arrived from Germany, unaccompanied by his

wife and daughter. They had been prepared to celebrate the
baptism that had been delayed by Peter's many hospital visits,
but found they could not face a memorial.

"I lie in bed and send my poor husband to fight," Heidi
whispered as she pulled the covers higher and heard Claus
plead with his father in the sitting room, "*Vater,* I tell you it
was from both of us. It takes a gene from both parents so I
inherited from you or *Mater,* although the cousin with this is
on your side. There is no blame. It is just sadness now."

Harsh mutterings from Herr Vogel. The bedroom wall
vibrated as he paced in the living room. Heidi reached out her
hand and pressed it hard against the wall. She squeezed her
eyes shut as Claus said, in a voice that had risen an octave in
his distress, "Yes, we *will* try again, but when *she* is ready.
There is a seventy-five percent chance another baby will not
have this."

"I decide. I decide *when,* I decide *if* and when," Heidi
repeated over and over as she rolled her head on her pillow.

"There was no need for this. You should have checked her
family. You knew about my sister's child," she heard her
father-in-law say with controlled fury. "All this time and all
this pain wasted on a child so sick; it is fair to no one."

She wanted to open the bedroom door and shout, "I thank
God Peter never had to meet you, you evil, controlling, bad,
bad man. *No one* loves you and you can go to hell. Peter was
more loved than you will ever be."

She almost got up; she almost went to the door.

"*Wann habe ich angefangen Geheimnisse zu haben?*" she
asked Peter, 'When did I start to have secrets?' She poured his
ashes out of the ornate urn on the mantel into a fine white
linen handkerchief, which she tied with a ribbon and tucked
into the knitted yellow cap that had been a newborn present
from Karl and Beppe. The cap was interwoven with red
thread, so when Peter wore it, his little round head had

resembled her favorite apple, a Cox's orange pippin.

The 5.3 ounces of powdery grey ash became a firm and comforting presence in her hand. Claus would never know the urn had been emptied. He'd never look. She was sure of that. The little, round apple of ashes would accompany her to work, to the market, on her walks through the park. Was it safe to carry something irreplaceable in a pocket? Was anything, was anyone ever safe?

"I must go to work, but as a mother, you should take the time you need," Claus told Heidi gently when she insisted on returning to work sooner than he thought she should. "The kitchen staff understands you need more time to mourn."

"I will mourn every day until my last breath, but I will not lie in this apartment and mourn. It will smother me to do that," said Heidi, speaking almost absently as she looked out the window to the geraniums on the fire escape across the alley. The crimson red ones had been replaced by pink. Geraniums were tough, but the red ones must have died. How sad, she liked them better.

"I will mourn as I walk down the street," she said. "I will mourn as I kick dead leaves aside, as I pass that poor creature who drinks in the doorway of St. Andrew's. I will put my empty arms to work and mourn as I bake, but today I go back to work."

Claus looked away. He didn't know what more to say to her. She had been so absorbed by the health of their child, she had distanced him, and his arms were no longer able to bridge the divide. Her cousin and his homosexual lover had flown in for Peter's funeral, and when they arrived, the two men and Heidi had stuck together, looking through him like he wasn't even there. What did they talk about? Men like that couldn't possibly understand what it was like to lose a child.

Heidi smiled sympathetically at her husband's solemn face. Poor Claus. He tried so hard to walk a safe, acceptable path, always looking for approval. He had never gotten it from his father, and now she feared he would no longer get it from her; she simply no longer had the energy give. He would have to learn to stand on his own. She opened the widow wide, small figures on the pavement, a man and child walking a black dog. She gave a sudden gasp of pain as an ambulance sped by, its siren piercing the air. An emergency had rent the fabric of a family somewhere.

Claus left the apartment before her, almost certainly to prepare the kitchen staff for her arrival. She knew he was afraid they would think less of her for returning a week after Peter's memorial, but Karl and Beppe had left yesterday and she had no doubt the staff would understand her need to work. She had interviewed each of them herself, giving personality equal weight to expertise; the latter could be learned, the former could not.

During her last months of pregnancy, she had taken to sitting more often, allowing the others to assume some of her tasks. She taught Rosita and Gabriel how to make *Sachertorte* and *Donauwelle*, with its sour cherries and rich chocolate glaze. They mimicked her accent and she mimicked theirs. She tried to learn some Jamaican Patois, some Spanish, and they learned some German. Her shortbread went home to an aunt or grandmother upon request. She listened to advice on parenting, laughing at the arguments that arose. Although only three in the kitchen had children, in America *everyone* had an opinion on how to raise a child.

Americans. There was a directness about many of them that crossed boundaries of gender, race and religion. They were a friendly, informal people. Her friends had warned her that New Yorkers were pushy and rude, and they were, but also boisterous, welcoming, and to her mind, generous and kind.

They had become her friends, the Jamaicans, the Puerto

Ricans, the runaway from California, the native New Yorkers, including the black veteran with one eye. She needed them now. Claus didn't feel the richness of their lives; he didn't hear as they joked, told stories, and teased each other as they chopped vegetables, stirred sauces, carved meats and seasoned stews.

The staff politely returned Claus's greeting whenever he walked through the kitchen to his office, but Heidi knew they didn't think much of him. They would watch in amusement as he turned to give his customary shy wave before firmly closing the office door.

"It's like he's scared of us," one of them once said to Heidi, and the others agreed.

"Not scared," she had said out of loyalty. "He just does not know you." But he was scared—he feared their talent and their heart.

In the evenings, Claus remained out front, charming guests with his attention and European poise. He kept an eye on the waitresses, filled water glasses when needed and followed Heidi's script when recommending a wine to complement a specific dish. During the occasional lull, Claus sat at the bar and shared insights with the bartender—a man, he told Heidi, who understood the differences that naturally separated people and made them more comfortable with their own kind.

On this day, her first foray outside alone after Peter's memorial, New York loomed large, the buildings almost met overhead, blocking the sun, traffic flew by. As she walked briskly down litter-strewn blocks toward Café Claus, Heidi longed for the intimate quiet she and Peter had shared in his desperate struggle to breathe, the hours they'd spent gazing at each other, his fist gripping her finger with surprising force. They had cocooned themselves in her hope, and what she finally came to accept as his weary resignation. Her hand enclosed the bundle of ashes in her pocket, a fist-full of minerals, the elements her child had left behind.

Someone had forgotten to water the large terra cotta pot outside the travel agency. The flowers had wilted, their heavy heads drooping as if searching for water in the dry soil at their feet. She would send someone back from the kitchen with a pitcher of water. Down the block she saw the restaurant's wooden sign jutting over the sidewalk and as she approached, she heard it protest a sudden gust of wind. She opened the glass outer door and crossed the atrium to stand by Peter's door. She traced the garland of Edelweiss with her fingers, as she had done with her son's tiny, perfect hand some weeks ago.

The kitchen staff looked up with a collective intake of breath as Heidi pushed through the swinging doors and stood before them. The tears that had refused to fall this morning traced a slow path to her collar. One-by-one, they came forward; Rosita led her to a chair, Sebastian brought a towel to mop her face, Leah made tea. Gabriel gave her a tape of prayer songs about children in heaven. A hand-written label on the front of the plastic case said *Kayode*.

"It means 'he brought joy.' My family gathered the songs when they heard Peter was born so sick. We made the tape for you, for comfort when the time came for him to go to God," said the earnest young man, enveloping her in the comforting scent of curry, as he leaned over to kiss her forehead.

He *brought* joy. They had made the tape when Peter was born, so *they* had known Peter wouldn't live long. Were the Jamaicans a wiser, or merely a less sanguine, people? Why her baby, when God allowed so many others with cystic fibrosis to survive?

She looked up to see Claus watching from the office window, the one that didn't open. He pursed his lips in a kiss and they smiled at each other. Heidi held up the tape and waved it at him. He shrugged and pressed his hand to the window; the glass tinted his white palm green.

As he was about to return to his desk, Claus frowned and pointed to call Heidi's attention to Sebastian and Gabriel as they exited the kitchen's backdoor with large water pitchers. Surely, they should be prepping food. Was another friend waiting in the alleyway in a decrepit American car, hood up, radiator steaming?

Heidi mouthed, "Flowers" and made the motion of using a watering can, but Claus shook his head. They could talk of this later. He had work to do. His father would be anxious for his weekly business report.

The exhilarating and frenetic world of a busy restaurant kitchen absorbed Heidi in the months that followed Peter's death. Her walk to work in the morning was spent in silent communion with her child, his bundle of ashes nestled in her pocket. Peter had taken on a wisdom untethered by his hundred and eighty-two days in corporal form. He clarified his mother's thoughts, urged her to consider new and bold food pairings, suggested ways to resolve the occasional conflict that arose between her and his father, warned of vendors who promised more than they delivered. The little handful of minerals had developed a wicked sense of humor and occasionally Heidi found a passerby smiling at her as she grinned when Peter suggested a particularly pithy rejoinder to one of her father-in-law's dictates.

Dissatisfied with Heidi's progress in easing their son's death into the past, Claus insisted they attend a grief counselor to process the seven stages of grief listed in the glossy booklet given to them by the hospital. Heidi felt they could skip some of the stages, but Claus and the counselor said all the stages needed to be addressed and checked off the list. To their counselor's nodding approval, Claus dutifully explored every benchmark; denial of Peter's diagnosis, anger that their family would be afflicted, bargaining with a higher power. Heidi tried to add to the exhumation, but as she saw no value in sharing her daily conversations with her son, she had little to offer.

Heidi understood Peter's voice was her voice, and that he had come to reside in a small part of her psyche where he could continue to participate in her life to the degree he was needed. But she feared if she spoke of him, he would be reduced to a 'coping mechanism,' placed on a timeline and a date would be suggested after which his presence would no longer be considered healthy. She wasn't going to give him up.

CHAPTER NINE

HEIDI MEETS NARA DE'NAE CROW: RIVERTON 1990

One year in Riverton led to two. Heidi had gone to visit Karl and Beppe twice, but she wasn't yet ready to move on. The history etched into the faces that came through the food line fascinated her. Some patrons were regulars, others disappeared after a meal or two. Some of the regulars had their favorite meals and voiced their gratitude when she managed to accommodate them. There were always comments when she tried something new and bold. She made sure to have a backup meal for the less adventurous.

Her morning routine had come to include an escape into her office mid-morning to listen to a portion of Wyoming Public Radio's classical music hour. For the first week of June, the station was featuring Austrian composers and Mozart's Piano Concerto No. 21 would be coming up after a short pledge break. Heidi ordered a delivery of eggs, milk and butter, hung up the phone and turned around to raise the volume on the radio behind her desk. She would settle back to listen to the first two movements before returning to the kitchen to check on lunch preparations.

At Gering's growl, Heidi looked up to see a dark shape looming in the doorway. Closer inspection revealed a young woman with lovely red-brown skin, dressed in bulky clothing, with a backpack slung over her shoulder. Long, black braids spilled down the front of her open navy blue, puffy jacket and, under the jacket, she wore a grey sweatshirt that came almost to her knees. Heidi wouldn't have been surprised if there were more layers of clothing under the sweatshirt. Many who came to Saint Gemma's Kitchen wore most of their wardrobe all day long, either as an added barrier to an intrusive world or because they simply had nowhere to secure their belongings.

"So, you're Heidi, right?" the young woman asked, her face glistening with sweat.

Heidi admitted she was and turned down the volume on the radio. She smiled, ignoring the slight challenge in the voice.

"Okay, well I'm Nara Crow. One of the guys out front said you'd be in here. He gave me this to fill out." Nara held up an application. "Your dog going to object to me coming in?"

Although the young woman's hands were delicate and her face and neck lean, from the little dog's perspective, she must have appeared enormous, even bearlike, in her bulky clothes. Gering rolled back his lips and rumbled. Heidi told him to hush and gestured to the chair in front of her desk.

"Come in and sit. You will be okay. Gering has the growl worse than the bite. All the clothes make you look so big to him."

Advancing into the room, Nara glanced at the dog and said, "Clothes stay on, little man."

She handed over her application and sat, placing the backpack on her lap and wrapping her arms around it as if it were a recalcitrant child she feared would bolt.

"We are lucky. The piano concerto that is about to start is one of Mozart's most popular," said Heidi. "The second movement is the Elvira Madigan part, from the Swedish film. We will not have time for the third movement, although it is very lovely too. If you are in too much of the hurry, you can leave the application and come back to discuss it after two

83

o'clock."

"Not in a hurry," Nara said, looking down to avoid the intense blue of this woman's eyes.

She suppressed a shiver. Eyes that blue reminded her of the curacao cocktails she had knocked back with the bartender at the end of her shift at the casino, blue margaritas, sapphire martinis. Taking a deep breath, she tried to relax in her seat, wondering what they were going to do while the music played. Stare at each other for however long two movements lasted?

To Nara's relief, Heidi bent down to pick up the dog and settled him in her lap. When the music started, Heidi leaned her head back and closed her eyes. Nara looked at the blonde woman in amusement; she sure wouldn't have closed her eyes with a stranger in the room. She surveyed her surroundings. The desk was extremely tidy. A cup sat neatly on a coaster, the few papers resting on top of a file folder would probably be filed in one of those metal file cabinets as soon as they were read, or checked off, or whatever. A big comfortable chair with a footrest occupied a corner—is that where Heidi would be sitting to listen to her music if she were alone?

Nara's face itched and she drew a hand over her upper lip to wipe off the salty beads of moisture. She should have asked how long a movement was. She winced as one of the babies kicked and glanced at the dog. He had his eyes fixed on her and gave her a look like he knew what was going on.

"Fuck you," she mouthed at him.

"You do not like Gering?"

Startled, Nara looked up to see the blue eyes locked on her. She couldn't fake it, a 'fuck you' was unmistakable, so she tried, "It's a term of endearment for dogs in my culture."

The corner of Heidi's mouth twitched, but she held up a hand to halt further talk. "Second movement, less than ten minutes," she murmured, closing her eyes again.

Nara put her backpack on the floor and quietly removed her outer jacket, heaping it on her lap. She wiped the sweat off her forehead with the sleeve of her sweatshirt, conscious of the dog watching her every movement. His nose sniffed the air with rapid little twitches. Nara wrinkled her nose and sniffed right back.

After the concerto's second movement, Heidi turned the music down and returned Gering to the floor. She thanked Nara for her patience and asked if she'd enjoyed the music.

"Yeah, they play it in the bathrooms at the casino where I used to work, but softer and more smoothed out."

The dog approached cautiously and started to sniff at her ankles.

"Aren't you just so cute?" Nara said, forcing a smile and glancing at Heidi to see if her remark had registered.

"He is the beguiling little fellow," Heidi agreed. "He is my first dachshund. He comes with my house when I rent it."

"Like, he was left behind?"

"Left behind, but the tenant takes the rose bushes from the garden."

"Weird. Well, he looks purebred. Maybe you can sell him," suggested Nara.

"No, we stay together," said Heidi mildly, picking up Nara's application. She read the name across the top aloud, "Nara De'Nae Crow. De'Nae, I have not seen it with the apostrophe before. Danae was the mother of Perseus, for Americans it is the same with a different spelling?"

"Excuse me?" asked Nara, struggling for polite, instead of 'What the hell are you talking about?'

Heidi laughed. "The nonsense with the names never leaves me. It is the hobby I think," she said, smiling.

Nara released the breath she hadn't realized she was holding. An Ice Queen. She bet men liked that smooth blonde hair, those straight white teeth.

She probably should try to be more sociable, but she wasn't going to ask who Perseus was so trying to appear casual and interested, she asked, "What does Heidi mean?"

"Oh, it is one of those mantles parents drape over their children. It means 'noble born' or 'honorable.' Adelaide, the English version, is prettier and has the same meaning."

"Uh huh," said Nara, nodding. "Well, Heidi's not too bad. So, what are you?"

"I am not sure what you mean . . . Oh, I am from Northern Germany, a small village near the Baltic Sea."

"I'm a German," would have been enough and Nara controlled a snicker. If she'd had anyone to share it with later, she imagined the two of them laughing about how long this interview was taking to get going.

Heidi examined the nervy, nervous girl who sat swaddled in so much clothing, looking at Gering to avoid looking at her. She leaned forward for a better look at the lovely orange, red and blue beaded necklace that had been hidden by Nara's bulky jacket.

"A beautiful necklace. Is it from your family?" she asked.

"That would be a yes," Nara said, addressing Gering. She brought her hand up to her neck. She had forgotten the good fortune necklace would be exposed if she took off her jacket.

Heidi noted the sheen building up on the young woman's face. At least Nara could shed some of her clothing for a while if she came to work at Saint Gemma's. Each employee had a full-length locker with a combination lock.

"You have not listed your address. Do you live in Riverton?" Heidi asked.

"Sure do."

"Have you worked in the kitchens before?"

"That says I have," said Nara, looking meaningfully at the job application before remembering she'd just listed her most recent job, dealing cards. She squirmed under Heidi's assessing gaze. "Listen, I work really hard, really I do, and you obviously need help. Ask me anything, I'll fill in the blanks, go right ahead," Nara said, hoping her cooperation was being duly noted.

"You have experience in the kitchen?" Heidi asked again.

"Yes, I have. I've waitressed. I've helped in back. I do what needs to be done. I'm a team player." Conscious of sounding too eager, Nara slowed down and continued, "You need the help. It looks like you're down two people. Only saw the big white guy with the red beard the first day and I haven't seen that Asian-looking guy with the crew cut since Wednesday. Last night, you guys were super slow to serve."

"You have been eating with us?" asked Heidi in surprise. "I serve on the line; I have not seen you."

"You've looked?" Nara forced herself to meet the blue eyes. "Have you really?"

Heidi gave a slow exhale as she mulled over whether Nara De'Nae Crow was going to be more of a liability than an asset. Cooperation, a touch of humility, a friendly attitude, all made working in a kitchen more pleasant and so, more efficient. She did need to hire someone but she had a good crew at the moment. They all got along. Heidi glanced at the clock. She'd have to check on the lunch preparations soon.

"Thank you, I will look this over," she stood up, "and now I must go and check on the preparations for lunch."

Clutching her jacket before her, Nara rose awkwardly to her feet, trying to quell a rising panic. "I will look this over" for a stupid-ass job at a soup kitchen, washing dishes, wiping tables, chopping, serving? Jesus, if she couldn't get this job, she swallowed hard, horrified as a hot tear traced its way down her cheek.

"I'm not saying you didn't look at us, sure you did, but you were running all over," Nara said, swiping at her cheek roughly, avoiding those eyes by concentrating on the wiener dog. "And I'm not saying you weren't on the serving line, just that you had to keep bringing stuff out of the back, because, you know, not enough help. You missed seeing me, so what?" she flicked a look at the blonde woman and tried a smile. "But you were cool, like you didn't yell. You looked like, you know, a good boss," her voice trailed off. "You looked like you were doing your best to keep it all going."

Nara pressed her lips together and looked at the tree out the window behind before fixing her eyes on Gering, who responded by stretching his head out toward her and vibrating the tip of his tail. A pause hung in the air. The announcer on the radio said something about donating money. Sounds from the idiots in the kitchen intruded into the office, a laugh, a hoot, more laughter.

"Nara." Her name spoken quietly, as if this blonde woman, with her pale skin and perfect teeth, knew her.

"What?" Nara said around the ache in her throat.

"Tell me, have you always had the chip on the shoulder?"

Nara looked away from the dog, preparing to fling, 'A chip, *your* shoulder,' at the German whose overuse of '*the*' had become beyond annoying. But she halted, unprepared for the smile and the softness in the blue eyes. Well, what the hell? She had the job!

Nara opened her eyes wide to prevent another traitorous tear from falling. She shook her head, bit back a grin and said, "The chip? Probably." She reached to her shoulder for an imaginary chip, and pretended to heft it in her hand before handing it over. "My chip is your chip now, Boss," she said.

When Nara reported to work for the afternoon shift, she stuffed her jacket and backpack away in her new locker. She felt Heidi come up behind her and taking a deep breath, she pulled her sweatshirt over her head and turned to face her new boss. In the dead silence that ensued, some of kitchen staff paused to look over at the new girl.

"*Ach mein Gott*! Pregnant. How did I miss that?" Heidi exclaimed after a moment, staring at the swollen belly that stretched Nara's T-shirt to the limit. "Nara, you are really, *really* pregnant!"

"I never said I wasn't pregnant," Nara pointed out. "You gave me the job and fair's fair, now you gotta give me a try. And I'm not that pregnant. They're twins, haven't slowed me down yet. You'll get your money's worth."

"Twins, did you get that?" whispered one of the staff to the others, who gave a collective nod.

Heidi let out an audible breath and asked, "How long before the babies come?"

"They're due mid-October, give or take. Two baby boys. The clinic says identical, one placenta," said Nara, ignoring the rest of the staff. Learning she was carrying two babies had been a blow, but at least they were boys. She'd never gotten along with girls, and now she was working for one, go figure. Well, she'd make it work.

"Time to put me to work, Boss," she said cheerfully. "Kindly give me an apron and I'll show you what I got."

Nara's first two days proved she was an efficient worker, although the kitchen crew didn't warm to her particularly, nor she to them. Inez called her a cold fish, an expression that made Heidi laugh. A woman said a friend of hers had worked with Nara Crow at a casino and she had a reputation as a party girl, drank with the bartender after her shift, probably got knocked up by him too. He split faster than a ripe banana when Nara started to show.

"A ripe banana does not split. And we do not trot out the dirty laundry that other people make," Heidi reprimanded. "As long as Nara can do the work, she may stay and we will be friendly with each other."

"Then tell her to be more friendly to us," said Massimo. He found pregnant women almost unbearably sexy and had tried to get Nara to notice him.

That afternoon, when Heidi asked Nara to try to be a little friendlier to the rest of the kitchen staff, Nara shrugged and said, "This is me being friendly."

To run interference, Heidi found herself working side by side with Nara most of the time. Surprisingly, she didn't find the thought of two babies, *two*, gestating so close to her distressing, perhaps because she realized how alone the young woman was.

CHAPTER TEN

YOU ARE A WE NOW

The following month, Heidi and Gering were taking an early morning walk in the park when they saw Nara coming out of the public restroom.

"Hi, Heidi and little brown dog," Nara called, yawning and strolling over to them, towel draped over her arm and a cup, with a toothbrush and toothpaste, clutched in her hand. "Chilly," she remarked, giving a brief shiver, her long black hair fluttering in the wind.

"*Guten Morgen,* Nara. Yes, it is chilly. You have the plumbing problems?"

"No, the plumbing works fine," replied Nara, casting a puzzled look at the restrooms.

"I mean, where you live."

Nara nodded toward a battered van parked at the curb, "That's home for now." Reading Heidi's stricken face, she added impatiently, "It's not a problem, Heidi. You're a worrier. Don't worry—not about me."

"But is this a special camping place where you park? A safe place?"

"Anywhere with a bush is fine. I have to move every two or three days so it doesn't look like I'm settling in. Freaks people out if you try to claim a few yards of asphalt. I lock the doors at night. I have bear spray, for people not bears obviously."

"Not the bears, but a pregnant woman sleeping in a van. This is okay?"

"And this is your business because?" Nara said, a note of resignation in her voice.

"Because you are not a me now, you are a *we*. There are three of you."

Nara gave Heidi a bemused smile and shook her head, parent to child. "Okay, well, thank you for your input and now, if you don't mind, *we* are chilly and *we* need *our* jacket." As she walked away, she called over her shoulder, "See you at three o'clock pronto."

Nara opened the back doors of the van, mimicking under her breath in what she considered a close approximation of a German accent, "You are not a me now, you are a we."

She crawled on top of her sleeping bag, lay down on her back and stared at the ceiling. Well, if Heidi Vogel was so concerned about the *three* of them, maybe she had a room to rent. Nara released a long sigh and allowed herself to envision what Heidi's house might look like inside, clean, really clean, the bed in the spare room would have a thick quilt, a comfortable couch in the living room, everything in neutral tones, like in a department store, maybe a few splashes of color here and there, a fridge, spotless, no spills, a washing machine. She had no doubt the German woman had a washing machine, and thick white towels in the bathroom. Everything warm and safe and clean.

"I'd be a perfect roommate," Nara said to the inside of the van. She had hardly any stuff, nothing of value besides her necklace and her book. She'd sell the van for whatever she could get, fork over most of her salary, pay Heidi whatever she wanted. After the twins were born, she'd hit up her dad for some money. If she didn't cause trouble with New Wife, he'd pony up for his grandsons. Better yet, maybe New Wife was gone. Six years of living big, her dad's money was probably running low by now.

"Slow down girl," Nara muttered under her breath. Heidi Vogel might not have a spare room. Or if she did, would she even want to rent it out? Reality at the moment was an old Ford Econoline panel van, a thin foam mattress and a sleeping bag, couldn't live any cheaper than that.

Nara unhooked the corner of a king-sized pillowcase she used as a curtain over the two small back windows and enough light entered to allow her to read the *National Geographic* she'd picked up at the laundromat. The magazine looked almost new, but it was from 1980. Where'd it been hiding for a decade?

The cover showed a baby orangutan having a bath in a green tub with a baby human, neither one of them seemed to be enjoying themselves, looking at the camera with big, wary eyes. The human baby apparently belonged to a primatologist. Orangutans are the most solitary of the Great Apes, the article claimed. The closest bond is between mother and baby. "Duh," said Nara, patting her belly. Males take no role in raising young, but do not practice infanticide like other apes are known to do. "Holy shit," whispered Nara, patting her belly again. Nesting, diet, uh oh, logging, habitat destruction, highly endangered.

"*Fuck*," she said, tossing the magazine aside. Ecosystems collapsing, primates going extinct so exotic wood could be made into furniture only the uppity ups could afford. She rolled over and stared at a rusty patch on the side panel that looked as much like Australia as it had yesterday, last week, last month. And there were the Solomon Islands off to the side. She touched the space between the continent and the islands. Six of the seven species of marine turtle could be found right there, in the Coral Sea. The hawksbill, endangered from being the primary source of tortoiseshell for decorative purposes, the green, some of the most accomplished travelers on the planet, the leatherback, the flatback, the olive ridley, the . . . the . . . shit, shit, she was drawing a blank. She slid the book out from under her mattress and opened it to the chapter on the Coral Sea, and there it was, the loggerhead with its big ol' head and flipper-like limbs.

Nara set the alarm so she wouldn't be late for work and wrapped her arms around the big book that had been her escape for so many years. She had thought about stealing it the first time she discovered it on Fat Dick Guy's bookshelf in Chicago, but the backpack she'd had then had been much too small. But the last time they'd stayed in that Chicago apartment, she'd come prepared with a bigger backpack.

A bigger backpack and a knife. A knife . . . if Fat Dick Guy came into the little room where she slept when they stayed with him, and did the same things he did last year and the year before, Nara intended to use it.

The men left the apartment so her dad could go show off being an educated Indian and talk down to Fat Dick Guy's students. While her mother got ready to take a shower, Nara went into the little room and closed the door. She practiced whipping the knife out from under the pillow on the cot. How would she do it? In the back, in the side, in the face? A ten-year old girl with a knife, she was ready.

Soon as she killed him, she'd grab the book, run down the stairs and out into the night. She'd head toward the lake. There were big houses all along the shore. She'd find food somewhere, sneak into the houses like Goldilocks, except she wouldn't get caught. There were foresty areas all around the lake. She'd seen them from the car. She'd make a den, steal blankets, stuff to keep out the rain, maybe find a dog, not everybody wanted their dog. She'd hide out until she was old enough for someone to give her a job. She'd save money, buy a camper, travel around, seeing the country with her dog. Her *big* dog.

Jab, jab, jab . . . she remembered jabbing the air with her knife. "Die, die, take that, take that," she had danced, parried and laughed. "Die, mother fucking, mother fucker, die," like a movie, like a movie but real.

She had whirled around when she heard her mother's voice from the doorway, "Nara, my God, what are you doing?"

For a long moment, they stared at each other, her mother small, wrapped in a towel, long hair loose, still dry. She hadn't taken her shower yet. When her mother advanced and tried to take the knife from her, Nara held tight and finally the words that had been silent for two years broke free, "He hurts me. He *hurts* me, Mama. I'm going to kill him this time."

"A mouse," Nara had heard women whispering about her mother in one of the nameless places they'd stayed as they followed her father to wherever his 'business' of being an example of real Indian took him. "Can't believe Danny would marry such a mouse."

"And dragging that poor little girl back and forth. No friends, no school."

"How's she even reading?"

"She must have been an accident, only way a mouse could trap Danny Crow,"

Well, her mother hadn't sounded like a mouse when she said in a voice Nara had never heard before, "I'll dress. Leave the knife on the pillow so he sees it. Use the bathroom. I'll get the suitcase. Hurry."

Nara had darted to the bookshelves on her way out the door. The book fit in her backpack perfectly. As they scurried down the back stairs, they heard the elevator rattling and whining its way up from the lobby. They stepped out a side door. The night wind blew from the lake and followed them down dark passageways and across broad boulevards. They kept pace, right foot for right foot, her mother no taller than she, but carrying their suitcase effortlessly with one hand and holding on to her with the other.

The bus station materialized in a harsh yellow light, grease and diesel, discarded newspapers and coffee cups, white people, brown people, black people, all the same, sitting on benches or quietly queuing, looking down at their shoes.

Her mother had raised her eyebrows when Nara took the book out of her backpack somewhere in Missouri. "That man give you that book, or did you take it?" she asked, her narrow, dark eyes sharp.

"Took it."

"Good," murmured the woman who had once made her daughter walk a mile to return a stolen pack of gum. "The ocean, a different kind of life there."

As the sun came up, the light played off the silver threads that wove their way through her mother's long black hair and Nara leaned over to glimpse a small portion of the good fortune necklace that hung around her mother's neck. Her mother caught her looking, grabbed her hand and gave it a little squeeze.

"Good fortune?" Nara had asked when her mother first made the claim for the orange, red and blue beaded necklace. They had been in a dirty hotel room in Albuquerque, cockroaches scuttling across the floor. "Good fortune, like good luck?"

"I don't know," her mother had admitted, arranging her hair and shirt collar to hide the necklace before they ventured outside to find food with what was left of the twenty dollars her father put on the dresser before he had left two days ago. "It keeps us safe from whatever's worse than this. Women in our family live long enough to pass it on to the next woman in line, so I guess it brings good fortune."

Halfway through Kansas, Nara tapped her mother's arm to show her the picture of a sea otter using kelp to bind her baby to her so they wouldn't drift apart as they slept.

"Now that's a good mama," her mother had murmured before turning her face away.

"You are too. You chose me," Nara remembered wanting to say. But she hadn't told her mother she was a good mama. They had left her father behind and her mother's sorrow was a soft, dark thing seated between them.

They picked up another bus in Denver and took it north to Rock Springs where her uncle had picked them up in his silver Chevy truck with the extra big tires and bumpers. "Good to have you home, Sister," her uncle had said as they stepped off the bus.

Then he had turned to Nara and done something astonishing; he had put his hand on her head, his brown, weathered face softened when he smiled. *"Hótousíhi?"* he asked.

He had asked her for her name. Her mother's own brother hadn't known her name! Her mother hadn't spoken to her family for years, but she could have picked up the phone to share the news, "It's a girl, my brother. Her name is Nara De'Nae. Tell the family, she's seven pounds, beautiful and strong."

Tell the family. Nara had thought they were going home to family, people who knew of her, who looked like her, who couldn't wait to be her aunts and uncles and cousins. People who, until now, didn't even know she existed.

Nara tuned the grownups in and out as she sat sandwiched between them, the high prairie rolling by, her book in its backpack held tightly on her lap.

"Your man ain't welcome here," her uncle said at one point, hunching over the steering wheel. "Not after selling Micky and Chester to the Feds at Pine Ridge to keep outta jail."

Her mother sounding tired, "You don't know . . ."

"We all know. Nobody gonna to let him rent a house . . ."

her uncle angry.

"... won't need one ... not coming ..."

"People don't care he's parading as an Indian for white folk, that's just embarrassing and sad, but you can't reform an informer. He better not be following you here, better not be hiding out among our people." Her uncle had rolled down the window to spit. The scent of the sun, the sage, dry dirt and brown, broken grasses filled the cab, the smell of summer on the Reservation.

"Can't reform an informer," her uncle's words had chased themselves around Nara's head for years. Now here she was, thirteen years later, living in a van, and as her babies grew bigger, her bladder got smaller. Nara sat up with an effort and unlatched the van's back door. She wouldn't make a dent in Heidi Vogel's orderly life, she thought, her flip-flops flapping in her hurry to get to the restroom on time.

How about, "Boss, can you write me a reference?" Damn, no toilet paper. She reached for another paper toilet seat cover. "I'm thinking of, no ... I am going to need to find a room for a few months, paying whatever's fair."

Indirect, yup, that was best. That way she wouldn't have put herself out there if Miss There-Are-Three-of-You Vogel, didn't want her.

CHAPTER ELEVEN

LET'S NOT TALK ABOUT WHEELS

"The situation this Nara finds herself in is enough to ring alarm bells," Karl stated firmly when Heidi phoned him and said she might be getting a roommate. "Many homeless are mentally ill and unpredictable."

"I work with her. She is predictable, Gering likes her and she is as mentally well as the rest of us," Heidi protested, trying to sound equally firm to cover her growing doubt. She was used to living alone, reading in the evening, taking a long bath with the bathroom door open so Gering, usually curled up on the bathmat, could run out to investigate if he heard a sound. She didn't really want to share her little house with anyone and she wasn't naïve enough to suppose living with the prickly Nara Crow would be anything close to easy.

"At the very least put a lock on your bedroom door," Karl urged.

"What do you think a woman who grows bigger every day is going to do to me as I sleep?"

"*Guter Gott,* Heidi," Karl huffed. "I don't know, but I suppose we can use our imaginations."

"I am sorry I even told you of these plans, and now you will tell Beppe, and he will have his things to say. Nara plans to go back to her father on the Wind River Reservation after the babies are born. We are close to the hospital here so staying with me makes sense."

"And if she doesn't go back? You'll be stuck doing her laundry, preparing her meals, picking up after her," Karl warned. "She'll be dependent on you for everything and you'll never get out of that dreary little town."

Heidi almost howled in frustration. It was so easy to think the worst of a stranger. They didn't know Nara . . . but then again, neither did she, not really. She breathed in deeply, exhaled slowly.

"When does this Nara move in?" Karl asked.

"Stop calling her *this* Nara. She is coming to see the house this afternoon. She may not even . . ."

"May not what?" Karl interrupted. "Of course she will want to move into your house. She will be there on your doorstep with her suitcase in hand. At the very least you must put a lock on your bedroom door."

"*Stop!* Karl, please, stop. Riverton is not so dreary, the garden is in bloom, there are three fruits forming on the quince tree."

Despite his love of quinces, Karl let out a grunt of disbelief that a small town in Wyoming could be considered anything but dreary.

The temperature warmed enough for Heidi to work in the garden with just a T-shirt under her overalls. The lavender and roses were in full bloom and buzzing with bees. A Western Meadowlark called from atop one of the clothesline's wooden supports, its yellow breast swelling as it released pure whistles that descended into series of short warbles. The grasses in the cemetery beyond the back fence followed the orchestration of the wind.

Heidi had just finished removing dead insects and leaves from the fountain when Gering's barks alerted her to Nara's arrival. She pulled off her work gloves and wiped her face with the back of her hand as she made her way into the house. She raised her eyebrows at her reflection in the hall mirror and puffed out her cheeks. *'Auf geht's,'* she told herself, here we go.

Nara stood with her back to the front door and turned around with deliberate casualness. "Nice get up, Boss," she said, eyeing Heidi's overalls.

"They are useful. My landlord's daughter is now allergic to the bees so I inherit her work clothes."

"I see. Practical is good." Coming up the path to the front door, Nara had reminded herself to appear only mildly interested in the room at first, not desperate, definitely not desperate. "You ready for me to check out your digs?" she asked.

"You want to see the garden first?" Heidi asked in surprise.

"No, I mean, thanks, but not necessarily. Digs, as in your house. It's an expression, your house, your digs."

Heidi laughed. "Yes, of course. To use dig like this is a new way for me. In English a word can have so many meanings. I think I can also ask you if you dig the spare bedroom you may want to stay in."

Nara vowed to reduce her vocabulary to the very basics or they'd be chasing their tails all day long. She just wanted a room, a warm shower, a . . .

"Follow Gering," said Heidi. "He wants to show you the living room."

Obediently, Nara followed the little dachshund's purposeful trot down the hall. She halted at the entrance to the living room.

"Orange. Unexpected." She turned to Heidi with a grin.

"The landlord's sister . . ."

Nara held up her hand. "Don't explain, unless of course you feel the need to. Weird as hell, but I love it. Please tell me there's more."

Heidi nodded and led the way to the spare bedroom. She pushed open the door and stood back for Nara to enter. Nara laughed out loud. The bed had a thick orange corduroy comforter, an orange shag carpet lay on the floor; she peeked in the bathroom, and the towels and bathmat were orange too.

After Nara had admired the fountain, the roses and the tiny clusters of berries beginning to develop on the elderberry bushes, the women sat on two kitchen chairs on the patio and had some lemonade.

"Ray Dolan, my landlord, has offered two garden chairs. I think I may tell him to please bring them over if you will be staying here," said Heidi.

"Well, okay then, if there's a garden chair for me to use, guess I'll have to agree to move in for a few months. After the boys get here, we'll go back to my dad, so yeah, a few months, maybe like four or five, is all I'll need and I thank you." Nara took a sip of lemonade, feeling almost weak with relief. In her last conversation with her dad, he'd said coming back to his house was a no go as long as New Wife was there. But one thing at a time. She'd figure it out.

"The guy at the gas station says he'll give me four hundred for the van," Nara said. "That's more than its worth, so I'm takin' it. Will that buy me four months? You need more, deduct it from my salary. Please."

"The van money is more than enough." Heidi hadn't expected rent but she understood Nara's need to pay it.

"More than? How about utilities then? It can cover those too."

"Of course," said Heidi.

"I have a few things in the van," Nara pressed on. "Are we thinking of me moving in now or waiting for the van money?"

"Oh, I think now. Gering will be disappointed if you do not move in right away."

"Yeah, I can see that," said Nara, looking over at the dog

busily digging a hole with his rump in the air, tail wagging madly. She rested her hand on her belly and felt a twin give a little kick of approval that their van days were over.

Gering jumped off Heidi's bed before midnight and did not return. As the warmth from his presence under the sheets cooled, she told herself sternly that to share a dog was a good thing. In the morning, when she called the little dog to come to the kitchen for his breakfast, Nara trailed behind.

Seeing the look Heidi cast Gering as he trotted over to his bowl, Nara took pity. "I'll keep my door closed from now on so he can't come in, but I tell you my ancestors, especially on the Arapaho side, slept with dogs. He knows that," Nara said, looking at Gering affectionately. "Some tribes called the Arapaho the 'dog eaters.' Ever hear that from your doggy friends, Gering?"

Heidi watched Gering look up from his kibble to gaze at Nara in adoration. She felt somewhat mollified when the little dog turned his gaze to her and wagged his tail before going back to his bowl.

"Did these ancestors really eat dogs?" asked Heidi, wondering if Nara was going to get up this early every morning, unnecessary since her shift didn't start until mid-afternoon.

"Eat dogs, who knows? Probably. They lived with dogs. Dogs may have eaten Arapaho too, sometimes." Nara chuckled. "They shared shelter, warmth, food. Dogs pulled sleds before the horses came. A *travois*—a kind of drag sled." Catching Heidi's doubtful look, she added, "There's all kinds of dogs Heidi."

"Of course, I understand about the different kinds of dogs," said Heidi impatiently. "I know that a dog like Gering could not pull a drag sled, but I think bigger dogs also would not be so happy dragging a sled along the rough ground."

"Oh for God's sake," Nara groaned. "I do not, repeat do

not, want to get into a discussion with a European about why we didn't invent the wheel and carts and all that crap. You guys didn't invent it yourselves; you just copied some genius Sumerian."

"I was not going to talk about wheels," said Heidi. "I just make the comment on friction from the point of view of the dog."

"Oh, pardon me."

A gust of wind rattled the window over the sink, momentarily silencing the click of the teapot-shaped kitchen clock. Nara wiped the spotless counter with the kitchen sponge and Heidi took a clean dishtowel out of a drawer and hung it on the oven door. Gering finished his breakfast and walked over to Heidi to have his collar put on.

"You take his collar off on purpose?" Nara asked, leaning back against the kitchen counter, hands resting on her belly. "I thought his collar had fallen off in the bed. I looked through my blankets, everything."

Heidi felt a wave of irritation and didn't think it necessary to explain the vet had suggested removing Gering's collar at night when little dog had developed a bare spot on his neck. "Would you like to wear a collar to bed?" she asked, attaching the leash to Gering's collar.

"Nope, got me there," said Nara cheerfully. "You can leave him home. I can bring him when I come to work this afternoon."

But Heidi declined the offer, saying Gering had to walk off his breakfast.

As Heidi buttoned up her coat, Nara returned to the topic she had said she did not want to discuss with a European, "All you guys talk about wheels. Like people ask why the Jews didn't fight back, or why there weren't more slave revolts, or why white Americans don't have a culture or for Indians, well . . . let's just say, give the wheel a rest. Anyway, it's not about the wheel. It's all about the axle. Once you have an axle, a wheel makes sense, and it wasn't like a bunch of different people were inventing axles. They just copied that Sumerian guy, and if that guy had lived this side of the world, we'd be wheeling while you eastern hemisphere types would be dragging."

"I think this morning you build the mountain out of the molehill," said Heidi, tying her scarf securely around her neck so it wouldn't blow away in the wind. "Also, I think that you must be a very good student in school to be knowing about the Sumerians and axles."

"Yeah, I was a great student. The Rez teachers loved me. The kids were crap. Anyway, we won't have a problem if you stop with the wheel talk."

"I will try not to bring wheel talk up ever again," Heidi promised solemnly, winking at Gering who had scratched at the door and was now looking at her hopefully.

As Heidi turned to say goodbye, Nara said, "And if we walk home together tonight, you can walk fast if you want to, leave me behind. Don't feel you have to slow down for the woman pregnant with twins who still works harder than just about anybody in the kitchen."

"We all work hard in the kitchen. No one is the deadwood millstone albatross." Gering looked up at Heidi imploringly and tugged on his leash.

"Did you say 'deadwood' then 'millstone' and 'albatross'? Pretty sure you have to choose one of the three," said Nara, trying to infuse as much incredulity into her expression as possible.

Heidi shook her head and flashed a grin. "No, I stay with the three, for emphasis."

Nara let out a hoot of laughter, "All right, have it your way, Boss."

Watching Heidi and Gering open the gate and step onto the sidewalk, Nara called after them, "See you at three, and I'd appreciate not prepping salads with that Raffi anymore."

Heidi flapped her hand behind her, not turning around. She had already promised Raffi he wouldn't have to work with Nara again.

CHAPTER TWELVE

SACAJAWEA'S SAND DOLLAR

The house was too quiet after Heidi and Gering left. Nara turned both the radio and television on to the news and went to take a shower. She'd already made her bed, straightened the stack of magazines in the living room and plumped the pillows on the couch. She'd make sure to leave the bathroom immaculate. Her mother's mantra had been, 'Leave a place cleaner than you found it. That way they can't say anything bad about you.'

The warm water steamed up the glass shower door and Nara drew a smiley face. Thick orange towels, soap that smelled of roses and shampoo with a hint of peppermint. She was just going to accept it, this was hers for a while.

"I'm not a complete fuck up, Mom," she muttered, running her soapy hands over her huge belly, feeling the movement under her surface. "Abracadabra. Hi, guys," she murmured, imagining the knees, feet, elbows and hands that pushed at her from inside, tethered, floating in their dark amniotic ocean.

With a towel wrapped around her head, Nara used a dry wash cloth to wipe down the shower door so no soap residue remained. She needed a bathrobe and a nightgown. Two pairs of sweat pants, a sweatshirt and several extra-large men's T-shirts was the sum total of her wardrobe at the moment. She'd see if she could borrow Heidi's car, go to the thrift store or Walmart, and maybe, just maybe, buy a couple of baby outfits as well. Twins. Unbelievable. She glanced at her face in the mirror. Did that woman look like a mother?

The modulated cadence of the news announcers kept Nara company as she considered what to have for breakfast. She took a carton of eggs out of the fridge. How many eggs should she have, three? One for her, one for each baby, three pieces of toast. "You are a we now," she mouthed to her reflection in the toaster.

She opened the cupboard to search for something to make the eggs more interesting. She shifted a bottle of olive oil aside. Suddenly, her hand froze. At the back of the shelf were two unopened bottles of wine, stored on their sides. A third bottle, a bottle of port, stood upright in the corner, and . . . it had been opened. Breathing shallowly, Nara picked up the port. The bottle was a little sticky. Sticky? She couldn't believe Heidi hadn't wiped down a sticky bottle. She held the bottle up to the morning light. Warre's Tawny Port. Didn't Heidi know it wouldn't keep forever once opened? The liquid looked black against the dark green glass of the bottle, but she knew its true color. A golden reddish-brown. It had been her favorite after-dinner drink. She had dressed well at the casino; she hadn't been a cheap date.

Nara sniffed the sticky neck of the bottle, apricot, peanut brittle, raisins. She tried the cork. It was stuck. She walked to the sink and dropped the bottle in, giving a whimper as it shattered. She turned on the tap and left it running as she went into the living room to stare blindly at the television. Oil prices rising, stock market dropping.

"No car, no stock, what the hell do I care?" she said aloud to the television, angrily wiping tears from her cheeks. If the cork hadn't been stuck, would she have taken a taste? What if she couldn't stay off it when the babies arrived? What if . . .?

When she considered it safe, she returned to kitchen. She

turned off the tap and picked the glass out of the sink with a paper towel. A few drops of port had splashed up onto the tap and she touched them, licking the barely perceptible residue off her fingers. Yup, apricot, peanut brittle and raisins.

"Broke a bottle of some kind of sweet wine when I was looking in the cupboard. Sorry. Tell me what I owe you," Nara said breezily as she arrived for her afternoon shift.

Heidi watched Nara make a business of tying an apron over her distended belly and said, "You owe me nothing. I forget the bottles are there." She doubted the port would have broken accidently.

Nara shrugged and got to work, not believing for a second someone could forget a bottle of Warre's.

The clouds that rolled over western Wyoming that day had released enough rain to clear the dust from the air. The sun had sunk below the mountains but the sky still retained a faint light. As they walked home from Saint Gemma's, Heidi and Nara stopped frequently so Gering's quivering nose could assess the smells released by the damp ground.

When Heidi removed a plastic bag from her pocket and picked up the waste Gering deposited under a crabapple overhanging the pavement, Nara said in astonishment, "May I just say, gross?"

"It is gross to leave it. The man who owns this house lets me pick his little crabapples for jelly when they are ripe."

"Yeah, nice guy to let you have his sour little apples, but it's not like Gering poohed right in the middle of the sidewalk."

"When I am a child in Germany, I have a dog. I am used to picking up."

"Damn, you running for Citizen of the Year? Bet your friends found you real annoying."

"Growing up, my friends and I fight sometimes," admitted Heidi, "But not about picking up the poop."

"Hard to believe you fighting," Nara scoffed. "About what? Somebody say something mean about somebody else and you had to teach them a lesson? Or some girl's boyfriend make eyes at you and she beat you up? Anybody actually hit anybody?"

"Oh yes, I punch my friends, I pull out the hair and I bite and I scratch. You had better be nice to me," Heidi warned, trying for a scowl.

Nara grinned. She didn't think Germans were known for their humor, but Heidi could hold her own. Had to respect her for that.

"We cross the road for a minute," said Heidi. "Be careful, because there is not the sidewalk on that side. The garden with the broken fence has honeysuckle. In the dark, the flowers release their scent to call to the moths."

Wanting nothing more than to get back to the house and put her feet up, Nara followed dutifully. Might as well humor the boss. She stumbled, almost went down but Heidi dropped Gering's leash and shot out a strong arm to steady her.

'I am sorry, this is too rough walking for you so pregnant," said Heidi, holding tight until Nara gasped, "It's okay. I'm okay."

Keeping her hand securely around Nara's upper arm and bending down to pick up Gering's leash, Heidi said, "It is my fault. We must be more careful."

Nara shook her head, unable to speak. Jesus, if she'd gone down crossing a road in the dark to smell some fucking flowers . . .

Heidi said softly, "If you shut your eyes and take the deep breath, you will see we are in heaven."

Conscious of the gravel through the worn soles of her shoes, grateful for the pressure of Heidi's hand around her arm, Nara closed her eyes and filled her lungs with the sweet, sweet scent of honeysuckle. Again, she inhaled the warm, sensual fragrance. It was well worth the danger of the trek across the road. She held the air in her lungs, imagining the floral essence crossing into her blood and being carried down to her babies.

At Nara's deep sigh of satisfaction, Heidi laughed. She pinched off several sprigs of the small, trumpet-shaped flowers from the profusion that tumbled over the derelict fence. Nara held the honeysuckle and Heidi grasped Nara's arm firmly with one hand and the Gering's leash with her other, until they had reached the safety of the sidewalk.

"We sleep with heaven's scent tonight. When we get home, I will make us warm milk," Heidi promised. "I will add a little cinnamon, a little vanilla and honey. Or I make it with chocolate if you prefer."

Nara said with a grimace, "Thanks but no warm milk for me. I've got calcium pills from the clinic. I hate milk, can't digest it."

"We have soymilk. Inez goes out this afternoon to buy it for us and she put it in the fridge at my house. She said you are lactose intolerant."

"I never told Inez I couldn't digest milk," Nara protested, trying to quell a rising panic that her life was being taken away from her by the good intentions of pushy people she barely knew.

"No, you say to her, 'Milk gives me the shits.' You say this to her when she offers you hot chocolate with whipped cream."

"I'm sure I added a thank you in there somewhere," said Nara, although she wasn't sure at all, something about Inez's easy give and take with Heidi bugged her. "So, Inez has a key to your house?"

"Yes. She runs errands for me if I am too busy."

"You trust her not to . . ." Nara searched for something Inez might take or do if she was allowed to wander unfettered through Heidi's house.

"Yes, I trust her not to. Now we stop the dilly dally," said

Heidi. "Look how dark and Gering wants his biscuits."

They walked the last block home in silence. Nara resigned herself to a hot beverage, soymilk no less. She'd tried it once and was not a fan. All she really wanted to do was relax and watch television. She hadn't watched television in months and the evening news had been the only ritual she'd shared with her dad, exchanging observations with him on how dangerously clueless the rest of the world was. Still, if being sociable with Heidi was one of the prices to pay for having a place to stay until the twins arrived, it was worth it. How long could having a little chat over warm milk take?

Heidi stifled a sigh. She tried not to regret she wouldn't be running her bath the moment she got in the door. Sharing a house with one bathroom meant a lengthy evening bath would be impractical; she remembered the urgency of needing the bathroom during her last weeks of pregnancy. For the next several months she would substitute a quick shower for her bath and give up her evening glass of port. She hoped she'd be able to escape to her room with Gering and her book before she became too tired to read. Bringing a person into your home came with the obligation to be sociable. How long could having a little conversation over warm milk take?

As Heidi heated their soymilk, Nara sat at the kitchen table, thumbing through *Das Fenster*, a German language magazine that Heidi claimed she didn't have the time to read. Heidi said the name meant, 'the window,' which Nara thought was a pretty good name for a magazine that promised to keep German expatriates connected to the news, entertainment and culture of their homeland. A lot could be learned from peeking in windows.

When Nara wrinkled her nose at the steaming mug placed before her, Heidi laughed. "I will go to the garage to fill Gering's food jar from the big bag and then I will join you," she promised. "You will take some little sips of your chocolate, just a few and I will be very happy."

Nara closed the magazine and sighed. Did she want to make Heidi happy? She felt she was in danger of falling into the trap most of the kitchen crew had fallen into, trying to make Heidi laugh, which was surprisingly easy at times. Her laugh lightened the air, like a kid's laugh, got everybody going. It made up for the times she fell silent; then Heidi still worked quickly and efficiently, but she wasn't really there. They let her be then. No one wanted to think she was as wounded as the rest of them.

Nara took a sip of her hot chocolate. It was pretty good. She'd watched Heidi add a little vanilla. She'd have to remember that. What were they going to talk about? Not her dad, that was for sure. Her dad had been left at a rest stop in Utah when he was two or three. He had never gotten over the humiliation of being abandoned. That small child still looked out of her father's eyes and hurled cruel words from his mouth. But that child had never been able to get her father to raise a hand against her or her mother. That was something to be grateful for.

Her dad had been raised by a Mormon couple in Provo, who had named him Daniel. In the college they had paid for, he'd dropped the 'e' from Crowe, their last name, to distance himself from them and their whiter than white lives. Shortly after Nara and her mom fled Chicago, her father had phoned the Reservation with the news his parents had died and left him their sizable estate. Her mother had held the receiver so Nara could listen in. "I made it easy for the lawyers, kept most of my parents' last name."

Just like that, the people her father had wanted nothing to do with for over twenty years had become 'parents' upon their death. Although only ten, Nara had been vocal about the cruel irony. Her mother had defended her dad, as she always did, insisting he was not to blame. "Your father doesn't know who he is, even having us hasn't healed that in him."

But her uncle had been wrong when he said no one would lease to Danny Crow. The money had allowed her father to move into the blue house on the river bend, and to pay for her mother's cancer treatments. And it had allowed him to find a new wife just months after burying his first.

Heidi returned from the garage with Gering trotting beside her, wagging his tail in approval. He looked on with satisfaction as the canister full of his food was placed in its proper place on the counter. Nara glanced at the clock. The nine o'clock news had started ten minutes ago.

Putting her own mug of hot chocolate on the table, Heidi took a seat opposite Nara and said, "This morning you talk about people in your family on the other side. Who are these people on this other side?"

Knew it, Nara nodded to herself, family stuff. No sweat, anything got uncomfortable, she would just make something up.

"Well, I can really only talk about my mom," she said slowly. "My dad's a City Indian, is all I'm saying."

"City Indian?"

"Yeah, not a big deal. I'll fill you in on my mom."

Heidi nodded. She brought her mug to her lips and paused. She could detect bean-like, slightly sulfury odor through the chocolate. She tried to control her grimace and took a sip. There it was, the soymilk undermined the very fine Dutch cocoa powder Karl had sent in one of his care packages. Tomorrow she'd heat cow's milk for herself. She wasn't lactose intolerant.

"You listening?" Nara asked. "You seem a little distracted. We could do this tomorrow. I could just go watch a little news and let you get ready for bed, read your book or whatever."

"No, I like to listen about another person's family," said Heidi, trying another sip of her drink. It would be a challenge to drink the whole thing.

"Okay, well here goes," said Nara, stifling a sigh, the ten o'clock news would have to do. "My mom was born on the Rez, so if there is another side, I'd say Shoshone, since they and the Arapaho share the Wind River Reservation. You know, handsome young Arapaho dude, gorgeous young Shoshone chick catch sight of each other swimming in the river, or bringing down a musk ox."

"A musk ox?" Heidi let out a peal of laughter, soymilk temporarily forgotten.

"Yeah, whatever, anyway we can guess the rest," said Nara, pleased with herself for throwing the musk ox in there. Who knew she could be funny?

"And the tribes share the Reservation in a friendly way?" Heidi asked.

"Pretty much. We have some differences. Language is really different. Shoshones speak a Ute-Aztec type language, the roots of Arapaho are Algonquian. We're from different places."

Heidi watched Nara take a deep swallow of her hot chocolate and asked, "You like this drink?"

"Pretty damn good." Nara ran an appreciative tongue over her lips.

Heidi looked at her in amusement. "Good, and I will send away for some lavender honey. We do not always have to make the hot chocolate. Lavender honey, a little cardamom and cinnamon, this will be very nice I think," she made a note on a little pad sitting on the table before looking up with a smile. "Tell me more about these native languages," she said. "Are no Shoshone words and Arapaho words the same?"

"I bet some of them are. I mean, languages change, borrow from each other, but nothing's coming to mind right now," said Nara frowning. Lavender in milk? And what was cardamom?

"Do many of the people on the Reservation speak

American English and their Indian language?" asked Heidi, pretending to take a sip from her mug.

"Depends what you mean by speak. They teach Shoshone and Arapaho in the Rez schools, and some people learn on their own, but to be fluent, it's like you have to be older before you realize how important it is to speak the language of your people. Young people are too busy being young. And why do you say American English? English is English."

"I would say no, not all English is the same. One time when I visit Scotland, I feel I need an interpreter, especially in the little towns."

"Hard to believe."

"But true, never is the less."

"None the less," corrected Nara.

"Thank you, none is the less."

"No, you have to dump the 'is'."

Heidi muttered something in German to Gering before turning her attention to Nara. "Now teach me a word in Shoshone and then the same word in Arapaho."

"Okay, but first translate whatever you just said in German to Gering. I'm up for learning another language."

"I say *'Wen kümmert schon ein ist?'* It means, 'Who cares about an 'is,' but of course I do not mean this, because I . . .'"

Nara held up a hand, "No need to explain, *Fräulein,* just say it again so I can get my pronunciation down."

Heidi did as requested and Nara repeated the phrase perfectly.

"Now my turn for the Arapaho and Shoshone word," insisted Heidi. "Just a word, I am not ready for the phrase."

"Good call, so like what? Make it simple. My Arapaho's great. I'm a little out of practice with Shoshone."

"Dog," suggested Heidi. "Say the words and spell them."

Nara rolled her eyes, 'dog' everybody's first word after Mama and Dada. She said dog in both languages.

"We use a symbol like a three for a *'th'* sound in Arapaho,

116

so it's *he3*," she said, scribbling the word on the back of the electric bill. "*H* – like in hay, *e* like in bed, *3* like the *th* in Beth or death. Dog's *sadee'a* in Shoshone, but there are a bunch of other dog words in both languages."

"A number in a word looks odd."

"Not really, you guys sprinkle those dot things on top of letters, willy nilly."

"An umlaut, it shows a vowel shift," explained Heidi. "Tell me a few other words, hello, goodbye, those sorts of words. In Shoshone too."

Nara obliged, writing the words down, saying them slowly.

"I did not do well in English in my school," Heidi said ruefully when Nara released an exasperated breath after guiding her through the pronunciations far more times than should have been necessary. "The woman who teaches us English in *Grundschule*, this is our elementary school, told my father that I do not have the good ear for language. Later, in *Gymnasium,* I was in the special class, for students who are very far behind in foreign language."

"Embarrassing," said Nara, sympathetically. Who would have thought this woman had been in Special Ed?

Heidi shrugged. "It is not so much embarrassing. I was good at athletics, mathematics and history, and I have an excellent palate. But I think I can learn to pronounce a few greetings words very well in both Arapaho and Shoshone. As well as, I want to learn more about the Reservation, but . . ." she looked at the clock, stood up and collected their cups, managing to hide the fact hers was still almost full. "I think tomorrow is best. I have to be at Saint Gemma's very early for the dairy and egg man in the morning."

After Heidi and Gering had left for the bathroom, Nara murmured under her breath, "Thank you, Mr. Dairy Egg Man," although she had to admit, having the obligatory third conversation of the day hadn't been so bad. She had been polite, sipping her warm soymilk, imparting knowledge. She'd learned her boss had been in a remedial language class and wasn't even ashamed of it. Nara smiled in satisfaction. She, on the other hand, did have an ear for languages, English, Arapaho, decent Spanish and Shoshone, and with the help of *Das Fenster* and all the German Heidi spoke to Gering, she'd soon have passable German.

Nara went into the living room and turned on the television, musing about how they would have looked to someone peeking through the kitchen window; two women, roommates no less, sitting at a kitchen table, cozy, cozy, cozy.

Keeping the volume low, she found the news. "War is heating up in the Persian Gulf," said the perfectly coiffed female anchor, her voice flat to show she could deliver bad news just as ably as any male.

Native boys would be going, fighting for their country. Not her twins, though. She'd take them to Canada or Mexico if war threatened when they were of age. Plenty of veterans from Twentieth Century wars were buried at the Arapaho cemetery on the Reservation. Veterans who'd come home to what? The boys would be ten when the Twenty-first Century dawned. New century, world peace? She doubted it.

When they got home the following evening, Nara complained her feet were puffing up, so Heidi told her to stretch out on the couch while the milk heated.Gering followed Nara into the living room and stood by as she settled herself onto the plush orange couch. She leaned over awkwardly and lifted the little dog onto what remained of her lap. She looked longingly at the television. How rude would it be to have it on in the background, volume low? Maybe tomorrow she'd put it on as soon as they got home, just matter-of-factly, no big deal.

Heidi came in with their drinks and handed Nara her cup before settling in at the end of the couch. She had made her hot chocolate with cow's milk and was looking forward to it. Nara took a sip and grinned down at her belly, "Here it comes, me wee laddies. Scottish English, am I right? Am I getting the hang of it?"

Heidi chuckled and said Gering thought she was a silly girl. Hearing his name had the desired effect and the little dog got up and made his way down the couch to Heidi's lap. Heidi gathered him in her arms, nuzzled his head until he made a contented grunting sound.

"He says he would like to learn more about the Reservation now," Heidi said, looking up with a smile.

"No shit, I mean, no kidding," Nara corrected quickly. "But make sure Gering listens up, because I don't want to have to repeat myself."

At his name, Gering made as if to rise, but Heidi held him fast and assured Nara they would both pay attention.

Nara cleared her voice theatrically and began, "Well, now, the Wind River Reservation, as told to me by my mom and various teacher types." She blew on her drink, took a sip, too hot but excellent. She cleared her throat again and proceeded, "In 1878 the US Government moved the Northern Arapaho onto land they had already given to the Shoshone—who, I might add, had already been on those lands forever and a day. Anyway, moving us onto the Shoshone Reservation was supposed to be temporary, until Uncle Sam found a spot to stash us away, but delay, delay, delay and finally Chief Washakie, Eastern Shoshone Good Guy, let us stay. They're still more on the north end of the Rez. We're more in the south."

"Do many children have a parent from each tribe?" Heidi asked, glancing at the clock. Was it almost nine o'clock already?

"Not sure I'd say many, but if you are mixed, one parent Shoshone, the other Arapaho, you pick which parent you're closest to and choose that tribe. Closest to your Arapaho parent, you're Arapaho, if you more with the Shoshone side, you're Shoshone. I'd say we mostly get along. There are separate tribal councils, sometimes they see eye-to-eye, more eye-to-eye than a lot of you Europeans and your World Wars."

"You are tired of the wheel comments. I am tired of the World War comments," said Heidi, releasing a short, irritated huff of air.

"Apologies. I will cease and desist," Nara said formally.

"Thank you. Now, I tell you what I hear people say. Like you, they say Chief Washakie is the good guy, but then I hear about the little town called Crowheart. The woman at the library told me it is near the place where Chief Washakie killed an enemy Crow man and cut out his heart and put it on a spear tip to wave around."

Nara let out a snort. "First of all, he wasn't waving it around like a *jerk*. What happened was the Shoshone and Crow battled for days over hunting grounds and too many young braves were dying, so then Chief Washakie and the Crow chief decided just the two of them should duel it out. The chief who won the duel, won for their whole tribe, fighting over, go in peace."

"Duel? They have the swords?" asked Heidi, not sure if 'duel' meant something different to Indian tribes.

"What do you think, Heidi? You think two chiefs would just poke at each other with arrows?" Maybe that was a little too snarky. Nara took a deep breath and continued pleasantly, "But I must say, good question."

Heidi chuckled and grinned at Gering, who wrinkled his lip and appeared to grin back.

"You and Gering having a little moment?" asked Nara.

"We think you are trying so hard to be very well-behaved. We have the bet that you will not be able to keep it up."

"Well shit," said Nara, not knowing whether to laugh or make a show of being indignant.

"Exactly," said Heidi, exchanging a look with Gering. "Now

if you would please continue with the duel. You were saying about the swords . . . "

To register her displeasure that the pair at the end of the couch thought she was a suck up, Nara gave them a long, withering look before continuing, "Yeah, well Chief Washakie had a sword, a cavalry sword, and the Crow guy had a lance or something. Washakie, he was already like, in his sixties but a warrior, you know, strong, fierce, fair. He won eventually but the Crow chief fought like hell and to honor the bravery of his enemy, Washakie cut out his heart. Honor, Heidi, not being a jerk."

Heidi imagined the bloody scene. Flies would have gathered. The pain would have been unbearable. Honor, had honor ameliorated any of it? But her people had done so much worse, with not a shred of honor, the children, the camps . . .

"Heidi? Are you listening? Time's a-wasting." Nara's impatient voice dragged her back to the present.

"I am hanging on your every words," Heidi said, raising her eyebrows to indicate attention.

"I'm sure you are," said Nara, letting the 's' go for now. "I was telling you Chief Washakie lived a hundred years. I said he was handsome as hell. Sacajawea brought a sand dollar back from the West Coast for him and he treasured it, simple little sand dollar. He used it in ceremonies until he died."

"She was in love with him?"

Nara gave a snort. "You get that from her giving him a sand dollar and me saying he was handsome? She was sold to a French-Canadian when she was twelve, helped lead Lewis and Clark when she was around sixteen and pregnant. I'm not thinkin' she had a whole lot of romantic feelings for anybody."

"A very tough girl," Heidi remarked.

"Absolutely a tough girl. She and her boys are buried in the Shoshone graveyard near Fort Washakie. There's a big bronze statue of her up a hill near her grave. She's standing there looking down at a sand dollar she's gripping it like this,"

Nara held her own hand in imitation of the statue, her thumb and third finger holding the sand dollar by its border, her other fingers partially extended. "Some people try to say she died young in South Dakota, but we know the truth."

Months ago, the Riverton librarian had told Heidi about the controversy over how long Sacajawea lived and where she was buried. Sacajawea's husband had married two Shoshone women, one died early and was buried in South Dakota, the other lived almost one hundred years and was buried on the Wind River Reservation.

The librarian, a Shoshone woman herself, had said, "Just compare our beautiful bronze statue with what they put up in South Dakota, a cement spire. You go to our cemetery, see our grave, you'll know she's here with us."

Trying to envision the statue that had captured both the librarian and Nara, Heidi asked, "What does Sacajawea do with her other hand?"

"The other hand's holding up the hem of her dress because she wading in the Pacific Ocean. We'll go see her so you can pay your respects. It's half an hour, maybe forty minutes away. We have to take something to leave her."

"Something? Food?"

Nara shrugged. "I left my favorite hair tie. People leave flowers, real and fake, toys, pencils, all sorts of stuff, something with meaning. Once I saw a bunch of shells, another time a dried sea star, like you'd buy in a gift shop."

Heidi's eyes lit up. "Wait," she said, getting up and disappearing into her bedroom. She returned holding an object flat in her hand. "We bring Sacajawea this."

"Holy Hell," Nara breathed, looking at the perfect, white sand dollar Heidi thrust out to her. The shape of the animal that had inhabited it was delicately inscribed on its surface, like a five-petalled flower.

"It is a sign," Heidi said softly. "It is the sign that we must go and visit her."

A sign. The kitchen crew at Saint Gemma's got a kick out of the signs Heidi saw everywhere. "A human Ouija board," Massimo called her.

"So, where'd you get a sand dollar?" Nara asked, turning the disk over to examine the opening where the animal's mouth had been.

"A school friend brings it back from a holiday she takes with her family to Florida. We are good friends; we always bring each other something from when we are away."

Nara felt a stab of jealously. There had been a few kids who hadn't been so bad in some of the places she and her parents had stayed, but nobody who would have called her a friend. Nobody who would have brought her something back from a vacation.

"Except clothes and a few this and thats," Heidi continued, "my sand dollar is the only not necessary thing I bring from Germany and now I know why. It is for us to bring to Sacajawea."

Ah, Nara allowed herself a grin. What were the chances of a woman bringing a Florida sand dollar, by way of Germany, to lay at the feet of a bronze Sacajawea in the Shoshone cemetery on the Rez? Perfect, so mind blowingly perfect.

"They're Echinoderms you know," she said, returning the sand dollar. "They're in the same phylum as starfish, or sea stars, if you're going to be picky. They're basically flat sea urchins." She pointed out the mouth, the anus and the gonadopores. "Gonadopores, they're used for reproduction. External fertilization of course, gametes released into the water because what's an echinoderm going to do with a penis or a vagina." Nara winked at Heidi.

At Heidi's delighted laugh, Nara stopped. "What?" she asked suspiciously, "Indian girl not supposed to know about marine invertebrates? I have a book, a college textbook."

"I laugh because I like to learn about the life in the ocean from a smart girl in Wyoming," said Heidi, her eyes dancing.

Nara allowed herself a chuckle.

"You do not need to tell me what I think an Indian girl with a college textbook cannot know," Heidi pointed out.

Nara took a moment to work out Heidi's tangled syntax before saying, "Okay, I'll give you that you're different." She leaned over as much as her swollen belly allowed and whispered to Gering, "Your mom's really, really different."

She looked up to catch Heidi watching them. Her face had become still, her deep blue eyes unreadable, as if she hadn't been laughing just a moment ago. Nara had known this woman for almost a month and still found her sudden withdrawals unnerving.

To fill the lengthening silence, Nara said, "I think I came from the sea in another life. Seriously, never been to the coast but I know it. I feel it. I can smell it. I've been escaping into that book since I was ten."

"This is an unusual book for a child of ten to want," said Heidi quietly. She had bought Peter's first book while she was still pregnant, imagining herself teaching him his letters. It had been made of cloth so he wouldn't be able to tear the pages.

"I saw it in a used bookshop window in Chicago," Nara said, the lie coming so easily. "I begged for that book, went on a food strike until my mom finally gave in."

"How long do you not eat?"

"Can't really remember. I've tried to block it out. The whole ordeal was a horror show, but I got my book."

Catching Heidi's speculative look, Nara hurried on, "Let me tell you something else about your little German schoolmate's sand dollar. Sand dollars look totally different when they're alive, kinda purple, some are brownish. What your friend brought back was just the skeleton, or endoskeleton to be more accurate because there's this leathery skin with little spines on top. *Echino* is Greek or Latin for spiny, *derm*, meaning skin."

Heidi gave a big stretch and yawn. She stood up, gathered their cups and smiled. "Tomorrow you will please show me pictures of echinoderms with their spiny skin on, but now we talk for more than an hour, so I say goodnight." On her way to the kitchen, she said over her shoulder, "I think you did not get this book because you refuse to eat. A mother would be proud her little girl would want a book like this and she would buy it for you. And sometime you tell me about Chicago."

Nara sat for a moment. Chicago, nope, not talking about Chicago, but Heidi was no dummy, that was for sure. She heard the shower start and got up to turn on the news. Tornados threatened the Lower Ohio Valley, tropical cyclones were brewing in the South Pacific. She switched to the local news. A human hand holding a rabbit's foot had been found in a casino restroom. "Somebody's got a sick sense of humor," she could hear her father saying with a chuckle.

Poor rabbit.

CHAPTER THIRTEEN

LONE RED EAGLE SUN

"Would you like to read the new *Das Fenster*?" Heidi asked, holding up the glossy magazine that had just arrived. They were spending a lazy afternoon inside since sporadic showers had left the backyard too damp for Heidi to tend the roses.

"*Danke*," said Nara, reaching out a hand from where she reclined on the sofa. "I have yet to see you read even one of these," she remarked, examining the cover where a tall, lean impeccably dressed couple flashed wide, proprietary smiles in front of an aggressively modern, angular house. All looked to be peachy in the pristine land of the Germans.

Gering waited for Heidi to settle at the end of the couch before picking his way carefully from his snuggle with Nara down to Heidi.

"I tell you, I have no time. I read cooking magazines, and for the simple pleasure, I read a book," Heidi said.

"I won't ask the obvious," said Nara dryly.

Heidi laughed. "I do not order *Das Fenster*. My closest friend, Karl, he is also my second cousin on my mother's side, gives me the subscription. This is so I remember I am not American. Karl and his Beppe want me to come home to them someday."

"His beppe? What's a beppe, a wife?" Nara asked.

"No, Beppe, a man, the name of Karl's Italian lover," Heidi explained, with that bubble of laughter that broke at times, like she was really, truly happy, like whatever haunted her had just up and left.

"What's this Beppe look like, a little fairy guy?" Nara asked, wanting something to say to quash her alarm. In a few short weeks, Heidi had become important and she wasn't ready to lose this woman to Germany and some fairy cousin and his lover yet. They probably treated Heidi like a princess.

"Beppe? Oh no, he is very handsome, you know, the rough man with strong muscles and the big, dark Italian eyes. He has a vineyard and a winery in northern Italy. He works outside and in the cellar. A man of the soil and a winemaker."

"No kidding. And what about Karl? He a hunk too?"

Heidi shrugged. "He is the more . . ." she searched for a way to describe Karl. Finally, she settled on, "Karl calls me his doppelgänger. He has my coloring, the hair not as light but the blue eyes are the same. Beppe thinks our features are similar. A few years ago, an underwear model, who looks very like Karl, is on the billboards all over Munich. Karl is often the guest chef on a popular television show, so people know him and they think Karl and the model are the same person. Karl pretends this annoys him, but the model is so handsome and I do not think he minds so much. You would think people would know better, a chef who owns his own cooking school would not have time to model underwear."

Television show, fancy cooking, modeling seemed pretty much in the same ballpark to Nara, and not that hard, but she wasn't going to argue since apparently Heidi was sure Karl wasn't moonlighting.

Instead, she said, "So Karl's got his deal in Munich and Beppe's toiling away in Italy and they're boyfriends, like exclusive, or what?"

"They pledge to each other fidelity so of course, exclusive. They have been together almost ten years."

"How does fidelity work long distance with gay guys? Their whole deal is based on sex."

Heidi gave an exasperated sigh. "This is your experience? You know so many homosexual people?"

"Okay, not really, not that I know of," Nara admitted. She had never been close enough to anyone for confidences. What she claimed to know about other people was gleaned from overheard conversations and television. She was willing to acknowledge Heidi might have had more experience in the social arena than she.

"Karl and Beppe say there is a rumor that the Dutch will allow marriage between homosexuals by the end of this century," Heidi said. "They will marry then, in Amsterdam and we will have such a celebration."

"I'll invite myself. The twins can be flower boys," declared Nara, not imagining as she said it, there would be any possibility she'd be hanging with Heidi in a decade. But right now, she wanted to be a part of it, a celebration in Amsterdam, windmills, wooden shoes, men walking around holding hands. Lots of happy, smiling crowds, a fairy tale in which she would be surrounded by people who didn't know shit about her. She'd be with her boys, and Karl and Beppe would welcome her like family. She'd learn some Dutch, impress the hell out of people.

But Amsterdam? No way was she trusting an airplane to carry her and her boys to Amsterdam. Nara saw herself standing on the deck of a ship surrounded by nothing but ocean, and in the pitch-black water, thousands of feet down, bathypelagic fish would be using their bioluminescence to attract prey or a mate. She visualized the deep-sea creatures from her ocean book, a humpback anglerfish dangling a luminescent lure, a deep-sea dragonfish displaying the glowing barbel attached to its chin. And she would be on the surface, filling her lungs with the briny air, knowing they were there.

"The twins, flower boys?" she repeated, anxious for Heidi to buy into her fantasy.

"Yes, of course," Heidi said absently. After a pause she added, "Karl and Beppe are my only family now. My parents die a few years ago, together when their car crashes. It was the wettest month on record in our part of Germany."

Sensing a response was required, Nara said, "Sorry about your parents."

"They die quickly and they have no suffering the *Autobahnpolizei* tell me." Heidi flashed a tight smile. "I make this my peace."

Sunday was dry and considerably warmer than the day before. Heidi deadheaded roses in the garden with Gering stretched out in a patch of sunshine near her, his little sides fluttering as he panted.

From where she sat on the patio, Nara called, "Gering's too hot; his brain's going to fry."

Heidi looked from Gering to Nara and shook her head, as if not worried at all.

"Your mom doesn't love you, Gering," Nara called again.

The dachshund lifted the tip of his tail without opening an eye. Nara gave up and returned to her perusal of *Das Fenster*. She was trying to decide between two articles for a game she had invented. She and Heidi could play it after lunch. Panting rapidly, Gering got up and came on the patio to drink noisily from his bowl.

"How's your brain? Dodged a bullet, buddy," Nara told the dog when he collapsed in the shade of her chair. "Karl's phoning today because Karl *always* phones on Sunday," she reminded him, leaning over and just managing to touch the top of his head.

Thinking back to Heidi's description of Karl and Beppe, Nara felt a familiar wave of longing. It was rare to be an Indian without close relatives and here was old Heidi, managing to take some distant cousin *and* his lover, and make a family for herself. And here was old Nara, managing to get knocked-up with twins, no goddamn family to speak of. After the twins were born, maybe she'd try harder to connect with her mother's family, except she seemed to remember hearing they'd scattered to Montana or some such place.

The babies woke up and Nara flinched. She placed her hands on her belly, envisioning the perfectly rounded heads, curved backs and clenched fists she'd seen on the sonogram. Two little beings drifting together in their own little world. She'd stopped drinking the day she knew she was pregnant, early, four weeks gestation. The clinic thought it had been soon enough and she had to believe them.

At Heidi's howl, Nara looked up. A gust of wind had picked up Heidi's broad brimmed hat and now it was sailing into the crown of the oak that had pulled down part of the back fence when it fell. Heidi swiped at her face to get the hair out of her eyes and turned to look at Nara, a dirty streak over her brow and down her cheek.

Sighing, Nara got up and went into the house. She returned with a baseball cap Sean, the barman at the casino, had given her to wear the one and only time they had gone fishing. Gering escorted her back to the rose bushes and Heidi.

"Put this on, white girl, before you get skin cancer," Nara ordered, frowning down at Heidi, who was now on her knees pulling weeds from around the base of the rose bushes in preparation to adding mulch. Heidi looked up, trowel held in a muddy-gloved hand.

"Never mind, stand up," Nara said impatiently. "I'll do it, and obviously I'm not bending over."

"No, I take the gloves off and do it," said Heidi.

"Stand at attention, hands at your sides, Corporal," barked Nara. They had recently watched Goldie Hawn getting browbeaten in *Private Benjamin* and had agreed that Heidi looked like an army recruit in her olive green and mustard yellow overalls.

"Yes sir, Sergeant sir," Heidi barked back. "Thank you for the promotion from the Private to the Corporal, sir."

Nara went inside to use the bathroom and looked at the clock. She might as well make their lunch sandwiches. She cracked hard-boiled eggs and mixed them with mayonnaise, pickle, pepper and salt. She opened the tin of Coleman mustard powder and added a generous dash. Dried spicy mustard, purely for Heidi but not so bad.

"Made sandwiches," Nara called as she settled back into her chair.

Heidi waved her trowel in acknowledgement but didn't look around as she concentrated on grubbing in the dirt. Nara sighed and craned her head to see where Gering was. He was under the other lounge chair busily chewing on a green thing shaped like a toothbrush. It was supposed to make his breath smell better.

"You have to hand it to your mom," she said to the little dog. "One track mind, she always finishes what she starts. You teach her that? Is it a German thing, German dog?"

Germans, Nara let her mind wander, there must be black Germans, Asian Germans, or didn't Germany work that way? Did a black German call herself an *African* German? People hear 'German,' and they think white person, people hear 'American,' they think white person. Lack of pigmentation allowed you to drop your ancestral country of origin, if you so desired.

"Oh, hello, I'm a *European* American, no white invader says that," Nara said under her breath, finding some comfort in her irritation.

White people, she smirked. Now she had her very own little white friend. Blonde haired, blue-eyed, I-am-from-Northern-Germany, Heidi Vogel, who acted like she really wanted to be friends with a young, pregnant Arapaho from a little family who seemed to belong nowhere.

Nara squinted at Heidi coming up the slope toward her. Even sweaty and in overalls, with dirt on her face, she looked classy. But no boyfriend, no interest in men that Nara could see, although there were slim pickins in Riverton. The guy who owned the deli sniffed around; the head of the Chamber of Commerce had made a move. Heidi had finally made up a boyfriend, a paleontologist in Thermopolis, who was often away for months digging up fossils. Nara couldn't have made up a better lie herself.

"You have the big frown. You are uncomfortable?" asked Heidi, standing before Nara and looking concerned.

"Of course, I'm uncomfortable. I have two people growing inside of me and I'm hungry. I made the sandwiches half an hour ago."

"You should not have waited for me."

"You're welcome."

"*Danke, hohou,*" said Heidi, smiling prettily.

"Ooo, 'thank you' in German and Arapaho. I must rate."

"You rate," agreed Heidi. "I wash up and bring out the lunch and you choose your article."

"Already done," said Nara smugly, tapping the glossy cover of *Das Fenster*.

The phone rang in the kitchen and Heidi hurried inside. From inside the house, Nara heard laughter, German, private stuff, Karl right on cue.

"I tell Karl I phone back in an hour. Do not let me forget," said Heidi when she returned, having washed up and shed her camo gear for shorts and a long-sleeved white cotton shirt. She put the tray with their lunch on the crate that served as an outdoor table, and went back inside to retrieve her binoculars before settling into her chair.

Heidi took her first bite of sandwich. Egg salad, she would have added a touch of curry, but otherwise, it was very good, just enough mayonnaise, a hint of mustard, and salt and pepper. "Excellent," she pronounced with a happy grin, basking in the luxury of having someone prepare food for her.

Nara nodded and took a big bite herself to hide her pleasure, 'excellent' from the Food Queen, high praise indeed.

"You say you have chosen the article for us?" Heidi asked.

"That I have, *Fräulein*. We'll do it after the excellent sandwiches, during cookies and whatever beverage you're going to force on me."

"Tea. Chamomile?" asked Heidi. Nara shook her head. "Peppermint?" Nara nodded.

As they ate, they watched several little birds flutter about in the fountain and after a few minutes Nara said, "Okay, I'm going to ask the name of those little birds, but I want name only please, not the whole song and dance."

"I understand," said Heidi, picking up her binoculars and adjusting the focus. "They are Blue-headed vireos. You see the yellow bars on the wings and the white ring around the eye?" She handed the binoculars to Nara. "They will leave for Mexico soon. They are similar to the White-eyed vireo, except that one has more yellow and it does not have the white eye ring. They both . . ."

"Cease, Nature Girl," Nara held up her hand, "just let me just look at the birdies."

Nara remained outside with her feet up, while Heidi went inside to make tea. Flying south for the winter, that must be nice. Wyoming winters were damn cold, damn long. Winter, the twins would be here, Nara released a long sigh. She was supposed to quit work next week and sit around and wait. She'd better get used to a whole new flavor of boring. She wasn't too concerned about the pain of childbirth, couldn't be that much worse than getting a fat guy's dick shoved in you at eight years old, couldn't be worse than that.

Nara gathered her long black hair in both hands, twisted

it and piled it on top of her head, enjoying the breeze on her neck. Strong hair, beautiful hair, the hair of a woman who could do anything.

She let her hair fall. She'd never even babysat. Did some kind of animal instinct take over so you knew what to do? There'd be a lot of laundry. She could do that. Hopefully she'd be feeling too tired to care about hanging around in a house in a Riverton neighborhood. The babies would keep her busy. They'd surely fill up that anxious feeling that something was going to drop any minute. But rarely did.

Heidi returned shortly with a tray of tea and cookies.

With a cup of tea in one hand and a large oatmeal cookie in the other, Nara nodded to the open magazine. "Game time," she said, pointing the cookie at the title of the article she'd selected.

Heidi dutifully read the title aloud, *"Kuhfurz erhöht den atmosphärischen Kohlenstoffgehalt."*

"Thank you very much," said Nara primly. She took a sip of her tea and cleared her throat. "Ahem . . . okay, now we see these photos of cow butts, and a Germanish kind of 'atmosphere' word shows up in the title. Last week you said *Kuh,* meant cow, so cow butts plus atmosphere, and butts fart and farts release gas into the air, sooo . . ." Nara scowled at the article and looked up at Heidi. "Am I on the right track? Is *furz* a fart?"

Heidi nodded.

"You Germans like your long words, is *rischen* like 'rising? *Atmosphärischen* is like 'atmospheric rising'?" asked Nara.

"No, it's a big word just for atmospheric. *Erhöht* is rising and carbon levels . . ."

"Hold on Susie Q, I'm getting there," said Nara, pointing to '*Kohlenstoffgehalt*'. "Another hell of a long word, all stuck together, meaning 'carbon levels'?"

"German is . . ."

"Never mind, I got it, so apparently, cow farts are increasing the levels of carbon in the atmosphere, and since you guys are such science geeks, I'm thinking it may be true," Nara placed her hand on her swollen belly. "So we better start raising less beef, if Mutt and Jeff here are going to have a chance."

"Matt and Jeff? These are the baby names?" asked Heidi, disappointed. She had hoped they would discuss names together.

"No, *Mutt*, not Matt. They're from some comic strip. I never saw it but my father got a kick out of it, nitwit white guys getting up to no good. I'm not one hundred percent opposed to German names 'though, unless they're Adolf or Engelbert or something like that."

"Adolf, it means 'noble wolf.' Engelbert means 'bright angel,'" said Heidi innocently, selecting another cookie for herself.

Nara snorted. "Jesus, nobody'll know that here. Give these little Native boys a break. I'll find an Elder when they're older to give them their Indian names. I'm letting you weigh in on the regular, whatever, name, don't screw it up. We're looking for something a little different, not too long, not too short, something with class."

Heidi already knew the names she would suggest if she was asked. For a month she had used them when she'd thought about the twins. Wanting to hold the names in her heart a little longer in case Nara didn't like them, she didn't suggest them now and instead asked how Nara would find the Elder to give the twins their Indian names.

"My mom's side will cough up somebody. They kind of cut us off because of my dad, don't ask, but I'll look 'em up when the twins get older," Nara said as she avoided looking at Heidi.

With her Uncle gone, there was no one, not a single, solitary Elder she could think of, but she'd figure something out, maybe even her dad would step up. Although an Elder had knowledge and wisdom, her dad had smarts, but not much more than that.

"It has to be someone special, not just any old Elder," she continued. "Someone with a connection. They'll spend time with the boys, dream, pray. Like, maybe the Elder will have a vision of a single eagle, a red silhouette maybe, flying past the sun, and one of the babies will be Lone Red Eagle Sun."

"So beautiful," said Heidi.

Nara nodded; she liked the image too. What spirits would she insult if she came up with the boys' Indian names herself? Better not, better work harder to connect with an Elder, better not challenge the old ways. She looked at the cookie plate, one cookie left.

"Do you mind?" she asked, reaching for it.

"No, it is for you," said Heidi.

"*Hohou, danke* and thank you."

"I will now try to get my hat from the tree." Heidi stood up and to Gering's delight, brushed the crumbs from her lap onto the patio.

"No, what you need to do is phone good old Karl. Give him my best, Beppe too if he's there. Let the tree keep your hat," Nara held her hand palm up in offering, "I bequest . . bequeath? . . . I bequeath you my ball cap."

CHAPTER FOURTEEN

BIRDS OF A FEATHER

After Nara stopped working, her days became insufferably long. Every part of her body had swollen, fingers, feet, breasts, belly. The babies weren't due for another four weeks and she swore she couldn't possibly get any larger. Her skin had stretched to breaking point. She shuffled around the house either barefoot or in the enormous pink slippers Heidi had purchased at Walmart, along with a bra so large Nara had burst out laughing, until she tried it on and found it barely fit. During the day, she spent hour after hour lying around, radio on, television on, newspapers, magazines scattered, neatly arranged, scattered, arranged.

Just her and the beings commandeering her body, waiting for Heidi to come back. Rarely did she and Heidi talk about anything of a personal nature, preferring to stick to news articles, politics and the goings on at Saint Gemma's, but they were roommates. Nara was pretty sure Heidi would call her a friend, but what did they really know about each other? That part of her soul that should be occupied by family or friends was impoverished, she knew that, and she needed something to offer the twins when later they asked about her life and their babyhood. And what would she have to offer them? A rabbit?

The rabbit had entered her chest quietly from the shadows as she lay on her side that first time in Chicago, hurting down there, staring at a textured white wall that offered nothing. When eventually she could move, she had tiptoed to the shower, locked the door and washed and washed and washed. In the steamy bathroom the soft grey presence behind her breastbone huddled, waiting, alert. It had been a comforting presence at first, exerting pressure but no pain, reappearing after each violation . . . but it had followed her onto the Reservation, where it was no longer needed, and its restless shifting sometimes made it difficult to breathe. As a high school student, she had flung it from her body as she ran laps around the track, the fastest girl on her team by far, and it absented itself for hours, days. The relief of having enough space in her chest to inhale and deliver oxygen to the very core of her being had made her higher than any drug.

After leaving school, making money, alcohol and sex had suppressed the rabbit and later, when the babies had taken up residence in her body, their ever-growing presence had banished it—forever she had hoped. But on occasion she was conscious of it waiting, just off stage.

Heidi ate at work and brought home a plate of the evening's offerings for Nara.

"Perfect," said Nara, "Pasta primavera plus Alfredo sauce. Where'd you get enough yellow peppers for a Saint Gemma's sized batch?"

"The yellow ones are just for you. For the patrons, I use only the green."

"Thank you kindly." Nara used a piece of garlic bread to sop up the last of the creamy sauce.

"And thank you kindly for two loads of laundry, ironed and folded."

"The pleasure was all mine." Nara gave a winsome smile. "So, let's make our evening's hot beverages and you can tell me about this Vogel you married."

Heidi cast her a long look and Nara chuckled.

"C'mon Boss spill, then I'll tell you some stuff," she said over her shoulder as she went into the living room to stretch out on the sofa.

Handing Nara a cup of hot chocolate, Heidi picked up Gering and sat down with him at the end of the sofa. She held the dachshund to her face and nuzzled his warm sleepy body. She glanced at Nara. How much did she really want to know about this narrow-eyed Indian girl, so smart, bitter and beautiful, with her long black hair spilling over her shoulders and down her breasts to her enormous belly, where two babies waited inside? Two babies who would come into her house for what, a few weeks as Nara healed? Then Nara would take them away. Babies she didn't know if she'd be able to bear holding. Two babies who weren't Peter.

'*Hör auf, so ein Feigling zu sein,*' she chastised herself, stop being a coward. What was the harm in getting to know Nara a little better? The young woman had already established herself in her heart; she would always be more than a memory.

Nara poked Heidi with her toe. "Ready?"

Heidi sighed and nodded, "I will tell you a little," she said, "and then you will tell me why you left the Reservation, pregnant and no job."

"Then you will have to tell me why you came to America," countered Nara. "Now, let's get this party started. The rules are, we take turns talking. Just talking, no questions."

"Why this rule?" Heidi asked. "Why do people who talk have to have rules?"

"Rules, because I've been in groups, I've done group work. You let people talk, they figure out what they want to say. It's just better. They say more that way, and now you broke the rule, so you have to go first."

"What kind are these groups?"

"Oh, for God's sake, Heidi, you've done it again. No questions. Get with the program or this will take forever."

"Okay, I get with the program and first I tell you the name Vogel means bird."

Nara grinned and said, "Nice, so we're two birds of a feather."

"Yes, the two birds of feathers."

"No, of a feather, we're . . . oh, never mind, continue," directed Nara.

"I understand, bird of a feather friend."

Nara rolled her eyes.

"Okay, I keep going. Claus Vogel, ex-husband, comes with baggage. Big baggage. His father, Herr Emmett Vogel, is a domineering and horrible man. The worst kind of German."

"And you are the best kind," said Nara loyally. "So, why'd you marry Claus if his dad's such an asshole?"

"You say no questions and you break the rule, but I will answer. I meet Claus at Klein Kartoffeln. This is Karl's cooking school in Munich. Emmett pulls the string with Karl because Claus does not really have the talent for cooking. He is more the business person. Alice, Karl's cousin on the other side from me, is Karl's assistant. She makes the mistake and she seats Claus at my table. This is a mistake because Emmett has said to Karl he wants Claus to meet a nice, smart German girl in the class, a girl who looks a certain way, and Karl does not want that girl to be me. But it is too late, Claus and I and Andre, the other man at our table, make friends right away. And I find out the coincidence, both Claus and I have internships at the restaurant at his father's famous hotel in Hamburg. When Karl tries to move Claus to another table the next day, we protest. We do not understand the big deal Karl is making and he gives up."

"This is sounding way complicated," interjected Nara.

"Yes. I think so. You take a turn now," said Heidi, relieved to abandon the naiveté of her early twenties.

"Complicated, but you haven't dropped a clue on this baggage you said Claus came with, or why Karl's all upset."

Heidi closed her eyes a moment. She had never tried to summarize to another person the steps that led to her absorption into the Vogel family. Gathering her thoughts into English and listening to herself now ...

"Let's go, Boss," Nara prodded impatiently.

Heidi sighed. If that early version of herself had ever existed, she had become a stranger.

Anxious to get her tale over with, she said quickly that after the course was over, Claus invited her on a holiday to Italy and his father arranged for them stay with Beppe Biro at his winery,

"Wait, wait," Nara's eyes widened, "*Karl's* Beppe?"

Heidi nodded.

Nara looked at the little dog. "You following this?"

Gering did something with his lip that was hard to interpret. A smile? A sneer?

"Gering follows because he has heard this already," said Heidi. "He knows how I first meet Beppe. Although Karl and I are related on my mother's side, we only make the very good friends when I start at his cooking school and we see all talent for food that we share. Karl is eight years older, the son of my mother's cousin, living hundreds of miles away. Before this, we hardly know each other and we do not know of each other's boyfriends. Karl is just the second cousin, I think."

"*Just* the second cousin?" Nara shook her head. "Why do you guys always do that? On the Rez, your mom's best friend's sister's kid is your cousin. No firsts, seconds, thirds. No once or twice removed shit."

"So, you must have many cousins?" asked Heidi, wondering why she had added the 'just the second cousin,' when describing her relationship to Karl. A brother couldn't have been closer.

"Me? I don't have lots of anybody. My parents were not

that social so I didn't have to put up with all that family business but I felt obligated to point out how picky whites are with how they rank family members."

"Thank you," said Heidi. "May I continue?"

"By all means continue." Nara bowed her head graciously.

"When I tell Karl that Claus and I will go on this holiday and will stay with Beppe Biro, Karl hits on top of the roof. This is when I find out that Beppe is his boyfriend."

"Hits the roof. You're not actually on top of anything," Nara corrected.

"Thank you, so when . . ."

"Hold on," said Nara, shifting her weight. "So, it sounds like Karl, Beppe and this Emmett, who also happens to be your father-in-law, have a pretty intense thing going on."

"Yes, they know each other for years. Emmett is the moneybags investor. He helps Karl start his business and he owns a little part of Beppe's winery."

In truth, the relationship between the three men was much more complex than that, but their painful history was not hers to share, so Heidi said, "I am done now. It is your turn."

"Whoa, Nelly, you don't get to leave the other person hanging. You need to tell me why Karl had his panties in a bunch over you staying with Beppe and getting it on with Emmett's boy."

Heidi sighed. It was no use. Nara was relentless. She explained that because Beppe knew Karl didn't like Emmett, Karl thought he should have refused to host Emmett's son. But then he got over it and decided to join them at the winery and the four of them had a very nice week together. Claus began to relax . . .

"What did Claus have to relax about?" Nara broke in. "You guys were on vacation."

"Karl and Beppe's relationship upsets him. His father teaches him homosexuals are an aberration."

142

"*Aberration?* What a fucking asshole." Nara shook her head and Heidi nodded.

On the last day, Heidi continued, Karl had taken her aside and warned her that Emmett Vogel was a ruthless man, who was not to be trusted. But by then, it was too late because she and Claus were beginning to fall in love.

"We are so young and Claus is so handsome, and very sweet in the bed . . ."

Nara interrupted, "Sweet? You're losing me here."

"I think your groups would not like so many interruptions while the person in the cat's bird seat is talking," said Heidi with a frown.

"Catbird, one word, and I was just making an observation." Nara wrinkled her nose. "Calling him 'sweet' doesn't sound like Claus rocked your world."

"I say 'sweet' because he is eager for me to teach him about what a woman wants. I have boyfriends before him and he says he has girls before me, but I think maybe not even one."

"Okay, Sex Kitten," said Nara with a grin.

"Also, I am ambitious. I know I can wear the pants. I say I will go to America someday so Claus says this is his dream also. Of course, then I was just the stupid little girl. I thought I could control everything in my life."

At her tone, Nara raised her eyebrows and Heidi raised hers back. She wouldn't mention Peter. You didn't talk about a dead baby to a pregnant woman. She shifted Gering on her lap. He opened a sleepy eye and yawned, his long pink tongue furling at the tip.

"Your turn now," Heidi insisted.

"In a sec," said Nara, placing her hand on her belly, "*Ouch!*" She shifted her position and grimaced, "Ow, Baby One just kicked Baby Two, little buggers," she winced and pushed herself to a sitting position. "Gotta pee, be back in a sec and don't you move."

"You will be more comfortable in bed?" asked Heidi, when Nara returned. "We can have more group talk tomorrow."

"Nope, we're on a roll and I'll be less, *way* less comfortable in bed. I think maybe I'll sleep here tonight."

Heidi nodded. She remembered the last weeks of her pregnancy. The pressure, the sudden tightening of her uterus in practice contractions, sharp stabs of pain from deep down in her body, her heavy breasts, the difficulty of taking a deep breath.

Nara adjusted her cushions before leaning back. "I'm ready for my turn, but are you going to be able to listen?" She looked at Heidi critically. "You got that anywhere-but-here look."

"I listen."

"Okay, well Baby Guy and I weren't married, surprise, surprise. The guy, first name John so I guess last name Doe, was a good-looking, mostly charming, mostly white guy. Well, maybe half, the rest was probably Native. He helped me change my tire when I got a flat one night and followed me home. We drank and screwed for a week then he said had to leave for boot camp in South Carolina. Boot camp, who knows? I'd say 'I gotta get to boot camp' if I wanted to move on. Anyway, he left me with twins."

"You have not tried to find him?"

"Now why would I do that?" asked Nara incredulously. "I don't want a man to take care of." She stopped, not sure she understood the expression on Heidi's face. "What? You think I should tell him? Because I can tell you, he was not daddy material. That charm came with a big dose of bad boy and I've already wrestled my demons. I screwed up by getting pregnant but I'm not screwing up as a mom. I'm staying healthy, keeping my babies strong, not drinking anymore."

Despite her discomfort, Nara glowed with health and Heidi had no doubt the twins would be strong. Peter had fought so hard for life and she had not been able to give him enough of her strength to survive. Would it ever not hurt?

"Heidi, what's wrong? Your turn," Nara said, prodding Heidi with her toe again.

Heidi grabbed it and squeezed, letting go when Nara howled.

"Hush, I do not squeeze so hard, you drama girl," chided Heidi. "My mind drifts and now I call it back. I will tell you about Claus's father, Big Bad Herr Emmett. You are ready?"

At Nara's petulant nod, Heidi continued, "He sets us up in business in New York, a restaurant, German. I choose the neighborhood and Claus and his father choose the name, Café Claus."

"Stupid name," remarked Nara.

Heidi shrugged. The name hadn't been her first choice, but it had placated her father-in-law when she insisted on a location he didn't think was ideal.

"We do well the first year and make a profit," she said. "We make a higher profit the second year. This is very good. Many restaurants fail early, but it is not good enough for Herr Emmett Vogel, the big man, the famous restaurateur. He wants more."

Heidi paused. As long as there had been hope of a healthy grandson, her father-in-law had stayed in the background, but after Peter's death, he couldn't wait to get rid of her. Her genetics made her useless to him.

"So, then he sends Anke," she resumed, anxious to get her dreary tale over with. "Anke Mueller is the young business consultant with the fresh face. She takes over Claus and the business and she gives them back to Herr Vogel. There is no place for me."

"Sounds like ol' Claus needs to grow a pair," Nara snickered.

"To grow the testicles?"

"That's what I'm saying."

Heidi smiled and nodded. Claus had been well endowed

but she understood the expression. She looked at her watch and stifled a yawn. "We wrap this up after your turn, feather friend."

Nara chuckled and moved a pillow to the small of her back, which seemed to alleviate some discomfort. "Right. Well, my mom died eight years, two months and um . . ." she frowned a moment, "a few weeks ago. I was sixteen. She'd been sick since I was thirteen so I guess it was time, but life was a hell of a lot better when she was around."

"I am so sorry," said Heidi.

"Yeah, well anyway." Nara gave a tight smile. She missed her mom every day. Her drinking hadn't been able to assuage the feeling she'd lost the only person who would ever truly love her. But it had helped.

"After your mother dies, who takes care of you?" asked Heidi.

Startled by the question, Nara laughed. "Get a grip, *Fräulein*, I was sixteen, didn't need anybody to take care of me. Good thing, because a couple of months later, my dad takes a new wife. There's something about my dad, women like him, but two months?" She held up two fingers and waggled them for emphasis. "Why my mom put up with him is one of life's great mysteries. Danny Crow, he's got zero loyalty to anybody but himself. But he's tall and handsome. He gives off some kind of vibe a lot of women go for, and he's got money. Anyway, New Wife moves in. We don't get along. She's always on at me. My dad tells us to work it out, to leave him out of it. Like with you, I knew there was no place for me. I was bored anyway. My dad and I aren't close. It broke my biology teacher's heart when I dropped out. She even offered me a room, hoped I'd be a marine biologist, probably thought we'd sit around in the evening worrying about the destruction of the Great Barrier Reef."

"A place to live and to finish school? This does not sound so bad," observed Heidi.

"Yeah, well I wasn't having her take my mom's place at my graduation, I'll tell you that. My mother left a hole and I was about to jump in it if I didn't get going. You get what I'm saying?"

Heidi nodded. "When a person you love so much dies, sometimes you must leave to live."

"Exactly. Sometimes you have to leave to live. Get what we're saying, Gering?"

Lying equidistant between the two women, the dog raised his head and looked from one to the other with half open eyes. Was it time to follow Heidi into the warm steamy bathroom while she took her shower? When Heidi didn't make a move to get up, he went back to sleep.

"Then what do you do after you leave your father's house?" asked Heidi.

Nara didn't reprimand her for asking yet another question. That rule had gone by the wayside long ago. Nobody had followed the rule in rehab either. She told Heidi she'd done restaurant work until she was old enough to serve drinks at a casino, pushup bra, the works. She caught the eye of the manager who told her she'd make more money working the gaming tables. The tourists would like a Native girl as pretty as her dealing cards. She'd had a fling with the bartender, then with Boot Camp Guy. When she found she was pregnant, she tried to go back to her dad's house.

"New Wife wasn't having any of it," said Nara, placing her hands protectively on her belly. She rolled her head to look at Heidi, "So there you go, Nara 101. Now we need to start thinking of baby names."

"Amadeus and Marcel," said Heidi, unaware she had spoken until she saw Nara's grin.

"Amadeus and Marcel. Marcel and Amadeus," Nara repeated. "I wouldn't have thought of those in a million years. Not too girlie, I guess. So, Amadeus Mozart and Marcel who?"

"Marcel Tyberg. My mother hears him play the piano

when she is a young girl so she is always a biggest fan. He is also a conductor and a composer."

"Never heard of him, must be pretty old if he's still alive."

"He dies in Auschwitz, one-sixteenth the Jew. When I drive here from New York, I stop in a church in South Dakota and hear the choir singing Tyberg's Mass No.2 in F minor. Marcel Tyberg's music in South Dakota. A sign of something good, I think."

Nara shivered. The holocaust part of Marcel's life might be a little hard to get past. Not like her own people hadn't suffered, but who'd even heard about this guy before?

Aware Heidi was waiting, she said slowly, "I'm thinking Amadeus is a go. Marcel I'm not sure about yet."

After a moment's pause, Heidi stood up. "Okay," she said with a bright smile.

"I'm not saying no to Marcel, Heidi, I am just saying keep the names coming."

"No, thank you," replied Heidi, looking at Gering and gathering their cups.

CHAPTER FIFTEEN

THE BUSH WOMEN OF THE KALAHARI

With a gloved hand probing Nara's cervix, the doctor announced, "One centimeter, bigger than a Cheerio, and I'd say, sixty percent effaced, but we've got a long way to go."

Spinning around on his low stool, he peeled off his gloves and tossed them into the trash with a flourish, beaming at Heidi as he scooted his way across the room toward her. Heidi glanced at Nara over his shoulder and tried to suppress a laugh when Nara mouthed 'Spiderman.' Round tummy, no neck to speak of, the four legs of the stool . . . with two more legs, he could well have been a giant spider.

"Will the babies have to stay in the hospital long?" Heidi asked when the doctor arrived in front of her.

She felt her smile slipping as she recalled Peter's long days in the Neonatal Intensive Care Unit, a hushed grey world of machines, barriers, fear and kindness. She looked down at the unexpected pressure of the doctor's hand on her knee. She raised her eyes to his, and whatever he saw there caused him to back his stool up rapidly and retrieve his chart from the counter.

"I shouldn't think they'll have to stay long," he said frowning at the chart in an apparent attempt to mask his embarrassment. "They're around five pounds each. At thirty-seven weeks, they should have enough surfactant in their lungs to breathe without assistance, but no guarantees. We'll release them once they've proved they're competent feeders, gaining weight, maintaining their temperatures on their own."

"What do the Bush Women of the Kalahari do when they have twins?" Nara managed to say before placing her hands on her belly as everything from her breasts to her thighs contracted powerfully.

The doctor turned to look at her, then glanced at his watch. "Good, now let's make this a nice long contraction."

After what seemed to be an eternity, Nara released a sharp breath and managed to add, "And how do twin Bush babies prove they're competent?"

"What is she talking about?" the doctor asked, casting a puzzled look at Heidi. He wrote the length of the contraction in his notes.

"We have the *National Geographic* magazines at home," Heidi explained.

"Oh, okay," he said, trying on a smile. The Native woman was odd, but the blonde woman was so pretty, perhaps out of his league, but he was a doctor so he might have a chance.

Maybe he shouldn't have touched her knee, but she had looked so sad for a moment.

He stood up and spun the stool back into its corner with a little too much force. It bounced off the wall and returned to him, so he gave it a more moderate shove before going to check the clipboard hanging on the wall.

"It looks like Joni's going to be your nurse," he said to the women. "You're lucky, she's a champ with multiple births, nothing fazes her."

"Yay, Joni," muttered Nara.

"If you're up to it," he said on his way out the door, "I recommend you ladies walk up and down the hall for a bit. It may move things along."

"Thank you, Doctor," called Heidi.

He stopped, turned and looked at her uncertainly, blushing when she gave him a warm smile.

After the doctor left, Nara swung her legs over the side of the bed and remarked dryly, "Although I'm the main event here, you must secrete a pheromone so I'm not going to take it personally that Spidey directed most of his attention at you. And that knee thing was a grope by the way."

Heidi shrugged. "You make a mole hill into a mountain."

"Oh, you're adorable, you are," said Nara, pushing herself into a standing position. "And what do you think he was referring to? What things might faze other nurses but not good old Joni?"

"He refers to nothing. It is just the extra talk. You are ready to walk?"

"Indeed, this is precisely why I'm standing, Boss. Now where's the TV remote? We need a quick check of the news before we go."

"We may walk up and down the hall for a while," Heidi pointed out. "We will turn the news on when we get back."

"Oh Heidi, Heidi, Heidi," said Nara with a sigh. "We can still walk if the TV's on, *Liebling*." She spied the remote control tethered to the bed and clicked through the channels until she found the one she wanted.

Heidi didn't argue. If a television playing to an absent audience offered comfort, the waste of electricity was a small price to pay. Shortly after Nara moved in, Heidi had asked her why she wanted the television on all the time when she very rarely paid attention to it.

"In case they have to alert us. You never know, nuclear attack, flood, wildfire, President going ape-shit," Nara had replied. "Don't want to be out of the loop. It'll give us time to evacuate, shelter in place, drink our purple Kool-Aid, whatever. And I'll save you from asking if I'm serious by saying, *Was denkst du, mein kleiner Schatz?*"

'What do you think my little darling?' Despite the sarcastic tone, Nara's adoption of the question she accused Heidi of constantly asking Gering had caused Heidi's stoic practicality to soften into something akin to tenderness. And the feeling had grown as Heidi had come to realize that this smart, edgy young woman attempted to hide deep and abiding fears under her frequent apocalyptic references.

With Heidi by her side, Nara walked up and down the corridor with the rocking, waddling motion adopted by near term women, pausing a moment each time they passed the open door to her room to squint at the television. After that powerful contraction of half an hour ago, the others had been infrequent and mild.

Nara was tempted to ask how long Heidi's labor had taken, but she didn't. She had discovered Peter's existence on her own. Heidi had never actually spoken about him. After she first moved in, Nara had listened for several nights to Heidi's soft murmurings through the thin wall separating their bedrooms. She had snooped one morning after Heidi and Gering had left for work and found the little bundle wrapped in a yellow knit baby cap stuffed into a small wooden box on Heidi's nightstand. Carefully she had opened it. Ashes. Oh my God, ashes. She had tied them back up, blowing the tiny, tiny bit of grey dust that had somehow transferred itself to her finger tips, into the air.

'Peter Son of my Heart,' using Heidi's German-English dictionary Nara had managed to translate the words carved into the front of the box. Now both she and Heidi shared two sides of the same secret. That was okay. All friendships had their limits.

When Nara tired of walking, they returned to her room. With an animated reporter gesticulating in the background, Nara lay in bed and thumbed through the most recent *Das Fenster* magazine and Heidi sat in the reclining chair and worked on a crossword puzzle.

"What is an eleven-letter word, starting with 'c', then three letters, then 'l' and 'a' and it ends in 'y'?" asked Heidi.

When she started to ask the question again, Nara responded tartly, "I'm not answering because I'm waiting for the clue."

"I say the clue," Heidi protested. "I say 'gratification or smugness.'"

"Actually, you did *not* say the clue." Nara looked up from her article, which appeared to be about Steffi and Sylvia, identical twins separated at birth and adopted into different families, one in Bonn, the other in Frankfurt. "See if the word 'complacency' fits with whatever else you have going."

Heidi penciled in the word and beamed. "I tell you with complacency that you are the very smart girl and the twins will have the best vocabulary."

"Not sure that's the best use of the word," said Nara, "and don't sound so surprised. I said I did well in school. I started reading at three, if my mom is to be believed."

Nara went back to her magazine, sounding out some of the words under her breath, *verlassen von ihrer jugendlichen Mutter*. Something. . . by their. . . something mother. "Boss, help me out," she pointed to the two words she didn't know.

"Abandoned and teenaged," translated Heidi. "You are reading about twins abandoned by their teenaged mother?"

"Give her a break, it appears she was only thirteen at the time," said Nara, "The babies found each other last year, on a *Kreuzfahrtschiff*. What's that?"

"A cruise ship."

"Of course, it is. Look, now they're fat and sassy women in their fifties." Nara held up the magazine. "They even have the same hairstyle and they both married *Feuerwehrmänner*. Which are, or I mean, who are?"

"Firemen," said Heidi.

"*Feuerwehrmänner*," Nara repeated the word several

times. Memorization was easy for her and she liked the harsh, guttural sounds of German. When Heidi talked to Karl on the phone, it sounded like they were about to take their shit out to the street and kick ass, or it did until Heidi gave one of her light, bubbly laughs, which precious Karl would probably describe as effervescent or delightful.

Nara closed her eyes and grimaced as another contraction gripped her, longer than others but not as intense as the one an hour ago. She bowed her head forward and placed her hands on her belly. It felt incredibly hard, her back ached, heat radiated down her thighs. When the contraction eased, she leaned her head back against the pillow and released a long breath.

"Seventy-three seconds," said Heidi.

"How do you know when it started?" asked Nara irritably.

"You make the contraction face."

Nara grumbled, "Yeah, well I'd like to be making more of the contraction faces if it got the twins to evacuate the premises sooner." She took a sip of apple juice and looked at Heidi thoughtfully. "You should talk German to the babies from the get go. Develop their brainpower. Arapaho, German and English, they'll be ready when the revolution comes."

"The revolution?" Heidi chuckled and looked up from frowning at her crossword puzzle. "This is why you work so hard to learn German?"

Unfazeable Joni poked her head in to introduce herself and said she'd be back in a few minutes to check Nara's progress, she just had to look in on a lady down the hall. Nara gave her a salute and the nurse grinned and waved.

"Seems a jolly sort," observed Nara, wincing and shifting her weight before snapping her fingers at Heidi to hand over the crossword.

"No, it is too easy for you. You will just fill them all in," protested Heidi.

"I only did that once and I apologized but, okay, just read

the clue."

"A ten-letter word meaning faithless or disloyal, starting with 'perf' and ending in 'us.'"

"Perfidious," said Nara instantly. "Bingo, always got A's in English."

They were still grinning at each other when Joni returned to say Patsy McKee was on the phone sounding very upset about an incident that had just occurred at Saint Gemma's.

"What sort of incident?" asked Heidi and Nara together.

"She wouldn't say. I'll check your effacement and dilation Nara, while you," she nodded at Heidi, "find out what poor Patsy's all het up about."

Heidi returned to the room to find Joni straightening the bed and Nara in the restroom.

"We're making progress. She's almost three centimeters, sixty percent effaced." The nurse looked at the partially closed restroom door and lowered her voice, "What's going on at Saint Gemma's?"

"Wait, wait for me," Nara wailed. "Don't start talking about what's going on without me."

"When she comes out, she can walk around a bit, or sit in the chair, if you're going to be here," said Joni.

Heidi shook her head. "I will have to leave for a while. A man with a knife. . ."

"Stop," Nara howled from the bathroom. "Don't start talking about a man and a knife. I'm almost done here."

Heidi smiled at the nurse and shrugged.

Joni smiled back. She liked this couple. Not overly affectionate, but she could tell the commitment was there. They would be good parents. The millennium was only ten years away, and even people in Wyoming were becoming more tolerant. Reluctant to go before hearing about the goings on at Saint Gemma's, she made a business of smoothing out every last wrinkle on the bed.

"I'm standing for a while," said Nara, emerging from the bathroom. She walked behind the lime-green recliner, gripped its back and bent over with her arms stretched out. She released her breath in a series of short pants, her long hair almost touching the floor.

"Okay, I'm done," said Nara, standing erect and placing both hands on the small of her back. "Spill, *Meine Liebste,*" she ordered Heidi.

"When the lunch is over, a man stays behind in the dining hall. When Edith tries to get him to leave, he pulls the knife and starts to run into the kitchen." Heidi grimaced as the scene played out in her mind. "Edith chases him and she grabs him from behind and the cut from his knife goes down her arm. It will have to be stitched up."

"Why didn't anybody run out from the kitchen with a meat cleaver or a frying pan and take him on?" asked Nara, sounding exasperated. "Edith's like a hundred years old."

"I'm sure she's not much over seventy-five, if that," corrected Joni. She loathed hyperbole and her mother was a friend of the McKees. "But I agree," she continued. "There must have been a man in the kitchen who could have helped."

"Saint Gemma's men are useless, except for Mr. Tolentino," said Nara disparagingly. "Where was good old Leo?"

Heidi reminded her Mr. Tolentino was still recovering from his hernia operation and would be gone another two weeks.

"Right, well I told you letting Inez take a day off when Mr. Tolentino was out was a bad idea. She would have disarmed a crazy with a knife in a heartbeat. Edith's lucky she just needs stitches in an arm."

"The police took the man away and Patsy and Edith are on their way here to the hospital for stitches," Heidi said, adding that a policeman was staying at Saint Gemma's until she got there because the kitchen crew was very upset. They wanted to go home but were prepared to stay if she got there and stayed until the doors were locked for the night.

Nara snorted. "Oh, for God's sake. So, they're thinking a whole army of crazies are going to descend on Saint Gemma's wielding knives? If a zombie apocalypse is on the rise, no offense Boss, but even you can't save them. Better sacrifice the cop, let him hang out there and hold everybody's trembling little hands until it's over."

"Well, I'd say get going," said Joni firmly. "Your staff is traumatized; they need you and people have to eat, and Saint Gemma's always provides a hot dinner during the week. At three centimeters, we have a ways to go here. We may be looking at an all-nighter and then some. It's hard to gauge with twins. Sometimes they take longer, sometimes they egg each other on and they're both out before you know it. I'll be here all night. You get on your way."

When the dinner line abated, Heidi went into the office. She had stopped to pick up Gering on her way back to Saint Gemma's and was grateful to have him on her lap. She looked at the phone and released a long breath.

"Okay, we phone now," she said, lifting Gering up and touching her forehead to his. She held him cradled in one arm and dialed.

She was told the twins had arrived forty minutes ago. They were loud and healthy and Nara was as comfortable as could be expected. Would Heidi be coming back this evening? She promised she would, when she could get away.

"They're here," she whispered to Gering, putting down the phone.

She walked down the hall and announced the babies' arrival to the kitchen crew, then returned to the office to make a list of supplies that needed to be ordered for the following week. Inez would be back tomorrow and could place the order then. Massimo had already taken over the responsibility of meeting the early morning delivery trucks and later in the week he would be there to unlock Saint Gemma's and put the perishables away. She started another list of extra chores to be completed as time permitted.

The babies had arrived and Nara was resting. Heidi realized she was no longer in a hurry to get back to the hospital. She locked the doors after the last of the crew had departed and gave each of the sinks another scrub. Her mind drifted . . . she had promosed the McKees another year . . . two babies, two adults, it made sense for Nara to continue staying with her . . . did she want Nara to stay? Hearing two babies crying during the night, neither one of them Peter, would she be able to bear it?

Did Nara even want to stay? She never referred to the house they shared as 'home.' It was always, 'your house' or 'the house.' Nara had insisted on paying rent while she was working at Saint Gemma's, but soon after the doctor recommended she stop working because her feet had begun to swell, an envelope had arrived from her father.

"Aw, I didn't know Danny Crow still cared," Nara had said, removing a stack of hundred-dollar bills. "This will help until we decide what we're doing here."

Heidi had refused the five bills Nara pushed toward her, telling Nara to save it for the babies. At the time, she had wondered if Nara's 'until we decide' had included Danny Crow. Was he the one who would determine if Nara and the babies stayed in Riverton or returned to the Reservation?

Heidi had just finished polishing the giant Hobart mixer when the McKees let themselves in through the backdoor of the kitchen with their key. After Heidi had exclaimed at Edith's black eye and admired her stitches, the sisters said they'd stopped because they had seen Heidi's Mercedes in the parking lot. They were surprised she hadn't taken herself back to the hospital.

"I miss the main event and since the nurse tells me Nara and the twins are well, I stay to make sure everything is ready for you tomorrow," said Heidi.

"And I must say, the Hobart has never looked better." Edith leaned forward to catch a glimpse of her black eye in the gleaming machine and grinned at her distorted image. "I, however, have seldom looked worse."

Patsy nodded her agreement, before saying, "Nara was in a talkative mood when we stopped to look in on her and the twins on our way out of the hospital. The babies are two peas in a pod, lovely little things, perfect as baby dolls. How anyone is going to be able to . . ."

"Nara said she's done with having kids," Edith interjected. "She wants to have her tubes tied, sensible girl."

"But the doctor says she's too young to make that decision," Patsy amended. "Perhaps she'll just have to abstain from that sort of life until the doctor thinks she old enough for the operation."

"And perhaps a woman in her twenties should be allowed to make her own decisions," retorted Edith, before turning her focus to Heidi. "She didn't say so, but I'm sure Nara is expecting you back at the hospital before too long."

Heidi refrained from saying, "And perhaps a woman can decide when she is ready to face a new mother and her 'peas in a pod' perfect babies.

Heidi stopped to drop a dejected Gering off at home. This was not part of their routine.

"You would not like a hospital," she told the little dog as he followed her into the bedroom, his round eyes blinking up ay her. "Those are not the smells a dog likes, the disinfectants, all sorts of unpleasant things. You will like my smell so much better," she said, taking her nightgown out of her closet and arranging it into a nest on the bed.

She knew what he would do when she left. He'd go to the

front windows to peek out, he'd take a trot out to the patio, water a bush and come back in. Then he would jump on the bed, rearrange her nightgown to his liking, settle in and forgive her for leaving him.

Amadeus and Marcel, Heidi tried to envision the babies as she drove slowly away from the house. Would she be able to forgive Nara's babies their strong, lusty lungs when Peter had fought for every breath he had taken? No, he hadn't fought for every breath. There had been some better days, some days when his cheeks had a hint of color and his little chest rose more easily, days when she had dared to hope he was getting stronger.

She turned into the hospital parking lot.

"Here we go, here we go," she whispered, waiting for the elevator, too tired for the stairs.

She walked into Nara's room and found the babies, wrapped tightly as burritos, fast asleep in the same bassinet next to their mother's bed. Heidi took the hand Nara reached to her and squeezed it.

"Sorry we couldn't wait," said Nara cheerfully. "After you left, Joni said I dilated faster than anybody she'd ever helped deliver. The twins just took over, made me push, push, push, nothing I could do about it. I told Joni not to put their caps on until you got to see their hair. They have kind of an updo going on."

Heidi leaned over the bassinet to take a closer look at the twins. Oh . . . she felt tears prick her eyes . . . they were lovely. From their rosebud mouths and the black, thickly lashed crescents of their closed eyes to the slight ruddiness of their round, light brown cheeks—every feature radiated health. She gently touched the silky black hair that had been washed and brushed into a swirl on the tops of their heads.

"Don't wake them up," Nara cautioned. "They just went to sleep."

"How did you decide who is to be who?" Heidi asked,

unable to find a single distinguishing mark.

"First baby out, Amadeus, three minutes later, baby two, Marcel. Alphabetical order, they have wristbands for now, we'll figure it out later. Now come sit by me and tell me what went on at Saint Gemma's."

"I look at them a minute more, then I sit. They have had your milk?"

Nara nodded, reliving for a moment how the babies had rooted at her, their tiny fists, their tiny little fingernails perfect as fish scales. The babies had known just what she was there for. Marcel had fed first because he was the loudest. Joni had helped him latch on, holding Amadeus until it was his turn.

"Weird feeling, being tugged on like that," observed Nara softly.

She watched Heidi leaning over the bassinet, murmuring to the twins in German, and allowed herself to relax. She could keep house like a good little roommate for now. She'd make herself useful. Her dad had said he'd send more money when the boys arrived, but he made it clear, she couldn't take the twins back to his house with New Wife there.

"This breast-feeding thing's pretty wild," Nara said, trying to get Heidi's attention. "Somebody came by with some pamphlets to look at with tips on how to feed them both at the same time." Nara nodded at her bedside table.

"Two at once, this is very efficient," said Heidi, longing to pick up one baby and then the other, to feel their weight in her arms and inhale the warm, sweet scent of their skin. She hadn't been prepared for the strength of her visceral reaction. Down to her very core, she ached to hold them, to rest her lips in the palms of their hands and feel their tiny fingers close around her. She pulled herself away and drew a chair up next to Nara.

"How's Edith?" Nara asked, once Heidi got settled.

"Twenty stitches down her arm. She is very sorry she wears her favorite shirt to work today. Her eye is black because her face hits the chair when she slips in her blood."

"Her blood? She slipped in her own blood? Did she hurt the guy at all?"

"Her blood, she is the only person who gets cut. She did not lose so much that she needs the transfusion, but people who are helping her step in it, so it is all over. The poor man who did this is the stranger to us."

"Poor man? Surely you jest, *Fräulein,*" Nara protested. "Poor Edith."

"Edith will recover, the man with the knife will not. The man takes his medications in jail, but not afterwards. They release him last week, but he has no one, nowhere to go. He will not take his pills because he thinks they are the little spies that enter his body and take over his mind."

Nara whistled. "How'd you get all that info? You sit down and have a chat with him?"

"No, I do not see him at all. They take him away before I get there. Jason, the policeman who stays behind, tells it to me. He is very kind. He helps me clean up the blood. His sister is the same, Jason says, the paranoid schizophrenic. He says the symptoms are similar to all these people. Voices inside them tell them the pills are bad and try to control their thoughts."

"Well, isn't that the point?" asked Nara, impatiently.

"Yes, the point unless the voices . . ."

"The cop good looking?" Nara interrupted.

"Very handsome. Florence makes the eyes at him."

"Is Jason single? He ask you out?"

"He asks," Heidi looked over at the bassinet when one of the babies grunted, "but I tell him about my boyfriend in Thermopolis."

Nara gave a long, theatrical sigh. "Heidi, I worry about you. You're going to wind up an old maid."

Heidi raised her eyebrows and shrugged. She stood up and went to look at Amadeus and Marcel again, hoping one would awake.

"What color are their eyes?" she asked.

"Kind of greenish at the moment. A dose of John Doe, his were pretty light as I recall, but they will probably darken in time and become regular." She looked at Heidi hopefully and said, "I don't suppose you brought anything back from Saint Gemma's to eat?"

Heidi apologized. She hadn't even considered Nara might be hungry. She looked at the clock, almost midnight. She went to the nurses' station to see what food might be available and returned carrying a tray with applesauce, crackers and cheese.

"Just a snack, but there is a potpie and a chicken piccata in the nurses' break room you may have. There is a microwave. Joni says the chicken piccata is better than the potpie, and crust in the microwave is not good, but I think the piccata will not have the capers."

"This will do, thanks," said Nara, sitting up a little higher, wincing as Heidi arranged her pillows.

"*Danke,* my poppet, I am internally grateful to you."

"Internally?" Heidi chuckled.

Nara felt a rush of warmth, Heidi was always more tuned in than you'd think.

"Joni says you did so well with the labor," Heidi said. "You are comfortable? They say there was some little tearing, but you have good painkillers."

"Love the painkillers, can't even feel the tears," said Nara. "They may send us all home in a couple of days if Amadeus and Marcel do their thing competently. They'll send me home with pain meds if I still need them. I take them only as prescribed, wait 'til *after* breastfeeding, so the babies only get a trace."

"Just what Joni tells me at the nurses' station." Heidi yawned and blinked rapidly.

"And exactly *why* is Joni talking to you about *my* pain medication?" Nara asked, her voice flat.

Heidi closed her eyes briefly. It had been a very long day.

163

She ached to hold one of the babies, to rest her lips on his soft hair. "You are right. We overstep your boundaries. I am sorry," she said carefully. "Joni tells me because we are being friendly."

Nara looked away. She'd only dabbled with painkillers, there was no record of that, and it hadn't been a problem. 'Let it go,' she told herself, she and the twins needed Heidi for now.

Nara caught Heidi watching her and noted the dark smudges under her eyes, the lines at the corners of her mouth. Heidi had come back after Saint Gemma's. Nara hadn't been sure if she would. She had been prepared for Heidi to just show up tomorrow morning with a balloon and offer to take her from the hospital back to the Reservation when they were released.

"Look at this, a plastic spoon wrapped in plastic," Nara said, picking up the spoon and waggling it at Heidi, anxious for a distraction. She pointed at the snacks on the tray. "Five plastic wrapped packets of two crackers each, five individually plastic wrapped slices of cheese. All this plastic will wind up in the ocean, in a whale's stomach, or being regurgitated by an albatross into its baby's mouth. We'll piss off the Gods if we don't get a grip."

Heidi nodded and watched Nara rip open the wrapping around a slice of cheese with her teeth. "Do you want me to help open the snacks?" she asked.

"I do not, Comrade, but I do want to hear about . . ." Nara craned her head to read the title of one of the breast-feeding pamphlets, "*The Double Football or Double Clutch Hold*,' if you would be so kind. Not if you're too tired, of course, just saying babies will want feeding in an hour or so."

Heidi opened the trifold pamphlet. After frowning at it a moment, she held up a diagram of a smiling woman sitting in a chair with pillows under her elbows and a baby at each breast.

"Well, she looks happy enough," remarked Nara, making

a cracker sandwich and devouring it in one bite. "Read what's going on with that perky little Miss or Mrs. as the case may be."

"Position a pillow on your lap and each side of your body," Heidi read. "Place each baby on the pillow beside your body so that the babies' legs point backwards." Heidi held up the picture again and Nara stared at it a moment before nodding and lying back. "Keep the babies' heads at nipple level. Support each baby's back on the inside of your forearm."

"Wait, what am I doing with the inside of my forearms?" asked Nara, starting in on her applesauce.

Heidi showed her the diagram again. Nara nodded. "Got it," she said.

"Secure the babies' bottoms with the insides of your elbows. Support the back of each baby's head by placing the palm of each hand at the back of each baby's head."

"Picture," said Nara and Heidi obediently held up the diagram.

"I'm thinking they could have done a better job with the instructions," Nara said critically. "This each baby, each hand business is confusing. What if I was the *blind* mother of twins? I wouldn't be able to understand the instructions at all."

"I have the confidence you would manage very well," Heidi assured her.

"Yeah, I would," said Nara comfortably. "And I'm thinking when one of the Bush Women of the Kalahari has twins, she just figures it out for herself, blind or not."

Heidi smiled. "I know for a fact that the Bush Women of the Kalahari *always* have twins and they are very talented at feeding both babies at the same time."

"They have to feed them at the same time because they have to spend so many hours digging up roots for water," Nara said, giving a yawn so big it made her eyes tear. "Bush Men out there hunting antelope, they probably don't help dig for water at all," she added sleepily.

Heidi picked up the next pamphlet and examined the diagram of the 'Cradle-Clutch Combination Hold.' She heard Nara's gentle snore before she had a chance to read.

Almost staggering from her own fatigue, Heidi rose to look at the babies one more time. She bent over and kissed one baby on his cheek, starting back guiltily when he stretched his mouth into a lopsided grimace, but then he settled, no harm done. She got a blanket and pillow from the closet, removed her shoes and collapsed into the chair. The babies would be waking soon, probably both at the same time. She could hold one of them then.

Heidi awoke and called to Joni as she was leaving the room. The nurse turned and said with a smile, "You missed two feedings, diaper changes, the lot. Nara insisted we let you sleep. I envy you being able to sleep like that."

"I am so sorry; I sleep like the log. Did she manage to feed them both at once?"

"The second time, yes. The first time Amadeus was very demanding and wanted his mother all to himself, but he fell asleep in less than ten minutes, so Marcel didn't have to wait too long. I'm heading out. Victoria will be taking over. I've really enjoyed working with you ladies."

"Yes, we enjoy you too. We will see you again?"

"I have a week off and I'm camping with my boyfriend near Pinedale. He's got those big wheels on his truck. We'll go off road. I can't say I'm looking forward to it, except for the snuggling," Joni said cheerfully. "I imagine you all will be released within a few days. I'll pray for that. And I pray there's lots of family to help at home. Tell Nara goodbye for me when she wakes up. Your girl's a firecracker."

Nara looked at the clock, 8:15 a.m. Heidi had managed to curl herself up to fit in the chair pretty well and was back asleep. The babies probably wouldn't wake for another hour.

She'd heard Heidi saying goodbye to Joni earlier but had kept her eyes closed, not feeling it necessary to join in the love fest. Joni praying for lots of family to help out at home, yeah, right.

Everything ached. Nara ran her hands over her empty, loose belly and felt a gush of blood soak the pad between her legs. Joni had warned her she'd be bleeding for a few weeks. "Totally normal, unless it's too much," the nurse had said as she massaged Nara's abdomen for the third time in half an hour.

"Ow, is this really necessary?" Nara had tried to bat Joni's capable hands away.

Joni continued with her massage. "It will reduce the size of your uterus down from a watermelon to a cantaloupe."

"What's too much blood?" Nara thought Heidi would have appreciated the fruit reference.

"More blood, more often, that's too much. You've had twins, we'll keep you here some extra days. Just press your button if you need a cleanup."

But now Joni had gone camping in the snow with her boyfriend, so someone else would have the joy of cleaning up the new mother of twins. Nara pressed the button by her bed.

After the nurse left, Heidi said, "I have good news. Bathsheba is back to Riverton for a month before she drives with her boyfriend to Florida for the winter. If I continue with the ordering and the books, she will fill in at Saint Gemma's and I can stay at home and help you for a longer time, if you wish to stay with me for a while."

"The McKees going to go for Bathsheba filling in?" Nara asked, turning her face to the wall and biting her lips hard so she wouldn't cry at the relief of being able to stay at Heidi's another month. Heidi would be home and she wouldn't be alone taking care of the babies right away. In a month, she'd be ready.

"Of course, they do not mind," said Heidi. "They are happy

Bathsheba can help so then I can help you. They think this will make me stay in Riverton longer. Edith and Patsy think they have their claws into me, but I make my own bed to lie in." Heidi curled her fingers into claws and raked the air at Nara.

"If you say so, *Kriegerprinzessin*," said Nara, attempting a grin.

Heidi laughed, enjoying the label 'Warrior princess.' She imagined herself in a short tunic, a sword in one hand, a shield in the other, the wind blowing her hair back, Nara and the twins cowering behind her as she protected them from . . . from what? Ah, the *Drude*.

"I will protect you and the babies from the *Drude*," she promised. At Nara's questioning look Heidi explained a *Drude* was a demon that attacked people as they slept.

"So, we sleep and you stay awake to protect us?" Nara looked dubious and Heidi grinned and crossed her heart. Nara sighed, eyelids suddenly very heavy. Heidi and a home for another month, whose God did she have to thank for that?

CHAPTER SIXTEEN

DOUBLY BLESSED

The twins each lost a little more weight than was typical for newborns and Nara developed a persistent low-grade fever, so the hospital kept the little Crow family for five additional days. Heidi visited in the morning and evening, and took the rest of the day to ready Saint Gemma's for her prolonged absence. At night she relaxed once again in a long bath, Gering curled on the bathmat. Before bed she stood in Nara's bedroom, imagining Amadeus and Marcel in their crib. Nara had been adamant the twins share a bed since they'd shared her womb. The doctor agreed it would do no harm and many twins found comfort in staying together. He added that the increased risk of suffocation was negligible.

But negligible was not zero, and Heidi knew she would be stealing in to Nara's room during the night to check on the babies.

Nara and the twins were discharged from the hospital into a blustery, grey day that was still much too bright. As they waited for Heidi to arrive at the curb, the nurse responsible for their welfare kept a grip on one of the wheelchair's handles and continued with her cheerful chatter, her words raining down from above.

"Life with twins, imagine that. Did I tell you my sister

almost had twins? Lost one, some people weren't very kind, told her life would be easier with only one baby, but I think they were just being thoughtless, not intentionally cruel. People might say 'double trouble' or 'rather you than me,' but they're just making conversation, like they want to be a part of it all. I say you're doubly blessed. Two little angels from above, come to sweeten your life. Two times the work, but two times the fun. An instant family, you'll get all the potty training done . . ."

Hoping to stem what promised to be a stream of platitudes, Nara craned her neck to look up and interrupted with, "Heard a rumor that they're planning to cut your benefits."

After a moment's silence, the nurse asked carefully, "Where did you hear that?"

"Two administrators walking down the hall. Yakety yak. They better be careful, never know who's gonna rat you out," said Nara, turning her face into the wind so her hair would blow away from her eyes. A baby in the crook of each arm robbed her of the use of her hands. She vowed to wear her hair in braids for a while.

They waited in silence until the black diesel Mercedes pulled noisily into the passenger-loading zone and Heidi got out, looking elegant in a sweatshirt and jeans. She smiled at the nurse, introduced herself and took one of the babies out of Nara's arms. Peter's pale image danced momentarily at the edge of her consciousness as she bent her head to the baby she held and inhaled a light scent of vanilla, powder and something slightly sweet.

"Hello, little one," she whispered.

As Nara prepared to rise with the other baby, the nurse clamped a hand on her shoulder and said, "No, you don't, Miss Crow. *Both* babies get safely tucked in first and then I assist you."

While the other two women strapped the babies into their

car seats, Nara took the opportunity to get herself out of the wheelchair and into the car unaided, feeling ridiculously pleased with herself as she fastened her seatbelt. She flashed the nurse a grin when Heidi started the ignition and the car rattled to life.

"Thank you kindly," she called out the window. "I may have misunderstood about the benefits thing. Just wanted to give you a heads up."

The nurse clamped her mouth into a hard line and gave a brief nod.

"I am not going to ask what you said that made that poor woman look so concerned," Heidi said as she pulled the car away from the curb.

"Good call, Boss. But you heard me try to fix it, right?" Nara murmured, leaning her head back and closing her eyes. She wondered idly what would come next in the land of motherhood and twins. She wasn't worried, not yet. Heidi still had more than three weeks off, and after that maybe things would settle in, maybe the four of them would just kind of settle in.

Regardless, three weeks was a long time. Three weeks would be multiple life times if you were a marine gastrotrich, living your days in the space between grains of sand on the ocean floor, sustaining yourself on whatever was small enough to enter your teeny, tiny gullet. Two or three gastrotrich life times, it shouldn't take longer than that to get the hang of being a solo adult dealing with two babies at the same time, maybe having to look for a place to live.

She opened her eyes and looked over to see Heidi's lips moving, probably some German incantation praying for patience or guidance or some such thing.

"Know what a marine gastrotrich is?" Nara asked to distract Heidi in her attempted liaison with the spirit world.

"Gastro means the stomach so I think it is a creature with a magnificent stomach," said Heidi, slowing to allow a cattle truck to pull into the lane ahead of them.

"Then you would be wrong, although I appreciate your logic," said Nara generously. "Gastrotrichs kind of forgot the whole stomach thing. They draw food, detritus actually, in with a nice muscular little pharynx, then it goes straight to the intestine for digestion."

"You have a picture in your big book we can look at?" asked Heidi.

"Indeed, I do, highly magnified. They pack a lot into a very short lifespan. Sexually mature in just a couple of days, except they're parthenogenic, well, some are hermaphroditic, but either way, not a whole lotta fun in that."

"They both are the virgin birth?"

"Not really. Parthenogenesis means the egg requires no fertilization; hermaphroditic means the organism can fertilize itself, although sometimes, you know, they can help each other out, exchange sperm or whatever. "

"Your mother is the smart pants," Heidi called to the sleeping twins.

"The smartest of pants," agreed Nara.

As they pulled in front of the garage, Nara pleaded, "Can we sit a minute in this warm comfy car? Babies sleeping, we can wait 'em out. I need a moment before starting on this one-way path to adulthood."

Heidi looked over her shoulder. The twins had been strapped into their car seats facing the rear window and all she could see was the top of their silky, black heads. She longed to go inside and sit on the sofa with one of them in her arms, to place her finger into a tiny palm and hope the little one would give her a squeeze. Before she resigned herself to sitting in the car for a few minutes however, Gering released a volley of agitated barks, his little face peeking out between the living room curtains.

Heidi tilted her head at Nara, who released a sigh and

unbuckled her seat belt, muttering, "You wouldn't believe how easy a gastrotrich would be as a companion animal."

"Wait," Heidi placed a hand on her arm and Nara's slumped back. Here it comes, Bathsheba can't fill in after all, by all means stay for a few weeks, but you're on your own. Nara put a finger on the custom mahogany dash and traced the grain. Jesus this car must have been expensive. A night's rest and she'd be okay.

"As long as Gering and I live in this house, you and Amadeus and Marcel may live here too," Heidi said quietly.

Nara's throat constricted. Without meeting Heidi's eyes, she opened the door and managed to stand before Heidi could get around the car to help her.

The next day the skies cleared, the winds died and the temperature became unseasonably warm for mid-October. Heidi parked a wheelbarrow full of mulch near the flowerbeds partway down the slope and went back to assist Nara in bringing the twins outside.

"In Germany, we call this warm autumn weather '*Altweibersommer,*'" Heidi said, taking one of the twins and tucking him into a sling around her neck. "It means 'Old Women's Summer.'"

"Think you can garden with a baby laminated to you like that?" asked Nara dubiously as Heidi arranged the sling to shade the baby's face and support his head.

"I am absolutely positive I can," Heidi responded cheerfully, helping Nara settle into her chair with the other baby.

"Not that I have a thing against old women," said Nara, "but the name '*Altweibersommer*' sounds kind of pathetic."

"Do you like better *pastirma yazi*? In Turkey, a warm autumn day is the best time to make pastrami so they call it Pastrami Summer," said Heidi, examining the baby in Nara's arms. "Which baby do I have?"

"Fifty percent sure you have Amadeus." Nara adjusted her sunglasses and looked up at Heidi. "So what are *you* going to call this frickin' fantastic autumn weather?"

"Indian Summer," responded Heidi promptly.

"Atta girl," Nara said comfortably. "Do you think you could bring out some water and snacks before you get to grubbing in the dirt. I meant to do it myself, but my baby's already asleep and yours isn't."

When Heidi didn't respond, Nara squinted up at her. She watched as Heidi's eyes strayed from one baby to the other, to the fountain, to the elementary school beyond the old cemetery down the slope. *My* baby, *your* baby. It had just been an expression, but apparently not an acceptable one. Not while Peter's spirit still hovered.

A sudden cold front kept them inside for the next few days, but then the winds dropped, the clouds went elsewhere and temperatures once again hovered in the mid-seventies. The sounds of *Carmen* projected from the radio Heidi had perched in the open kitchen window. In a lounge chair, Nara reclined with the twins.

After pulling out her spring bulbs and gently brushing off the dirt, Heidi, escorted by Gering, brought them back to a box she had waiting on the patio. Singing softly in Italian, she placed the bulbs between layers of newspaper in preparation for storing them in the garage for winter.

"Do you even know what you're singing?" Nara asked suspiciously, dropping a cracker with cheese surreptitiously on the ground for Gering.

"I understand some of the words and I know the Carmen story inside and outside, so I understand what I sing," Heidi said, dusting off her hands and pouring herself a glass of water. "Will you please make me a cheese with cracker?"

"Then I suppose I have to feed it to you, which I am happy

to do."

"This is not necessary; a little dirt will not hurt. A bite and it is gone," said Heidi, frowning down at the dachshund. "What is Gering eating?"

"Clumsy me, musta dropped a piece of cheese. You have a tape deck, let's get some *Phantom of the Opera* or *Westside Story*. I've heard those a few times. I'll sing too and we can have a real hootenanny."

"Hootenanny?" Heidi let out a peal of laughter. "I love this word. It means you sing along, yes?"

"And shake your booty if you're so inclined, but not so loud with the yucks, *Meine Liebste*. Both babies sleeping. I'm thinking we have half an hour tops before its cleaning-changing-feeding time. Better go do your mulching."

Nara watched Heidi raking around the base of the roses. Another week and Heidi would be back at work. "Easy peasy," Nara muttered to herself. Taking care of two little beings solo would not be a problem. She knew the drill, sleep when the babies slept, remember to eat something before or after nursing, drink plenty of fluids, engage the babies with talking, singing, making faces. "No problem at all," she whispered, letting out long, shuddering sigh.

CHAPTER SEVENTEEN

BLUE HOUSE ON THE RIVER BEND

The twins slept a lot and when awake, spent most of their time fixated on each other, babbling and waving their arms, leaving their mother plenty of time to lie on the sofa and stare at the ceiling.

Nara imagined herself flying above the unnamed gravel and dirt road that led from the highway toward her father's house on the river bend. She saw her father coming out his front door and looking up, sensing she was there. The sun on her back as she hovered above, her arms making gentle corrections in the buffeting wind, the sound of the water. A stone's throw from her father's backdoor, the Wind River tumbled by relentlessly, never quiet due to its rush to get over and around the boulders that fell periodically from the high red rock cliffs in this part of the Reservation.

Except for the last months of her mother's illness, she had been happy at the blue house, she realized in hindsight. She'd had a boyfriend for a while, an older boy who dropped out of high school to go to California with his cousin. He had been polite. Her mom had liked him. Hard to tell about her dad.

An earlier memory also revisited her these days, one she thought she'd managed to shut away. Her father phoning them at her uncle's house to announce his arrival on the Reservation, her mother hanging up, her uncle saying, "Leave

Nara with us, we'll take care of her. No one will visit you if you're living with him. Don't lose your family. You're choosing to move in with Danny Crow, your girl shouldn't have to."

Then her mother turning to her and asking, "Nara?" And she felt it again, so many years later and no longer a child, but she felt it again, that punch to the gut. That punch when she realized her mother had given her the choice to be left behind.

She remembered her uncle looming dark and sinister, her mother at his side, both of them waiting. And suddenly she was running out the door with her backpack, which carried nothing but her book on the ocean and the creatures it allowed to live within its depths . . . jumping into the old red pickup her uncle had said they could have, huddling on the front seat, her cheek on her backpack. Page 131, a dolphin fighting a shark to save her calf; page 223, a sea lion mother returning to a rookery after feeding in the ocean and managing to find her own pup among hundreds of others by its unique smell.

Her mother driving off, grinding the gears, the gravel giving the hard crunch of broken glass, her mother's soft voice, "Your uncle is a good man Nara. I didn't know if it was fair to take you away." Her mother repeating herself, again and again, as if trying to excuse the fact she would have allowed her daughter to stay behind.

For years Nara had told herself that if she hadn't gotten in the truck, her mother would have come back for her. Her mother had left Chicago to bring her to safety. That was motherhood. You chose your kid, no matter what. That was what she was waiting to feel for her boys, her flesh, her blood.

She was just so tired.

One of the twins began a faint whimpering. The other joined in. The whimperings became full-throated howls. The package of baby wipes was almost empty, not enough for two messy little bottoms. She had forgotten to buy more, but wait . . . baby wipes, four packages of them sitting on the changing table. Heidi must have gone out last night to buy more. Another responsibility had been taken away from her—now Heidi would always make sure there were plenty.

As Nara fed the babies, both at once, the 'Double Clutch Hold' having become second nature, she watched the news. Prize Brahma bulls had been found with their throats cut near the Colorado border. "Damn Zombies," she muttered, although it was probably a human revenge thing of some sort, but if you got an animal involved in your human shit, you had no heart, you had no soul, so you might as well be a Zombie.

She put the twins on their blanket on the floor, rolling them onto their sides so they could look at each other and went back to lie on the couch. She tried to concentrate on breathing deeply to prevent herself from closing her eyes and floating away. She didn't hate Heidi's house, she told herself; it was comfortable, safe and clean. She hated the neighborhood.

"Here a house, there a house, everywhere a house house," she murmured, placing the heels of her hands over her eyes, knowing outside the front door would be tidy little front yards and the people looking out their windows, wondering what a Native girl was doing in their midst.

At about four months the babies began to sleep for longer stretches at night and the gloom Nara tried to hide when Heidi was around eased. But the respite was short-lived. A few weeks later the twins began to wake more and more frequently, crying for food every hour or so, tugging at her desperately until they fell into a fretful sleep.

After an evening of listening to the twins almost constant crying, Heidi suggested they weren't getting enough to eat.

"I know," said Nara, wearily. "Take Gering and go to bed. I have a doctor's appointment for them the day after tomorrow."

An hour later, Heidi and Gering returned to the living

room to find Nara on the couch, her bathrobe splayed open, one baby still latched to her nipple, the other had apparently given up and lay in a heap at her side. The light from the television reflected off the tears Nara hadn't the energy to wipe away. She looked up at Heidi, then down at Gering.

"What's up Doc?" she asked the little dog, her voice hollow with exhaustion. "Mean lady and twins keeping you up?"

Gering wagged his tail tentatively before crawling under the coffee table, rather than taking his accustomed spot on the couch. He had been wary of Nara lately. Heidi picked up the sleeping baby and sat down, resting her lips on his forehead. Aside from a grimace, he didn't stir.

"Amadeus?" she said, nodding at the baby still attached to Nara.

"No, you have him. No, wait," Nara looked down and scrutinized the baby at her breast. "Yeah, you have him. He usually gives up first." She released a long, slow breath of air, swallowed hard and said, "Who cares who's who anymore?"

"We make the doctor appointment for tomorrow. It is the first thing we do in the morning," said Heidi.

"The Kalahari Bush Women breast feed their twins for years. Then the twins go to college, usually Harvard, unless Oxford nabs them first," Nara said dully, her voice fading as she continued, "They always get scholarships, because, you know, it ain't easy being a twin in the Kalahari."

"I phone Edith early tomorrow morning," Heidi said. "The McKees can open up and get the lunch preparation started and I will take you to the doctor. After tomorrow this will be easier. They will give you formula to supplement your milk."

"Gering doesn't like me anymore," Nara said tonelessly as the little dog peeked out from under the table. She didn't really care. It was just one more thing not to care about. "I'll take them in tomorrow, I don't need you to come. I just need the car keys, I'd prefer to go alone anyway, just me and the boys, the boys and I, what fucking ever."

Before leaving for work, Heidi backed the Mercedes out of the garage and checked that the infant carriers were secured properly in the back seat. It was bitterly cold, but trucks had already salted the roads and Nara was a good driver, the babies would be safe. Heidi grimaced. 'Vertraue ihr, Nara ist eine kompetente junge Frau,' she told herself. 'Trust her, Nara is a competent young woman.'

Still, Heidi wished she could be present to carry one of the babies to the car, to check they were both correctly belted in, to warn Nara one more time the road might be icy. But Nara had rebuffed her offer to accompany them to the clinic, and Heidi knew she must be careful. Amadeus and Marcel weren't hers. Nara could take them away whenever she wished.

A very slight tension had developed between the two of them regarding the babies, very slight. Heidi could almost convince herself the tension was her imagination, except she'd had a dream two nights ago. She and Nara were standing on a blacktop road that led nowhere. Each of them held onto an arm of a doll and they were tugging in opposite directions and tugging and tugging until suddenly the arms pulled off, releasing a choking cloud of dust.

"We will not come home after lunch today, Gering," Heidi told the little dog as he trotted before her in his warm black and red plaid jacket. Of course, it would be natural to come home briefly, just to find out what the doctor had said, just to hold one of the babies for a few minutes, to rest her lips on the silky black hair that would smell of Johnson's Baby Shampoo. But she would not come home after lunch. She was not the mother.

The twins were silent as Nara stripped them down. They were weighed, prodded and probed before they were handed back to Nara to dress and place back in their infant carriers.

"They're plenty alert, but are they always this quiet?" the doctor asked.

"We haven't been sleeping that much. We're pretty wiped," said Nara with a yawn. "Believe me, they can make plenty of noise."

The doctor nodded slowly and went to sit behind his desk, waiting for Nara to take a seat.

"They've hardly gained any weight since you brought them in, let's see. . ." he looked at his chart, ". . . three weeks ago. Not good, Nara. You're going to need to supplement. Some women can breast feed twins for a year or more, you can't," he said, pragmatically. "Continue to give them the breast, that's important for both you and them, bonding, immunity, all that good stuff, but we'll send you home with bottles, instructions, a couple of cases of formula. My nurse will put them in the car for you."

He pressed the intercom and gave instructions to his nurse before turning his attention back to Nara. "Are you eating enough?" he asked, leaning back in his chair. "Have you always been this thin?"

"Never been a porker but I try to eat," she said. "Sometimes it's just too much work, all the chewing and swallowing. I'm not that hungry."

The doctor steepled his fingers and narrowed his eyes. "Depression," he diagnosed.

"Not depression," Nara replied. "I don't have the energy to be depressed."

"Then we'll get you the energy to be depressed," he said, grinning at his attempt at humor. He was rewarded by Nara's snicker.

"We need you on a good diet, a variety of fruits and vegetables, dairy, cheese, nuts, eggs, at least three servings of protein a day," said the doctor cheerfully, plucking a booklet from a holder and shoving it over his desk toward her. "You need five hundred to a thousand calories more per day than a non-lactating woman, just to maintain your own weight. You'll see that salmon is considered a perfect food for nursing mothers, but they warn you to stay away from swordfish and shark, too much mercury."

"How about I just limit my swordfish and shark intake to once a day," Nara said, dutifully opening the booklet and pretending to read. She heard the doctor's chuckle and then his pen scratching rapidly.

"I suggest we get you into a group for new mothers. There are a couple to choose from," he said, handing the piece of paper to her when she looked up. "Try one of these, they're free. An Arapaho woman runs the second one, but you'd be welcome of course, at either. It can be very helpful to talk to other women who are also feeling overwhelmed."

At that, Nara laughed, perhaps a little too loud and a little too long. She stopped abruptly when she saw the concern on the doctor's face.

"Sure," she said, waving the numbers at him. "Maybe I'll go to both of them, then start one of my own. Moms helping moms, I like it."

Marcel took to the bottle right away but Amadeus wanted his mother's breast. Heidi thought each baby should have a share of breast milk, but she only said it once, because they both knew it wasn't her decision to make and Nara thought the babies had figured out how to allocate resources just fine.

For another few weeks, Nara was able to produce enough milk for Amadeus alone, but when he began demanding to be fed more and more often, it became obvious he was going to have to transition to the bottle too.

"The doctor said if you don't continue to try to breast feed, the milk will dry up all the way," said Heidi. She tried not to react to Nara's flippant, "Oh well."

With both babies on the bottle, Heidi offered to take over

more of the feedings, allowing Nara to go to bed early. When one of the babies awoke during the night, the other woke too, but Heidi was there before Nara could even reach for her bathrobe, so what was the point in getting up? She drifted back to sleep listening to Heidi's quiet crooning.

With not even a mole to tell them apart, the twins were so similar, Heidi and Nara occasionally argued about who was Amadeus and who was Marcel. When the twins started to teethe and the doctor recommended Tylenol to ease their discomfort, Nara wrote an A on the hand of one with a sharpie, and an M on the other, so neither baby risked being overdosed.

Once they had definitely settled on a name to go with each child, other differences began to appear. Marcel was a little more adventurous, sat up a few days earlier, he was more willing to try different foods. The more cautious Amadeus watched his brother and wouldn't try any food Marcel pushed away. Marcel preferred to use a spoon while eating oatmeal, Amadeus preferred using his hands.

Marcel was the first to say a word. "*Da da*," he said one day, pointing at Gering.

"Could he be trying to say dog?" wondered Heidi aloud.

"More likely he thinks his dad is a dog," Nara responded.

When Amadeus said "*ma ma*" several days later, also pointing at Gering, Heidi and Nara agreed the twins were probably practicing with sounds rather than wrestling with meaning.

CHAPTER EIGHTEEN

THE BROTHERS GRIMM

"Why is she so anxious they learn German?" Karl asked, when Heidi relayed over the phone Nara's request for children's books written in German.

"She speaks Arapaho to them, they hear English all the time and she says, and I quote her, 'There is no law against Indians speaking as many languages as they damn well please,'" Heidi replied.

When Karl relayed the conversation later, Beppe observed, "I'm uncomfortable with how defensive Nara appears to be. I hope she treats our Heidi well. And are you sure she used the word Indian? They preferred First Nation people or Native American to Indian when I lived there, not that I had Native friends, or any friends for that matter, although I was very good at American football."

"A handsome, athletic Italian in Wyoming, I would have thought both girls and boys would have been swooning," said Karl loyally.

"Oh *mio caro*, I had so much anger and so much to hide, I may not have given them a chance," Beppe admitted. "Now, isn't there a bookstore near that new Moroccan restaurant that just opened? You promised me we'd try something exotic for dinner before I leave you tomorrow. We will pick up some fairy stories for the babies and mail them, gifts from their uncles. We always send clothes."

By the last weekend in July, the heat wave had broken and the temperature hovered in the high seventies. Heidi lay stretched out on a blanket on the patio with the twins while Nara read *Daumesdick* out loud from her lounge chair, pausing frequently for Heidi to explain the meaning of a word or correct her pronunciation.

After she had finished, Nara rendered her critique. "*Der Brüder Grimm* are some kinda weird," she announced. "First the mom asks the powers that be for a son who's no bigger than a thumb. Then his dad, who claims to love him, *sells* him after Tom Thumb tells him to, which is a problem in itself. Who gives a kid the power to make that kind of decision? Then after a series of misadventures, Tiny Tom winds up in a cow stomach, not digested by the way, just hollering away, then the cow stomach gets eaten by a wolf, so now he's hollering in a wolf stomach, then the dad kills the wolf with a *punch*. I was almost buyin' it until the end. No way can you kill a wolf with a punch."

"This version says the punch, other versions say an axe or a mallet," said Heidi, sleepily.

"Oh, well, way more plausible with . . ." Nara paused when the phone rang inside the house and Heidi scrambled to her feet and dashed into the house.

"Cousin Karl phoning from Munich on Sunday like clockwork," said Nara to Amadeus, who had been watching his brother practice a commando-style crawl toward the fountain. At his mother's voice, he turned his head to her.

Nara got up, stretched and walked over to the blanket to position Amadeus on his tummy. "Go on, don't let your bro always take the lead," she urged.

Amadeus bobbed his head vigorously before rolling himself over onto his back and looking up at his mother victoriously.

"Does Nara like the books?" asked Karl.

"She says the Brothers Grimm are grim," said Heidi.

"Well, of course they are, and all English speakers love that play on words. Beppe insisted we go the traditional route, I advocated for something mild and modern, trains and dogs." He paused then said, "And now I have some disappointing news about our visit."

Alice was taking longer than expected to recover from her recent lung infection and a delay of a few weeks would bring them to an inopportune time for Beppe to be away from his vineyard. They would plan to visit next year, in the early spring. Heidi hid her relief; dealing with Nara's mercurial moods was enough to cope with at the moment.

When she went back outside to lie on the blanket with the twins, Marcel laboriously turned himself around from his mission to crawl off the patio and pulled himself toward her. He arrived with a triumphant grin and draped himself over her.

Nara laughed and got up to retrieve Amadeus, who gave her a beneficent moist grin. The new teeth he and his brother were cutting were having their effects.

"More drool than a hagfish makes slime," Nara said, returning with him to her chair and wiping the slippery saliva off his chin. "So, when's the Cuz and his boyfriend coming?"

"Not next week. Karl's distant cousin on his mother's side has been unwell. She is still weak from her hospital stay. Karl's cooking school is closed for the month, but she will not be able to do all the planning that is needed for the next session. I have told you about Alice Lykke."

"Cystic Fibrosis Alice? Karl's right hand woman, good at everything except breathing, Alice?"

At Heidi's look, Nara demanded, "What?"

"It is cruel to take a whole person and label them as this."

"Look, if I met her, I'd be nice. I didn't know you were best friends. If I knew her, I wouldn't describe her like that," Nara protested. "You haven't given me anything else to work with."

"I have said to you more. I tell you how artistic she is and brave and smart and patient."

"You forgot to mention she's Danish, Karl gave her a cat that's missing a paw, and she and Beppe like the same books, so okay, you're right, I shouldn't have reduced her to a disease even though you just mentioned she'd been sick. Now you'll have to accept my apologies." When Heidi didn't respond, Nara implored, "C'mon, Boss, really . . ."

"In the north of Europe, more people have this disease," Heidi said as just a point of information, uttered softly on a warm afternoon.

Nara watched Heidi gently caressing Marcel's back. Well, what the hell—was *this* why Heidi's baby died? Had cystic fibrosis killed Peter? Were they ever going to talk about him? Maybe not. Some things were too painful to push to the surface, so you avoided talking about them, leaving other people a minefield to navigate.

She got up. "Going inside to pee," she said, placing the sleepy Amadeus next to Heidi and his brother on the blanket. "Make sure the little dudes don't drive off while I'm inside and when I get back, maybe you'll be up to answering my original question."

The twins were sitting up when Nara returned with two glasses of lemonade and a box of saltines on a tray. Holding the tray high with the expertise of one who had waitressed, Nara sat down cross-legged and placed the tray before her on the blanket. She opened the box and removed one of the wax-wrapped rectangular columns.

"Marcel gets a cracker, Amadeus get a cracker, Heidi gets a cracker, cute little wiener dog gets a cracker," she doled four crackers out like playing cards, "and Nara gets a cracker." She popped one in her mouth.

Heidi frowned. "Gering should not . . ."

"Eat people food, I know. He's only getting one." Nara grinned as Gering darted over to the babies and bolted down their saltines too. "No, oops, okay three. Not the kids' fault, they're not up to competing with a wiener dog yet. Now, when are Karl and Beppe coming?"

Heidi reached half-heartedly for the cracker box, but Nara whipped it out of her way and repeated, "Karl? Beppe?"

"I live with three children and a very bad dog," said Heidi, with a resigned release of breath. "The delay for Alice to get better will make it difficult for Beppe to leave his vineyard, so they postpone their trip until the spring. They send their love," Heidi said, leaning over to take a leaf out of Marcel's mouth.

"They're delaying their trip half a year or more?" With Heidi focused on Marcel, Nara waved a cracker at Gering and he slunk furtively toward her. "You think they really want to come?"

"They absolutely do. They are very busy men, but Karl says that they will buy the tickets for us all to go to Germany for Christmas if we wish."

"Are you kidding me? Fly to your homeland? No, I don't think so, Kemosabe. If I wanted to fly, I would have come back as an eagle."

"I have two questions," said Heidi with a bemused smile. "The first is, what were you before the human, and the second is, what is this Kemosabe?"

Nara grinned. Well okay, they'd negotiated the minefield and it was back to the races. She took the end of her braid and gently played over Amadeus's face, eliciting a sneeze. She picked the baby up and nuzzled him, wiping his face with her shirt before turning her attention back to Heidi.

"You don't remember what you were before, until you're in transition, then you get to see the whole pantheon, or panoply, or whatever, of lives, according to my religion of me, myself and I," Nara said matter-of-factly. "And Kemosabe was

Tonto's honey-bunny term for the Lone Ranger. You've heard of Tonto, right?"

"Yes, I know him. He rides the horse named Trigger."

"Got to tidy up your Americana, Boss," Nara scoffed. "Scout was Tonto's horse, Silver was the Lone Ranger's horse and Trigger was Gene Autry's horse."

"No, I tease before. Trigger is Roy Rodger's horse. Champion is Gene Autry's horse," Heidi contradicted, picking up the cracker Nara threw at her and popping it in her mouth.

"Fancy a German thinking they know that. And you're only right if you're one of those people who's been tricked into believing Roy Rodgers and Gene Autry are two different people."

"Ridiculous girl," said Heidi, yelping when, to the delight of Gering and the twins, Nara started to throw a barrage of crackers.

CHAPTER NINETEEN

A DOG KNOWS

As the boys became more independent, entertaining each other with their babbling, alternately grabbing food and toys from each other, then offering them back, Nara became increasingly restless. Life was beginning to close in. It wasn't the boys; they were the best thing she had ever done. It was being unable to measure up, to be the alert, calm, well-mannered. . . and what? The optimistic, joyful mother Heidi and the rest of the world expected her to be?

To be fair, she knew Heidi was on her side—the German woman had been on her side since day one—but her trust in her only ally was shaken when Heidi came home to find Marcel outside by himself, sitting in the fountain, trying to grab at the water as it rained down. When she heard Heidi's cry, Nara ran outside immediately to find Heidi, ghost white, holding a dripping Marcel.

She explained to Heidi that Marcel had thrown one of his tantrums. He hadn't wanted to come inside for the few minutes it would take to transfer clothes from the washer to the dryer, so she left him sitting on the patio, surrounded by toys. Amadeus had been perfectly happy to accompany her inside.

When she reached for Marcel, Heidi turned away, refusing to give him up. They argued. Did it make a difference if Marcel had climbed in or fallen in? Nara said sure it did, Heidi said it surely did not. Regardless, Nara said, she never, ever would leave either twin alone outside again. Still Heidi held onto Marcel, and just when Nara was going to demand her baby, Heidi handed him over. Then Heidi had walked over and drained the fountain.

Nara refilled it after Heidi left for work the following day. She loved the fountain, the babies loved the fountain, the birds loved the fountain, the backyard was dead without the sound of falling water. Heidi didn't say anything when she came home after lunch to find them outside, Nara with eyes trained on the children, everybody yards away from the fountain. But in the morning when Nara went outside to turn the fountain on, she found it had been drained again, and this time, the motor had been removed from its housing. Her shock opened up the space in her chest for the long absent rabbit to again enter and settle behind her sternum.

For the rest of the day, the rabbit remained huddled and complacent, but the next morning after Heidi left for work, the animal began an agitated circling, kicking hard each time it passed Nara's heart. Without alcohol or the distraction of work, she knew the only way to quiet the rabbit was to move to the point of exhaustion. With one baby on her back, the other in a stroller, Nara walked to the park and followed the asphalt paths for hours, a rat in a maze, a hamster on a wheel, the same bushes, the same dented garbage cans, the same women in the playground pushing toddlers in bucket swings, wiping sand from snotty little faces. She didn't stop, she couldn't stop, she walked, fast, relentlessly and the twins went along for the ride. She hadn't packed a diaper bag, she hadn't packed snacks, but the babies remained quiet, stoic, waiting for their mother's agitation to quiet.

Hours later, as they walked home, Nara said to the rabbit, "I'll tolerate you for now but no circling, no kicking, *capiche*? Or we do this whole rigmarole tomorrow, except longer and harder." Then another thought occurred to her. "Listen up," she said, feeling a little cheered even though the twins had begun to fuss. "Another reason to cool it—I live with a dachshund now. Hunting dogs, they go after burrowing animals, don't know what he will do if he discovers you."

It took a few days for Nara and Heidi to hide Marcel's misadventure in the fountain under a veneer of normalcy. Nara was the mother. Heidi was the mother's friend who also loved the twins, but knew her place. Nara could tell Heidi was trying to curtail her open affection toward the children, talking to them more moderately, picking them up less often.

The alternator for the Mercedes had finally arrived at the mechanic's and Heidi picked up the car Friday afternoon and brought it home before going back to work.

"The weekend weather will be good," she said, finding Nara on the sofa and the twins napping. The television was on. Nara muted the sound, sat up and looked at Heidi politely.

"I think we should go on a picnic," Heidi continued. "Anywhere. Wherever you like."

At the thought of getting out of Riverton, Nara felt such a wave of relief she was momentarily speechless. She got up and slowly walked to the window to look out at the silent fountain. Could they really get back to where they had been—a family of sorts? She remembered the lake in the in the photograph in the office at Saint Gemma's. She'd never been to that side of the Wind River Range. On the Reservation, the Wind River Range lay in the distance, a long blue-grey serpentine form crested in white, separating modern Native people from what had once been theirs, the rich hunting grounds of the Green River Basin. Nara turned and caught Heidi watching her, waiting for her response.

"If it's anywhere, I say let's get the hell outta Dodge," Nara said. "Let's go to that lake by Comfrey."

Heidi's eyes lit up. "This is such a good idea," she said and the smile that had been so guarded lately broke through. "Beppe calls Comfrey the only tolerable place in Wyoming."

"Oh, well, Beppe would know," Nara remarked, biting back her grin.

Heidi laughed. "Yes, a man who spends only the very short part of his life in Wyoming is smacked with this arrogance."

"You're priceless," said Nara. She'd given up checking Heidi on her idioms months ago.

The next morning they packed a hamper and headed out of town, Gering in the back seat between the twins, taking turns licking himself and each baby in turn. Nara chuckled to herself as she watched the scrubby high prairie grasses and forbs zip by. Who'd have thought Ms. Cautious would be a speed demon? She listened to Heidi going on about the numerous picnics she had shared with her folks by a lake outside their German village and the school friends she would meet up with. Nara tried to envision her own parents taking her on a picnic. Never in a million years, and even if they had chomped on sandwiches by a lake, there would have been no friends to meet up with.

Lake Cheynook was less crowded and way more beautiful than Nara had imagined it would be. The sound of leaves rustling in a light, warm breeze, the gentle lap of water against the rocky shore, the smell of pine laced with damp. Minerals sparkled in the silt, the air was alive with dragonflies and butterflies, raptors and songbirds.

They spread their towels on a flat rock that extended into the water. Heidi had worn a swimsuit under her shorts and sweatshirt and didn't mind the cold. They stripped the boys down and Heidi walked into the water holding them both, their little brown legs clinging to her as they attached like limpets. She bobbed up and down when the water reached her chest and the boys screeched with delight, each with one arm wrapped around her neck, the other free to bat at the water.

"We should stay here," Nara murmured to Gering, stretched out beside her. "Live by a lake like this. No one watching us, just the big ol' sky overhead."

She felt a wave of desperation. They'd be back in Riverton tonight, and in two days she would be hauling the twins across the street with a pie. Charise, the white woman in the grey clapboard house opposite Heidi's had a baby, a dull, fat thing, older than the twins but hardly even standing yet. To please Heidi, Nara had invited Charise and baby Walter over for a play date, but other than being adults, or being babies, they had nothing in common. Then yesterday, Heidi had offered to bake the woman a pie. A pie Nara would deliver on Tuesday, a pie that dictated they would have to suffer through a repeat performance of sharing the joys of motherhood. Was this now to be a weekly occurrence in claustrophobic, suffocating Riverton?

"You bite that fat baby on Tuesday," Nara whispered to Gering. "That should do it."

Heidi emerged from the water. With a twin on each arm, she looked like a woman advertising a family vacation, except the babies would be blond not little black-haired Native kids, and definitely, they would not be naked. The babies, swaddled in towels, lay sleepily sucking on their bottles. Closing her eyes, Heidi stretched out on the rock to dry in the sun and Nara looked at her critically. Strong body, narrow waist, full breasts, flawless skin covered with goose pimples. Plucked chicken, Nara turned away, cold white skin always reminded her of plucked chicken.

And before she could stop herself, Nara asked the question she knew every mother of more than one child must torture herself with, but never, ever asked out loud, "If the babies were drowning, who would you save first?"

She felt Heidi stiffen and forced herself to meet the deep blue eyes, wide with shock, and something else—fear.

It broke Nara's heart how easy the answer was for her. She loved both her boys absolutely, completely, without reservation, but Amadeus, just that little bit more. If Heidi would only say, "I would save Marcel first," somehow it would all balance out.

When Heidi closed her eyes and turned her face away, Nara knew she was feigning sleep. She was too quiet. It was rare for Heidi to be so dishonest. The rabbit shifted uneasily and Nara pressed on her chest. She straightened her spine, tipped her head back and drew in as much air as she could, using her lungs to check the soft, grey creature. She glanced at her children lying apart from her, sleeping on their towels, depending on Heidi as much as they depended on her.

Is that why she asked that stupid question? Nara wondered. To punish Heidi for the way the twins lit up when she came home, the ease with which she picked them up and smothered them with kisses? And then a thought dawned that made the question she had asked Heidi even worse and the rabbit sat up and took notice. Peter's little ball of ashes . . . Were they the ashes of a baby who had drowned? Had he drowned in a fountain? Had he drowned in a goddamn lake?

When the wind picked up, Heidi rolled to her side and suggested it was time to leave. They changed the babies' diapers for the ride home. As they walked back to the car, Nara said she and Gering had made a deal, since she rode in the front on the way to the lake, he got to ride in the front going back to Riverton. Neither Heidi nor Gering protested, and Nara squeezed in the back between her children and watched Comfrey's main street come and go, only one car parked at Toot's Lucky Thirteen, no activity at the air strip, the hills rolled their way down to the highway where the cars would be zipping east and west . . . .

On Tuesday, Nara took a pie across the street as had been promised. She managed to carry both of her babies and the pie, a feat she thought should surely deserve something in the afterlife. As she kicked the front door with her foot, she was already planning their escape.

Charise opened the door with a shy smile, her pale eyes blinking rapidly in the cool morning air. She took the pie and ushered them into the sitting room. Walter sat on a blanket in front of a television where three women discussed how to make Thanksgiving table decorations with gold spray paint, ribbons and mini pumpkins.

"We haven't even started on October. Aren't we a little early to be planning Thanksgiving?" asked Nara, depositing Amadeus and Marcel next to Walter on the blanket. The children stared at each other silently.

"You have to be prepared," said Charise. "You can at least gather the paint and ribbons, but you're right, mini pumpkins won't be in the markets yet."

"A month at least," Nara agreed.

"I'll get our coffee and some snacks for the kids." Charise looked at Nara uncertainly, as if asking for permission to leave.

"That would be lovely, thank you so much," said Nara, toying with the idea of switching the channel while Charise was out of the room. She wouldn't do it, but the thought that if she did, her hostess wouldn't protest pleased her. Weren't they polite women?

Charise returned carrying a tray with two cups of coffee, sugar and cream and three small plastic bowls of Cheerios. She placed a bowl in front of each child.

"You know that James Bond movie where the woman is painted all over with gold paint and she suffocates?" Nara asked, adding cream to her coffee. "You think pumpkins have spirits? You think they'd rather suffocate than rot away, return to the cycle of life?"

Did Indians think pumpkins had spirits? Charise hoped she wouldn't offend her guest when she uttered the only reply she could think of, "Well, most get eaten and at least a gold pumpkin would be pretty."

Nara nodded her head at the profundity of Charise's observation and said, "You sure got me there, Charise."

The babies dumped their Cheerios out onto the blanket and started to use their pinchers to pick them up and put them in their mouths. The television ladies moved on to uses for a wedding dress after the wedding. Two advocated for saving it for their daughters. One said for wedding number two, which elicited titters from the other two.

Charise furrowed her brow. "I don't think divorce is funny, do you?"

"Funnier than being left a widow," said Nara. "And, you know what? I'm thinking I may have left the iron on, so we'd best be going."

"Do you want to leave the kids here while you run over and check?"

"Better not." Nara got up. "I've got stacks and stacks of ironing to do. Then the house to clean, the gardening, the babies will need their hourly medicine."

"What do they need hourly medicine for?" Charise looked at the twins with concern.

"They prefer me not to discuss it. I'm sure you understand," said Nara, hefting a baby onto each hip.

Amadeus and Marcel had their first birthday a week later. Heidi asked Charise to come over for cake but she begged off, saying Wayne had a cold and she'd spare the twins his germs. Edith and Patsy dropped by with two red fire trucks, big enough for the children to straddle. The sisters partook of the Black Forest cherry cake Heidi had baked, Edith taking pictures of the twins with whipped cream covering their faces and their arms up to their elbows.

Saint Gemma's did a bang-up feast at Thanksgiving, everybody pretending they had plenty to be thankful for. Nara drove the twins down to the dining hall and a great fuss was made over them. A new generation, unspoiled, maybe one will be president someday, more than one person said. Others agreed. A Native American president in the next century, it would be about time.

At Christmas, Karl and Beppe sent Italian slippers lined with sheep's wool for the four of them.

"Good God, these must have been expensive," Nara said, shaking her head. "The twins will outgrow theirs in a heartbeat. Not saying I'm not grateful, but those men need a dose of common sense."

"We will keep the babies' slippers as reminder of how small their feet once were," said Heidi.

"And where will we keep them, *Meine Liebste*," Nara responded, avoiding Heidi's eyes as a chill settled in the air.

The boys toddled, ate, pooped and peed and entertained each other. Famine in Somalia, War in the Balkans, flooding along the East Coast, a windstorm in Norway was the worst ever recorded, a mother and two of her children died in a house fire in Cheyenne. Only the dog and the baby survived.

When would it be different? Nara imagined the pages ripping off a calendar, the way they showed time passing in old-fashioned movies. October. Rip . . . gone. November, December, rip, rip . . . gone. The rabbit in her chest moved less these days, maybe it was dying of boredom.

Snow and bitter cold kept Nara and the children inside for most of January, except for the hour or so after lunch when Heidi came home and insisted they all bundle up and trudge the few blocks to the park and back. Heidi suggested Nara might like to come back to work for a few hours in the afternoons. A change of pace might do Nara good; they could pay Charise to watch the twins.

"Hmmm," Nara put her fingers to her chin. "Let me discuss this with the twins and we'll get back to you."

And then Sean phoned. He had tracked her down through a girl they both knew from the casino, a girl who now worked at the health clinic.

"A girl who should be fired for giving out information on a patient," said Nara, and he laughed.

He missed her, he said. He'd cleaned himself up. They should have a little get together. I have kids now, boys, twins, she protested. Yeah, he'd heard, get a babysitter, have a little fun. She should have hung up, but she didn't.

"A good friend of my mom's is visiting her daughter in Lander and if I can borrow the car, I'd like to go see them," said Nara when Heidi got home that evening. "Would you mind having the twins on your own? Like you and Gering take them to the park or something?"

"Yes, of course we will do this," said Heidi, putting Gering's dinner down in front of him, "but this good friend of your mother's does not want to meet your children?"

"She has a tricky heart. The doctor wants her to avoid young children, you know, the noise, germs." Nara forced herself to meet Heidi's blue eyes, blue like a curacao cocktail, sapphire blue. Hard to tell if the boss was buyin' it.

Sean had cleaned himself up. He said he was looking for more casino work and they both agreed a bartender had options. They drank a little at a bar, then took a bottle to a motel room. Nara said no to the coke and took just one hit of weed. Sean said he was proud of her and she'd be good for him. He chuckled and said he forgave her for letting herself get pregnant by some other guy, twins no less. He was indisposed at the time. Who could blame her? Did her German roommate want the babies? he joked. Twins? *Jesus*, but you couldn't tell, she'd gotten her body back.

"Are your breasts a little bigger?" he asked, running his hands experimentally under her sweater and pressing himself against her. He wanted her to stay until dawn, but Nara said maybe next weekend. She'd have to see about the kids. Okay, he said. He'd phone at noon on Friday and see what she'd been able to work out. He thought he'd be able to bring a little hash, very pure, wholesome, but it'd be up to her if she wanted to partake. Otherwise, pizza, light beer and porn. They'd have a good time.

Nara returned to Riverton after midnight. Heidi had left her bedroom door open to hear the twins better and Gering crept out to greet her.

"You have to go back and sleep with your mama," she whispered, picking him up. He licked her face and sneezed. "Okay, you can come in with me, but hush."

She gently closed Heidi's door and went into her room. The hall light provided enough illumination that she could distinguish the twins, Marcel curled on his side, his head butting into Amadeus's back. She climbed into bed and held Gering under the covers and close to her chest. The grey bunny within stiffened and Nara grinned to herself.

"Relax, you delusional little weirdo and the dachshund won't even know you're here," she whispered.

The rabbit eased and allowed an exhausted sleep to descend.

On Thursday, New Wife phoned early in the morning and said, without introduction, "Your dad's sick. He wants to meet his grandsons."

"How sick?" Nara asked. Her pulse quickened; the soft grey rabbit perked up. Her father should meet his grandsons.

"You know, sick, his heart. He puts those pills under his tongue when the pain's real bad but he won't get the bypass surgery, so you know, he's not doing anything to help himself." New Wife sounded tired and more than a little pissed off.

"If you have a car, you can come and get us and I can help," said Nara, pressing on her chest and trying to inhale deeply. The twins had stopped playing and were staring at her. They must have heard something in her voice. They were intuitive that way.

She hung up the phone and looked at the clock. There was plenty of time. Since Saint Gemma's was once again short staffed, Heidi wouldn't be coming home after lunch today. And after the dinner rush was over, she and Gering were walking home by the farm to see if the piglets had been born. They wouldn't be back until dark. By then the house would have cooled and the smell of diaper rash cream and powder, the sounds of cries, coos and chuckles, would have evaporated.

Don't think of Heidi, don't think of her coming home to an empty house, don't think of her shock, don't think of her calling out their names . . . Nara avoided her face in the mirror as she gathered their toothbrushes, soaps and shampoos. She scoured the sink, put their towels in the laundry hamper, took them out and put them in the washing machine. She wouldn't turn it on. She didn't want wet clothes to sit and mildew.

She took the car seats out of the Mercedes and had them waiting on the sidewalk next to two suitcases when New Wife drew up in front of the house in a late model car. She waited behind the wheel as Nara put the suitcases in the trunk, strapped the car seats in place and carried the twins, one at a time, from the house.

They drove silently away, New Wife not remarking once on the babies. Nara looked out the window as they left Riverton. They'd be at the blue house soon, a world and forty minutes away. Heidi would understand a sick man would want to see his grandsons. A break would do everybody good.

The turning point . . . had it been the fountain or her question by the lake . . . or had it been Sean coming back into town? Thinking of Sean, Nara felt a tightening down deep and released a long breath. Yeah, Sean had looked good, eyes clear, and oh, he knew how to please her. Two babies. Nara couldn't see Sean putting up with one baby. It was just as well he wouldn't be able to find her at her dad's.

New Wife turned onto Highway 26 and within minutes they passed a sign welcoming them to the Wind River Reservation. Nara glanced at New Wife's profile. Blank face, not wanting to look at her, ignoring the babies, a woman itching to take off before all her pretty was gone.

"Good," said Nara, earning a quick glance from New Wife.

Nara relaxed in her seat. She'd see if she could convince her dad to have his surgery. She, Danny Crow and his grandsons in the blue house on the river bend, it might work.

As Heidi and Gering walked home that evening, they stopped by the small farm that had managed to hang on to several acres as houses sprang up around it. The sow lay collapsed on her side in her sty by the fence, surrounded by odor of damp straw and manure, made more pungent by the noisy heater the farmer had rigged up. The sow's flat, rubbery disk of a nose tilted slightly at their presence.

"Polka dot babies, you clever girl," Heidi called softly, picking up Gering so he could get a better view.

The sow's small eye opened a slit. She gave a soft huff before her mouth returned to its perpetual smile, the smooth, round curve of her enormous behind looking strangely seductive. Although their large pink mother had a solitary dark spot on her hip, the babies were liberally sprinkled all over with dots. Lined up at her teats, the piglets sounded like lawn mowers struggling to start, as they frantically tugged at their mother, tails spiraling as their little haunches strained to thrust their greedy mouths forward.

A special stillness emanated from the house as Heidi and Gering approached. Not a single leaf fluttered on the hanging plant by the front door, and the curtains in the front windows hung limp. Gering cast Heidi a look as she stood a moment with her head bowed and her hand placed flat on the door. He sat down and refused to get up when she pushed the door open.

Heidi picked him up and called, "We're home," a quaver to her voice. Television silent, air stale, the hallway extended long and dark to the kitchen.

"Nara? The piglets are here. They have polka dots. All over, the polka dots," Heidi's voice faded as she passed the living room. She couldn't bear to check Nara's room yet.

On the kitchen table, she found the note propped up against the vase containing the pink and purple hydrangeas she had bought from the florist yesterday to replace the daisies that had lasted for almost a week.

"New Wife phoned and came and got us. My dad is sick. I'll phone with our number and address.

Love you, Nara

The strollers were still there in the hall, the backpacks still in the closet, the car seats had been removed from the Mercedes in the garage. Heidi forced herself to check Nara's closet and the dresser with the twin's clothes, empty. Baby shampoo, toothbrushes, Nara's toiletries all gone.

Gering's rapid little steps on the wooden floors, the refrigerator, the occasional gust of wind rattling the windows were the only sounds in the house that night. Heidi hovered by the phone until bedtime, refusing to put on the radio, no distractions, just waiting. Of course, a sick man would want to meet his grandsons.

Nara knew her father's phone number and address. She

could have written them on the notes.

The following week, Nara phoned in the evening to say, "The Bitch left, pardon my English, New Wife has departed for Los Angeles. We're staying with my dad for a while. There's beauty on the Rez and I want the boys to feel it."

"Your father is very sick? I will come on Saturday with food and bring some of the boys' toys."

Nara gave a brittle laugh, a sound Heidi hadn't heard since their early days. The nervy, nervous girl had returned, but now she was a mother.

"Always the worrier, Heidi," Nara accused. "We're peachy. Dad's hanging in there, and the boys are doing great. Lots of clothes, toys, food, but thank you. No need to come to us. We'll come to you. Go take your bath, get ready for bed. Miss you."

"I miss you very much too. What is . . ." Heidi began, but Nara had hung up.

"Did you know?" Heidi asked Gering as he picked his way slowly across the floor toward her, head and tail held low. She picked him up and he trembled as he licked the salty wetness from her face with his rapid little tongue.

She didn't turn on the bath. She was afraid she wouldn't get out. Instead, she sat upright on the kitchen chair, staring at the wall, the fingers of one hand pressed to her lips. When had been the turning point? The moment she had fallen in love with the twins and tried to hide how afraid she was Nara would take them away? The forced domesticity of a brave, proud, frightened young woman? A party girl, the women in the kitchen at Saint Gemma's had called her.

Had the turning point been her own inability to hide how terrified she had been to find Marcel alone in the fountain that day last summer? Nara had been scared too, and Heidi knew she shouldn't have yelled so many times, "He could have drowned, he could have drowned." She couldn't make herself hand Marcel over right away when Nara had reached for him, but she knew she should have.

Or, had the turning point been when Nara asked her that question at Lake Cheynook in September? There was no answer to a question like that, so she had said nothing, but even so, Heidi knew she had failed some kind of test. She should have laughed. Nara couldn't have been serious.

She should have said, she should have said. . .

A note, a phone call, no number, no address, silence. In retrospect, Heidi realized she and Nara had never really talked about the future. They had lived each day watching Marcel and Amadeus grow. She had been able to ignore the distance that seemed to increase a little each day, because each day, the assumption that they would raise the babies together had grown stronger. It was best for the babies to have two adults tending them; a lap for each baby at night, two baby backpacks to take the twins hiking on summer weekends. At least that had been her assumption. Nara hadn't assumed anything.

The brittle laugh, the quick phone hang up, now Heidi understood what they meant. They meant no future, no family. They meant nothing came next.

And Peter would have been seven, if he had lived.

CHAPTER TWENTY

THAT TINY BIT OF HOPE

Munich was having a wet summer, although thankfully, it saved most of its rainfall for the evening hours. The morning sun warmed the damp earth and the garden cat had not yet emerged through the mist for his breakfast. Since the finicky beast preferred his fresh sardines at room temperature, Karl removed the fish from the refrigerator before making his second espresso of the morning. The single origin Ethiopian beans he purchased yesterday made a rich, dark, earthy brew with a hint of chocolate. He would have to control himself from having a third. He carried his demitasse to his breakfast alcove and placed his usual Sunday phone call to Wyoming.

Heidi picked up the phone sounding resolutely cheerful during their initial exchange of pleasantries until Karl asked if there had been any news of Nara and the twins. After a slight pause, she responded hollowly, it had only been forty-three days since they had left, thirty-seven days since Nara's call from her father's house. It had not been so long.

"Heidi . . ." Karl began.

"I am fine," she interrupted.

"You do not . . ."

She cut him off, "I am *fine* and what are you drinking?"

"An espresso, my one and only. And how can you say you are fine? You do not sound fine; you sound like the life has been sucked out of you."

"I say I am fine because I eat, I work, I sleep with a little dog who is a dear."

"Then bring the dear little dog and come home to us, you silly girl," said Karl, exasperated. "Work for me. Think of how much better your life will be in Munich. Or help Beppe with his tasting room. You have been in your little western town eons beyond the year you originally promised those McKee women. How long can you possibly stay at a food pantry in Wyoming?"

"How do I know how long, Karl? Honestly, this is an impossible question." Heidi heard the note of desperation in her voice, but she couldn't stop, "Another thirty-seven days, and then thirty-seven more, and thirty-seven more after that? And on and on, until Amadeus and Marcel are little boys, until they no longer remember me?" She put her hand over her mouth, to prevent herself from saying more.

Yesterday she had driven through the Reservation on Highway 26. Nara could have been down any of the little roads that disappeared behind hills or down arroyos. Heidi had stopped and talked to a woman hanging laundry on a line strung between two cottonwoods outside a trailer near the highway. A plump puppy and two small children stood silently by as she had asked the woman if she knew of Nara Crow and identical twin boys.

"What's she done, this Nara Crow?" The woman narrowed her eyes.

Heidi hastened to assure her Nara had done nothing wrong. She was Nara's close friend and wanted to see if Nara needed help taking care of her sick father, but she had lost the address.

The woman told the children to take the puppy and go inside. The trailer door opened with a squeak and closed with a clatter and the woman went back to hanging up her washing, saying over her shoulder that there were no Nara Crow's around here.

Heidi returned to the car. "Did you hear, Gering?" she said to the dog sitting erect on the driver's seat. "She tells the children to take the puppy inside too. What would we want with that puppy? You should have made the loud woof so she knows I already have the best Wyoming dog."

"*Du bist ein Narr*," she told herself bitterly, 'you are a fool.' A pale, blonde woman driving a Mercedes, looking and sounding too foreign and too eager, not knowing the address of a close friend.

"Heidi?" asked Karl after his apology for posing his "impossible question," had been met with silence.

"I am here," she said tonelessly.

"We are concerned about you," Karl said, measuring beans into the grinder. "We will fly out to visit you as soon Beppe is done with moving the more mature Barolo onto new racks in his second wine cellar. We will finally make the trip we planned before Alice fell ill last summer. She is well and more than capable of planning my next sessions and allowing me two weeks away."

"But before you and Beppe were coming to here to meet Nara and the twins. They may not . . ." Heidi paused, unable to admit Nara might not be coming back, ever. "You hate to fly; you will have to take multiple flights and we promised Beppe he would never have to come back here. Let me pay you a summer visit instead."

"Beppe has forgiven you for moving to Wyoming and I will put up with the flights," replied Karl. "Give me a moment. The cat has arrived for his breakfast."

When he returned, he said it almost seemed Heidi didn't want to see them. She protested she did, but she only had weekends off and they would have nothing to do as she worked.

"We will luxuriate in your little house, plant your garden and welcome you home in the evening," Karl said.

"Last year we got a frost in May."

Karl gave short laugh. "*Mein Gott*, what an unforgiving place. Then we will be forced to visit your soup kitchen, assist you in serving instant mashed potatoes from a box with canned gravy, and entertain your staff with tales of your naughty deeds."

"Nothing but fresh potatoes, my staff is trained in making excellent gravies, and there are not so many naughty deeds. You and Beppe will have to make them up."

"It will be our pleasure to do so." Karl smiled at the smugness in her voice. He turned the grinder on, trying to muffle the sound with a towel and inhaling deeply the scent of freshly ground beans.

"What are you doing?" asked Heidi suspiciously. "You said one cup. You know too much caffeine does not agree with you."

Karl said the sound was the garbage disposal and she insisted she knew the difference between a disposal and a coffee grinder. The darkness she had felt all morning began to lift and Heidi released a sigh of relief. She did want to see them, she realized, her closest friends, her family. They would not have to be entertained. She said she had found a new sheep's cheese, locally made, creamy and sweet and she would have some on hand for their arrival. Karl mentioned an article in *The Wine Spectator* that noted Beppe's winery as being one of the jewels of Italy's Piedmont.

"He must be crowing with pride," said Heidi with a chuckle.

"He is insufferable."

When it was time to ring off, Heidi said, "I love you."

When Karl responded with, "*Danke,*" she smiled. Unlike Beppe, Karl was not given to declarations of affection.

Out the kitchen window she spied a sleek, masked,

greyish-brown bird with a crest and red, white and yellow tips to its wings, peck around the bird feeder in a desultory manner. She picked up her binoculars. It was a Bohemian waxwing.

A Bohemian waxwing had visited Karl's garden the day she had gone over to say goodbye before leaving to join Claus in New York. She and Karl had been sipping their aperitifs on his patio when a handsome bird arrived to feed upon the blackberry bramble spilling over the back wall and they had identified it from Karl's bird book.

Normally the species preferred berries, fruits and insects and would not be attracted by the seed she put out for her usual visitors, mountain chickadees, goldfinches and black-eyed juncos. She would view its arrival today as a harbinger of Karl and Beppe's visit.

Beppe answered Karl's phone call that evening in a voice thick with worry. "This is what I get for using Czech labor. I should have watched every step. Now I'm afraid another rack may go down. I've lost nearly a hundred bottles, including a dozen of my *nonno's* Barolo. I'll hear his howl in my dreams tonight."

Karl offered words of sympathy. They had sampled a bottle of Beppe's grandfather's wine the first time they had met, and the loss was indeed a tragedy.

"How many of your grandfather's bottles do you have left?" Karl asked.

"Seventeen."

"And remember, I am storing two cases here. If we have one each year for our anniversary, we will be old men before we're done."

"Thank you. You're right, although I intend both of us to reach deep into our nineties," Beppe said with a rueful chuckle. "Now tell me about Heidi. Has Nara returned with the children?"

"No, and still no phone call, beyond the one Nara made a week after leaving. That was thirty-seven days ago. I can hardly tell you the number of times Heidi said thirty-seven days when I asked her how long she planned to continue on in Riverton? Thirty-seven days, and another thirty-seven days, and another, it was almost a mantra. I'm afraid she'll insist on staying in Riverton until she loses her youth altogether. She will not let go of *dieses kleine bisschen Hoffnung.*"

"Beyond my capabilities, *caro mio,*" said Beppe.

"She will not let go of 'that tiny bit of hope,'" obliged Karl, releasing a short, irritated sigh. After over ten years together, Beppe could have picked up a little more German.

"Such a long time without a phone call makes it appear Nara does not want to be found," Beppe pointed out. "And that is her right, unless Heidi thinks there is foul play. Are there any clues?" Beppe was a voracious reader of detective novels.

"Clues? What on earth are you talking about?"

"For instance, Heidi is positive the letter left on the kitchen table was written in Nara's own hand?"

"I am sure that is not even in question," said Karl impatiently.

"Then she needs to let Nara and the twins go. Heidi has no claim to Nara's children."

"Oh, for God's sake, Beppe, have some sympathy."

"I am not going to respond to that, except to say if you don't think I weep for Heidi, you hardly know me," said Beppe mildly.

"I am sorry," said Karl, rolling his eyes at being compelled to issue two apologies in a day.

"Apology accepted. It is a painful situation, and allow me to add, I miss you very much."

"It goes without saying I miss you too," said Karl. "How much longer do you need to take care of your wine?"

Beppe promised he'd get to Munich within a week.

Alice, Karl's invaluable assistant, had worked hard to find the men acceptable flights to Riverton from Munich but the best she could do was to have them fly from Munich to Newark, Newark to Denver and Denver to Casper, where they would rent a car and drive three hours to Riverton. Everything about traveling to the least populated of the fifty states appeared to be lot of work.

"You know I would have preferred to fly nonstop," Karl grumbled as he packed. "I hate the takeoffs and landings; you know I do."

"Nonstop to Wyoming?" Beppe chuckled. "To Riverton, no less? Alice did her best. We're flying first class so we will have special lounges to wait in for our layovers."

"Lounges, layovers, plural," Karl said bitterly and Beppe decided it was the moment to go into the kitchen to prepare a snack. Karl would calm down more quickly without an audience.

He returned carrying two glasses of dry sherry and a plate of cheese, crackers and fresh figs on a black lacquered tray that he partially balanced on his right forearm. The hook that usually replaced his missing hand had needed a tune-up and wouldn't be ready until tomorrow, when they would pick it up on their way to the airport. He waited for Karl to remove several pairs of neatly folded socks from a small round table so there was somewhere to place the tray, then he sat down to wait for Karl to finish packing.

Beppe had found it easy to pack, three pairs of black jeans, dress clothes unnecessary, as they weren't going to Jackson Hole. Thermal undershirts, a couple of sweaters and he'd wear his leather bomber jacket. He understood selecting what to wear was a more considered process for Karl. Every item of clothing made a statement. Since childhood, Karl had been complimented for his extreme good looks, and he carried that burden and responsibility with him.

Karl accepted his sherry and pondered his outerwear.

Beppe looked ruggedly handsome in his leather, but that wasn't his style. Karl held up a charcoal-colored, single-breasted, three-quarter length light wool coat for Beppe's approval.

"One of my favorites," said Beppe, dexterously adding a generous smear of Brie to a cracker and holding it out to Karl.

"Will we have to hide who we are?" asked Karl, waving away the cracker.

"It will be safer if we do," said Beppe, eating Karl's cracker and preparing himself another. He got up and examined Karl's closet, selecting a grey cable-knit scarf and a lighter weight Italian cashmere, also grey, but with several bold red stripes toward the ends. "Do not protest," he said, as he removed two colorful silk scarves from Karl's suitcase and replaced them with the woolen ones. "These will be much more suitable for the Wild West. When the sun goes down, Wyoming can be colder than anything you can possibly imagine."

Their flight over the Atlantic was uneventful. Karl slept peacefully, Beppe finished one novel and started another. During their first layover, Karl roamed the Newark airport, poking around in shops, thumbing through magazines, pacing restlessly, Beppe stayed in the first-class lounge and read.

As they boarded the flight to Denver, Beppe hung back to have a quick word with the stewardess. He arrived at their seats to find Karl settled into the window seat.

"I suggest you move to the aisle," Beppe said. "The stewardess told me they are expecting severe turbulence over the middle states and you will find holding my hand more of a comfort than holding the hook."

Karl paled and shifted to the aisle seat without comment.

Within half an hour, the plane began to shudder and pitch. Babies from the coach class wailed, an adult or two joining in. Karl held Beppe's hand so tightly Beppe had to gently pry Karl's fingers open several times to restore blood flow.

After a particularly dramatic jolt and wobble, Karl cast Beppe a desperate look and fumbled with his seat belt.

"Use the air sick bag," said Beppe, reaching for a neatly folded, plastic-lined bag tucked into the pocket of the seat in front of them.

"I will not," said Karl through gritted teeth. He managed to set himself free and staggered to the bathroom as the stewardess shouted at him to remain seated.

He returned to his seat during a moment of calm and gave Beppe a wan smile. "I am officially purged and I have retained my dignity," he said, buckling his belt and reaching for Beppe's hand again.

The plane made a relatively smooth landing and taxied to a stop. "Well, that was perfectly dreadful," Karl observed. "And you read the whole way. Are you even human, Beppe?"

"Very," said Beppe, giving a quick look around to see they were unobserved before giving Karl a quick kiss. "I am proud of you, not a peep."

"I was too terrified to peep. Babies are to be forgiven but I must say, there should be a law against adults howling on a plane."

"You are very hard on people."

"No harder than I am on myself."

"Exactly," said Beppe, feeling around with his foot for his second shoe.

Karl squatted down and extricated the expensive Italian loafer from where it had become lodged under one of the seats in front of them. He slipped it on Beppe's foot, straightened up and looked anxiously toward the back of the plane where people were opening overhead bins and beginning to advance down the aisle.

"If you could see your way to standing up, Beppe, we may be able to vacate before the hordes make their way to us."

As they walked off the plane, Karl grumbled, "And why

are we *flying* to Casper? To save three hours of driving time? Was that Alice's idea or yours?" Karl gave an elaborate shudder at the thought of getting on another plane. "Going home, Beppe, we must . . ."

"Yes, I know. We will drive from Riverton directly to Denver. Now let's get your ginger ale."

And he, himself, would have a beer, decided Beppe, imported, something with some flavor and heft.

CHAPTER TWENTY ONE

HEBEKA

Heidi had forewarned Karl and Beppe of her monochromatic surroundings, courtesy of her landlord's sister, but still they raised their eyebrows as they stood surveying her sitting room.

Beppe picked up Gering, who hadn't offered even a semblance of a growl. "Dogs like me," he said, unable to keep the hint of pride out of his voice and Heidi and Karl shared a grin.

"And you said all the linens, blankets and towels are orange also?" Karl asked.

"Yes, also orange but of very good quality," replied Heidi, who had no interest in putting money and effort into decorating Ray Dolan's house. Besides, Nara had professed loving the orange.

"Would you perhaps allow us to help you dilute the color?' asked Karl. "Turquoise, cream and grey come to mind."

"Not necessary," Heidi stood with her arms crossed. "If the color is too much, buy what you like, but Gering and I are used to it now."

"Carmela's vet told me a dog's color vision is limited to blues and yellows," said Beppe, who had only bought toys for his beloved Italian Greyhound in those colors.

For the first three days, Karl and Beppe cooked and cleaned and enjoyed taking Gering for walks in the park, not linking arms, Karl concentrating on what he derisively called his 'macho walk.' They helped serve meals at Saint Gemma's, entertaining the kitchen crew and patrons with their accents and comments.

Inez insisted she was in love. It didn't matter if Heidi's cousins batted for the same team. She'd take either one. Heidi almost said, 'Only Karl is my cousin,' but remembered Nara calling her attention to the rules whites constructed about who could and could not be considered kin.

When Massimo admitted that for gays, Karl and Beppe didn't throw it in your face, Heidi demanded, "Throw what in whose face? You be respectful to them or I beat you up."

"Yes, Boss," said Massimo with a broad grin.

By their fourth day, Karl and Beppe admitted to each other they couldn't see Heidi leaving Riverton anytime soon. She insisted adamantly she wasn't ready for a comfortable life of exceptional food, fine wine, ballet, opera and fully functional people.

"If she won't come home, we must give her something more here," Karl said, arranging in a vase the red roses they had bought at great expense. "A small business, and we will be silent partners, help with the start-up costs, offer advice. She feels like a victim now, not in control of her life."

"Her own enterprise will make her feel more powerful," Beppe agreed.

"She will resist at first. She said if Nara doesn't come back by the time the boys turn five, she will leave Riverton, but they're not yet two. *Mein Gott*, can you imagine another three years here?"

"Absolutely not," said Beppe fervently.

"When she leaves, she can liquidate the little business." Karl cut another inch off the stem of one of the roses and tucked it back in the vase. "She certainly won't lose money; we'll take the risk. This is just to fill the gap until she moves on with her life."

Beppe had already gotten out his notebook. "We will make our plans irresistible," he said.

"A German Chocolate Cake is a revolting beast," said Karl, returning to the house later the next day, exhausted from making two dozen layer cakes, with the traditional coconut pecan frosting. Baking the cakes at Saint Gemma's, using ingredients they had purchased themselves, had provided an opportunity for Karl to assess the kitchen's suitability for the plan he and Beppe had concocted.

"I suppose I should have made sheet cakes, easier for everyone, but regardless, I'm done with production work," vowed Karl, accepting the glass of wine Beppe brought to him in the bath. "It's only satisfying for those trying to claw their way up, or for Heidi, who claims to get such satisfaction from feeding the masses."

"That's why you own a culinary academy," soothed Beppe. "You train others to be the workers of the world and you don't have to deal with the masses. Now tell me, is the kitchen suitable? I have found a lawyer who is prepared to help us."

"The kitchen is ideal, actually," said Karl, sipping his wine. He held up his glass. "What is this? It is excellent."

"Charles Krug, Cabernet. Napa Valley. The man with all the teeth at the deli offered it from his private stash when he found out we are staying with Heidi. He wants to know if she really has a boyfriend, a paleontologist in Thermopolis."

"Thermopolis? The dinosaur place? Oh, that *is* lovely. Rare of our girl to lie so creatively. She must have been desperate."

"I'm sure she didn't want to hurt his feelings. He said he's asked her out several times."

"Well, he can't have her," Karl stated emphatically. "The

teeth, those tiny eyes, most unattractive. Now about the kitchen, there's even an empty storage room I'm sure we can commandeer."

After the lawyer had summarized his clients' proposal to the McKee sisters, Edith and Patsy enthusiastically agreed to allow a small shortbread company to operate out of Saint Gemma's Kitchen on the weekends since the ovens weren't in use, anything to tie Heidi to Riverton longer.

"Will it be difficult to convince your third partner?" the lawyer asked Karl and Beppe after the McKees had left the meeting. It seemed risky to plan a business without the presence of the woman who was to run the operation.

"Perhaps," said Beppe, "No," said Karl, both men answering at once.

That evening Heidi sat curled up with Gering under a blanket in an armchair and tried to appear she was still listening to Karl and Beppe's proposal. She restrained herself from asking incredulously, 'Are you on crack?' a question Massimo's brother Raffi used every time something surprised him in the kitchen. Every day she got up and went through the paces. Saint Gemma's had not suffered, but she couldn't imagine having the energy or the will to do more than what she was already doing.

Images of Amadeus and Marcel floated before her. They would now be talking, running, getting into mischief. She saw their grins, heard their chuckles, felt the smoothness of their soft skin. Would they be plump, or would they be lean like their mother? Would Amadeus still be cautious, would Marcel still take the lead? If they and Nara had truly disappeared, she and Gering would take off, wander the earth, head north to the Arctic Circle, disappear. Suddenly she felt faint and she bent over Gering with a groan.

"She's gone pale. Make her some tea," said Karl to Beppe,

leaping up to move Gering to the floor and pull Heidi to her feet.

"Gering doesn't like the floor," protested Heidi weakly as Karl led her to the sofa.

"*Mein Gott!* It's a floor in a cottage, not a cave in the Alps," said Karl impatiently, arranging the blanket over Heidi's knees and plopping Gering next to her.

"Why did you put her on the sofa?" Beppe whispered when Karl went into the kitchen to check on the tea makings.

"Because she was sinking into herself. She wasn't hearing what we were saying, couldn't you see that? On the sofa, we sit on either side of her and apply pressure, that way she'll know we are not giving up."

"Open your eyes, Heidi. You will spill your tea," said Karl firmly, settling on one side of Heidi and nodding to Beppe to sit on the other. "We will start over. You will listen to us. We will go through it all again and then you will respond."

Heidi looked at Beppe, who gave her an encouraging nod and smile.

"Then I choose Beppe to talk," said Heidi, grimacing at the trace of petulance in her voice.

Beppe looked pleased. "We will be limited parents," he began. "We will make a financial commitment, especially at the beginning."

"Limited *partners*," Karl said.

"As you say, *partners*," Beppe corrected himself. "We will help with marketing. We can do that from Europe. Shortbread rounds, your mother's recipe with a twist. They are easy to ship and if stored properly, they last well. Five ingredients will be all you need."

"I will ensure a source of the *Preiselbeermarmelade* from Germany," interjected Karl. "How do you call it here?"

"Lingonberry jam," Heidi muttered.

"Lingonberry jam evokes Germany," Karl continued.

"People are always attributing shortbread to Scotland."

"Lingonberry evokes Sweden. That is what people will think, and my mother got her recipe from a Scottish cookbook. It is a Scottish biscuit or cookie, as they say here," said Heidi, coming out of herself a little. "You know this, Chef of All Things on This Planet and the Next. Anyway, I prefer the raspberry jam with my mother's recipe."

The men grinned at each other. Their girl was fighting back.

"Raspberry would be an excellent complement to the hint of almond in your mother's recipe but it is also a much more common flavor," said Karl. "With the thin layer of lingonberry, your *German* shortbread will be the only one, a separate niche."

Beppe added, "For marketing, a separate niche is so important. And we have thought of a name. "

Despite herself, Heidi laughed. "Tell me."

"The company is Hebeka," said Karl. "The first two letters of each of our names, Hebeka Golden Shortbread Rounds, German shortbread baked in Wyoming."

"Scottish, Swedish jam," Heidi protested feebly, grabbing Karl's hand when he tried to poke her.

"Shortbread from Wyoming, *buon Dio*, who ever heard of such a thing?" said Beppe, still struggling to view anything to do with Wyoming in a benign light.

CHAPTER TWENTY TWO

YEARNING TO BREATHE FREE: 1995

When the Native man with the impressively scarred face questioned why the words engraved on the plaque at the base of the Statue of Liberty were so prominently displayed at the entrance to the dining hall, Heidi said, "The woman who gave the starting funds for Saint Gemma's Kitchen claimed to be descended from Emma Lazarus."

She placed a dinner roll and two balls of whipped butter on his tray and waited for him to continue making his selections, but he fixed her with his bloodshot eyes instead.

"Interesting, since Emma Lazarus died unmarried at thirty-eight," he said. "What does that say about a rich, New York Jewish girl in the nineteenth century?"

Heidi had learned in America, the most unexpected people liked to share the most unexpected information, true or not. He was the last to shuffle through the line with his tray, so they had time to talk.

"Unmarried? Thirty-eight? You are suggesting perhaps she was not interested in men? Are you suggesting she was the lesbian?" Heidi asked. "It could be that her family did not introduce her to an appetizing man."

The man shrugged a shoulder and gave what might have been a grin on his rather immobile face. Heidi handed him a small bowl of applesauce, which he took with a trembling hand.

"And you know about Emma Lazarus because you have studied the women poets?" Heidi asked, shifting down the food line in step with him, waiting for him to point to what else he wanted.

"Wrote a paper in college, English Literature. Know your enemy." He waited for the surprise in her eyes, which didn't come. He figured her for a European, one of the North Country ones, blonde, blue eyed, cool. She didn't have the heat of the Mediterranean.

"You have a lesbian for an enemy?" Heidi asked, innocently. "She must be one of the tough ones."

"She can be tough, but she can't take my land," said the man and he and Heidi shared a grin at how inane their conversation had become.

He pointed a dirty finger toward a meaty oblong. "What's that?" he asked.

"*Rouladen.* It is beef rolled around the pig's belly slice, with onion and pickles. Then we brown and then we simmer. The *blaukraut,* the red cabbage, makes a very good complement. It offers just the correct amount of sour for the meat. In Germany, sometimes a chef will use veal, but not I. Ever."

"Too expensive?" *Germany*, he'd pegged it, amused with himself at how much that seemed a victory.

"Too expensive and too wrong for the baby cow."

He nodded. A veal calf had a miserable life, his ex-wife would have agreed. He looked at the woman dishing out his food, the woman who was not afraid to meet his eyes.

"You ever think of the irony of having the last lines of a sonnet written for immigrants on the wall of a soup kitchen that serves a healthy dose of indigenous people?" he asked, wondering when the last time was that he'd had an actual conversation with anyone.

"Yes, I have thought of this irony, but the words are not at fault," she said. "You are saying there are more lines to this poem?"

He wasn't surprised at her defense of the words. Immigrants loved the Statue of Liberty.

"Yeah, *The New Colossus,* there's another two-thirds. It starts with a reference to the original Colossus, on the island of Rhodes. Lazarus wrote it in 1883," he said, putting his hand down heavily on the counter as he felt his legs about to give way. He glanced at her and flinched at the sympathy in her eyes.

"Now I need to sit with my beef rolled around a pig belly slice with its complement of sour enough cabbage," he said, wanting to prove to both of them he had some intellect left, wondering how he was going to carry a tray while he still had the shakes. Three days without a drink, three days of nausea, headaches, sweats, three days of hell, three steps toward forgiveness.

The German woman pointed to the nearest table. "Sit. This afternoon it is my pleasure to carry your tray to you. But do not tell the other guests or they will all expect the Cadillac treatment."

'Cadillac treatment,' if he'd been less tired, he would have laughed out loud at a German knowing the term. He shambled off, made it to the table she had indicated and sat down with relief. He waited with his eyes closed, waiting for the pleasure of being seen to ebb, waiting to feel nothing, waiting for his food. When she placed the tray in front of him, he saw she'd added a glass of water, a glass of juice and a cup of coffee, saucer on top to keep it hot.

"*Aishenda'ga,*" he said, lacking the energy to translate, but hey, immigrate to my country, learn my language.

Heidi swallowed her disappointment. He was Shoshone, not Arapaho. Nara had taught her to say 'thank you' in both languages.

"Are you from the Reservation?" She could tell he wanted to be left alone to eat his meal in peace, but she had to ask.

"At times," he said, stifling a sigh. First food in three days at a free soup kitchen and he was going to have to pay for it.

"I have lost touch with a friend, Nara De'Nae Crow," she said, sitting opposite him. "A young Arapaho woman with identical twin boys. She is lovely, a little taller than me, a little scar by her left eye. The boys are now five years old. She left Riverton almost four years ago to stay with her father on the Reservation. Have you heard of someone like that? I know Wind River is a big place, but identical twin boys, there cannot be so many."

To avoid the plea in her eyes, he used both hands to bring the glass of juice to his mouth. He put it back on the tray, spilling only a drop. Another victory, he was racking them up. He looked at her and shook his head.

Should he tell her he had been MIA for over five years? Two months in a hospital recovering from burns, until he had healed enough to spend four years, three months in jail for Aggravated Homicide by Vehicle. It hadn't been enough time, he knew that. He could have gotten twenty years, except nobody did, not for a first-time DUI. Not when his passenger, the young hitchhiker who ended up dead, had no identification, no one to stand up for him.

After jail, he hadn't returned to the Reservation like he had planned from his cell. For several years, he had crawled the gutters in Laramie, Cheyenne, in places he couldn't recall. He didn't remember how he'd gotten to Riverton, but three days ago, as he lay shaking, feverish and freezing under a thin wool blanket at a shelter just down the road, the skinny white boy had come to him. He thought he heard himself speak or cry out, but the young hitchhiker had remained silent, looking at him from the foot of his cot.

So, the boy had not left him. The boy was out there somewhere and waiting to forgive him when he crossed over. He was no longer alone; he knew that now.

The Shoshone looked at the German lady, who hadn't given him her name, and managed to say, "I don't know of your friend."

Her mouth twisted and she stood up. "I interrupt your meal with my questions. I am sorry and I think you would tell me if you knew of Nara and her boys," she said, her eyes searching his face.

He thought he probably would have.

"I ask people less often than I did, and soon, I will stop asking all together," she said. A smile flashed and faded, then she told him to enjoy his meal. She added that Saint Gemma's was not open for hot lunches tomorrow and Sunday because the kitchen was used to bake shortbread for Hebeka, a business she shared with her cousins. Bags of peanut butter or cheese sandwiches would be available, however, and could be picked up by the back door.

"Then we are back to the normal hot lunch and dinner schedule for the week. On Monday, we have the American favorite, tuna casserole with noodles. Canned tuna, but in Wyoming, the can is better, I think. I hope we will see you."

He shook his head. "Moving on," he mumbled.

The shelter where he'd spent the last three nights had found him a place at a halfway house in Rock Springs. He could stay there if he arrived sober, remained sober. One day at a time.

"Then I wish you good luck," she said.

He bobbed his head. "You too."

He watched her walk back to the kitchen. She was a nice lady. She had looked at him, she'd talked to him as if she assumed he would be interested in what she had to say. Yet another victory. He'd think about writing *The New Colossus* down for her and dropping it off before he left town. If he remembered, if he could find a pencil and paper.

Heidi liked to do some of her prep in the quiet of the dining room after the last meal of the day, away from the good-natured banter of the kitchen. She glanced periodically at their final patron as she chopped stale crusty Brötchen rolls into small squares for their transformation into garlicky croutons.

'*Geschädigter Mann der Würde,*'she dubbed him, 'Damaged Man of Dignity.' She tried to remember customers through the descriptive names she gave them. If he were still here when she locked up for the night, she would show him to the door, but for now he could sit after his meal.

"Let him stay," she told Mr. Tolentino, who had paused in his mopping to catch her eye. "He will not be a trouble." Mr. Tolentino nodded and went back to work.

The man cleaned his plate, took his dishes one at a time to the bussing tray and looked over at Heidi when he was done. She smiled and gestured to his seat, indicating he could sit if he wished. He returned to his chair and leaned back, eyes half closed, nodding his head periodically to some internal dialogue, she thought, but he may just have been trying not to fall asleep.

The Shoshone had said he was moving on, but if he'd become a regular, she would have liked to hear more about the papers he'd written in college. If he were on a different part of his journey, if he had managed to come out of himself, she imagined he would have asked her how she had come to work at a soup kitchen in Riverton. That was a question she commonly got.

Would she have said she had followed a tumbleweed? Poetic, but inaccurate since she had gotten the job before the tumbleweed was even a factor.

If she and the Damaged Man of Dignity had eventually become friends, would she have told him about Peter and how holding Amadeus or Marcel had helped soothe that ache? Would he have told her how an educated man who had studied women poets had come to fall so far?

PART TWO:
THE LITTLE CROWS

CHAPTER TWENTY THREE

THE SOONER IS THE BETTER

Saturday, the morning after serving the Damaged Man of Dignity his beef *Rouladen*, Heidi came to work and found Massimo had already stacked the shortbread baking pans on the counter and turned on the ovens.

"Thank you," she called and heard Massimo's reply from deep within the large walk-in refrigerator. Hebeka had proved a success. Five ingredients, one baking temperature, a product easy to wrap, store and ship, and Heidi had a select group of clients as far away as New York. With Massimo's help today, she would get at least one batch of shortbread done before two of the counters would be needed for assembling the bag lunches.

"Hey, that guy from yesterday with the messed-up face knocked on the back door about half an hour ago," Massimo said, placing fifty pounds of butter on the counter. "Gave me a poem for you, said to give it to the German lady. I put it on your desk."

"A poem?"

"Yeah. *The New Colosseum* or something. He didn't make it up himself. The last lines are the same as on the wall in the dining room." Misreading Heidi's silence, Massimo added defensively, "Figured it was okay to read it because it wasn't exactly in an envelope. Didn't even have your name at the top."

"*The New Colossus*, and yes, of course, okay," Heidi assured him.

Gering was delighted to see her in the office so soon after they had arrived and got up from his nest to greet her. Automatically, she picked him up and held him as she scanned the lines written in a shaky but legible hand. Clean paper, black pen, where had the Shoshone gotten them? Pain and resignation had danced with a fierce pride in his eyes, and although a few words were crossed out, she had no doubt he had recalled the poem perfectly—he would not have dropped it off otherwise. Would this be enough of a reminder of whom he had once been to carry him through the day?

She sat at her desk, and spun around in her chair to look out the window. Over the six years she'd been at Saint Gemma's, the Western Catalpa had grown tall and broad enough to obscure the chain-link fence behind the narrow car park. The tree was just beginning to produce its sweet clusters of bell-shaped flowers. Its seedpods would stay through the winter and cling to the tree like brown icicles. She was the only one at work who considered the tree especially beautiful, but she thought someone who wrote down The New Colossus for a stranger would also see its beauty. Feeling as if she'd lost a friend before she had gotten to know him, she read the poem again.

Two days later, after organizing the lunch clean up, Heidi went to take an inventory of the spice cabinet. Looking at the shelves, she sighed. People hadn't put jars back where they belonged and no one had noted on the list hanging on the wall that they were almost out of bay leaves and paprika. She wiped down the big sticky bottle of vanilla and tightened the cap, wondering idly what Claus and Anke would think of where she worked now.

She didn't envy her ex-husband and his not-so-new wife their upscale New York restaurant. For six years, the McKee sisters' generous budget permitting, she had been putting the finest culinary training available in Germany into feeding the huddled masses. She wasn't sorry she had traded a city of eight million people for one of ten thousand, but she was ready for a change, taking Gering of course. It was a great mistake to let people convince you that you were irreplaceable. It was a trap set for security and convenience.

She had almost decided on Toronto, Gering had his vaccination records, Karl had a connection with a restaurant in Montreal. She would dissolve Hebeka. She didn't want to sell the shortbread recipe, the client list, Hebeka's reputation. A buyer might lower her standards, substitute margarine for some of the butter, use imitation almond extract.

Inez, Massimo and Mr. Tolentino could run Saint Gemma's Kitchen. They had developed enough tolerance to forgive mistakes in the kitchen. Massimo had become a creative and skilled chef, Inez had a good business sense, and Mr. Tolentino had a nose for spotting trouble, putting out embers before they flared into fires.

Heidi added cinnamon sticks, peppercorns and allspice to the list, pausing when she heard the phone ringing in her office.

"Will you get that Inez, please?" she called. "Take the message. I will phone back. I am almost finished here."

A moment later, Inez appeared wide-eyed at the pantry door. "Holy Jesus, it's a WHP officer," she said in hushed tones.

"WHP?"

"Wyoming Highway Patrol. He's waiting on the phone. C'mon Heidi, hurry up."

Autobahnpolizei. Heidi stood staring down at the pink princess phone, such a serendipitous addition to the mission of saving those who could not save themselves. It now appeared a menacing presence and she had to muster the courage to reach for its handset lying so recklessly on the desk.

"Hello? May I be of help to you?" she asked cautiously.

"Hello ma'am. This is Officer Clayton Brown of the Wyoming Highway Patrol. Is your name Heidi, ma'am?" Not an unkind voice, deep and businesslike.

"Yes," said Heidi frowning, meeting Inez's eyes. "I am Heidi Vogel." At Heidi's tone Gering got out of his basket, stretched and sat down at attention.

"Spell that last name for me?"

"V-o-g-e-l. Tell me, please, what is this about?"

A pause, then, "Ma'am, I'm sorry to say there's been an accident. We have two small children here and one of them has the name 'Heidi' and your number written in sharpie on the inside of his forearm. They're twins. The one that talks says they're five years old."

Gering slunk under the desk. Numbly Heidi heard that a young woman, mother of the kids, had been driving the car. The crash had occurred about eight miles west of Ten Sleep. The family had been taken to a hospital in Casper and the mother had yet to regain consciousness. The kids were bruised, a little cut up, but fine. The boy with the number on his arm? He said his Aunt Heidi would come and help them.

"Social services are on their way but, if you could come ma'am? Sooner would be better. Should take you maybe two hours," said Officer Brown.

Very carefully, Heidi replaced the handset and sat down. Her hands trembled so much she closed them tightly into fists. She looked up and stared at Inez.

"What?" whispered Inez. "Holy shit, Heidi, what? You want some water?"

Heidi bit her lips and slowly shook her head. "Phone the McKees and tell them Nara and the twins are in the hospital in Casper. Nara is hurt, unconscious. The policeman said this telephone number and my name is written on the arm of one of the boys. I do not know how long. . ." she paused, scooted her chair back and pulled Gering from under the desk. "The policeman says I must go to Casper, the sooner is the better. I will take Gering home and get the car. I will leave the back door unlocked and the key on the kitchen table. If you stay at my home with Gering, you can bring your boyfriend too, but you both have to only smoke outside."

Inez promised to phone the McKees. Nikko was last week's news so she and Gering would bunk down solo, no smoking inside. Now Heidi should hightail it to Casper.

CHAPTER TWENTY FOUR

PRONOUNS

At Heidi's request, the nurse at a brightly lit station agreed she could see Nara first before going to the room where the children waited. As they were walking down the hall, the nurse chatted, "There seem to be no internal injuries. Surprising since the car is totaled. The kids got out of the car and scrambled up the bank to the road and waited for help. Their mother may have been conscious for a bit, one of them says they saw her struggling and almost went down to help, but then she stopped moving and they didn't want to be separated and thought it better to try and stop a car. Poor little boy cried. He thinks if they had gone back down, she would have been all right. It does look like she struggled to get out initially, but a BAC that high, would have made it difficult."

"BAC?" asked Heidi.

"Blood alcohol content," the nurse explained.

"No," said Heidi, horrified. "Nara would not do that."

"Listen to me. I just talk and talk. The good news is the kids were safe in the back seat, belted in and Mom's blood pressure is good." The nurse smiled at Heidi as she pushed the door open into Nara's room. "Mom hasn't regained consciousness but the doctors couldn't see a bleed on the scan so now we wait. The bruising's mostly lower down so she looks good, doesn't she? Really cute kids, people must tell you that all the time."

"Yes, all the time," Heidi said softly, approaching the bed where Nara lay shrouded in sheets, small and perfect, attached to beeping machines.

One hand peaked out of the thin white blanket. Heidi brought it to her lips and kissed the palm. It gave no response. She leaned over and whispered, "Nara. It is Heidi. I am here, Nara. It is Heidi."

"I'm going to give you a few minutes, Hon, then I'll take you to the kids," said the nurse as she checked Nara's IV. "One of them still hasn't said a word."

They were little boys now, no longer the babies Heidi envisioned when she prayed for them each night. They sat side by side in jeans, striped long-sleeved T-shirts and sneakers, identically dressed, identical twins. Officer Brown, WHP, sat across from them and rose to shake Heidi's hand. A small, plump woman with dark brown skin leaned against the wall writing on a clipboard. Her hair was done in a myriad of braids interwoven with red ribbon and beaded at the ends. The beads knocked against each other when she moved her head, a lovely sound like tiny hooves on a wooden bridge. Officer Brown introduced her as his wife, Lily.

"She's the social worker involved in this, uh, situation," explained Officer Brown. "Thought I'd stick around, take Lily to dinner in a bit."

Heidi stared at the twins. "Hello," she said softly. They looked at her expressionlessly, their eyes hooded.

"Thank you for getting here so quickly, Miss Vogel," the social worker said, stepping forward.

"It is Heidi, please." Heidi shook the hand the woman held out to her and turned her attention back to the boys. Would she have even recognized them if she'd passed them in the street?

"Heidi, this must be such a shock. I'm so sorry," said Lily

Brown, trying to recapture Heidi's attention.

"Oh yes. I too, I am sorry. The boys have grown so much, I . . ."

"Of course, this is all so difficult."

Heidi suddenly focused on the social worker and gave a smile. She recognized the slight Jamaican accent. Two of the kitchen staff at Café Claus had been Jamaican. They had been so kind when Peter died.

Lily Brown regarded Heidi with eyes so dark, the irises were indistinguishable from the pupils. "I understand from one of the twins that they and their mother were coming to live with you. Is that right?" she asked.

Heidi tried to mask her surprise. Was this true, that they were coming home after almost four years? She glanced at the twins and one of them tipped his head back and brought his chin to his chest in a slow emphatic nod.

"Yes, they were coming to me," said Heidi, her eyes darting between the little boy and social worker. "We have not spoken for a while, but yes."

She saw Nara now—in their heart-shaped faces, high cheekbones, narrow eyes, the shape of their mouths. There was perhaps a hint of the father in their skin tone, slightly lighter than Nara's, but mostly, she saw Nara.

"Remind me, I haven't seen you since you were babies," Heidi said. "Who is Amadeus and who is Marcel?"

"Marcela. I'm Marcela," said one softy, emphasizing the last vowel.

"She says she's a girl," said the other, looking at the adults. "She is a girl too, 'cept she got man parts."

Startled, Heidi stared at Nara's children. Surely, she had misheard. For more than a year she had changed their diapers. She knew they were little boys. Identical twins, so similar she and Nara had difficulty telling them apart. Was Marcel saying he was a homosexual, at five? She looked from the nurse to Lily to the WHP. The nurse shrugged, the social worker nodded, Officer Brown shifted uncomfortably in his seat.

"I . . ." Heidi started to say, before clamping her lips together. Nara would explain when she got better. Could children so young be teasing the grownups? Not under these circumstances, not while their mother lay unresponsive in a hospital bed.

Lily made a note on her pad. So, Heidi Vogel had been surprised by the addition of an 'a' to Marcel's name, that called the closeness of her relationship to the children into question. "When did you last speak with Nara?" she asked.

Heidi pulled her attention away from the twins, "I am sorry?"

"Your last conversation with Nara?"

"I cannot remember. It is some time."

"She was living on the Wind River Reservation?"

Heidi nodded yes, as Amadeus broke in, "No, in Ten Sleep. We were in Ten Sleep."

Heidi quickly said, "Yes, of course, in Ten Sleep."

Lily looked thoughtfully from Heidi to Amadeus. She moved over to stand in front of the boy, blocking him from Heidi's view.

"When did Nara and the children move from the Reservation?" asked Lily.

Heidi frowned, as if trying to remember, before responding, "Recently."

Amadeus spoke up from behind the social worker's back, "Aunt Heidi is the charming white guy's sister. He was our dad. That's why she's white and not Indian looking."

'The charming white guy,' Heidi's breath caught. Amadeus had parroted Nara's term for a man she had claimed to know for only a week. What had happened since Nara took them away? What made Marcel say he was a girl?

Lily considered Amadeus's description of his father, who apparently was Heidi Vogel's brother. 'Charming white guy' from a five-year-old? She turned to look at the little boy who looked back at her boldly. She regarded Heidi. The German woman was holding back, struggling, someone not used to lying. But shock had such differing effects on people. Some couldn't stop talking, others gave robotic responses, still others vacillated between lucidity and staring into space.

"And the charming white guy's name?" Lily asked after a moment.

Marcela whispered, "Mama said *mostly* white guy," shrinking when the adults turned their attention to her briefly.

Heidi said, "He has a name, but I have not heard from him, from my brother, in a long time."

"And your brother's name?" Lily asked doggedly.

Heidi looked at her hands a moment before raising her eyes and saying almost defiantly, "Claus. Brown. His name was . . . it *is*, his name *is* Claus Brown."

Lily examined Heidi's face and shook her head slightly, wooden beads dancing. "How do we get hold of the children's father, Heidi?" she said patiently.

"I am not sure."

"How long have you resided in this country?"

"How long? I was born in Germany. I married and came here, to America."

"You speak English well. How long have you been here?"

Heidi looked at her as if she hadn't heard, so Lily repeated herself.

"I am sorry. I have been here since 1982—so it is thirteen years? I learn English in *Grundschule*, German primary school."

"Your husband's name?"

"Ex-husband, Claus Vogel."

"Uh huh," said Lily Brown. She clicked her pen rapidly a number of times until she heard a soft, "Lily," from her husband and stopped.

"And did Claus, the brother, come to America with you and

Claus, the husband?" she asked.

Heidi opened her mouth, but closed it before speaking, and the social worker repeated the question. Heidi released a soft exhale. The hole she was digging had become very deep. She caught a glimpse of Amadeus's little face as he leaned over to see around Lily. He held out his arm so she could see her phone number. He sat up as the social worker turned to see what Heidi was looking at.

"We are not playing a game here," said Lily sharply.

"Of course, not the game and I will tell you . . . it is that we all come to America, to New York City, together," said Heidi, watching the social worker write on her pad.

"It sounds like you used to be close to your brother," Lily observed.

"Our lives change." Heidi shifted under Lily's steady gaze. "I am sorry," she said, trying to swallow a sigh of despair.

And she was sorry. Sorry for being such a poor liar and giving her 'brother' the same name as her ex-husband. And had she really named her brother, Claus *Brown*? Had she really used the social worker's last name? Heidi looked at the floor. She could hear one of the twins whispering something to his brother. Sister? Brother-sister?

The twins were getting restless. Anxious to proceed, Lily Brown started to speak but halted when Heidi raised her remarkable blue eyes and said, "It is sad, but later my brother and I became not so close and we did not visit nor talk. This terrible thing, this terrible accident that has hurt Nara, it is a very big thing to wrap around in my arms, and so now my thoughts in English are not so good."

Lily shared a look with her husband. He raised his eyebrows as if asking how long this woman was going to continue with her charade. Lily sighed. If there was even the remotest possibility of Claus Brown's existence, she would have to spend time trying to track him down.

She said, "Of course, a serious accident, young children, it is very overwhelming but I need your help in making the proper notifications, Heidi. We need to try to reach your brother and we need to determine the resources we're going to need for the children."

"I am here. If we do not reach my brother, I have the resources. When Nara is well, they will come back to Riverton with me. The babies are born there. They live with me for more than a year. Their crib is . . ." Heidi looked at the children, and thought of the crib that still stood against the shared wall between her room and Nara's. She barely went in that room anymore, just to open a window, just to dust. She met Lily's eyes and said, "There is space in Nara's room for two more little beds. We have a big back garden. The school is nearby."

Lily started to click her pen rapidly, but stopped when she heard her husband's soft, "Lily."

"You're saying you are prepared and capable," Lily gave her pen several clicks, looked at her husband and placed it on her desk, "and that's all good to know. However, there is a process to follow until we can determine Nara's status."

A process to follow . . . Nara's status to determine . . . Heidi nodded and said she understood, but she'd only seen Nara for a few minutes when she arrived and now she would like to go and sit with her. The twins got up and moved close to Heidi.

"Mama wants us too," said Amadeus.

Lily glanced at Officer Clayton Brown, who gave her the smile she'd married him for, part admiration, part empathy, a big dose of tenderness. He looked at his watch and cocked his head at her. Lily nodded and her husband crossed his arms, stretched out his long legs and closed his eyes.

"Your husband . . ." began Heidi.

" . . . will be just fine," finished Lily. "He understands I need a quick word with you in my office before we go." She stood up and smiled at the twins. "We won't be long, I promise. I'll bring your Aunt Heidi back here in two shakes of a lamb's tail and then the three of you can go and be with your mom."

On the way to her office, Lily told Heidi of recent research that showed stimuli from young children sometimes found a passageway into their comatose parent's brain, especially at night. The neurology department at Casper General was interested in trying a new protocol; the twins and Nara could remain together through the night if an adult family member stayed with them. If Heidi was prepared to spend the night, she could be considered the adult relative for now. Otherwise it would be emergency foster care for the kids, and they could be brought back to the hospital for a visit tomorrow.

"But I *am* the adult relative. I am the sister of . . . I am the Aunt. Of course we stay together," said Heidi, concentrating on breathing deeply to clear the light-headedness that must surely be attributable to having no food or water since Riverton.

Lily unlocked the door to her office, pushed it open and ushered Heidi inside. "Water?" she asked, opening a little fridge and getting out a bottle.

Heidi nodded her gratitude and waited as Lily picked a pile of folders off a chair, looked around and added them to a low pile in the corner. She gestured for Heidi to take a seat, and removed another stack of folders from the chair behind her desk, placed them on top of a file cabinet and sat down.

"You are busy," Heidi observed, looking around. She couldn't imagine working in this clutter. She filed invoices away as soon as goods were checked off, recipes were placed back in the file cabinet after each meal had been prepared, equipment maintenance manuals and warranties had a drawer of their own.

"True, I am always busy, but trained in triage and little Marcela and her brother rise to the top." Lily sat down and leaned back in her chair. "Now, about the kids, any questions?"

Heidi took a long drink of water, and wiped her mouth with the back of her hand before asking, "This is questions about Marcel?"

"Marcela, yes, or better yet, what do you think?"

"I think . . . " Heidi paused, and Lily nodded encouragingly, beads bouncing.

"I think," Heidi tried again, "Marcel thinks he may be the homosexual but he is so young, so I think also, this might be *der Fehler*. The mistake. Do you think this also?"

"That Marcela is mistaken? No, I don't think so. Some children may go through periods of gender confusion, but in her case, I sense *she* is who *she* says she is, genitalia to the contrary. And a transgender child is no more likely to be homosexual than any other child." At Heidi's frown, Lily added, "I'm saying they are two different issues, or perhaps it would be better to say, two different ways of being a person."

Taking in Heidi's look of confusion, Lily sighed. Would it ever be different? At her brother's insistence, she had shared with no one his secret, that he had been born anatomically female. Twice in America, he had been brutalized by ignorant people who thought it their business to dictate who was acceptable to live peacefully within their midst, and now he trusted almost no one, not even her husband, who given a little time, she was almost certain would take the information well. Still, it was her brother's tale to tell.

She glanced at her watch. Although her husband was a patient man, he would be hungry for his dinner. "We will save our longer talk for tomorrow," she said. "For now, briefly, fill me in on how Nara has described Marcela's transition."

Heidi released a short breath, relaxed her hands and forced herself to meet the social worker's eyes. "I tell you earlier that Nara and I do not talk recently about the children, but I do know that Amadeus and Marcel are the number one priority for her."

Lily picked up a pen and began her nervous clicking, until she caught herself and put it down.

"We both need to recognize that these children have been neglected due to their mother's illness," she said, holding up her hand when Heidi started to protest. "I am *not* saying Nara does not love her children. I am saying her disease has gotten the better of her. We don't have the time to discuss alcoholism now. We'll save that for tomorrow, but let's deal with what you can do to be helpful to the children tonight."

Heidi nodded, trying not to let her relief show. Tomorrow she would be able to convince Lily Brown that Nara had learned her lesson. When Nara realized the danger she had put the children in, she wouldn't want to drink anymore.

Lily waited for Heidi to meet her eyes before continuing, "Tonight you need to let Marcela be who she claims to be."

Heidi nodded. "Yes, of course. Whatever he wants."

"No, Heidi, listen to yourself." Lily swallowed her exasperation. "To gain the trust of these children, you need work on getting your pronouns right. Amadeus is a little boy who is attempting to shoulder way too much responsibility at the moment. He considers Marcela his *sister* and you need to stand with him in this. Don't concentrate on what's between the legs, concentrate on who Marcela is, in her brain, her heart, her relationship to the world."

Heidi looked at her water bottle's label. It claimed to be 100% mountain spring water. She doubted it. She met Lily's eyes and said boldly enough to convince them both, "I will concentrate on the heart and the brain."

Lily nodded. "It will get easier the longer you are with her," she promised, pushing her chair back. "Marcela will show you who she is."

As they walked down the hall past a cart stacked with the detritus of partly eaten meals and the murmurs of televisions and visitors, Lily pondered the issues she'd be dealing with in the days ahead. A comatose mother, abuse, neglected children, alcoholism, a German woman who claimed kinship and who was frankly a terrible liar. If she was a blood relative, it was hard to see much white in those children. If Nara didn't make it, tribal rights would be a major factor. She glanced at Heidi. The woman hadn't written Aunt Heidi and her number on that little boy's arm. His mother had done that. When notified of the accident, Heidi had dropped everything to get to Casper, and although shocked to her core, she hadn't denied outright that Marcela was a transgender child.

"I just took her vitals, no change," said the nurse as Heidi and the twins entered the room. "I'm about to go off duty and Richard is taking over. He's Lily Brown's brother. You'll love him, a real sweetie and so handsome. That touch of the exotic in Casper, all the ladies love him." She checked her watch, noted something on a chart on the wall and waved goodbye.

There were two large lime-green padded chairs in the room and Heidi and Amadeus dragged them close to the bed. Heidi sat on one, the twins on the other. Heidi watched Marcel get up, stroke Nara's hair and put his forehead on his mother's shoulder. '*Her*,' Heidi reminded herself, *her* forehead, *her* mother. Marcela.

Amadeus walked to the window that overlooked the parking lot. Using his breath to mist the glass, he traced circles, zigzags, points, lines with his finger on the pane. As Heidi came to stand beside him, he looked up with a weary little face.

"Amadeus," she said softly. "Were you really coming to live with me?"

He shrugged. "I think so. When we get in the car, Mama always says, 'If anything happens, we say we're going to live with Aunt Heidi.' You remember us, right?"

"From when you were born, I think of you every day. Your mother wrote my telephone number on your arm?"

"Yes. I said she could." Amadeus pushed up his sleeve so the number was exposed.

"Is my number always on your arm?"

"No. Just sometimes." He puffed moist air on the glass and drew triangles this time.

Heidi returned to sit with Nara and Marcela and eventually Amadeus joined them, sharing Marcela's chair. Heidi got up, closed the door firmly and sat back down.

"Listen," she said to the children, "I told lies."

Amadeus and Marcela nodded.

"It is a bad thing to do."

They nodded more tentatively this time. They were used to lies and lying.

"It is just that, I do not understand what this is about. I love your mother and I saw you born. Beautiful babies you both. I do not often lie. I am not good at it."

Amadeus said, "You did okay."

"Yes, okay," whispered Marcela.

They stopped and the three of them looked at each other guiltily as the door pushed open and a tall, lean black man in scrubs came in.

"I'm Richard, your nurse. I'll be here overnight. I met the kids earlier. You're Nara's sister?" He looked at Heidi doubtfully.

"It is the sister-in-law. They are my brother's children. I am Heidi."

"Ah," said Richard, walking over to check Nara. He placed a thermometer in her ear and gently brushed her hair off her forehead. He checked her IV and then lifted her sheet and nodded.

"Listen, I need to make Mom more comfortable. Your social worker, Lily? She's my sister. We're probably the only two Jamaicans in Casper." He gave a deep chuckle and made a note on the chart on the wall. "Lily will take good care of you. She dropped off clothes for the kids and we have towels and toothbrushes here. There's a shower down the hall you may use. Those chairs? They pull out into a kind of bed. Let me get the clothes, then you can take the kids to shower while I take care of Mom."

The clothes were gently used and very clean. Heidi imagined a social worker would have a big box of used clothes for children in need. Red pajama pants and a white sweatshirt with a bison for Amadeus, yellow pants and a pale green sweatshirt with hearts and stars for Marcela.

The shower was cavernous, with two detachable showerheads. The children looked around curiously. Amadeus hooted. There was an echo and he grinned at Heidi and hooted again.

"This is so big, probably for the person who is in a wheelchair," Heidi explained, regulating the water as Amadeus and Marcela stripped naked.

"Bug bites," said Amadeus said when Heidi questioned the scattering of angry, round marks on Marcela's back. "Stupid bug bites, huh Marcela."

Marcela looked at her brother silently.

"The water might make them sting," Heidi warned.

"I don't care," said Marcela.

The twins delighted in spraying each other with warm water as Heidi sat on a white plastic chair in the corner, trying to stay dry. They danced around, holding their skinny little brown legs high, hopping, twirling, little penises dangling on both the boy and girl. The girl? Was Marcela a girl? Heidi closed her eyes and concentrated on her breaths.

She heard her mother's voice behind her, saying, "Things always look more hopeful in the morning, *meine Schatz*."

Was that the pressure of her mother's hand on her shoulder? Heidi looked at the tiled wall behind her, nothing. She felt almost nauseated with fatigue. *Would* things look more hopeful in the morning? So much depended on Nara.

She went back to studying the twins. They had changed.

As babies, Amadeus had been the more cautious child. Now he took charge. Marcel had been a confident baby, brave, adventurous.

As the shower progressed, Marcel responded to the water as most children did, becoming louder, laughing, splashing his brother. *Her* brother, Heidi reminded herself, Marcel*a*. The children came over to her for the liquid soap she squirted in their hands and washed, at Heidi's direction, 'every nook and cranny.' The phrase sent them into fits of giggles.

"Is this a nook Aunt Heidi? Is this a cranny?"

She wrapped them in towels and held their slender little bodies close, drawing in their warmth as they burrowed into her. Did they believe she was their aunt? Is that why they allowed her to hold them?

Someone had left wrapped sandwiches, Jello and apple juice on a tray inside Nara's room. Pillows and blankets were stacked on a chair.

"Mama can't eat if she's sleeping," whispered Marcela.

Heidi showed how fluid from the bag on the pole dripped down the tube into Nara's arm. "It is not just water. It is sugar and good things. Your mother will not be hungry," she promised.

Reassured, the twins excitedly told Nara about the shower as they ate their dinner. They giggled that they had washed every nook and cranny. Aunt Heidi got wet too even though they tried to be careful.

As the children chattered away, Heidi watched the rise and fall of Nara's chest, as shallow as a neap tide. Nara had tried so hard to make her understand the influence of the sun and the moon on the oceans. If only she had paid more attention, if only . . . spring tides were the greatest, twice a month, new moon and full moon, spring, not named for the season, named for . . . for jumping, for height. No, Nara's chest did not rise and fall like a spring tide. It was a neap tide, the shallowest tide . . . first quarter moon, last quarter moon, the gravitational pull was so much less, so very much less. Why had she not paid more attention when Nara tried to explain the world to her? She should have paid more attention. The book—Nara wouldn't have left her book on the oceans behind, unless, unless . . . if it had been left in Ten Sleep, Heidi vowed she would drive there and get it.

The twins pulled their chair out into a bed and lined it up as close to Nara's as they could, refusing Heidi's help.

"Aunt Heidi, you put your chair there," Amadeus pointed to a spot between their bed and the door. "When Mama wakes up, she has to climb over all of us."

Marcela added, "Then we'll be in the way and we can yell, '*Stop.*'"

"Yeah," said Amadeus, "and then she can't get away."

Richard came in to survey the arrangement and agreed they'd given him enough room on the opposite side of the bed to take care of Nara. He told Heidi there was a call for her from Riverton at the nurse's station and he would wait with the children until she got back.

When she heard Inez's voice on the phone, Heidi apologized for not phoning earlier. She explained how grave the situation in Casper was.

"So, Nara's going to be okay?" Inez asked cautiously.

"Yes, of course, but I just don't know how long . . ."

"Shit Heidi, we got this," Inez interrupted. "We like a buncha little Heidis now. We're all efficient, all getting along. Edith says she's getting me check writing privileges," she added proudly. "Massimo's strutting around with his inventory list, checking things off. He can pull together the order for next week, no problem. Gering's okay, kinda quiet. I think I'm ready for a dog, less trouble than a boyfriend. "

"Inez, I am so . . . "

"Heidi, forget it. You help me out all the time, like with my

mom going nuts about that thing last month, but phone me tomorrow and like the day after, you know, keep in touch."

The children were already dozing when Heidi returned to Nara's room. Richard greeted her quietly and slipped out. She woke every time Richard entered to tend his patient. At one point, she felt his hand on her shoulder.

"You are strong enough, I know you are," he whispered. "God knows it too."

CHAPTER TWENTY FIVE

MY KIND OF INDIAN

Lily arrived the next morning, her dancing braids silenced by a silver and jade hair clip. She announced she would be taking the children down to the cafeteria for breakfast and then to the park for a little airing out. When Heidi moved to accompany them, Lily raised her hand.

"Just us, the kids need some Lily time," she said. "We probably won't be much more than an hour. You take a break. There's pastries and coffee machine in the lounge, but if you're looking for a really decent cup of coffee, you should try the bagel place down from the gas station on the corner."

"Thank you," said Heidi. She glanced at the twins, hoping one of them would object to her exclusion, but they said nothing. They stood shoulder-to-shoulder, expressionless, staring at a point somewhere between Nara's bed and the door. She was conscious of them waiting. Waiting as plans were being made around them, waiting to see how long their mother would take to awaken. They had been concerned last night she might get up and walk out of the room, so they must think it would be soon.

Heidi watched from the doorway as the twins scurried down the hall after Lily. They were so very small and the social walker was walking much too fast. Just as they were about to disappear around the corner, Marcela stopped, turned and raised a small hand. Heidi pressed her hand to her mouth and blew a kiss.

She returned to the peaceful form lying in the hospital bed and whispered fiercely, "We stay together now. Do you hear me, Nara? We *all* stay together now."

Heidi left the room when the morning nurse came to bathe Nara. She intended to go to the lounge, but an elevator stood open and invited her in. Perhaps she did want decent coffee at the bagel place after all. The lobby was empty save for a young man with a name tag that read 'Elias,' seated at the reception desk. He wished her a nice day, without looking up from his magazine.

"And I wish you the very nice day too, Elias," she said, smiling when he rewarded her with a startled look.

A crisp wind blew dried leaves into the lobby as the glass doors slid open, and Heidi stood blinking in the watery morning light. On the opposite side of the broad boulevard bordering the hospital's parking lot, she spied a large, round, yellow sign announcing '*Super 8 Motel*' in bright red script. More than a decent cup of coffee, she needed to stretch out on a bed for a few minutes. And she needed a shower, although she had brought no clothes or toiletries with her. She could have packed a small bag in no time at all.

The motel was not far. She would leave her car parked in the hospital lot and walk, breathe, walk and breathe. '*Hast do nichts gelernt, dumme Gans?*' she heard the Mercedes chastise as she passed it by. 'Have you learned nothing, you silly goose?' She had left New York similarly unprepared.

"Are you from the hospital?" The receptionist looked at Heidi with a sympathetic smile. "We're used to people needing a room after spending time with a loved one over there," she said, nodding at the window.

"Yes. It is my sister-in-law who is the loved one."

"Well, we hope she is resting comfortably," said the

receptionist as she took an imprint of Heidi's credit card. "When the rodeo comes next month, we'll book up fast, but your room is yours for as long as you want it, and we wish your sister a speedy recovery."

'Sister-in-law,' Heidi almost corrected, but why exchange one lie for another?

The motel had a gift shop, which displayed an assortment of clothing for the guests' convenience. T-shirts in bright pink for women, blue for men, both with a bucking bronco and *CASPER* written prominently across the chest, sweat pants, men's boxer shorts. The only female undergarments on offer were flimsy, black-laced panties, what her mother would have referred to as *'Sexy Unterwäsche.'* It was impossible to imagine the panties covering anything of note, so Heidi purchased two pairs of men's boxer shorts, holding them up to her waist and choosing extra small. She also purchased a T-shirt and a pair of grey sweatpants.

The motel room smelled faintly of cigarette smoke and strongly of chemical cleaners so she opened the windows wide. She peeled back the rough maroon bedspread. It had tiny broken golden metallic threads that stuck up in the air, ready to snag any pair of *Sexy Unterwäsche.* She collapsed face down on the bed and wrapped her arms around a pillow and whispered, *"Mein Gott, Mein Gott"* over and over, too tired to cry.

Heidi woke with a start and looked at her watch, half an hour gone. She took a quick shower, dressed and returned to the hospital to find Lily sitting with Amadeus and Marcela in a waiting room near the elevators.

"We had a good breakfast, didn't we?" said Lily, smiling at the twins who nodded solemnly. "Not much conversation, but good appetites, and we got some fresh air in the playground a few blocks down on Wyoming Boulevard."

The twins exchanged a look but remained silent.

"Heidi, we'll talk this afternoon," Lily continued. "See what the doctor has to say at eleven, spend your time with Nara. I have to go to court on another matter, but I should be back around three this afternoon."

At 11:15, a very young Doctor Singh entered the room. He greeted Heidi and turned to Amadeus and Marcela. He held out a hand to them and looked a little embarrassed as they shrank back.

"The children should walk down to the nurses' station. You can take them. They have some books and cookies there. Cookies," he repeated to the children for emphasis. "Your aunt will come and get you when we're done."

The twins' confidence was ebbing, Heidi could feel it as they each took one of her hands and held tight. She returned to find Dr. Singh had placed the twins' chair at the foot of the hospital bed. The children had insisted on folding it up in the morning with the blankets still inside and blanket fringe poked out all around. He slouched in the chair with his eyes closed and his legs stretched out, perhaps to avoid the fringe. He opened his eyes when she said, "Doctor Singh?"

He sat up and drew a hand over his face, exhaustion settling on his handsome, dark features.

"Sorry, end of my shift," he said, sitting up. "The kids settled with cookies and books?" He yawned and clasping his hands, stretched his arms above his head, holding them there as he twisted several times, side to side.

He gave himself a little shake and continued, "We have some good children's books for cases like this. Impairment of the mother, hospital stays, that kind of thing. The social worker will be giving you more information this afternoon. Is it Lily who's working with you?"

Heidi nodded. She sat down at the head of the bed, turning her chair sideways to face Dr. Singh. She placed her hand on Nara's forearm and asked, "What is this impairment? Yesterday the nurse said that the tests do not show damage to the brain. That the brain and the internals are not bleeding."

Avoiding Heidi's eyes, the doctor looked at Nara as he spoke, "We have this current injury, the accident. There's not an obvious cause for her lack of consciousness, not from the scans, and yet she is nonresponsive. It has only been two days. She may regain consciousness at any time."

He spoke of similar cases. Even those with more obvious injuries could have a positive outcome, but on the other hand, on occasion, a case that should end well, did not. There were so many variables to consider Hope for the best, prepare for the worst, he cautioned.

He glanced at Heidi. "I'll leave Lily Brown to address the other concerns."

"What other concerns? Please," Heidi felt a wave of panic, "Nara will get better, like these others who healed."

"Lily will be here this afternoon. She will address the alcohol issues, the BAC at the time of the accident, whatever social service protocol needs to be followed for everyone's best interests. It is her kind of Indian that has such a problem with alcoholism." He regarded Heidi a moment. "My kind of Indian is like you Europeans. Our risk is much less than for her kind."

Heidi understood what he meant. She was familiar with the statistics for alcoholism on the Reservation, but she did not want to be 'a kind' with this man, this very young, tired, superior man who couldn't say when Nara would return. She stood up, holding Nara's hand in hers.

"She is not a *kind* of Indian,"Heidi said, striving to control the tremble in her voice. "She is Nara De'Nae Crow, an Arapaho. She fought her demons for her children. She says this before they are born and she delivers healthy babies."

Dr. Singh leaned forward, using the chair's arms to push himself to his feet, his eyes a mixture of sympathy and exasperation. "Look, I am just the doctor, forget the Indian stuff, very unprofessional, stupid, I don't know why I even said it. Jesus, I'm tired, unprofessionally tired."

He winced as Heidi wiped at her eyes. "Listen, we'll see what she can do. Nara is a young woman. Medically, I'll tell you this, her liver is already somewhat fatty and her liver enzymes are elevated. Her uric acid levels are too high. The blood in her urine may be from the accident or from alcohol abuse, we don't know. Not surprisingly, she's deficient in B vitamins, which are now being added in the IV.' He heaved a deep sigh before adding, "She was significantly damaged before this accident, but as I said, she is young."

After he left, Heidi sat with her hand covering Nara's, watching the IV's slow drip, the trace of Nara's beating heart across the screen of the monitor, the gentle rise and fall of her chest. She rose and applied Vaseline to Nara's lips the way Richard showed her the night before.

"We are all part of her village," he had said. "In Jamaica, if someone is sick, we all care for her."

"Do you remember, Nara, when . . ." Heidi began, and talked and talked, reminding Nara of their first meeting, the meals they had shared, the games they had made up. She talked of Gering, the issues he was having with his back, how happy he'd be to see her and the twins.

The children had placed two chairs in front of the nurses' station, facing the way Heidi would come. They sat erect, legs dangling, and silently watched her approach.

"I am sorry I take so long," she said as she stood before them. "After the doctor leaves, I sit with your mother and I talk."

"Okay, but that was too long," said Amadeus.

"Too long," echoed Marcela.

"Oh, don't worry your auntie," chided the nurse as she tucked papers into a file folder. "They were just fine," she said to Heidi, beaming with efficiency and good will. "We had cookies, juice and read a book. They're the ones who didn't want to color. Just wanted to sit right there and wait for you. Quiet as can be, good as gold, wish my two were so well behaved. You have children of your own, Hon?"

CHAPTER TWENTY SIX

ALL POSSIBLE CONTINGENCIES

"How would you like to do this?" asked Lily when she arrived in the afternoon, briefcase under her arm. "I need some private time with you, and the children can't be left alone."

Before Heidi could reply, Amadeus spoke, "We can go back for the cookies and books, but Aunt Heidi, you come get us sooner. Not like last time."

Heidi took the children to the nurses' station and returned to find Lily leaning over Nara, calling her name softly. Nara's cheekbones had become more prominent, the outline of her lips more defined. The softness that overlaid her features just a day ago was retreating. They arranged the chairs next to each other, Heidi taking the one nearer the bed.

"You met with Dr. Singh this morning?" Lily began.

"Yes, a very young man and very tired. He did not say much about Nara. He just says about her kind of Indian and alcohol." Heidi was unable to keep the bitterness out of her voice. "He says we wait for Nara, to see if she comes back, and she will. It has been only two days."

"He's a good doctor, Heidi. He hasn't been here long but time will humble him."

Heidi shrugged, biting down on her bottom lip as her eyes traveled from Lily to Nara. She got up and walked to the window. The Mercedes sat forlornly in its parking spot, the little white tufted seeds from the cottonwood trees covering its hood attested to its prolonged wait. She hadn't noticed the seeds when she walked by on her way to the motel. She could feel the dread that started that morning slowly compressing her chest as she tried to inhale.

Without turning around, she said, "Dr. Singh said you had things to tell me about Nara."

"Yes, I do. Please come and sit."

Lily made a show of removing some papers from her briefcase, although she knew the numbers. Some days and some cases were harder than others, and for anyone in social services, papers were a helpful prop.

"Nara's blood alcohol was 0.17 when she was brought into the ER," Lily began. "That is over twice the legal limit. It would have been higher when she was driving. And the children were in the car. She was driving above the speed limit when the car went off the road. Heidi, if Nara recovers, there are child endangerment charges that need to be addressed."

"They will all stay with me and we will address the charges," Heidi said, wrapping her arms tightly around herself.

"Yes, I understand that's your intention." Lily put papers in her briefcase and removed a list of questions. "Now I'm going to ask you some of the questions from yesterday over again. See if you can give me more definitive answers now that some of the shock has settled."

Heidi nodded.

"How long were Nara and your brother together?"

"Not long."

"How did you meet Nara?"

"Through my brother."

Lily sighed. "You are not close to your brother, but you are very close to Nara, but they were not together long?"

In a voice husky with exhaustion, Heidi answered, "Nara

lives with me in Riverton, before and after the babies are born. Four months before and fifteen months after. I saw them born."

Yesterday she had told the twins that same lie too, but surely saying she had actually witnessed the babies' emergence into the world would confer legitimacy to her claim of being family. There was no point saying that after she found out she had missed the twin's birth; she had taken several hours to prepare herself for meeting them.

"Witnessing a birth is very special," agreed Lily. "Now tell me, why did Nara leave Riverton when she did?"

"Her father becomes ill and he wants to meet his grandsons."

"Why had he not seen them before? They were fifteen months old when Nara took them away. Her father's house was less than an hour away. "

Heidi looked at Lily Brown in shock. They had been so close? She had driven through the Reservation a year to the day after Nara and the twins had left her, an anniversary of sorts. Through Kinnear, through Crow Heart. The Reservation was almost 3500 square miles, a few small towns, dirt roads disappearing off Highway 26, over hills, down arroyos, houses and trailers in the distance. Those near the highway had little to distinguish them except the patterns of the rust on their propane tanks. She didn't approach any homes this time, but she stopped in a few stores in Ethete and Fort Washakie. Her questions were met with shrugs. Nara Crow and twins? No, not around here.

All those many, many months, could they really have been so close? A sudden thought struck her. Had Nara come into Riverton to shop? Most people from the Reservation did. Had Nara seen her, but ducked out of the way to avoid being seen in return? How long had Nara stayed at her father's house after he had died? The social worker would expect her to have an answer to this question. As Heidi's thoughts fluttered, she imagined little birds battering themselves against glass and grimaced at the image.

"*Halt! Reiß dich zusammen,*" she told herself fiercely. 'Stop! Pull yourself together.'

The accident had happened. It was an opportunity, a sign life must now change. When Nara was released from the hospital, they would take a trip to the ocean. California, Oregon, Nara could choose. If they liked it there, they could open a small restaurant in a seaside town, family style, no alcohol served.

Lily watched Heidi with interest. The frowns, the small shakes of her head, lips moving, the occasional German word or phrase. The woman was an open book, albeit written in a foreign language. Like so many well-intentioned people, Heidi would try to shoulder Nara Crow's illness, sweep the house daily for alcohol, think of moving the family away to escape the addiction. The German woman was enterprising; she'd think of opening a business elsewhere, probably a restaurant, family style, no alcohol served. The children helping in the kitchen, adorable, doing their homework at a table after hours, everyone happy and healthy. What Heidi Vogel didn't realize was that the disease moved with you, there was no escape.

The sounds from Nara's machines were a constant, almost hypnotic presence. Heidi looked up when she became conscious of the social worker's eyes upon her. The last question had been something about Nara's father, she was almost sure.

"Nara has the more deep feeling for her mother," Heidi offered. "She goes to help her father, but they are not so close."

Lily Brown gripped her pen and resisted clicking it. This wasn't getting them any further down the road. She withdrew a copy of Danny Crow's death certificate from her briefcase and put it in Heidi's lap. Heidi was forced to grab it before it slid to the floor.

"Daniel Crow died on June 18th, 1994." Lily pointed to the document. "No one seems to know exactly when Nara left her father's house, but when the landlord goes to pick up the rent check, the house is vacant. After Nara's father dies, she doesn't contact you. Why do you think this is?"

"I am not sure. I am sorry." Heidi shook her head and sat up straighter. "I have these same questions also. Nara will have to tell us." She handed the death certificate back to Lily without looking at it.

Lily went on, "Nara's tie to the Reservation is very important when we consider the welfare of the children. The community is very tight-knit; aunts, uncles, cousins, grandparents, close family friends, they all gather round when needed. The isolation of the Crow family is most unusual. It may stem from animosity directed specifically toward Danny Crow. There is a rumor he worked with the Feds to stay out of jail during the altercation between the government and AIM, the American Indian Movement, at Pine Ridge in the 70's."

"I do not know of this altercation when I am the child in Germany," said Heidi. "And again, I tell you, she does not talk about her father so much."

"Okay," Lily bit her lips and checked her watch. She didn't have the time to discuss even briefly the unrest of the 70's. Since Heidi Vogel might well wind up becoming the repository of family history for Amadeus and Marcela, right now she needed to relay the rest of the information she had been able to glean on Nara Crow's family.

Lily summarized where she could. Danny Crow had been abandoned in Utah as a little boy. His tribal affiliation was unknown, but the social worker that interviewed him wrote in her file that she thought the child had been trying to say he was Choctaw or Chippewa. To a small boy, the words could have sounded similar. Regardless, he may have been very far from home. He was adopted by Mormons, received a sizable inheritance his parents passed away, although he was estranged. He met his wife in college, and apparently learned some Arapaho from her.

"Nara is fluent in Arapaho," said Heidi, finding the story of Nara's father as an abandoned child heart wrenching. "She probably has taught it to the twins."

"Probably? You don't know?" At Heidi's silence, Lily sighed. Was she really going to be able to sign papers claiming Heidi Vogel was a relation? Nara had an uncle who moved to Montana with his immediate family several years ago, but Lily had been unable to track him down.

She asked if Nara had ever talked about relatives, friends, anyone from Wind River.

"Why do you ask me questions about her reservation life and the people she knows?" Heidi retorted. "Why do you not wait for Nara to answer them?"

Lily stared at her, eyes wide and Heidi flinched at the frustration she saw there.

"Because Nara *obviously* can't help us right now, that is why Heidi, and it's right now that counts for these kids."

"I know." Heidi swallowed. "I am sorry."

Lily wrote on her form, tucked it into her briefcase and took out another.

She continued, voice controlled, patient, "If Nara's recovery is delayed, we may be able to arrange for the twins to go with you under certain parameters, but for this to occur, we will need a background check, fingerprints, that sort of thing. If Nara recovers sufficiently to live with you, social services will continue to monitor her and provide wellness checks on the children."

"But the children are healthy. They love their mother." Heidi could hear the plea in her voice.

"I'm preparing for all possible contingencies here," Lily said evenly.

"What does this mean, these contingencies? Nara has only two days since her accident." Heidi then addressed Nara, "Dr.

Singh says you can come back at any time."

Lily's pen went click, click, click, as she tried to control her exasperation. "Heidi, *listen* to me. Nara may not be able to take care of the children for some time. She may *never* wake up or she may live and keep drinking, keep endangering those children."

Heidi took Nara's hand, shocked that Lily would talk like this in front of Nara. But she didn't protest, not now. When Nara was better, they would jump through Lily Brown's hoops together. They wouldn't have alcohol in the house. They would concentrate on raising the children.

"Have the kids mentioned 'That Shit Sean' to you?" Lily asked.

Heidi shook her head.

"Because that's how Amadeus refers to the man they were living with in Ten Sleep. The twins may have heard Nara say it, maybe just once, but I'll bet it describes him perfectly. I think he's responsible for the cigarette burns on Marcela's back."

The bug bites. Appalled, Heidi realized she should have made the connection. A waitress who had worked at Café Claus had the same small round scars on her arms. She said they were childhood burns from her father's cigarettes. But one day she came to work wearing a scarf and Claus had asked her to remove it, saying waitresses didn't wear scarves. Fresh wounds had been revealed, fierce red marks. Claus had sent the girl home. She had been absorbed into New York's faceless crowds and never returned. Heidi had been haunted for weeks. She knew she should have done more to find the girl and offer help, but then Peter had been born and there was no time to care for anyone else.

"Something tipped the balance," Lily continued. "There are no old scars. These wounds are just a few days old. They may well be the reason Nara took off so suddenly. The twins refused to talk about the marks to the intake nurse, but the trained eye can detect cigarette burns every time."

"Why do they not tell me Marcela is burned with the cigarette when I ask about the bug bites when they take the shower?"

"Because they're five years old, Heidi, and their little five-year-old selves could well think they did something to cause the burns. They may think they're at fault, that they're responsible for getting their mother hurt. They have clammed up. They're just trying to get through this."

Heidi looked at Nara in the bed, remote, absent, and said softly, *"Es ist gut, Nara hört das."*

"Heidi?"

"I say, 'It is good Nara hears this.'"

Lily closed her eyes and prayed for patience before saying, "The kids were very anxious at the park this morning, did I tell you that? After fifteen minutes, they wanted to come back here where we're taking good care of their mother. Their Aunt Heidi has arrived and That Shit Sean can't find them, not here. Outside the hospital, they're afraid."

"Do you think he will come looking for them?" Heidi looked to the door in alarm.

"The kids? Not for the kids, but who knows what he thinks his claim to Nara is." Click, click went Lily's pen. "Without her, the kids are nothing, just pawns, bones of contention to beat the mother with. The children, of course, don't understand how unimportant they are to him."

Heidi remained silent. They would have to move, find a life elsewhere. It was the only way to be safe.

"Heidi, so are you?"

"Sorry, again please?"

"The kids. They're little survivors; they're viewing you as their back-up plan. I don't know what it's going to look like, but if necessary, are you willing to try for that?"

Heidi nodded. "Yes, to be the back-up plan."

"Then listen carefully because I can only say this once,"

Lily said, venturing into territory she hoped never to enter again. Her pen clicked rapidly until she grimaced and dropped it in her briefcase.

Heidi steeled herself and forced her eyes to meet Lily's. "Yes?"

"You and the children claim you are their aunt. Remember this and own it. If I, too, choose to believe you're Auntie, I won't have to beat the bushes looking for your brother. You understand me, am I correct?"

Heidi nodded wordlessly. She had absorbed the lie so completely she would swear to any authority that her bloodline flowed through these children.

"Then, we get you fingerprinted today. The police station can do it and the children will need to come. They can't be left alone in the hospital, so I will have to accompany you off the premises until you're cleared."

"I have a motel room just over there." Heidi pointed out the window.

"Good, but let me repeat, the kids can't be there alone with you until your fingerprints clear. They can go into emergency foster care tonight and we can regroup tomorrow, bring you all back together then."

Heidi stood up with alarm at the threat of placing the children with strangers. Would they believe strangers would protect them from Sean?

She sat down on the edge of Nara's bed and faced Lily directly. "May we stay again together with Nara in the hospital tonight?"

"This new protocol of having young ones stay by their mother works better if there are some signs of response from her." Lily got up to check the chart on the wall. "The doctor and the nurses haven't seen any."

"The machines cannot tell how she hears. They are for the heart and oxygen."

Lily returned to her chair. "Okay, you've been by her side.

You need to clearly tell me you see indications of response."

"I do. I see indications of response."

"And these indications are?"

"When I talk and hold her hand, I feel she is with me."

Lily, such a loyal Agent of the State, fed Heidi her next lines, "She squeezes your hand, doesn't she? She does that when you talk. Heidi, *you* need to say it."

Heidi looked at the monitor, the trace of Nara's heartbeat, and affirmed, "Yes, she squeezes my hand when I talk."

Lily sat back down and wrote rapidly. When done, she dropped her pen in her briefcase, put the papers away and gave Heidi a determined smile.

"Okay, get the kids, Aunt Heidi, while I arrange another night here. The fingerprint guy closes shop in an hour so we have to hustle. Richard is working the night shift again. He'll help. He thinks Nara hears us too."

CHAPTER TWENTY SEVEN

NARA SLIPS AWAY

They slept by her bed as Nara slipped from life in the weak light of early dawn.

That evening Amadeus had put a thin arm around Heidi's neck and buried his face in her shoulder, his little body trembling. Heidi shut her eyes tight as she heard him say, "She's going away. I can feel her going away."

Marcela turned from stroking Nara's hair and said, "I want to lie with Mama."

Heidi nodded and Marcela climbed onto the bed. She wormed her way under Nara's arm and laid her head on her mother's breast. Amadeus watched his sister settle and walked over to claim Nara's other side. He curled up and draped his arm protectively over her stomach.

Heidi pressed her forehead against the cold glass of the window. Outside the world stretched endlessly. Inside this cloistered room, life telescoped inward, the beep of machines, the air temperature fluctuating less than a degree, the light: bright, dim or off. The reflection of her face in the glass was alien, her haunted eyes enormous, the dark smudges beneath them absorbed by the night.

The cottonwoods that bordered the lit parking lot beckoned, their limbs waving in the wind that swept down from the high prairie. She had heard their wood was weak and a litter of smaller, broken branches lay on the pavement amid the fluffy white cotton of the cottonwood seeds. Through the trees' black silhouettes, she could make out the bright red and yellow sign of the Super 8 Motel. She still needed to move her car.

Marcela began a gentle chant, *"No no no noooo . . . No no no."*

Every second 'no' was a low note, every fourth 'no' faded, then a high, a low and a high until she began again. She continued as Amadeus fell asleep, the rhythm unfaltering until she raised her head and said, "Aunt Heidi?"

Heidi quickly wiped her cheeks with her palm and turned from the window.

"When Mama's heart doesn't beat, is she dead then?"

Heidi caught her breath and nodded.

"She's not dead," said Marcela. "I can hear it."

She wriggled her way back under Nara's arm and soon Heidi could hear her breathing match her brother's, and they lay, limbs entangled in the bedding and their mother's limp arms.

Richard came in as the nursing shift changed.

"I will need one side to tend to her," he said, looking at the sleeping children.

He and Heidi made up the children's bed and as they tried to remove Amadeus without waking him, his mother's arm suddenly contracted, holding him in place.

Heidi's heart leapt. "Is this the response? She is trying to hold him?"

The pity she saw in Richard's eyes pulled a sob from her throat.

"Even comatose patients may have contractions," he said gently. "Her heart is beating and she breathes on her own because there's activity in her vital reflex centers. Her lower brain retains some control over her muscles."

"But we do not know it is a contraction without meaning."

"I'm talking from experience, but no, we don't really know. Her arm has relaxed now. We can move Amadeus."

As the night progressed, Heidi dozed but she sensed Richard coming in more frequently. At one point she got up and helped him move Marcela from Nara's side and they tucked her in next to her brother. Heidi awoke to Richard's hand on her shoulder and she sat up. With the dim hallway light behind him, his face was so dark she couldn't make out his expression.

"Come," he whispered and drew her by the hand into the hall. "She's gone," he said gently, holding Heidi as she sagged against him.

She heard a sound, more animal than human, a ragged wail that she muffled by clamping her hands over her mouth. Then fiercely, shaking her head, she whispered harshly, "No, she stays, she stays. She has just returned to me."

She pressed her forehead into Richard's bony shoulder and they leaned against the wall, she could barely breathe, smothered under a cloak of exhaustion and loss.

In time, Richard said, "We need to wake the children and tell them. You may stay with her for a while, until you're ready. There is no rush."

But they didn't stay long, not after Nara had gone. As she cooled, she curled in on herself, her lips tightened, exposing even white teeth. As she withdrew, blood vessels constricted, her skin became sallow and waxy, and her spirit became clearly defined by its very absence.

Richard found an empty waiting room with a couch and brought blankets.

"I do not know what we do now," said Heidi, putting a blanket over the children on the couch. She glanced at the children and whispered, "How to we take care of her body?"

"I phoned Lily," said Richard. "She'll be here in a couple of hours and she will guide you on what needs to be done with Nara and what you and the children will do after. Now you try to get some rest."

He left the room silently on crepe-soled shoes. Did nurses always wear them when they dealt with death?

And Peter would have been ten, if had he lived.

Lily found Heidi sitting upright on a sofa; her head tipped back, eyes shut and mouth slightly open. Her arms enclosed blanketed bundles on either side.

She called a soft, "Hello."

Heidi started, opening exhausted red-rimmed eyes, underscored by smudges so dark they looked like they had been painted on.

The children's heads lifted and they tried to nestle even closer to Heidi, refusing to look at Lily when she said, "I am so sorry."

Marcela whispered, "I have to pee."

Heidi nodded to the bathroom door, "Leave the door open. I will be right here. Amadeus, you go with your sister."

Heidi watched them as they took their blankets with them, wrapped tightly around their shoulders, the exemplar of Native children from an era past.

"With Nara gone, what is it that we do now?" Heidi asked.

Lily reached for her hand. "You will have to make decisions regarding her remains and we have to discuss options for the children until your clearance comes through. Richard's shift has ended but he's staying to take the kids to the cafeteria for breakfast. There is coffee in my office and I brought muffins, so we can eat while we make our plans."

Lily had expedited Heidi's fingerprint clearance, but it would still be several more days before the results came through. A preliminary background check listed Heidi Vogel as a Permanent Resident Alien. She had arrived in New York with her, now ex-husband, Claus Vogel, in 1982. The couple opened a very successful restaurant in Manhattan. In 1985, she buried a baby boy, Peter Vogel, death due to pneumonia complicated by cystic fibrosis.

Later records showed Heidi managing Saint Gemma's Kitchen, a charity in Riverton. In 1992, a business license for the Hebeka Shortbread Company was issued in Riverton to Heidi Vogel and two limited partners residing in Germany and Italy, Karl Engel and Beppe Biro, who had provided financial backing. Heidi owned sixty percent of the business and the men forty percent. Hebeka now distributed to high-end food purveyors in major metropolitan areas on both coasts. Heidi continued to manage the charity kitchen. It appeared she was a woman of both enterprise and mission, and she was more than financially secure.

When Lily had arrived in the U.S. as a young child with her mother and brother, social services had provided for them and she didn't hesitate when it came time to declare her major in college. Social workers saved lives.

She knew the necessity for checklists and rules. If a rule no longer worked, it needed to be re-evaluated and, following specific procedures, it could be changed. Lily worked by the book but, in the case of the Crow children, the book needed new chapters and it needed them immediately.

No man was listed as father on the twins' birth certificates. Heidi wouldn't have been thinking about that when she made her claim to the sister of a Claus Brown and twin's aunt. Nara's death made it next to impossible to track down the real father.

After a long history of Native children being stolen from their families, placed in boarding schools and forced to lose their culture, the adoption of Native American children by white parents had become a complex and lengthy process and required tribal consent. Danny Crow's history made him a pariah, and his daughter hadn't done anything to mend that. Nara's wishes, if they could be defined, carried weight in determining the future of her children and she obviously had a strong relationship with Heidi. She had written Heidi's phone number on Amadeus's arm, a lifeboat masquerading as a black sharpie pen.

Foster care was an option. The State would maintain legal custody of the children, provide financial support and continue to monitor their health and welfare. However, the State was ill-equipped to advocate for transgender children and Heidi Vogel had shown the strength and commitment to parent. Given the woman's financial resources, Lily thought they should pursue a legal guardianship and award Heidi all physical, legal and financial responsibilities.

The Rule stated that the twins should be placed in emergency foster care until Heidi's fingerprints cleared. Lily didn't bend The Rule, she broke it and allowed Heidi to take the twins back to her motel room that evening.

At eight o'clock, Lily arrived at the motel to find two little cots had been moved into the room and the twins taking a bubble bath. She saw a child's pink T-shirt that matched Heidi's and another in blue and two pairs of small navy-blue sweat pants, neatly folded on a little table.

"Are these Richard's chocolate chip cookies?" Lily asked as she sat on the bed, talking to Heidi through the open bathroom door. She took a large cookie from the several dozen sitting on a plate by the television and thanked God for her brother.

"Yes. He drops them off on his way to work and I am so lucky. They are all for me because the children say they do not like walnuts. Please help me eat them."

"Happy to lend a hand." Lily unabashedly reached for another.

A squabble broke out in the bathtub as Amadeus blew a handful of bubbles at his sister and she claimed they hurt her eyes. When Heidi threatened to pull out the plug, Marcela's eyes no longer hurt and Heidi agreed to five more minutes.

After their bath, Heidi settled the children in front of the television and she and Lily stepped outside so Lily could check the seat belts in the car.

"I always wanted a Mercedes," Lily tugged at a seatbelt. "Don't see many of them around here." She breathed in deeply. "Smell the leather. Red leather, unbelievable."

"I worked hard for this car," Heidi said. "It will be a good one for us now."

They leaned against the side of the car and spoke in low voices.

"How are they doing?" Lily asked, nodding over at the motel room.

"They will not talk about Nara. They like the motel. They want snacks from the gift shop, soda, candy. They whine and argue. When I sit down, they are there right away, hanging on. They do not ask questions, they just say, 'I want, I want.'"

Lily saw the fatigue etched on Heidi's face, but there was a glint of humor too. "This will get harder, Heidi," she warned. "They know their mother is dead, but they don't really understand she is gone forever. They're afraid of answers, so they don't ask questions. We don't really know what their days have been like for the past three and a half years. Are you up for this? They may regress. They will act out. They will push at you, and they'll be angry."

"You know that animal, with beautiful hair and a tail like the rat, but it is much bigger than the rat?' asked Heidi. "Lots of teeth?"

At Lily's look of confusion, Heidi added, "The one with a pouch. She keeps her babies in a pouch until they are older, then they cling to her back as she travels."

"The opossum?"

"Yes, that one. Nara and I are the opossum. She is the pouch; I am the back. I carry them now, until it is time for them to let go."

Lily reached for Heidi's hand and drew her into an embrace. They stood in the stark blue light of the mercury vapor lamp that bathed the motel's parking lot and Heidi drew comfort from Lily's soft scent of nutmeg and vanilla.

A chorus of "Heidi, Heidi, Heidi" started up inside the motel room. The door opened a crack and a little brown face peeped out.

"Just two more minutes," Heidi held up two fingers, "then we walk to the office and buy the chocolate."

"*Yay.*" The door slammed shut.

Heidi walked Lily to her car, parked opposite the Mercedes.

"This morning you said cremation," Lily said as she opened her car door.

"Yes, I will take the ashes with me. You can arrange this?"

"Yes."

"I will be there, but I think not the children."

"No, not the children. You can explain the ashes when they're older. My brother spent more time with Nara than I did and he wants to go with you. I will wait with the twins."

The motel door opened wide.

"Chocolate. You said two minutes, Aunt Heidi," Amadeus whined. "It's been like two *million.*"

Marcela pushed in front of him. "We each get our own chocolate. It's no fair sharing *all* the time. You got cookies, so we get chocolate."

"Marcela gets to be on piggyback down there, and I get piggyback on the way back," said Amadeus.

Lily chuckled. "Oh, I have *such* respect for opossums now. Be sure they say thank you."

CHAPTER TWENTY EIGHT

FROM CASPER TO RIVERTON

When Heidi was allowed to take Marcela and Amadeus back to Riverton, Lily Brown came to see them off, bringing chocolate chip cookies *without* nuts from Richard for the children.

"Marcela's situation is not unique," Lily murmured to Heidi as she gave her a hug and pressed a letter from Richard into her hand. "My brother's story. He says to phone him anytime."

On the way out of town, Heidi and the children stopped at the Highway Patrol Headquarters to pick up a box containing what had been salvaged from Nara's car.

"Just some clothes, a real pretty beaded necklace, and an envelope of photos," said the woman behind the desk as Heidi signed for Nara's belongings. She checked Heidi's driver's license carefully, looking from her to the license several times before nodding and handing a small cardboard box over the counter.

"No, wait," said the woman, as they prepared to leave. She grabbed a big book sitting on a desk. "You'll have to forgive us. We were looking at some of the pictures yesterday. Hard to believe all those creatures live in the sea."

Heidi took Nara's book, and unable to speak, nodded her thanks.

"You'll all be just fine now. God is with you. You just talk to Him," the woman said with an encouraging smile.

The children wanted to look at the photos right away but agreed to wait until lunch. Of course, that meant stopping at the first roadside restaurant they spied. Heidi opened the trunk and wedged the urn of Nara's ashes a little more securely behind the spare tire before retrieving a manila envelope from the box. Their belongings were so few that she knew the twins had seen the urn when she opened the trunk, but they didn't remark on it.

She handed the envelope to Amadeus, who held it away from his sister and said, "First we have to order our food, right Aunt Heidi?"

A waitress led them to a booth and watched as the three of them arranged themselves on the same side of the table, with Heidi in the middle.

"Me and my sister, we always put our mama in the middle too," she said, handing out glossy menus with large colorful pictures of burgers, sandwiches and milkshakes. "You kids want crayons and placemats you can draw on?"

Marcela shook her head and Amadeus answered, "No, thank you. We're busy."

After ordering, the twins took turns reaching into the envelope to pull out a photo, explaining the people they recognized to Heidi. Marcela pulled out a picture of a handsome older couple seated on a sofa with a television set on in the background. The man had a narrow face, deep-set eyes and grey braids. He wore a plaid shirt and his long legs were stretched out before him, boots crossed at the ankles. He had his arm around a small woman who leaned against him, smiling shyly into the camera. Her feet barely touched the floor.

"That's Grandpa," Marcela said. "We lived with him in the blue house. The lady wasn't there. She was dead already. She was our Grandma. Mama's mama."

Amadeus said, so quietly that Heidi had to lean close, "Grandpa was old. Sometimes he was fun but sometimes he got mad."

"He liked Amadeus more. He only got mad at me. And Mama sometimes," said Marcela, looking down at the table, as if ashamed.

Amadeus bowed his head under the burden of being the favored child and murmured, "I don't think so."

"Yes, he *did*." Marcela glared at her brother before turning to Heidi. "He said Mama was soft on me and he said it's Mama's fault I'm a girl."

Amadeus continued to shake his head slowly back and forth as he reached in the envelope for another picture. He drew out a photo of a slender teenaged girl leaning against the side of a battered red pickup truck. She wore black boots, and a short, ruffled skirt. Her denim shirt was tied high to expose her navel. Her long black hair was swept over one shoulder and she laughed into the camera, head tilted. The orange, blue and red beaded necklace she wore around her neck was now safely in the box in the trunk of the Mercedes.

"It's Mama," the twins cried in unison, their eyes bright with delight.

Heidi looked at Nara's young, carefree face, full of life and possibilities. Was the joy she saw there just for that one moment in time? Or had there been days, weeks, even months of looking to a future where dreams held true? Heidi felt weariness settle in her bones. When had life for this beautiful girl become such labor?

When their food arrived, Marcela propped her mother's picture against the napkin dispenser so Nara could watch them eat their meal.

"Restaurants have good food, don't they Aunt Heidi?" said Amadeus, tucking into a hamburger almost too big for his mouth.

Marcela offered Nara's picture a French fry, then grinned

279

at Heidi. "Mama says I have to eat it," she popped it in her mouth, "and she says she doesn't need it because in Heaven she has that hospital bag in her arm."

"Sugar," nodded Amadeus wisely, "and water."

They looked at Heidi uncertainly and she shrugged and smiled, trying to find her voice.

"Aunt Heidi, maybe it's just water in the bag, huh, because she doesn't need the food part anymore." Amadeus looked at Heidi, his eyes wary.

"But everybody always needs water," said Marcela. "Water and sleep, and Mama gets to sleep as much as she wants to now." She reached over and adjusted Nara's picture, which threatened to topple on its face.

The children wanted pie, although they hadn't been able to finish their burgers, and Heidi had managed only half an egg sandwich. Heidi pointed out they had Richard's cookies in the trunk, but they sighed in unison, crossed their arms, pouted, until they thought better of that tactic, smiled at her winsomely and said, "Aunt Heidi, *please?*"

"Pie is supposed to be apple, right?" Marcela asked Heidi, interrupting the waitress who began to list the pie offerings, starting with coconut cream, pecan and chocolate silk.

Heidi wondered if a good parent would say yes to pie if more than a half of each burger and most of the French fries hadn't been eaten. She was relieved when the waitress offered to cut a slice of apple pie in half and put it on separate plates. It seemed a reasonable compromise.

As they waited for their dessert, the children turned back to the envelope. They didn't know who the faces were in the next few pictures, friends or relatives perhaps? Then Amadeus pulled out one Heidi recognized. She had a copy at home and she remembered that day. She and Nara had taken Gering to the park for his morning walk, the weather windy and crisp. Bits of dry leaves had clung to Gering's determined little form and he stopped frequently to shake them off.

They had strolled arm in arm, laughing so hard at something Heidi could no longer remember that they literally ran into a neighbor, who had said, "Whoa", then, "You look so happy, you two. Let me take a picture."

He dropped two prints through their mail slot the following week.

"I asked him for two," Nara had explained. "It's better to have two, just in case."

'Just in case.' Nara had been thinking even then, that she and her babies might go away.

"Look how big Mama is. We were in there," the twins pointed at Nara's belly with wonder. "Right in there."

"I know. I tell you before, I am there for your birth." She described how brave Nara was, how beautiful they were. The nurse had bathed them and brushed their hair on top of their heads. They looked so much the same, no one could tell them apart.

"But you and Mama could tell us apart," insisted Marcela.

"No," said her brother. "Nobody could. Aunt Heidi just said."

They looked at Heidi for a response.

"We could tell just the tiniest bit who is who, but nobody else could," she said.

"How much more driving, Aunt Heidi?" asked Marcela as they piled back in the car after lunch.

"About one hundred more miles. It is less than two hours."

"But we've been driving already like a hundred miles." Marcela pursed her lips fretfully.

"No, only twenty. You take a nap, the afternoon siesta. Then you wake up and there we are, at our home."

Marcela gave a long-suffering sigh and refused to let Heidi help her with the seat belt. She reached for her blanket and draped it over her head with a little slit arranged for her eyes.

Heidi started the car and put a tape of Mozart's *Die Zaubertflöte* into the tape deck. The Magic Flute, a birthday gift from Karl and Beppe.

"Too loud?" She turned around and the twins nodded, so she turned the music down and pulled the car onto the road.

When the first aria came on, Amadeus said, "That's not English singing."

"It is German."

"You speak German?"

"Yes, I was born there, in Germany. I tell you this already."

"But you like it here better, you like being here with us."

"Yes, I like being with you and Marcela. You are American so I choose America."

"Okay," said Amadeus.

Heidi concentrated on the road and the rolling Wyoming landscape, comforted by her language and Wolfgang Amadeus Mozart's romantic tale of duplicity and foolery. Oh to have a magic flute to turn sorrow into joy. Such a flute had assisted the innocent and steadfast Tamino in his trials of fire and water.

She, Karl and Beppe had driven to Turin on New Year's Eve a year ago, a lifetime ago now. She had flown to Italy for Christmas and they had attended a production of The Magic Flute at the Teatro Regio Torino. As they entered the opera house's elliptical auditorium, they had been enclosed by arterial red, from the carpet to the walls, the curtain and the velvet seats that enfolded them. From the ceiling, thousands of translucent vertical stems of light shone down, like icicles.

After they took their seats, Karl leaned over and whispered, "Only the lights save me from feeling I have been swallowed by a great, bloody beast."

Beppe frowned but Heidi had to agree.

In Act One an enormous black serpent filled the stage, a puppet pushed and pulled by dancers in black leotards, and it as writhed around Tamino, his clear tenor voice cried out. To whom? Who did he implore with that beautiful voice to save him, as the snake raised its massive head to strike? Was it to God? Is there a God?

Heidi turned the music up a notch and the twins didn't protest. They drove by the exit for Hell's Half Acre, a nightmarish chaos of rocky spires carved by an ancient offshoot of the Powder River. Despite its name, the gorge covered three hundred and twenty acres. She imagined taking the twins there to explore the alien landscape, perhaps after winter but before the snakes woke from their winter sleep.

She was coming to love this land that humbled civilization, so much of it withholding the resources necessary for a comfortable life. The land commanded respect and crushed the weak or unlucky. It offered pockets of luxury in the Northwest corner that sequestered the rich and their tax dollars and protected much of the badlands from human interference.

Heidi glanced in the rear-view mirror, expecting to see the children asleep, but each looked out their nearest window, Marcela's eyes peeping through her blanket, Amadeus with lips in silent conversation with his reflection in the glass.

Marcela fell asleep before Act Two. Tamino had no idea of the trials to come.

Just before the evil Queen of the Night hit a high F in one of opera's most famous arias, Amadeus leaned forward and whispered, "Aunt Heidi?"

She glanced in the mirror and turned off the music when she saw his face wet with tears. She reached her hand back awkwardly between the front seats.

Amadeus stretched himself forward and took her hand and held it tight, "I stole girl clothes from the washing place for Marcela. She put them on and he saw and he burned her."

"Okay, Amadeus. It is okay." With a squeeze, Heidi withdrew her hand and pulled the Mercedes off the highway onto a gravel drive that led to a cattle guard and a metal gate.

She turned around in her seat. "Sean burned Marcela for this?"

Amadeus shuddered, looked out the window and nodded. Marcela woke up and dragged the blanket off her head.

She looked from her brother to Heidi, "Amadeus is crying, Aunt Heidi."

"Yes, we are going to get out for the moment. Do you want to come out too?"

Marcela looked dubiously out the window. "Too windy," she said plaintively, looking from her brother to Heidi. She sunk down in her seat and pulled the blanket up under her chin.

Heidi got out of the car and opened Amadeus's door.

"Come, it is not so windy," she said as her hair whipped around her face.

They sat side by side on the rough gravel, using the car as a windbreak. Heidi took a napkin from her pocket and wiped Amadeus's face. The wind claimed the napkin as she tried to hand it over to him. They gave each other a guilty smile.

"Okay, we litter, but see? The wind takes your tears away. There are many things more powerful than we are. Now you tell me."

She took his hand and they watched a tiny bird peek out from a creosote bush. It fluffed its feathers and hunched its wings, its stick-like legs and toes hanging on as the winds blew. It turned its head from one side to the other, examining them with impossibly tiny black eyes.

Heidi turned to the small boy at her side, "You tell me what happened, Amadeus."

He pulled his hand away and wrapped his arms around his knees. He said, in a voice hollow with exhaustion, "We were in the bedroom. We have to stay there when they drink and he's not supposed to come in, but he *did*. He pulled Marcela's dress off, then he burned her."

He clamped his lips shut to stop their trembling and rested his forehead on his arms.

Heidi placed her hand on his back. "You tell me all of it, Amadeus, then I help to carry it. You will see. It will be better."

He nodded and looked up as Marcela knocked on her window. Heidi smiled up at her and held up a finger.

Heidi started to speak but Amadeus interrupted and said quickly, "Mama hit him and he hit her and Mama yelled "get in the car, *get, get, get.*" Then yelling and the more yelling and the more and more, then she came outside with some stuff and we left. Then the car crashed when we were driving down the long hill. The part where it . . ." he made a curving motion with his hand. He stared at Heidi, his chin quivering, "And Mama's dead 'cause the dress made him mad."

Heidi drew him to her. "We will blame Sean for this. You hear me, Amadeus? It is *all* Sean, not us."

They leaned back against the car and watched the long prairie grasses weave and feint. The wind offered the scent of sage and a slight whiff of whatever had attracted the vultures circling over the ravine on the opposite side of the road. Puffs of cloud sped across the faded blue sky, casting shadows on low hills as they eclipsed the sun. When they heard Marcela wail from the car, Amadeus stood up and attempted to pull Heidi to her feet.

Before she started the engine, Heidi said, "In a few miles we drive through a beautiful canyon. We will stop at a park by a big lake and use the bathroom and see if there are frogs by the shore. We stretch our legs, there is a pretty walk along a river. I saw a puma track in the mud there once. So big," she rounded her hands to indicate. "If we are lucky, we see a track."

"Maybe we'll see the puma," said Marcela hopefully.

"For this we have to be very, very lucky. They are *such* shy creatures. We stay together and be very quiet and maybe we will."

As they approached the southeastern side of Boysen Reservoir State Park, Heidi pulled off the road and down a steep drive that led to a campground next to the Wind River. Cliffs of orange, yellow and brown strata protected the picnic area from wind. Sharp black rocks asserted themselves in sandy areas where the cliff had crumbled. Cottonwood leaves littered the ground and tiny purple flowers lay in mats along the border of the path that led to the restrooms. After using the restroom, they drank from a water fountain, the children complaining about the water.

"It is mildew," said Heidi, wrinkling her nose.

They walked down a dirt trail to the river, which flowed vigorously over slippery golden rocks. This part of the Wind River was shallow and the brown weeds under its surface added to the precarious slimy thrill of wading to a flat pebbly island in the river's center.

Marcela got there first, unscathed and hopped from leg to leg, shouting her victory as Amadeus and Heidi picked their way carefully through the water

"She's always the fastest," Amadeus said, "but she shouldn't boast, right Aunt Heidi?

"Hey, Marcela," he yelled. "You shouldn't brag about it."

He turned to Heidi and added proudly, "She's so fast. She's not scared of falling. Mama calls her a pronghorn. You've seen them, right? Sometimes they eat grass with the cows. They go where they want. You're not allowed to mess with them."

They lay on the island, listening to the water protesting as the island split it into two channels. The screech of a hawk, the shift of gears as trucks passed on the road high above, the tumble of rock sliding down a cliff nearby, the hum of flies, a fish jumping—the comforting sounds that life continued unabated.

"I want to live here," said Marcela stretching out fully, toes pointed and arms above her head.

"Mmm, me too," said Heidi sleepily, the sun warm on her

face. After a few minutes, she opened an eye and said, "But an island in a river would not suit Gering."

Heidi told them Gering knew them when they were babies. At first, they claimed to remember him. Big and black, said Amadeus; big, white and fluffy, said Marcela. When Heidi described the little dachshund, they said, oh yeah, they remembered him and they agreed, a little dog like that needed a house and a bed.

CHAPTER TWENTY NINE

BRINGING IN INEZ, MASSIMO AND MR. TOLENTINO

Heidi pulled into Saint Gemma's parking lot and told the twins to wait as she ran in to pick up Gering.

"We want to come in too," whined Marcela.

"No. I will be less than a minute."

"We have to pee," said Amadeus.

"If you can hold the pee, tomorrow we will buy chocolate. We will be home in five minutes."

Chocolate. The twins nodded. They could hold it, but Aunt Heidi had better hurry up.

Heidi dashed through the back door, calling hello to the kitchen staff as she ran down the hall to the office. She picked up Gering, who greeted her with barks, whines and wriggles.

"I woulda dropped him off, but I guess you couldn't wait to get your boy. Where are the kids?"

Heidi turned to see Inez grinning behind her. "In the car. I have a big hurry now because they have to use the toilet but I must talk to you and Massimo and Raffi and Mr. Tolentino before you meet them again."

She had listed the members of Saint Gemma's who had already met the twins and knew Marcela as Marcel.

The children agreed to sleep in the second bedroom if the bedroom doors remained open and Gering slept with them. As

Heidi passed their room that night, she heard Marcela whisper, "See? Told you Mama would get us a dog."

"Mama's dead," Amadeus whispered back.

"I know, but she got us one anyway. A good one. He remembers us. Do you remember him?"

"No," said Amadeus. "He used to be bigger."

"No, he didn't," Marcela protested. "He's always been little."

The next morning, Heidi phoned Saint Gemma's and asked Inez to come over to her house to become reacquainted with the twins.

"Why you?" demanded Massimo. "Why reacquainted? Like, she thinks we're gonna scare them or something?"

"I don't know, just sayin' what she said."

"Fuckin' weird," said Massimo,

"Better watch your mouth The boss is back."

"Where? You see her?" Massimo mugged and looked around. "And when's she comin' back to work?"

"In a few days. She's getting the kids settled."

"They're five years old. Why do they need to get settled? She brings them to work, sticks them in the office with coloring books and shit, maybe sets up a little TV. They can help with some chores. They should be going to Kindergarten soon. What's the deal?"

Inez shrugged. Heidi had been kind of mysterious on the phone. Maybe the twins had lice, worms or something.

"You will see. Marcela has changed from how we thought her to be," said Heidi when she opened the door to Inez's knock. "They are in the backyard. They will not remember you, but will you please also not remember them? We start fresh."

"Marcela? What the. . ." Inez began, but Heidi was now down the hall.

Inez returned to Saint Gemma's later than the one hour she said she would be away.

"Relax, I'll cover dinner and you can take off early," she told a disgruntled Massimo, throwing a mock punch at him. She had started boxing at the gym and her coach said she had talent.

"Ow," said Massimo, rubbing his arm.

"Didn't hurt," said Inez, restraining herself from throwing another punch. Maybe the first one had been a little bit more than a love tap. "We gotta go into the office and shut the door while I tell you about this situation. Heidi's going to take care of talking to the McKees but you gotta listen to me. After that, we bring Raffi and Mr. Tolentino in, and if any of you screw up, make this little kid's life any harder, Heidi and I will eat your balls for breakfast."

"Heidi can eat my balls. You can't."

"Shut up and listen. We got a Two Spirit situation here."

Massimo stared at her, mouth open, eyes wide with shock. "Jesus, if that's what I think it is . . ."

"It is. You know what I'm saying. I can tell by you goin' all bug-eyed like that. You got enough Indian in you to be cool with it." Inez was still shaken herself, but after spending time with the twins, she'd come away convinced Marcela was a girl.

'Two Spirit,' was a term that had shown up in the local paper a few years ago. A reporter had attended the third annual Native American/First Nations Gay and Lesbian conference in Winnepeg and brought it back. People still argued about exactly what it meant except, most agreed, it referred to someone who was probably going to have a lot of shit thrown at them.

"I'm Italian and Samoan," Massimo reminded Inez. "Raffi's dad and my dad are two different people. He got the Indian."

"Well, borrow it, Massimo. Jesus, man up. Why do you

always have to be so difficult?"

At first Massimo protested Marcel's transition, saying, "She got a penis; she's a boy, is all I'm saying. Maybe a little homo boy, that's okay, but a boy." They sat and bickered awhile, old friends who refused to acknowledge the attraction between them.

Massimo eventually came around, as Inez knew he would.

"What the fuck do I care?" he said with a shrug of his massive shoulders. "You and Heidi want Marcela to be a girl, so she's a girl."

"Good," said Inez. "Now go get Raffi and Mr. Tolentino, and this time you'll explain it and I'll listen and make sure you get it right. Don't make it so as I'm sharpening my knife and heating up oil in my frying pan."

Inez phoned Heidi that night and pronounced everybody cool. All three men had wanted to know what Heidi thought of Marcel's transition, and as usual, what Heidi wanted, Heidi got. They promised they'd get the pronouns right.

In turn, Heidi said Edith McKee had tried to hide her surprise. After Heidi had answered her many questions, Edith insisted Patsy would come around and certainly wouldn't cause any trouble.

"Trouble?" asked Inez.

"No trouble. Edith will not allow it, and she is the dog on the top. Now next week, I bring the twins to you for part of the morning when I go to enroll them in Kindergarten."

That night, as she had done the night before at the twin's insistence, Heidi counted off the number of steps from her bed to each of the twins'. Always twenty-three.

That night, as they had done the night before, the three of them prayed to Nara to watch over them.

CHAPTER THIRTY

THE DISTRICT OFFICE

"Birth certificates, two proofs of residency, vaccination records and, you're the aunt you say?" said the nasal voice over the phone.

"Yes, the aunt but also guardian," responded Heidi.

"Then we'll need proof of guardianship too. I assume you have those papers? And you do realize school starts in two weeks?"

"Yes, I do realize this, but the guardian papers have just arrived. This is the reason I do not register until now."

"All right then," the voice sounded somewhat mollified. "And a photo ID for you, for proof, driver's license preferred, but I expect you have a passport, and that will do if it has to." A heavy sigh. "Tomorrow we close at eleven for a staff meeting. We open at eight."

"Thank you, I . . . " but the registrar had hung up, no goodbye.

The official guardianship papers had arrived with the State Seal of Wyoming imprinted in the upper right-hand corner of the first page. The central figure of a draped woman holding a banner reading 'Equal Rights,' was in reference to Wyoming's distinction of being the first state to allow women the right to vote, but perhaps it could now represent the right of all to be given the dignity that was their due. In the last decade of the Twentieth Century, surely it was time to put prejudice to bed.

After the children were tucked in for the night, Heidi spread the guardianship papers on the kitchen table and drew up a chair. She read each word aloud, then again silently. There was her name, there were the children's names, social worker Lily Brown had signed as witness. The guardianship was unlimited, Heidi was *in loco parentis;* she had the legal right to shepherd the Crow children into adulthood.

Heidi ran her fingertips over the raised notary seal. An evening chill caused her to shudder and she reached for her sweater.

Nara's children were now hers to raise, to enroll in school, their health and welfare now her responsibility for life. Adulthood did not sever a tie like that. She was unaware of her tears until they began to dry, causing her cheeks to itch. She rubbed her palms vigorously over her face. She placed the guardianship papers, the twin's vaccination records, birth certificates, and a utility bill as proof of residency, into the embroidered shoulder bag Karl and Beppe had sent from Munich for her birthday, two years ago.

After a moment's thought, Heidi went to a binder she had put on the bookshelf by her bed. Lily Brown had copied a series of papers for her and Heidi had put them in the binder when they arrived back in Riverton. She selected a paper published by *The Harry Benjamin International Gender Dysphoria Association.* It would provide definitions, if needed.

As she tried to truly understand Marcela, Heidi took comfort from reading about Dr. Benjamin's most famous patient, Christine Jorgensen, who said in 1985, "I am trans*gender* because *gender* refers to who you are as a human." Included in the binder was a copy of a 1982 Associated Press article summarizing a lecture Miss Jorgensen delivered to college students in which she stated, "Sexuality is who you sleep with, but *gender* is who you are."

After Heidi presented her documentation to the school registrar tomorrow, she would bring the papers home, tuck the Benjamin Association definitions back into their binder and place the legal documents in the locked metal box under her bed. They would lie on top of her divorce degree, her citizenship papers, Nara's death certificate and Peter's birth and death certificates. Tomorrow she would approach that nasal voice. They would meet face to face and she would make her request.

Amadeus and Marcela were excited about going to school. Massimo had told them Kindergarten was a blast. They had ignored the punch Inez had given him when he added ominously, "It's all downhill from there."

They whined when Heidi dropped them off at Saint Gemma's in the morning.

"There will be no children there," she explained again. "It is just the grumpy adults at the District Office. Children are next week, when the school starts. Inez has work for you, and you will each earn a dollar."

Armed with all required documentation, Heidi walked the ten blocks to the school district office, practicing her request under her breath in German until she realized and switched to English. Two small additions would have to be made to Marcela's registration form, changes from the birth certificate to speak the truth.

Heidi pushed through glass doors into a small lobby and followed a sign pointing down a poorly lit hallway to the registrar's office. She arrived at a small, stuffy, mustard-colored room and found a woman, presumably the registrar, using a spray bottle and paper towels to wipe the petals of an elaborate arrangement of artificial flowers. The flowers sprang from an ornate, gold and black plastic vase, which stood on a pedestal in the corner.

"Hello, I'm Heidi Vogel to register. . ."

"The Crow twins, yes, your accent gives you away," said the voice, not so nasal in person. Heidi took an involuntary step backward as a long thin neck pivoted a face toward her. When she realized that the highly arched, darkly penciled-in eyebrows were responsible for its look of extreme alarm, Heidi relaxed and attempted a smile.

"So many flowers," she said, looking at the arrangement.

"And a lot of work," a shelf of false eyelashes shuttered the registrar's eyes momentarily. She jutted a firm chin in the direction of her long wooden desk. "You may start by filling in one of the registration forms on the clip board over there, black ink only, block letters. Twins, so obviously you'll need to do everything twice."

She went back to wiping her flowers as Heidi took a seat on a metal folding chair in front of the desk. A cup with a yellow smiley face held an assortment of blue and red pens, no black. Heidi dug through her bag and managed to find a black pen that worked after she shook it several times. She carefully printed the required information on a form for Amadeus.

The registrar returned to her comfortably padded swivel chair and looked a Heidi expectantly. "Two forms, Miss Vogel, one for each."

"I have to explain before I start the form for my niece."

The registrar listened in silence as Heidi asked to write two small corrections. Marcela's school form would not align perfectly with her birth certificate, but it would be very close.

Although impossible for the registrar to look any more surprised, her voice evinced her disapprobation, "Marcela can be his nickname, if that's what you think is best for the child, the kindergarten teacher can call him Marcela, if that's what you *really* want, but he must be registered with the school district in accordance with his birth certificate."

"But the birth certificate is not correct, her name and

gender are not correct. Gender is who you are and on the rare occasion, this is not the same as the anatomy. I have an article and some definitions if you would like to read about transgender people," said Heidi, but the registrar shrank from the papers she offered.

"*Gender?* You want Marcel to be entered into my computer as *fe*male?" The registrar's long neck periscoped her gaze from Heidi to the flower arrangement, as if asking it to share in her disbelief.

The face pivoted back in Heidi's direction, "You apply to the State for a correction to be made, Miss Vogel. This is not something we can do here. Gender is specified on a birth certificate at a hospital, where a baby is born."

The registrar blinked, pursed her lips and attempted unsuccessfully to increase the arc of her eyebrows as she continued, "You may keep your articles and definitions, Miss Vogel. A *doctor* can *see* gender. If an error is made on the birth certificate, you call it to the State's attention right away."

"We may not apply to the state to make the change official until Marcela is eighteen," explained Heidi.

"Even more reason why we cannot approach this very slippery slope, Miss Vogel," the registrar admonished. "We cannot start a precedent. We do not want to slide from information provided by a government document, into a . . ." she searched for what would be at the bottom of a slippery slope ". . . into a crevasse of chaos."

Heidi tried to imagine a crevasse of chaos. Would it be filled with defaced birth certificates? Shredded passports? Maimed driver's licenses? She could imagine Karl rolling his eyes and saying with a shudder, "*Mein Gott,* save us from the tyranny of the petty public servant." He had warned her this might happen; she had been so naïve.

Heidi tried once again, "Since we cannot request this change from the State until Marcela is older, this is just for school, to start at the school as who she is. The precedent? You have had this request before, from a parent or guardian, to change a child's identification on the school registration from male to female?"

"No, Miss Vogel, we have not. People here understand our protocol, so they don't ask. It may be different in some of your European countries, but in Wyoming, we have standards to follow."

"And to make a little girl's enrollment in the kindergarten more comfortable for her, a change that is surely our family business and will harm no other student, you say we have to sacrifice *this* for the protocol?"

The convolutions of that particular sentence and the accent that had become more pronounced, gave the registrar pause until she managed to dredge up, "The greater good, Miss Vogel. I have explained we cannot start a precedent for this kind of thing. In *our* country, in *Wyoming*, we understand the greater good."

The two women locked eyes until the registrar broke away with a shake of her head and began to enter Amadeus's information into her computer.

"We close in a half hour, Miss Vogel," she said without looking up. "Staff meeting. To enroll Marcel Crow, you must fill in his form correctly. Ask his kindergarten teacher to call him Marcela, if you must, but a little boy with a girl's name will be teased."

Heidi sat with her mouth clamped so tightly shut her jaws hurt. She almost crushed the nib of her pen into the paper as she transferred information from Marcela's birth certificate to the second form. She handed it to the registrar who made a show of checking it carefully, initially appearing not to hear as Heidi repeated her request for the name of the principal at Winfield Elementary School.

Perhaps realizing that Heidi was not going to go away until she got the name, the registrar said in a singsong voice, "Mr. Orrin Harris. He follows the rules too, Miss Vogel. We all do."

Heidi returned to Saint Gemma's Kitchen to find lunch well underway and the twins scraping dishes into a bucket before handing them to the dishwasher, a friendly old man who insisted on talking to them in Arapaho. He was pleased how much they understood, although only Amadeus would respond in kind. Marcela refused to speak any language but English, with a smattering of German.

"I have one more chore, not fun for you," Heidi said as the twins protested her second departure. "You finish helping Mr. Hosa and we go to the movie tonight. It is *The Little Mermaid* cartoon, and a mermaid becomes a girl. It is Walt Disney."

"Does she still have a tail?" asked Marcela.

"How's she gonna put clothes on with a tail?" said Amadeus, rolling his eyes. "How's she going to walk?"

"She can wear a dress, a long one and no one can see. The dress can hide the tail, or she gets legs. Or a man could carry her," answered his sister. "A handsome prince."

"We will find out if she keeps the tail," said Heidi. "After I come back, we help set up the dinner and then we take Gering to the park and then we will go to the movies. We will eat lots of popcorn, a big bucket with butter, butter, butter!"

She grabbed Amadeus in a fierce squeeze, but Marcela squealed and darted away.

CHAPTER THIRTY ONE

HONESTY

For the wooing of Principal Orin Harris and the kindergarten teacher, Heidi wrapped two ten-inch shortbread rounds in cellophane and tied each with a broad gold ribbon. Although no one was answering the school phone, from her backyard she had seen activity across the playing field all week. Teachers were preparing their classrooms for the new school year.

She walked home briskly to change into her most becoming blouse, muttering, *"Verdammtes, verdammtes Distriktbüro!"* Damn, damn District Office! The District Office could have their incorrect form. No one there would ever meet Marcela. To them she was just a piece of paper. The school would have its own files on each student. She would ask for modifications on those forms, an '*m*' changed to an '*f*,' an '*a*' added to 'Marcel.' She would make the principal and the teacher understand how important this was.

Rather than take the car, Heidi took a shortcut through her backyard, down the slope of the church graveyard and across the playing field. She inhaled deeply as she wound her way through the gravestones, some too mossy or worn to read, others tilting drunkenly into the earth. After returning to Riverton with the twins, she had crept into the graveyard one night to add some of Nara's ashes to the soil of the same grave that had received a dusting of Peter's when she had first rented Ray Dolan's house. Now she imagined the box elder and hackberry leaves, sustained by Nara and Peter, emitting tiny puffs of oxygen from their undersides. From above, the broken branch of an elderly oak clawed at her when she veered off the path to stop at the small grave, some distance from the others, where the sprinkling of Nara and Peter lay.

She had cleaned the gravestone herself, uncovering the inscription:

Griselda Pugh
Chosen by the Lord
November 12, 1902
Aged 1 year 4 months 3 days

Griselda's parents surely must be dead by now, but no one lay next to her in this, her final resting place.

Further down the slope, chamomile sprawled in the sunnier patches, releasing the musty scent of old upholstery as Heidi trod her way around a large family plot surrounded by a low, rusted, wrought iron fence. As she approached the school from the back, she saw several classrooms with adults at work, one hanging posters, another up a ladder painting what looked to be a large cat on a wall.

Previously named Fremont Comprehensive, Winfield School received its new moniker to honor proudly acclaimed native son and local rancher, Darrell Winfield, the famous "Marlboro man" in the Philip Morris tobacco ads. Two years ago, in its continuing effort to support the young, the tobacco company offered to underwrite the renovation of several Wyoming schools. The Riverton school district put its share of funds to good use at its oldest school, transforming Fremont into an attractive building, part brick, part cement. Through tall, double-paned windows, fitted with new venetian blinds, bright airy classrooms looked across the playing field and up the slope to the graveyard.

Marlboro money also funded the new gymnasium. The

painted image of a cowboy on a horse, holding a red and white banner proclaiming 'Marlboro Country,' greeted young athletes and their parents as they entered the gymnasium. Industry and education, working hand in hand.

Heidi skirted four drinking faucets aligned in a trough that separated two newly painted doors, BOYS on one, GIRLS on the other, blue footprints leading to the BOYS, pink to the GIRLS. She followed the smell of fresh asphalt to the front of the school and smiled at a young man who looked up from painting lines to delineate new parking spots. He smiled back and raised a friendly hand.

The door to the main office stood open. No secretary sat at the desk in front of the principal's office, but she heard the approach of a high-pitched metallic sound and a short, sandy-haired man walked rapidly around a corner, pushing a squeaking cart from which an ambitiously high stack of file folders threatened to topple. Heidi quickly placed her bag on the desk and rushed forward in time to clamp her hands on top of the folders, preventing most from sliding to the floor.

"Thank you so much. We've averted a disaster, you and I," the man beamed. "Orrin Harris," he held out a warm damp hand. "Principal," he added with satisfaction.

"Heidi Vogel. My twins are new pupils for your Kindergarten and it is my pleasure to help you with the *almost* disaster."

He gazed into the clear, deep blue eyes before him, and for Principal Orrin Harris, a tedious afternoon brightened. This was just what a 'Heidi' should look like, Nordic, long fair hair held in a braid, twisted into a bun, strong, slender arms extending beyond the short, puffed sleeves of her crisp cotton blouse. She wore a blue cardigan tied by its sleeves around her shoulders. Her dimpled smile exposed a glimpse of very white teeth.

He accepted Heidi's offer to help organize the more than two hundred folders from the cart, into his file cabinet. They worked efficiently and were done within twenty minutes. Before they left his office, Heidi withdrew a buttery golden shortbread from her bag and held it out to Mr. Harris.

"For you," she said with a smile.

"Ah, you're Riverton's famous baker, from Saint Gemma's!" he exclaimed. "Oh, my wife will be so pleased. She sampled your shortbread at the Rotary Club's fundraiser and positively raved. My files, now a great golden cookie, I tell you Miss Vogel . . ." he wagged his head, no further words necessary. He beamed and tucked the shortbread in his briefcase.

A man buffing the floors cautioned them not to slip as they walked down the corridor. Another man, descending a ladder with a spent fluorescent tube, called a friendly greeting.

"You'll like Miss Dodd," Mr. Harris enthused as they turned a corner. "Mary Ellen Dodd, old Riverton family. She's the very best Winfield has to offer, a remarkable young woman, not everyone has the gift to guide the very young."

Heidi agreed the twins were most fortunate to have such a teacher.

"But Mr. Harris?" she said, placing a hand on his arm so he slowed. "I do have a small and important request for you and Miss Dodd."

"Anything, Miss Vogel, anything we can do." He smiled at her. She really had a most attractive accent. "You may present your request to both of us, because here we are." He opened the door into the kindergarten classroom, with a slight bow.

Miss Dodd stood with her back to them, weight on her right leg, her left extended to the side, toes pointed, arms held gracefully in an arc before her.

"Used to do ballet," whispered Mr. Harris, "Very slim at one point, difficult for some of us to maintain our weight."

He called, "Well, well, Miss Dodd. Working your magic on the room, I see."

The young woman turned and allowed her arms to drop

as she shifted her weight to her left leg, circumscribing an arc on the floor with her right toe. As she brought her feet together, Heidi almost expected a bow but instead the kindergarten teacher stood erect.

"Just working out the kinks after being up and down a ladder most of the day, Mr. Harris," she said.

On the wall Miss Dodd had painted a passable 'Cat in the Hat' looking very pleased with himself, white gloved hands clasped at his belly. Under him she had added the quote,

"WHY FIT IN WHEN YOU WERE BORN TO STAND OUT?"

The principal nodded at the wall. "Doctor Seuss, quite right, welcoming, affirmative. Very nicely done, Miss Dodd."

"And you have brought me a parent, I see," said Miss Dodd, casting a smile in Heidi's direction.

Mr. Harris placed a proprietary hand on Heidi's elbow. "This is Miss Heidi Vogel, aunt and guardian to the Crow twins, students of yours next week. Just enrolled today. We need a moment of your time, if you please. She has a request of us, and a gift, I may add, for you."

Heidi and Mr. Harris looked at each other in puzzlement as Miss Dodd backed away from the proffered shortbread. She held up a plump hand and looked at them with agonized eyes. Two days on yet another diet, this one, which severely restricted carbohydrates and joy, was proving achingly tedious, yet her magazine had promised so much. The Before and After pictures told the story. Frumpy, pudgy women transformed into energetic, smiling beauties, with vastly improved fashion sense. Always a man in the background, lust in his dark, brooding eyes.

Miss Dodd frowned at the thick, luxuriously wrapped shortbread and breathed in a faint scent of almond, sugar and butter. She felt herself weakening. Perhaps if she changed to the new cabbage, onions and liver diet, the one that allowed a day's break every thirteen days for unlimited carbohydrate eating. Her neighbor's sister-in-law had lost twelve pounds in three weeks following that diet. The trick, the neighbor said, was to eat so many carbs on the allotted day that you were sick of them for the next thirteen days, no need to feel deprived.

"I believe you have another shortbread, Mr. Harris," said Heidi, as she made to withdraw her gift, but Miss Dodd had made her decision.

"I am so sorry, Miss Vogel, my mind is caught in a fog, so much to do," she said, reaching for the golden round with a small shiver of relief.

She would start the liver and cabbage diet today, but *beginning* with the day of unlimited carbs it allowed once every two weeks. That meant eating the whole shortbread tonight, but if she gorged tonight, she would surely be sick at the thought of cakes, cookies and pies for the next thirteen days. On her way home, she'd pick up the liver and cabbage, and yes, she was allowed an onion every other day. With the shortbread out of the way, she would be all ready for tomorrow. Twelve pounds in three weeks, her transformation starting with this gold-ribboned delight.

She turned her attention to the baker, who had just said something about the family having a special need and apparently causing Mr. Harris to evidence some confusion,

"Niece? I was informed they are both little boys," said Mr. Harris.

He hadn't really understood what that irritating woman from the district office was gabbling on about over the phone, but it did seem to involve the Crow twins being little boys.

"Marcela is just the boy on her birth certificate," Heidi explained. "When you meet her, you will see she is a girl. It will be much easier for her to start with you that way, and for the other children also. This is not a choice we make. Marcela is transgender."

The principal and the teacher looked at each other in bewilderment.

"Marcela is so excited about coming to school. She will do

her best for you in class," Heidi went on. "I have a transgender research paper with me. May I read you a small portion?"

After Heidi read the three paragraphs she had selected, she prepared to wait out the silence that descended. One slow minute and another, she looked out the window. The gusts of wind that rattled the windows had set the trees to beckoning from the cemetery up the hill. A door slammed down the hall, a telephone rang unanswered.

Mr. Harris cleared his throat. "Interesting, interesting Miss Vogel. This is a new one for us." Another throat clearing, then, "We who work with children know they are very malleable. They go through phases of all kinds. They try things on so to speak."

Her evening with shortbread temporarily forgotten, Miss Dodd asked, "Have you tried counseling?"

Heidi swallowed her frustration and said, "Yes, we have counseling after their mother dies, but counseling will not make Marcela into a boy. The change on paper we ask for is to recognize the person inside Marcela. I can bring more research for you."

The principal exchanged a quick look with Miss Dodd before saying, "With school beginning next week, we don't really have time to read more research, Miss Vogel, but we will certainly consider what you've shared with us and discuss it. I assure you, we value a child's privacy, although this might be a chance for the other children to learn about differences. We teach how important it is to be kind and tolerant."

Miss Dodd joined in, "Kindness, tolerance and *honesty*. We emphasize 'The Golden Rule.' Do you know it? Do unto others?"

"Of course, I know this rule, Luke 6:31, and I understand you work to teach children kindness and tolerance but Marcela should not have to fight for who she is in kindergarten. When you meet her, you will forget that we even have this conversation, because she is *honestly* a little girl. What is not honest is to . . ." Heidi bit her lips, struggling to find her words. "If a person finds out that the form in your office has my niece listed as a boy, it may be that this person cannot accept and understand who Marcela is. I ask that you let the form in the file cabinet in the school office have her name as Marcela instead of Marcel and her gender as female, and that you keep our confidence."

Heidi examined their faces and Mr. Harris and Miss Dodd averted their eyes. They were not bad people. Would they let themselves accept Marcela for who she was? After a long moment's silence, Heidi stood and thanked them for their time, saying again how much her niece and nephew were looking forward to Kindergarten. She trusted they would do the right thing by allowing Marcela to be enrolled as a girl.

Perhaps she shouldn't have added that last part, she worried as she walked back across the playing field. As she said it, she had seen a hardening of their features as if they were asking themselves, who was this German woman to say she trusted them to do the right thing, when *they* were the experts? How many children did *she* interact with day after day, year after year?

"*Lieber Gott, beschütze Marcela*," she prayed aloud. 'Dear God, protect Marcela.'

After Heidi's departure, Mr. Harris turned to Miss Dodd, "Well, *that* was unexpected."

"Most unexpected. Do you think the child might be homosexual? Although he's very young to make that choice, isn't he?"

"I'm not sure it *is* a choice, Miss Dodd, but if the issue is homosexuality, surely in kindergarten, that doesn't come up. And she read us some research. This sounds like it may be something quite different entirely."

"There's research of all kinds, Mr. Harris. This transgender business . . . well, let me just say that given that

Miss Vogel is foreign, you heard the accent and her overuse of the present tense, she may have a different definition of homosexuality. She acts as if this little boy thinks he's in the wrong body."

"And she believes him, Miss Dodd. Didn't it seem like she believes him?"

"But that poor little other twin. This must be very confusing for him. What does that poor child believe?"

"If Miss Vogel's the guardian, she's been vetted by the State, so I imagine the welfare of the normal twin has been assessed. My concern is what to share with the rest of the staff. If *only* adults know, we can probably . . . well, maybe they don't have to know. *Do* they have to know?"

"Mr. Harris, *honesty*, that's our standard."

"But we don't talk about any child's gender really, not in depth. It sounds like we may never have known of the issue with the Crow child if Miss Vogel hadn't brought it up."

"She told us because she wants us to *lie* on our copy of the school registration form," said Miss Dodd, concerned at Mr. Harris's naivety.

"It's just two small changes, Miss Dodd."

"I can call him by a girl's name, but what about the office form? Even if we change that, you'll have to tell the office staff this child's secret. They may have to help her, or him. Her? Him? If he? She? Oh my, this is so confusing. Let me try again, if the *child* has an accident, they may have to help him and they might see his, well you know . . . see the difference. Since he's coming to school pretending to be a *girl*, it would be such a shock."

Reluctantly, Mr. Harris had to agree and before the end of the day, he talked to his office staff, emphasizing discretion. His secretary appeared exceedingly worried about bathroom protocol and he attempted to placate her by suggesting they let the child use the private bathroom off his office.

He phoned Heidi that evening, "All taken care of, Miss

Vogel, and he may, or I mean *she* will be using the private restroom off my office. She merely has to ask my secretary, whenever she needs to go, she is welcome."

Heidi looked at the twins, sitting in the kitchen chairs, about to have a snack before bed and asked Mr. Harris to give her a moment. She asked the children to go into the garage and search the Mercedes for her small gold hoop earring that might be there. Chocolate tomorrow if they found it.

They scampered off, Gering at their heels, and Heidi spoke quietly into the phone, "Why does Marcela need the separate restroom? There must be a door for each toilet in the girls' room."

"Yes, of course there is, but this is a compromise, Miss Vogel. Now she has a special privilege."

"She does not want a special privilege. She is a little girl five years old. She wants to be treated the same."

"But she is *not* the same, Miss Vogel," said Mr. Harris softly. "And really, we are doing the best we can. I also have to consider my office staff."

"Your office staff? They are afraid for Marcela to use the girls' restroom?"

Mr. Harris attempted a small laugh. "No, not afraid, by no means afraid." At Heidi's silence, he added, "We are just trying to make this situation easier for everyone."

Heidi was so angry when she hung up the phone, she brought the side of her clenched fist down on the table so hard the saltshaker fell on its side and rolled on to the floor.

As babies, Marcela had been the bolder twin, usually the first to try new things, bright, lively, facing life with gusto. And now she was a solemn, fearful little girl. And whatever hurt his sister, hurt Amadeus too. Tonight they'd had a good time at the movies. It was a Disney movie and she had assumed it would be safe, although the original Hans Christen Anderson tale had contained so much cruelty. But in this version Ursula, the witch, was destroyed, Ariel the mermaid was allowed to become a human forever and she and the prince sailed happily away as Prince and Princess. And now to come home to this phone call; she would wait until tomorrow to inform the twins of Marcela's special privilege.

The children returned to the kitchen complaining they looked all over the car for the earring and it wasn't there, but they had tried so they should still get chocolate.

Heidi agreed. She bent down and picked up Gering to avoid meeting their eyes.

Marcela sat stone-faced at the breakfast table the next morning, her arms crossed. "What did you say to them?" she demanded. "I don't want to use his stupid bathroom. Why do I have to?"

Trying to keep her own frustration and disappointment out of her voice, Heidi explained once again. "Yesterday, the person at the District Office tells me the school papers must match the birth certificate that says you are both boys. I ask to write your real name on their form, but this district person says no. And we also know we have to wait until you are eighteen before we get you the official new birth certificate, so then later I go to the new school and explain who you are to the principal and your teacher. You will not meet the district people. It is the school that is important. I think Mr. Harris and Miss Dodd understand, but it seems they do not understand all the way. So tomorrow I will go back to the school and talk to the principal again, and to the people in the office, and I explain again and I say. . ."

"No, I don't want you to," Marcela interrupted, her chin quivering.

"If you go and yell, it will be bad," Amadeus warned.

"I am not going to yell," Heidi said. "I am going to explain quietly."

"I won't have to pee. I'm going to practice not peeing," Marcela blinked her eyes rapidly, her little fists clenched and trembling.

"Or if you have to go, I say I have to go too and then we will both go into the principal's dumb bathroom," said Amadeus. "And we'll tell kids we get to use it because we're special because we're twins and Mama died and you're just our aunt and you're not even from here."

Heidi didn't trust her voice until she got a drink of water and took some sips. She stood at the sink, watching the twins' reflection in the window. Their little mouths were moving, they were whispering to each other. They already had their new school clothes, special lunch boxes for their morning snacks and new barrettes for Marcela, but now their happy anticipation at starting school had come crashing down over which bathroom Marcela was allowed to use.

Heidi gave them a moment before turning around and saying, "When I go in to the office tomorrow, I will only talk to the adults. No children will ever know."

The twins stared at her. It was the adults who'd caused this problem in the first place.

"We don't want you to talk to them," said Amadeus. "If you do, we're gonna run away and we're gonna die or get eaten up by a big thing, like a monster."

In the end, Marcela resolved the issue herself by refusing liquids during the morning and not using any bathroom at school. Fortunately, kindergarten was over by noon.

CHAPTER THIRTY TWO

KINDERGARTEN WEEK THREE

Mr. Harris watched Marcela Crow curiously the first week of school, looking for glimpses of a little boy. He hadn't had much experience with Indian children, but he was of a romantic nature and he loved the *idea* of an Indian child and the Crows twins were particularly beautiful examples. Perhaps it was that dash of European ancestry, or was he imagining it because their aunt was so pretty? Although they were of the same height and had same shape to their features, he could almost swear one was a girl, the other a boy. Marcela ran with the girls at recess, dancing sideways at times, a graceful child, her black hair flying as she raced, laughing as she bent over to catch her breath with her hands on her hips.

Within a few days, Miss Dodd said she had had become so comfortable using female pronouns for Marcela, she now didn't even have to think about it.

After the first week of school, Heidi began to relax. Both twins seemed genuinely happy with Kindergarten. When she picked them up at noon to take them back to Saint Gemma's for the afternoon, she listened to their happy chattering in the backseat. For September, Amadeus and another boy had an extra five minutes of recess to gather up the balls and jump ropes and put them in the big tub in the cloakroom. There was an Open House soon and their artwork was going to be on the walls in the cafeteria. Oh, and her cookies were way better than anybody else's and all the kids wanted her to make extra.

On Friday of the second week, Marcela climbed into the car and informed Heidi that children could take home Rudolf, the class Guinea pig, for the weekend, if they were on Miss Dodd's list.

"He's not named after a reindeer. He's named after a man who used to do ballet, but he died," explained Marcela. "Miss Dodd dances ballet."

"Rudolf Nureyev, I think. He was a very beautiful dancer," said Heidi.

"Rudolf the guinea pig is a very beautiful guinea pig." Marcela nodded her head emphatically. "He has three colors and little legs and a soft body. He wrinkles his nose like this." Marcela demonstrated a rapid series of nose wrinkles.

Heidi laughed. "He must be very cute."

She caught sight of Amadeus chortling with a group of little boys as they strolled slowly toward the waiting cars. He was the only Native boy, the only boy with long hair, the boy with the unusual name, the smallest of the boys, yet he appeared to be the leader, fearless, fast, so easy in his skin.

"Everybody wants Amadeus to be their friend," said Marcela softly. She had been watching her brother too.

Heidi turned to look a Marcela. "Tell me how you get to be on Miss Dodd's list to take the Guinea pig home."

"You have to show her that you know how to take care of him," said Marcela, buckling her seat belt.

"And how do you show her this?" Heidi looked at her watch. She would give Amadeus a few more minutes with his friends.

"You take his water bottle down and wash it, then you fill it back up and put it back in his cage and it can't drip more than it's supposed to," Marcela explained. "Then you change his newspaper and sweep up all the bits that drop on the floor and then you wash your hands. Then you give him more food and you wash your hands again. I already helped Miss Dodd. She is going to watch me do it by myself tomorrow and then I get to be on the list."

Amadeus entered the car, breathless. "Are you talking about Rudolf?"

Marcela nodded.

"Marcela's going to be the first one on the list to bring him home because the water bottle is hard to hang back up, and everybody else makes it spill too much water," said Amadeus.

"It's not hard if you do it right," said Marcela, smugly. "Buckle your seat belt."

"I don't care if I never get on the list," Amadeus grinned at a boy who slapped his hand on the window, "because I don't want to take care of him. He's boring and he poops all the time and you have to sweep it all up because it all rolls around and falls on the floor when you try to get the paper out of the cage."

"You just have to fold the paper right and most of it stays inside," said Marcela, anxious for Heidi to get a good impression of Rudolf because she was going to ask for a Guinea pig for her birthday. "Miss Dodd says Guinea pigs love you a lot if you take care of them right."

Besides Gering, Marcela had decided a Guinea pig was probably the best animal in the world. She was going to get an orange, black and white one, just like Rudolf, but a girl. And then her Guinea pig could have babies with Rudolf, and there would be a whole family of Guinea pigs. And she would make them a house so they didn't have to just live in a cage, and they could have their own little beds and toys, and Rudolf could visit whenever Miss Dodd said it was okay.

Watching his sister, knowing what was going on inside her head, Amadeus said, "Marcela wants . . ."

"No, I don't," Marcela cut in, casting her brother a furious look. Aunt Heidi had to meet Rudolf first, and love him, or she probably wouldn't say yes to a Guinea pig pet. She leaned over and pinched Amadeus hard.

"Marcela, did you just pinch your brother?" Heidi had seen the pinch in the rearview mirror.

"No, I didn't and before Rudolf comes home you have to read a paper and sign your name. It's for permission and rules. Are you going to read it?"

Heidi promised she would, but no more pinching. She silently blessed Miss Dodd. How wonderful for Marcela to be first on the list to bring the class Guinea pig home for the weekend.

On Wednesday of the third week of school, Mr. Harris noted Marcela sitting alone on the bench during recess. Until today, she had been in the thick of things, playing tag, sharing her snacks, giggling over whatever little girls giggled at. When he approached her to ask if she was feeling unwell, she bent over to carefully refold the lacey border of the yellow socks that peeked out of the tops of her turquoise sneakers.

"I'm okay," she said, refusing to look up at him.

When the children were dismissed at noon, he went to talk to Miss Dodd and she concurred that the child appeared quieter today, but she had heard no bullying.

The next morning, Heidi sat on the edge of Marcela's bed, smiling at Gering who peered out from under the covers. She was trying to keep a growing sense of alarm in check. Marcela had spoken very little after being picked up from school yesterday, falling silent after dinner and refusing to participate in their bedtime prayer. Since school began, Marcela had been the first to sit down for breakfast, but today she was dawdling.

"I think the new red blouse will look very nice if you wear the jeans with the flowers on the pockets," said Heidi, leaning over and patting the bed next to her to encourage Gering to crawl toward her.

Marcela replied sullenly, "I can dress myself, go away."

Heidi picked up Gering and enfolded him in her arms. He attempted to lick her face, little tail wagging madly, as it always did when he was anxious. He sensed something amiss too.

"Of course, you can dress yourself, Marcela, and it is go away *please*." Heidi stood up. "Amadeus has finished his breakfast and you still need to eat. We leave the house in a quarter of an hour."

Heidi looked at the little girl sitting with her arms folded tightly across her chest, her face wiped of expression. Something was terribly wrong. Heidi would phone the office and request a meeting with Miss Dodd for this afternoon. She would worry all morning of course, but right now she had to help Marcela pull herself together for school.

Once dressed, Marcela trailed into the kitchen and handed Heidi a butterfly barrette. "It won't stay in," she whined, her eyes filling with tears.

Heidi clipped the barrette in place and kissed the top of Marcela's head.

"Sit, eat Marcela, soon we leave."

Marcela sat down and batted at the top of her cereal with her spoon, soymilk splattering. "I'm not hungry," she said. "I'm sick. I can't go to school."

"But Amadeus says today the class finishes the masks for the Open House next week," Heidi said. "I want to see yours."

"It's stupid. It's ugly."

"No. Amadeus says Miss Dodd holds your mask up for the others to see how beautiful and what . . ."

"Nobody plays with me," Marcela broke in, dropping her spoon on the table with a clatter. "They won't sit with me. They whisper and say things."

Heidi felt a cold wash of fear. Had children had found out how Marcela was different from the other girls? She put her hand to her throat where a hard ache gathered, and pulled out a chair.

Amadeus leaned back in his seat, crossed his arms and gave her a hard look. He still felt the satisfaction of punching his fist into the belly of that soft pink kid, the one whose mom worked in the office. That shut him up and Miss Dodd didn't see. Nobody would say anything; they liked him, but he couldn't stop the girls from moving away when Marcela tried to sit with them. You couldn't *make* someone play with you. And he had boys to play with, he couldn't just stay with his sister.

"What do they say?" Heidi asked quietly.

Marcela turned away and whispered, "Just *things*. Mean *things*."

"Amadeus? What are these mean things?"

"Don't tell her, Amadeus, don't talk about it." Marcela glared at her brother.

"When I come to get you after school, we will sit and talk to Miss Dodd. We will see how to make people more kind," said Heidi resolutely. Perhaps the worst had not happened. Marcela could be sharp, maybe she had hurt another little girl's feelings, maybe the children were jealous Marcela had been the first chosen to take Rudolf home, maybe many things.

"*Noooo*," Marcela wailed, "I don't want to talk to Miss Dodd. They just don't like me, nobody does. Only Gering does. Amadeus can go to school; everybody likes him. I can't go."

She pulled the barrette out of her hair and threw it at her brother. It missed and he picked it up and put it on the table.

"I don't have to go to school," said Amadeus to his shoes.

Heidi picked up a trembling Gering and handed him to Marcela. "You go to school today, Amadeus, and Marcela will come with me and Gering to Saint Gemma's this morning. I will phone the attendance office with an excuse for her. We drive today because we are late and Marcela does not feel well. Everybody get in the car."

Amadeus tried to suppress his grin. "Okay."

Cuddling Gering, Marcela slunk low on the backseat so no one would see her as Amadeus leaped out of the car, greeted by a chorus of calls. Heidi watched the little boy run to stand in line with his friends. He didn't look back.

At recess Amadeus was fastest across the monkey bars, he was picked first for kickball. Marcela's seat across the classroom was empty. He was going to say his sister was sick, but nobody asked.

Mr. Harris received Heidi Vogel's call that morning with a sinking heart. Little Marcela Crow's privacy had been invaded and he followed a suspicion that had been brewing since his secretary had said, several days ago, that the Crow twins seemed to be fitting in well. The note of defiance in her voice had been so unexpected, he thought he might have imagined it at the time, but now he thought not. He opened his door and waited for his secretary to return from the women's room. She had a son in kindergarten, an unpleasant boy who twice had been brought to his office for pushing children in the schoolyard.

His secretary stood in front of his desk, refusing to meet his eyes. Sniffing, twisting her hands, she insisted that she was as mystified as he, how it became known to the other children that the Crow girl wasn't like other girls in a most shameful way.

For this second meeting, Heidi did not bring shortbread. She, Miss Dodd and Mr. Harris sat on child-sized chairs in the kindergarten room, in the deep silence left behind by absent children. The meeting would be short; there wasn't much to say.

Miss Dodd and Mr. Harris shared how badly they felt on Marcela's behalf, and what a delightful child she was, artistic, responsible and well-behaved.

"She is first on the list to bring our Guinea pig home for the weekend, if you agree," said Miss Dodd, brightly.

The three of them looked at the little animal in his cage, and he wrinkled his nose.

"I do not think Rudolf will be coming home to us," said Heidi.

"Surely in a week or two, the children will forget . . ." began Mr. Harris.

"You do not believe this and neither do I," Heidi interrupted sharply. She swallowed, and closed her eyes briefly before continuing, "Three weeks ago you say that you model honesty. Honesty is not telling what is written on Marcela's birth certificate. It is allowing a child to be who she is as a human being."

"And we hope you accept that we are so very sorry, Miss Vogel," said Mr. Harris. "I assure you I have reprimanded the person who let the cat out of the bag."

"The cat?" asked Heidi, her voice icy. "My niece, the cat in the bag? A cruel expression Mr. Harris, although I think perhaps you did not mean it."

"It is a common American idiom, Miss Vogel," said Miss Dodd, rising to her boss's defense.

"Yes, I know this, but it is small, dismissive of the harm to a little girl. A bad person in your office talks about my niece and stirs the trouble. We do not meet now for Marcela; it is too late to mend this harm to her. We meet for another child. The child who comes next year, or in a few years, so perhaps that child will not have his or her privacy disrupted. Marcela's identity harms no one. You think about this. How does my niece, who you say is so artistic and well-behaved, who is so good with your Guinea pig, how does this little girl harm anyone?"

Heidi supposed the only true surprise was that it had taken two and a half weeks for Marcela to become the target of cruel words and behavior. Was it because it takes time for both children and adults to examine those around them and seek out their own kind, cementing their allegiance by turning on the unorthodox, the exotic, the nonconforming?

Amadeus finished his third week of school but he said he wasn't going back unless Marcela came back too.

"I get to stay and help Aunt Heidi and Inez and Massimo. I don't have to go back there," said Marcela. "Aunt Heidi says Kindergarten is optionable. She's going to find a different school for first grade. One that doesn't know about me. "

"Optional," Heidi corrected. "And yes, we will find a very good school for the first grade."

CHAPTER THIRTY THREE

LIFELINE

After a restless night, Heidi woke earlier than usual. She clutched the receiver, her lifeline, and wrapped its coils tightly around her fingers. "I am so sorry to wake you, Karl," she said into the phone. "It sounds like you were sleeping."

"Beppe just arrived a few hours ago. We were taking a nap before dinner. Tell me what has happened," said Karl, stretching and putting another pillow behind his head. "Heidi," he mouthed to Beppe.

"I am sorry, but there is no one here to understand how painful this is for us. Amadeus loves school but now he says he will not go back without . . ."

She stopped as she caught a flash of black rushing in from the soft grey dawn. It struck the kitchen window with a crack and she gasped and put a hand to her cheek as if she had been slapped. She watched as the dark shape slid out of sight leaving a red ellipse on the glass.

"Heidi?" Across a continent and an ocean, Karl heard her catch her breath. Beppe wrapped an arm around Karl's waist, drawing him close in the attempt to hear Heidi's side of the conversation, although most of it was in German.

Karl put a hand over the receiver and whispered, "A bird hit the window and left blood."

"Oh, our poor girl," groaned Beppe. Heidi was surely going

to interpret a dead bird as a dark omen.

He sat up and looked for his underwear. He found it on the floor in the hall with his jeans. After three weeks apart, he and Karl had been desperate to get to each other. He returned to the bedroom and sat on the edge of the bed to pull on his pants because Karl had said Giselle, the woman who tended his garden, would likely be working all afternoon. His shirt appeared to be nowhere. His hook was safely on the nightstand, but he didn't remember taking it off. He wouldn't put it back on until tomorrow. They would make love again before dinner and later take a bath, all activities far safer and more pleasant without his hook.

Beppe shook his head on the way to the kitchen. There was nothing good about Wyoming. *Mio Dio*, the relief he'd felt on returning to Italy. He waved at Giselle who was trundling past the kitchen window with a wheelbarrow and she flashed him a grin. He poured two glasses of mineral water over ice and put them on a tray, a twist of lime for Karl, lemon for him, and there was his shirt draped haphazardly off the vacuum in the corner. Two buttons would have to be found and sewn back on.

While Beppe was in the kitchen, Heidi told Karl she was taking both children out of school because kindergarten was not mandatory in Wyoming. "We will have to find another place to live before the first grade," she said, "but we will not go away like a dog with its tail between its legs."

"Of course, you won't. You are not defeated," Karl affirmed. "Moving is the only logical thing to do."

"I should not have trusted the school. I am so stupid when I think they will protect Marcela."

"It just takes one ignorant *Arschloch*," Karl pointed out.

Heidi nodded to herself. The secretary with the small eyes and the pinched mouth had been the ignorant asshole, she was almost sure of it.

"And because Marcela is so young," Karl went on, "*you* will be blamed for who she is, for letting her dress like a girl, for letting her be called by a girl's name. When she is older, more of the blame will land on her."

Heidi made a guttural sound of despair and disgust.

"You must be practical or this will happen again," said Karl, calmly. "Start by getting her a new birth certificate. You said the social worker in Casper has a transgender brother, a nurse. He will be part of a network to keep people safe. He will almost certainly know how to get an altered birth certificate, all underground, of course. Hold on," he said as Beppe came back into the room and held out a glass.

Heidi heard whispering, Beppe asking questions, Karl replying.

"Beppe wants to talk to you," said Karl, coming back on the line. "Don't hang up when he's done. We still need to say goodbye."

"*Cara mia*," said Beppe, his voice warm and deep.

"*Ciao, come stai?*" she asked, using the little Italian she knew.

"*Bene*, but listen, Karl said you think you behaved stupidly to trust people at this school, but you did not. You grew up a favored child, an easy child who met all the expectations of a pretty little German girl. You are not used to being on the outside. You are still learning what it is like for Marcela to be so very different. For Marcela, you must be vigilant. Riverton is not the place for you now."

"I know. Last night I talked to Edith McKee. She understands why we have to leave. I will give Saint Gemma's time for transition. Inez and Massimo are a very good team and Mr. Tolentino is always the grownup in the room. They are devoted to Saint Gemma's mission. I am not irreplaceable."

"Of course, she's irreplaceable," muttered Karl in the background.

"Have you thought of where to go?" asked Beppe.

"I am taking the children to Comfrey on the weekend for a picnic and to teach them a little swimming in Lake Cheynook. We will look at the town as a possible place to live, or perhaps go to a bigger place like Pinedale. The twins need to stay close to where they were born. Their grandfather did not have roots and he suffered. Karl and I can go wherever business takes us, but for you, and for the twins, there is a tie to the land. I already see it in them, at least I see this in Amadeus. Mr. Hosa, an Arapaho man who works at Saint Gemma's, pointed out to me how Amadeus listens to the plants and the birds and the wind."

Beppe understood. He was only ever truly at home in Italy, in the Piedmont, where his family had lived for centuries growing grapes. His vines talked to him. The crows that sat on the end posts at dusk, talked to him. He heard his grandfather's voice at his back at night if he walked through the rows, especially after a long, hard day. Heidi was right to keep the children near the soil of their ancestors. Comfrey was the other side of the Wind River Range from the Reservation but tribes had hunted and camped throughout those mountains before the whites came.

"At least in Wyoming, a town of seven or eight hundred is not really considered so very small," Beppe said.

"Comfrey has a thousand people now."

"Almost a city, then," Beppe laughed. "My friend, Ruth Creeley will not have moved away. She is descended from the original founders. She will introduce you to people and help you find a place to live. But surely it is too cold to swim in the lake now."

"No, we are in the Indian Summer," said Heidi, a catch to her voice . . . Nara lying on the lounge chair, the babies just a week old, the hot sun beating down. Five years ago, it had been a very late *Altweibersommer,* Old Woman's Summer—Indian Summer.

323

After Heidi hung up, Karl raised his eyebrows at Beppe. "She can take Hebeka with her wherever she goes, but you showed me Comfrey on a map once. It is on the way to nowhere."

"Route 80 is not so very far away, and I seem to remember an airfield," said Beppe, stretching out, pulling Karl down next to him.

"But making shortbread will not be enough for her. Once set up, with a few employees, Hebeka will almost run itself. What will she do, volunteer at the library, assuming they have one? Collect alms for the poor?" Karl ran his hands down Beppe's well-muscled abdomen. "She is a chef. Her talent almost rivals mine. Do they even have a decent restaurant in Comfrey? And if they do, will they know what to do with her? They might expect her to be a line cook for American food, slinging hash or whatever." Karl gave an elaborate shudder.

"Hush," said Beppe, pulling his lover on top of him and covering Karl's mouth with his. They had only a few days before he needed to be back in Italy to prepare for harvest. Ruth Creeley would take care of Heidi.

Heidi officially removed both children from Winfield Elementary the following day. The twins had spent a lot of time at Saint Gemma's before school started and the office was set up for them, but the last time they had put long days in at the food charity, they had been excitedly looking forward to the start of kindergarten. Now they were back to spending a whole day at work with Heidi, helping with little jobs in the kitchen, taking naps in the beanbag chairs set up in the office, watching a video in the afternoon on the little television Mr. Tolentino had procured from his neighbor. They were restless. They'd had a taste of something more and they watched the clock. The day at school would have started with music and letters and numbers. At ten o'clock, kids would be having their snacks on the benches, and after that they would play tag, dodge ball, jump rope and hopscotch. Before it was time to be picked up at noon, they did art and made things out of clay and finger-painted and colored. The coloring books Heidi bought weren't the same as the mimeographed sheets the teacher gave them, and didn't smell as good. The finger paints she bought didn't have as many colors. You couldn't play dodge ball or tag very well with just two people, although it was better if Inez and Massimo joined in.

But Gering was content. He found the beanbags more comfortable when occupied by a child.

The evening before going to Lake Cheynook, Heidi took the twins to Walmart to buy swimming suits. On the way, she told them she had taken them to the lake with their mother and Gering when they were babies. She had carried them into the water while their mother and Gering watched from the shore.

"Why didn't Mama go in the water too?" Marcela asked.

"I –I do not know," admitted Heidi.

Before they left Riverton the day she and Nara had taken the babies to Lake Cheynook, she had offered Nara her extra swimsuit, but Nara had rolled her eyes and said, "This is your gig, Babe."Babe, said in such a flippant tone, Nara had never used that term with her before. She had been sharpening her edges, more silences, tight smiles, more looking away. After the incident with Marcel getting into the fountain, they had ceased questioning each other about most things, living parallel lives with few intersections . . . until that day at the lake when Nara had posed the worst question of all, 'Which twin would you save first if they both of them were drowning?'

"Mama couldn't swim," said Amadeus, who had been sitting with feet crossed at the ankles, staring out the window, hands pressed flat on the seat as if bracing himself.

"How do you know?" asked Marcela.

He relaxed his hands and shrugged. "She just said it. Mama said she couldn't swim. She said you have to teach us, Aunt Heidi."

Although Heidi was getting used to Amadeus repeating something Nara had just told him, she always felt a brush of fear, very slight perhaps but it fed into the perception that Nara was watching. After one of Amadeus's pronouncements, Heidi sometimes recalled a whisper, nothing intelligible, a sound, a sigh. The grief counselor had said Amadeus had a powerful imagination. Was that all it was? Heidi rarely talked to Peter these days, but when she did, he always talked back.

Heidi smiled at Amadeus's reflection in the mirror. "I will teach you how to swim," she promised.

"Did you hear Mama, Aunt Heidi?" asked Marcela. "Did she tell you to teach us?"

"I think maybe . . ."

"No, you didn't hear her say that," said Marcela. "She doesn't talk to us, just to Amadeus because he's her dumb little boy."

"Do not be unkind," reprimanded Heidi.

"Okay, he is her *not* dumb little boy." Marcela swung her legs and stuck her tongue out at her brother.

Amadeus selected his swimming trunks immediately, navy blue with palm trees and sharks. He came inside the changing room with Heidi and Marcela and watched critically as his sister tried on suit after suit.

"That one's good. It doesn't show anything," he said when Marcela finally tried on a yellow two-piece suit with a frilly skirt.

"I wish the purple one had a skirt," said Marcela, looking longingly at a skimpy bikini with bows at the sides.

"My mother would say a little girl wearing a suit like that is growing up too fast," remarked Heidi. "You look very pretty in yellow."

"You're just saying that because nobody can see my penis," shouted Marcela, throwing the yellow swimsuit on the floor.

They heard tittering from the dressing room next door and the little girl's face crumpled.

"Ice cream?" asked Heidi, wrapping her arms around the child, unable to think of what else to say.

"Everybody hates me," said Marcela, her eyes brimming with tears.

"Not Inez, not Massimo, not Edith, not Patsy, not Karl, not Beppe. " Heidi looked at Amadeus.

"Not me, not Aunt Heidi, not Mr. Tolentino or Mr. Hosa," Amadeus supplied.

"Not Gering," said Marcela with a watery smile.

CHAPTER THIRTY FOUR

RESTAURANT FOR SALE

Saturday arrived, a perfect warm October day, a mild breeze, a cloudless sky. Heidi packed biscuits for Gering, peanut butter sandwiches, oatmeal cookies, oranges and water. When they were about to set off, Heidi asked the children if they wanted music and they said they didn't care, so she put in a tape Karl had recently sent her, Schumann's only piano concerto.

"Who is this guy?" asked Amadeus suspiciously when the music started.

"Robert Schumann wrote the music."

"Is he playing the piano?" asked Marcela.

"No, a very fine Polish man is playing the piano. His name is Krystian Zimerman. I went with your Uncles, Karl and Beppe, to hear him play in Munich two years ago."

"Why isn't the guy who wrote it playing it?" Marcela asked.

"Robert Schumann died a long time ago. He did play the piano but then he hurt his hand and he could not play anymore, so he spent the rest of his life writing music. Do you like it? You will also hear oboes and violins."

But the twins were more interested in how this guy Robert hurt his hand, and why a doctor couldn't fix it and if he was mad because he couldn't play the piano anymore. How old he was when he died? Did somebody shoot him or stick a sword in him?

With Schumann's lyrical, romantic music in the background, Heidi elected not to say the composer had spent the last years of his life struggling with hallucinations, suicide attempts and depression. Instead, she said she didn't think he had died a violent death, and although he died quite young, he had many children and a kind wife named Clara who lived a long time after his death and was a very fine pianist herself. For years she played his music all over Europe so people could hear what a wonderful composer Schumann was.

"Then why isn't she playing on the tape?" asked Marcela.

"Because she's dead," answered her brother. "A lot of people are dead."

Marcela seemed satisfied with that answer and the children lapsed into silence, Marcela absently playing with Gering's ears, Amadeus closing his eyes, his lips moving on occasion. In conversation with Nara? Heidi wondered.

Heidi turned up the volume, remembering back to the lively discussion she'd had with Beppe and Karl several years ago, after they had taken to her to hear Krystian Zimerman play Schumann's music in Munich. Beppe claimed Schumann had died of mercury poisoning from treatment for syphilis, but Karl disagreed. He'd always understood the composer died of pneumonia caught in a mental institution. Heidi said she'd read a book on how famous people had died, and it claimed an autopsy of Schumann's brain had found a tumor. A tumor could cause the hallucinations that plagued the composer, but, the book theorized, the tumor may have also stimulated creativity. As they moved into the kitchen to watch Karl whip up soufflés for a late supper, their discussion turned to why so many artistic geniuses were tortured souls.

Karl and Beppe, how she missed them, their loving concern and the fun they had. Heidi glimpsed the children in the rearview mirror. They had nodded off, trusting her to take care of them. Gering caught her eye from where he lay curled in Marcela's lap.

"*Du bist mein Verbündeter*," she whispered to him, 'you are my ally.'

Their family dynamics had changed since Marcela's privacy had been breached and the three of them had forged an unspoken agreement—the only way forward involved hiding and secrecy. The children were waiting for her to lead the way to safety and she had already taken some steps. She had found Ruth Creeley's number in the telephone book and left a message on Ruth's answering machine, mentioning Beppe. Ruth had not phoned back yet.

Heidi had also phoned Lily Brown's brother. When he heard of Marcela's experience in school, he asked, with a sigh, if she had really thought it would be any different. He said he would check around, people in the forgery business tended to come and go, fortunately Marcela wouldn't be enrolled in a new school until next year, so they had some time.

Richard's final words had been, "Wherever you end up, don't trust anybody with Marcela's story. Not until you can trust them with her life."

The twins perked up when they passed the airstrip, and a big billboard. This must be the beginning of Comfrey. The lake was nearing. They grinned at each other and wriggled in anticipation.

As they were driving slowly along Main Street, Heidi noticed the restaurant that looked out at the mountains had closed and there was a For Sale sign in the window. With the twins protesting, she pulled the car over and said she'd just be a moment. They could cross the street with her if they wished, or wait in the car, but she needed to look in the window of that restaurant across the road. Nobody's in it, hurry up, they whined. Heidi took a pad of paper and a pencil out of the glove box and walked briskly across the road.

Apparently, the entire building was up for sale. The upper floor had two office spaces that shared a bathroom, and a two-bedroom apartment, with one and a half bathrooms. A small diagram showed the apartment spanned the back of the upper floor, a pity because it wouldn't have a view of the mountains. An open lot behind the building was included in the deal. The realtor was listed as Ruth Creeley. "Ruth Creeley," Heidi breathed. Ruth Creeley, such a good omen.

Heidi jogged back across the street and opened the car's rear door.

"We just take a few minutes," she promised. "I need to walk around this building. There is an empty lot at the back and I want to see it. We will put Gering's leash on so he can lift his leg."

The twins howled their displeasure. Gering could lift his leg at the lake; she *prooomised* they were going swimming; they'd been waiting *hooours*.

Heidi reached over Amadeus to get Gering.

"Out, please," she said to the children and grumbling, they got out of the car, saying they were going to lift a leg too.

The lot had a tree that afforded enough privacy for the twins to relieve themselves as Heidi stood looking up at the building's second floor. Three large windows faced the lot, not a view of the mountains but plenty of light. With growing excitement, she envisioned the three of them living in the apartment while she got the restaurant going. She could try to rent out the offices. Eventually, they'd find a house and the apartment could be rented too.

She peered through the windows of the double backdoor. Supplies could be unloaded directly into the back of the restaurant. She saw what appeared to be pantries on either side of a short hall and ahead, she glimpsed part of the kitchen.

She turned around when she heard the loud, violent sound of glass shattering. The twins had found some bottles, lined them up and one of them had thrown a stone. They looked at her guiltily. Gering cringed at their feet.

"Do you know Gering, or another dog or a cat may get glass in its paw now?" Heidi demanded.

The children wiped their faces of expression and clamped their mouths into straight lines. The sound of the breaking glass had been shocking to them too. Amadeus picked up Gering and handed him to Marcela. The twins stood shoulder to shoulder, looking very small and defiant.

"There was a broken bottle by the tree and you said we could go over there to pee and we almost got cut on it," said Amadeus.

Heidi knew they felt guilty and they wanted her to feel guilty too. Broken glass, the hazards of an empty lot, she should have been more careful and checked around the tree before letting them go over there.

"I am sorry. We are lucky you do not get hurt," she said. "We will pick up the bottle so we do not make things worse."

She retrieved a plastic bag she spied flapping against a post in the corner of the lot. "One of you hold Gering to keep him safe, one of you hold the plastic bag and carefully, I pick up the broken glass. Then we ask the shop on Main Street that has the door open if I may use their telephone to call the number on the sign. This is just a few minutes more, then we go to the lake and swim and have our picnic."

The twins nodded solemnly and did not protest. They were in a little bit of trouble, Aunt Heidi was in a little bit of trouble, but she was still taking them swimming.

The shop with the open door turned out not to be a shop at all, but a lawyer's office. A man with a greying mass of wavy red hair tied back in a ponytail looked up from his desk and grinned at Heidi as she entered.

"Raul Diaz," he said, rising and extending his hand. "To what do I owe the pleasure?" He looked around the good-looking blonde to the Indian kids and their little dog, an interesting group.

"May I please use your telephone to call the number on the For Sale sign down the block?" Heidi asked.

"Oh God, yes," he said, pushing the phone toward her. The street had been almost dead since the closing of the restaurant last year. "Not sure if Ruth's back from her little sojourn but she's got a machine."

He listened with unabashed curiosity to the conversation. So, this woman was named Heidi Vogel. She had some kind of accent, probably German from the name. Apparently, she and Ruth knew someone named Beppe. She said she and her kids were going to the lake for a picnic and she wanted to take a look at the restaurant before they returned to Riverton, or she could come back next week. They could talk about Beppe later, but he was doing well. The blonde had a nice laugh, and what a figure. He looked over to see the little kids scowling at him.

"Thank you, Mr. Diaz," said Heidi, handing back the receiver.

"Anytime at all, Ms. Vogel," he replied, standing and giving a little bow.

"C'mon, Aunt Heidi," whined one of the kids.

Heidi Vogel gave an apologetic smile and allowed herself to be tugged out the door.

"You'll find we're a real friendly town," he called after her. "Good schools and hungry people."

Heidi opened all the car windows wide as the Mercedes slowly climbed the steep winding road to Lake Cheynook. The perfume of pine resins and sage entered the car. Light, dark, light, dark, the interior of the car flickered as sunlight pierced the canopy of the swaying trees. The car park was less than a quarter full. The children tore up the trail, waiting for Heidi at the top, excitedly shouting that they saw the lake.

Heidi walked slowly with Gering. According to the vet, the little dachshund had developed IVDD, Intervertebral Disc

Disease. The jelly-like cushions between the lower vertebrae in his spine were hardening, a risk with his breed.

"Keep his weight down, don't ask him to do more than he can do, and we'll see how he progresses," the vet had said.

Heidi stopped and looked up at the twins. They ran back down the trail, Amadeus took the small picnic basket from Heidi, Marcela the towels, and Heidi picked up Gering, who would walk more easily once they got to the top.

They spread their towels on the flat rock that extended into the water, exactly where Heidi said she had put the towels when she brought them and Nara to the lake when they were babies. Across the lake, people gathered to jump off big rocks into deep water, their shrieks echoing off the rocky cliffs behind them.

Heidi took the twins, one at a time, to where the water was over their heads and showed them how to float on their backs and how to roll over and paddle on their fronts. Before they were much older, she would teach them to swim properly, she promised. The question Nara had asked in this very spot four years ago, "Which twin would you save from drowning, if you could only save one?" would never be a factor. They would both be good swimmers; they'd both be safe.

The twins came out of the water for their lunch, sitting on the rock, towels wrapped around them, the sun warm on their faces.

"This is the best place," said Marcela, and Amadeus agreed.

Heidi lay down and looked up at the sky, smiling at the children's giggles and whispers. She felt Gering shift from where he lay nestled under her arm. He started a low growl and got to his feet.

"Aunt Heidi, look, somebody, a lady," hissed Amadeus and Heidi sat up. "She's waving. She's coming."

Gering continued his rumblings at a wiry little woman in a big hat, red-checkered shirt and faded jeans, who was heading purposefully their way.

The woman held up a bag and called with a grin, "Ruth Creeley. You're Heidi Vogel and kids, if I'm not mistaken. I come bearing cookies.

"May I approach your people?" she asked Gering before stepping onto their rock and Marcela giggled.

The woman grinned, advanced and sat down easily, looking very limber and fit.

Ruth said she had come part way up Wild Horse Valley Road to bring some cookies to her friend, Booker McNabb, but she couldn't get through his gate and she didn't feel like climbing over. She remembered Heidi had mentioned kids, so she thought kids, plus cookies . . . why not take a little trip up to the lake?

"Is Booker a kid?" asked Amadeus.

"Not to look at but deep down, there's a lot of kid in there," said Ruth. "He's a metal worker, sculptor, all around clever fellow. If you feel like sharing some of your cookies with him, you can follow me down the hill when you're done here. If he's back, his gate will be open. He's got a horse and a goat."

The children looked at Heidi, eyes wide.

"And," Ruth continued, drawing out the word, "I'm driving a big wheel open-air jeep. If it's okay with your mom, you can take a ride in it. Your mom and the little dog can follow us in your car down the hill."

"She's our aunt," the children chorused, and Ruth made a very formal apology.

They jumped up, ready to go, but Ruth told them to hold their horses and paddle a few minutes so she could have a wee chat with their aunt. Ruth fixed intelligent, bright eyes on Heidi.

"So, tell me, how much business experience have you had? I'm anxious to have a natter about Beppe, but one thing at a time. We'll stop by Booker's if his gate is open, then we'll check out what's on offer on Main Street."

Heidi trailed Ruth's jeep out of the parking lot and down the hill, the kids turning around frequently to check on her progress and wave. The gate stood open and Heidi followed Ruth up a steep gravel drive to the second person she would meet in Comfrey, no, the third person—she had already met Raul Diaz, the lawyer on Main street.

She rounded a bend and slowed to take in the wooden cabin ahead. It had a large front porch, a nice place to wait for guests. A stone building and a small barn with a white-fenced paddock were a short distance to the left. On the right she glimpsed a deck that extended beyond the cabin and into the sky. They must be high above Comfrey.

Heidi watched a tall, broad-shouldered, dark haired man advance on Ruth's Jeep. He halted, shaded his eyes and looked at the Mercedes. He gave his head a small shake before he continued to Ruth. The children were still buckled in the back, grinning and waving at her. Heidi parked behind the Jeep, got out of her car and stretched. The man glanced at her briefly and went back to talking to Ruth.

When the blonde woman came from behind to stand directly in front of him, Booker had no choice but to acknowledge her.

"Hello," he said.

"Hello, Mr. McNabb. I am Heidi Vogel, soon to be Heidi Crow. The twins are my niece and nephew, Marcela and Amadeus. May they get out of Ruth's car?"

Ruth looked on with a grin. "Booker say hello to Heidi, kids say hello to Booker. Then we'll be done and Booker can go on haranguing me about my Jeep. He thinks I got ripped off by the by, although I like it. I expect you're safe, Heidi. He'll consider your car an intriguing anomaly."

Booker turned dark eyes to Heidi, the corner of his mouth raised a fraction. "I do like the looks of your car, Miss Vogel soon to be Crow, and yes, I do think Ruth's ridiculous Jeep is going to be trouble. The speedometer stopped at 200,000 who knows how many years ago. Ruth should stick to her old trucks." He looked at the kids. "Get out by all means, run around. The horse is friendly, goat's not very."

"Can Gering come too? We'll hold him," promised the little girl. "His back hurts sometimes."

Booker raised his eyebrows at Heidi.

"Gering is our dachshund. He is in my car," she said.

Something tugged at Booker's memory, a small dachshund, a blonde shivering in her underwear, how long ago had that been? He narrowed his eyes at the woman, yeah, he remembered her. You didn't forget a woman trying to put a bra on under her jacket. For a couple of months, he'd hoped to catch another glimpse of her by the lake, promising himself next time he'd get off his horse and say hello.

"Sure, get the dog out," he said to the little girl before turning his attention to Ruth. "Is this a visit? I was just going to light the forge, but if you want, we could go inside or on the deck, make some coffee or tea."

"Well, that's a warm invitation Booker. I was hoping Heidi would see how friendly we are around here, and I'd like her to look down on Comfrey from your deck. I'll be showing her the old Taylor's Refresher building on Main Street."

Booker glanced at Heidi. Damn, she was a nice-looking woman, with an accent. German? Blue eyes to go with it. Was she becoming 'Crow' by marrying the kids' dad?

"Coffee, tea, water?" he asked.

Ruth was enjoying herself immensely. "Coffee?" she said, looking at Heidi.

"Mr. McNabb has a date with his forge," said Heidi. "We should not interrupt him."

"I'm sure Mr. McNabb would prefer to be called Booker, and he has time for coffee since we brought the cookies. Got any juice for the kids, Booker?" Ruth gave him a grin.

"Might," said Booker. "Come in the house, Ruth, and give me a hand."

Ruth winked at Heidi and followed Booker inside. She was going to get an earful.

"Just bringing you cookies, just showing a friend of a very old friend around, didn't mean to invade your manly little enclave. We'll gulp our coffee, thank you, and be off before you know it." Ruth got a bottle of apple juice out of a cupboard. "I wanted Heidi to see Comfrey from above, or we wouldn't have dreamed of dropping by unannounced."

"You never announce when you're coming. You just show up and Jesus, Ruth, I haven't even said anything yet." Booker looked for a can opener to open a new can of Folgers. Instant wasn't going to cut it.

"Saying it for you." Ruth opened the fridge. "You have cream? She looks like a cream girl to me, maybe sugar, what do you think?"

"No, I don't have cream. I don't use it."

"Ah, here it is," said Ruth, finding a small carton behind the rice pudding she had made for him a couple of days ago. "I put the cream in last week, when I brought up that apple pie. I told you to whip it."

"Well, obviously . . ."

"Never mind," Ruth interrupted. "I'll have to remember whipping half a pint of cream is too much cooking for you. I'll dilute it with a little milk and it'll be perfect for the lovely Miss Heidi." Ruth got a jug out of a cabinet. "Where'd you get this pretty little jug, Booker?"

"I have no idea. You probably gave it to me when you brought that box of dishes over."

"So I did. Coffee almost ready? I'd like to show her the restaurant before it gets too late. She's got to get back to Riverton tonight."

"The coffee was your idea. So, is she marrying the kids' father? Is he the Crow?"

338

"She did mention becoming a Crow," said Ruth thoughtfully. "She hasn't mentioned a current man. She used to be married, had a restaurant in New York with an ex-husband. He was the Vogel. She didn't talk about how she's connected to the kids, other than to say she's their aunt, which doesn't look likely but still . . ." Ruth put the cream back in the fridge, "the kids might be Crows. She didn't use their last name. I'll let you know."

"Christ almighty, Ruth, don't bother. I'm not interested in her or her kids. And what's with a dog like that in Wyoming? That's some coyote's lunch."

"You still bedding that agent of yours from Jackson, Booker?"

Was that a cackle he heard? Booker swore silently, Ruth could be so damn annoying sometimes. "Let's get this coffee over with. I've got a deadline, that elk piece is due to Rock Springs next week."

Heidi watched Ruth follow the *hübscher mürrischer Mann-Kind* into the cabin. She grinned at the epithet, handsome grumpy man-child, as she followed the children's voices to the horse paddock. The goat hadn't come over but the horse was standing at the fence, letting itself be petted. Gering stood on the ground, trembling, looking tiny and forlorn.

"You forget Gering," Heidi accused, picking the little dog up and holding him close.

"He didn't want the horse to sniff at him," said Marcela.

Heidi frowned. "Look how big this horse is. Compare it to Gering, of course he feels afraid."

The children looked at Gering, no bigger than a loaf of bread in Heidi's arms, and saw her point. "Sorry," Amadeus said.

"This nice man, Booker, and Ruth are getting us something to drink," said Heidi, starting toward the cabin with Gering tucked safely under her arm. "Come onto the deck of the cabin and see Comfrey from the top."

The children took off. They ran onto the deck and marveled at the view. They could see the whole town, and there was an airplane coming into the airstrip. A spotting scope was set up, but Heidi wouldn't let them touch it until their host gave his permission.

After Booker and Ruth came back with the drinks and a bowl of water for the dog, Booker got a box for the kids to stand on and let them look through the scope. He stood next to them with his cup of coffee and listened to the women behind him chattering about someone named Beppe.

"Who's Beppe?" he asked the kids.

"Our uncle," said the boy.

"He's going to get married to our other uncle when the world comes to its senses," said his sister.

Booker gave a burst of laughter and the girl scowled at him. "That's what Aunt Heidi says. She says the world has to come to its senses and then Karl and Beppe can get married."

"Yeah, I'd say she's right about that." Booker shook his head and tried to hide his grin.

Booker walked them to their cars and they said their thank yous and goodbyes. The kids waved from the back of the Jeep, the Mercedes followed behind. The woman, the dog, the underwear had been pale blue. She was a little thing. She'd looked bigger from the horse. But there was something tough about her. He chuckled. How long had it been? Five or six years? Maybe more?

The children chased each other through the lower floor of the building as Heidi and Ruth poked around. The room to the side of the main eating area had once been used as a bar. The kitchen was generous. There were three pantries, one had become a little office space, and several store rooms. Heidi remarked everything was very clean for a place that had been shut down for over a year. Ruth explained she had the Dubois brothers come in to air the place out weekly. Heidi would find the apartment and offices upstairs similarly fresh.

"You'll find Tyree and Armand Dubois very useful," said Ruth, as if Heidi had already made an offer and it had been accepted. "Every business in Comfrey uses them for something. They even help Booker McNabb take his art pieces here and there, but I don't think they can cook. I have another man in mind to help you in the kitchen, a gentleman who went through a bad patch, to judge from the burn scars on his face. He's in the Mandarin class I teach in Rock Springs three times a week. I'm filling in for someone on maternity leave."

"Mandarin? You speak Chinese?" Heidi was unable to keep the surprise out of her voice.

"I speak Cantonese too, courtesy of my Chinese father, but there's more demand for Mandarin. By demand, I'm not saying there's a lot of interest out here, but the Twenty-first Century is approaching. More people should learn another language or two."

"Yes, I agree but . . . You are half Chinese?"

"Do I look half Chinese to you?" Ruth grinned at the bright blue eyes, opened wide with disbelief. Girl probably thought she was a nutcase, better trot out the explanation. She told Heidi that Jerome Lee had been a stepfather, but he had helped raise her from five, so she wasn't making him a 'step' anything. He had been a very dear man and he had been her father pure and simple.

Heidi agreed the term stepfather carried with it a certain distance

Ruth beamed. She was enjoying getting to know this young woman, but the children would be demanding their aunt's attention soon, and she had more enticements to offer.

"Let's not get sidetracked," Ruth said. "I'd like to tell you about this man from my class, Esau Aoah. Shoshone. He has a way with food or I wouldn't have mentioned him. Each class we have a potluck because everything goes better with food and what he manages to create, in what he describes as a very minimal kitchen at the halfway house he currently lives in, is truly exceptional. He's a real find."

Heidi laughed. "I think the cart is put in front of the horse."

Ruth raised an eyebrow then chuckled. "Cart before the horse? No. I don't think so. My feelers say you're coming to us. Now, let's take a looksee upstairs."

The apartment had two bedrooms, appliances but no furniture. Ruth said she knew of three estate sales coming up in the surrounding areas. Heidi could easily find what she needed there, unless she was tied to a specific decorating scheme.

"Comfortable and no cigarette smoke smell is my scheme," said Heidi.

"Then two of the estate sales will suit you just fine. The Dubois boys will pick up whatever you buy and deliver it. Now, you said the kids are almost six?"

"Their birthday is in October."

"Good. They're young enough to still share a room and we'll have you into a proper house before it starts to matter. We'll find you a place near our excellent school, and I expect you'll want a nice-sized yard."

"Do people tell you, Ruth, that you push, push, push? I can not catch my breath," said Heidi, wondering why she wasn't finding the woman more irritating.

"All the time," said Ruth with a grin. "But I'm harmless."

Heidi laughed. What had Beppe said all those years ago about Ruth? That she sees who you are? That she had helped him when he was more lost that he had ever been? He hadn't mentioned how much Ruth talked.

Ruth invited them back to her house for minestrone soup, saying the children could have a run around and see her animals while Heidi looked over the inspections commissioned by the couple, who had backed out of the deal last month.

"You may want to get your own inspections of course, but I assure you there was nothing in the inspections that concerned them," said Ruth. "They got cold feet because their banker said we're a little out of the way here."

"You *are* out of the way here," Heidi pointed out.

"And it's never bothered us one bit, plus our airstrip brings in hunters, hikers, people who appreciate the outdoors but don't want all the posh Jackson Hole foists upon them. Now let's get some soup into you."

The soup was very good. Marcela got to bottle feed a kitten that Ruth had picked up cowering by a road leading into Farson during last week's unexpected downpour. At Ruth's request, Amadeus shinnied up a pear tree to get the pears at the very top.

After supper, Ruth followed them out to the car and pressed a slim volume into Heidi's hand. "It's my little foray into fiction," Ruth said, "but it's firmly rooted in fact. I've used the names of real people, two of them my direct ancestors. Most of the others are people who traveled on Captain William Hardy's wagon train in 1852. I wrote the tiny tome in a matter of hours, although of course, I was already well-versed in the history of the West."

"Hours? This is very fast," Heidi said.

"So they tell me, but I just closed my eyes and whole scenarios revealed themselves to me—the dialogue, people's thoughts, the smells, the sounds. Some gave me their names, others did not," Ruth shrugged, "then I sat up and typed until I was done. You will see I adopted a rather formal style, which amuses my friends to no end, but that was how people spoke at the time. I relied on primary sources, diaries, letters, but mostly, I was just listening to the people speaking to me in my head."

"Remarkable," said Heidi.

Ruth beamed. "It is indeed, and I'm proud to have been chosen as a channel of sorts. One word of warning, don't confuse the McNabbs in my writing with the McNabb you met today. Booker's more of a peach than he may have seemed, by the way. He's from a branch of the McNabb family that did not join the Oregon Trail. He arrived here a seven years ago on a motorcycle and turned many a pretty head."

"I will remember not to confuse him with the McNabb people in your book," Heidi said solemnly, holding up the little book for emphasis.

"You need to get yourself going." Ruth nodded at the children, already in the car. "Drive safely, not too fast. That little boy says you drive too fast."

Heidi looked at Amadeus through the car window and he ducked his head.

"I'm usually a no-frills, scientifically minded sort of person," Ruth was saying, "but, like I may have mentioned, I have feelers, and my feelers tell me you're destined to come here."

"We will see," Heidi said, getting in behind the wheel. She had learned from Karl never to appear too eager to close a deal, but she had come up with an offer, which was close to the asking price.

Ruth promised to present Heidi's offer tonight. Since a deal had fallen through last month, the owners were very anxious to sell. They were now living with their daughter in Evanston, and she needed their help with her mortgage.

As they drove out of Comfrey, Heidi told the twins they must say something if she started to drive too fast. They promised they would if she promised to take them back to the lake tomorrow.

"Not tomorrow," said Heidi. "Tomorrow is Sunday and I have too much to do. To buy a business will not happen over the night. Our offer has to be accepted by the owners. I need to review the building inspections. I have to arrange with your Uncle Karl to help with the money. We need to be patient."

"Why can't we just not have a restaurant and still move to Comfrey," said Marcela, frowning. "We don't have to have a restaurant. You can do lots of good stuff."

"What other job do you suggest I do?" Heidi checked the speedometer and slowed.

"You're always cleaning and there are a bunch of houses in Comfrey," said Marcela. "People would give you lots of money to clean their house."

"Comfrey seems like a place where people clean their own houses," said Heidi, biting back a grin at the thought of what Karl would say if she told him she was giving up her years of culinary training to clean houses. "What do you think, Amadeus?"

"I think I'm going to get a horse. Ruth says there are lots of horses around." Amadeus nodded at his reflection in the window. A horse.

"We don't have to have a restaurant if we move into Ruth's house," Marcela said. "We could help her with her animals. She said I could have the kitten I gave the bottle to if we move here."

"You do not want the Guinea pig for your birthday anymore?" asked Heidi.

Marcela shook her head. "No, a kitten. Please."

Or maybe they could live next to Booker, thought Amadeus, his chest beginning to swell with relief. They could build a cabin next to Booker's. There was lots of room and Booker could pay Aunt Heidi to clean for him. His horse could live with Booker's horse and the goat. Until today, everything had been pressing down on him—because of Marcela and not going to school anymore and Mama sometimes talking when he didn't want her to. Why didn't she ever talk to Marcela? Why couldn't they be the other kind of twins where one could have girl parts? Then Marcela's spirit would be in the right body and she wouldn't have to be so sad and mad. But a horse . . . if he had a horse and Marcela got the kitten, and they moved to a place where the school didn't know about Marcela, everything would be so, so much better.

CHAPTER THIRTY FIVE

RUTH'S TINY TOME

"Ruth," Booker said, picking up the phone in his shop, knowing it would be her. She always phoned at this time of night if she knew he had been working in his shop, just to check he hadn't dropped an anvil on his toe, she said.

"She's the children's aunt and their guardian," Ruth said without preamble. "They're 'Crow' so she's in the process of changing her name to match theirs. Sounds like she's claiming kinship with their father but she was much more attached to the mother who died in a car accident, fairly recently, I think. She was a little cagey about the whole business so I didn't want to press."

"You never press."

"Indeed," said Ruth. "Regardless, she's interested in coming to Comfrey. She actually made an offer, contingent on all the usual things. She's a sharp businesswoman. I gave her my little history, told her to read it to get a taste of our town."

"Yeah, that'll rope her in."

"Have you even read it, Booker McNabb? It's less than twenty pages including my introduction."

"Sure, I've read most of it . . . well, some of it. 1850, Greta Magroot and the founding of Comfrey, orphaned children, a dead ox, but you said you made a lot of it up on your intro page."

"I did not. I said it is a synthesis of Greta's diaries and other historical documents I researched, with some dabs of artistic license to smooth out the edges. It reads like a nice little story but it's an important document, the founding of Comfrey. Read it, all sixteen pages, you can bet Heidi Vogel Crow will. It will give you something to talk to her about the next time you see her."

Booker gave a snort and reminded Ruth he was a very busy man. He had a show coming up.

Ignoring this, Ruth continued, "She's got a little baking business in Riverton. She thinks she might want to move it here, in addition to reopening the restaurant. That's a nice dose of jobs for us. She has a cousin who will help with a hefty down payment. He and his Italian lover, who, as unbelievable as it might sound, I knew many, many years ago, are part of her baking business too. The children call them their uncles and they seem very closely involved with the family."

"Yeah, Beppe and Karl. They're getting married when the world comes to its senses."

"Say that again?"

"Can't, gotta work on the elk. Good luck with your sale," said Booker, hanging up with a broad grin. It felt good to have one up on Ruth.

He went into his studio, turned the radio on loud to country rock, and fired up the forge. He worked until midnight, stopping when he suddenly realized he'd missed dinner. He hadn't eaten anything since Ruth's cookies eight hours ago. He staggered to the house to take a long shower. He soaped and chuckled as he worked his shoulder. Heidi Vogel Crow, twins, gay uncles waiting for the world to come to its senses—if the woman bought the restaurant, maybe he'd stop by for a meal every now and then.

He grabbed a beer, made a cheese sandwich and fell asleep on the living room couch before finishing either.

***

Heidi carried the sleeping twins into the house, one by one. It had been a very long day. She lay them on their beds, removed their shoes and pulled their quilts up, letting them sleep in their clothes. She went back to the car to get Ruth's book and the rest of their belongings. Did Ruth use her book to reel people in, the way she had let Marcela feed the kitten and let Amadeus climb to the top of the pear tree? The way she had brought them to meet the brooding Booker McNabb. 'A peach,' Heidi chuckled to herself. Oh, Ruth Creeley was a conniver to be sure.

Gering accompanied Heidi into the bathroom and curled up on the bathmat. Heidi applied a dose of Epsom salts to her bath water and lowered herself in, sighing with pleasure as the soft water surrounded her. She patted her hands on a dry wash cloth and picked up Ruth's book. On the back cover, Ruth grinned into the camera from under a hat that might have been the same one she had worn today. Under her photo, a short paragraph described Ruth as a descendent of Toot and Greta Magroot, Comfrey's founders. Ruth spoke Mandarin, Cantonese and Urdu and in her younger years, she had trotted the globe, but now her duties as realtor and a member of the town planning commission kept her close to home. Since 1988, she had worked for Wyoming Fish and Game as the only certified opossum rehabilitation specialist in Sublette County. Heidi peered more closely at the photograph. On closer inspection, what she had assumed was a cat in Ruth's arms was clearly an opossum.

"*Mein Gott,*" whispered Heidi. 1988, the year she had fled New York, Ruth was in Wyoming becoming a certified opossum rehabilitation specialist. "Nara is the pouch, I am the back, and now Ruth Creeley is the opossum rehabilitation specialist," she said softly.

Heidi leaned back in the bath. If Peter had lived, would she ever have taken him to Wyoming? Perhaps they might have passed through if they had gone on a cross-country adventure, and they would have stopped to see Yellowstone and the Grand Tetons, but they would not have tarried. Now here she was, with two children very different from her son and she was considering taking them to live on the Green River Basin side of the Wind River Mountains for at least the foreseeable future.

She opened Ruth's slim volume and began to read.

***

THE FOUNDING OF COMFREY, 1852
A fiction rooted in fact
By Ruth Roos Creeley

It was a warm spring day in mid-May of 1852. This would be Captain William Hardy's seventh trip shepherding families to Oregon's Willamette Valley. His present group was a small one as it prepared to roll out of Independence, Missouri. Relatives and friends gathered to say goodbye and bestow one last basket of apples, dried fruit, or a freshly baked loaf or pie. Children laughed, dogs barked and wagged their tails. A cat in a cage looked fearfully out from back of one of the wagons and hissed at curious faces that came too close. Oxen shook their heads in their yokes and rolled their eyes, a cow bellowed and horses stamped their feet impatiently. The air was alive with cheerful voices, laughter, hope and trepidation.

A month before departure, the Captain had gathered his families and counseled them on the merits of oxen compared to mules. Mules were faster, but harder to handle and required better food. Oxen would eat most anything and although slow, they were mighty strong. Castrated young and trained early, they were tractable and resigned to being beasts of burden. For the most part, the wagons would be transporting food, water, some clothing, tools, weapons and perhaps a few keepsakes. The Captain warned of seeing fine china, furniture and family heirlooms cast by the wayside as the Rocky Mountains approached. He told each family what to pack, how much food to bring and what the rules would be to settle disputes.

For the first third of the journey, the wagons would follow river valleys. The valleys offered a walkable grade, and walk the travelers would, for two thousand miles. There would be fresh water and ample grass for the first month, but as the trail gradually rose in elevation before the foothills of the Rockies, the land became less forgiving and the graceful prairie grasses surrendered to tough blue-gray scrub, yellow dirt and red rock.

"Prepare for wind," the Captain cautioned.

Heat, cold, thunder and lightning, water that was sweet and water that could kill a person overnight. There would be dust. Oh Lord, there would be dust. Those wagon trains that set out a few weeks earlier had already broken through winter's suppression and now the earth was as soft as a blanket. On a calm day, for those at the beginning of the train, the dust merely encompassed feet and ankles. A small breeze elevated the blanket to the knees. About ten wagons back, the dust crept even higher, up petticoats, up noses, in mouths and ears. Captain William Hardy, impervious to bribery, rotated the wagons with a precision worthy of his rank. He temporarily blocked the sun as he rode up and down the ranks, leaning over to encourage, sitting erect in the saddle to chastise.

Usually they would travel through neutral land, but Lakota Sioux, Shoshone, Arapaho, Crow and Cheyenne people crossed the area from their recognized tribal zones. Each year brought an increase in tension between pioneers and Indians, but for now leaders like the Captain traded respect, blankets, weapons and tools for safe passage. Seven to ten days out of Fort Laramie, Captain Hardy planned to cross the North Platte and continue along the Sweet Water. They would avoid the Indian *unrest in the more northern parts of the Rockies and cross the mountains at their lowest point, South Pass, a broad valley at an elevation of just over 7400 ft.*

Most of Hardy's forty-seven families came from two small Missouri towns and knew each other, at least in passing, but the Magroots and the McNabbs came from Pennsylvania, and that may have been part of the reason they preferred each other's company and kept their wagons close. The Magroots and the McNabbs were unique in other ways as well. Mr. Faolan McNabb was a big red-haired Scot with a burr so pronounced few could understand him. Much was made of his Christian name, which they pronounced 'FOOL an,' though the jokesters quieted in the evening when the families gathered around the campfire and Faolan sang hymns in a rich yearning baritone, accompanied by his brown-skinned daughter on her violin.

Mrs. Cora McNabb was a Negress. In 1852, Pennsylvania was one of two states that allowed Negros and whites to marry, but no family on this wagon train had ever witnessed such a union. When the McNabb wagon joined the train, Mrs. Duncan declared she talked to Mrs. McNabb for several minutes before realizing that she was talking to a Negress because Mrs. McNabb's sunbonnet was so deep, her face had been in shadow.

"I feel for those children," Mrs. Duncan said to any who would listen. "Not knowing what they are. Not natural, that taking up with a Negress, but maybe the poor fellow did not know better, being from Scotland. Someone should have told him."

God spoke to Mrs. Duncan and she knew it was her duty, to make His feelings known. The Magroots shocked Mrs. Duncan even more profoundly than the McNabbs. Tiny Greta Magroot insisted she and her three daughters wear men's clothes just like her husband and four sons. And her great strapping husband, with the unlikely name of 'Toot,' went right along with it.

"Oh, I know you, Mrs. Duncan," Heidi said aloud. Narrow-minded self-righteous people, her father's side of the family was full of them. She turned off the hot water tap and continued to read.

When Greta had learned the trip was over two thousand miles and that they would be walking most of the way, she couldn't imagine her girls or herself wearing heavy skirts and aprons, tromping along in the dust mile after mile, week after week, month after month. Eventually Mrs. Duncan's accident would prove her point. The Magroots brought along two horses and all took turns riding them. The women rode the horses astride, just like the men.

"Immodest for a woman to ride like that," Mrs. Duncan sniffed. "Those girls will sacrifice their virginity if they part their legs and straddle a horse like that."

Heidi laughed out loud, but she quickly sobered. If the other settlers hadn't been so busy with their grim tromping, a woman like that could have caused real harm stirring up trouble against the perceived strangers in their midst. Heidi yawned; the warmth of the water was too enervating to continue reading in the bathtub. She was less than half the way through Ruth's little book, but when Ruth phoned tomorrow, she would like to be able say she had finished it. She closed the book, got out of the bath and dried herself on one of the orange towels that had belonged to Ray Dolan's sister. Ray had outfitted her house with his sister's things, Ray had cared for Gering until she had arrived in Riverton. People had responded to her kindly all her life, they had smiled and offered her a hand. Beppe was right, she had been a favored child and now she was a favored adult. Mrs. Duncan on the Oregon Trail would have liked her, Heidi was sure.

She put on her nightie, but rather than going to bed, she sat up in the easy chair in the sitting room, Gering under the orange blanket on her lap, and returned to Ruth's tale. Imagined or not, it rang true . . .

Clean water, enough food, good humor and luck kept Death at bay for the first eighteen days of the trip, but once he plucked little Sara Cox from her mother's arms in the late afternoon of June 3rd, he took up permanent residence on the train. He caused unbelievable misery, and everlasting peace. Some families he passed over, some he visited several times in a night. He drained bodies of their fluids, fomented fevers and painted spots on downy cheeks. He fractured bones, and lacerated limbs. He impaled, he caused guns to misfire. Five weeks into the trip, he caught Mrs. Duncan's skirts in a wagon wheel and pulled her under, cutting her almost in half.

When Death stole both parents from the four McNabb children during their attempt to cross the North Platte River, he changed the future of the Magroot family as well. Unlike the other families on the Hardy wagon train, the McNabbs had mules pulling their wagon. Tears filled Faolan's eyes when he confided in Toot that his wife's father had spent his entire life's worth on the gift of six mules. The old man believed each family member, even the baby, should have their own mule when they got to Oregon.

"Can't start out in life any better than that!" the old man assured each of his grandchildren as they gathered before him. "Each mule has a little part of me watching out for you."

It wasn't the mules' fault that it had been a particularly wet spring and that the muddy waters of the North Platte were deeper and swifter than usual for June. It wasn't the mules' fault that the back axle of the McNabb's wagon broke as they attempted to ford the North Platte, but when the axle broke, two mules were dragged under and the other four panicked. The water was whipped into a muddy froth as hooves flailed, mules brayed and squealed, and children screamed. The wagon tipped and Cora McNabb was thrown into the river. Faolan went after his wife as Toot and some of the other men managed to release four of the mules and get them to the other side. The Magroot boys rescued the three older children. The baby, swaddled in blankets, nestled in a basket, was found shortly thereafter bobbing peacefully in a bank of reeds. A tiny Moses, bright-eyed and smiling.

Greta and one of her daughters rode almost a mile down the riverbank until they spied a flag of cloth waving merrily from a partially submerged branch. The flag was of the lovely floral pattern Greta had complimented Cora on the first time they met. Faolan was lying face down on top of his wife just under the water's surface. The two, mired in the crown of a fallen cottonwood, had left this world in each other's arms.

The McNabb children stood wordlessly as their parents were laid to rest in a hastily dug grave. Captain William Hardy changed into his Sunday shirt and read a prayer from the Holy Bible as Greta washed the faces of the departed with lavender oil and placed a posy of comfrey and wild flowers in Cora's clasped hands. She led the children away from the grave so they wouldn't see their parents covered with dirt. She and her daughters sat with them on a small hill as the Captain, Toot and some of the other men discussed the fate of the McNabb children. The most difficult and longest part of the journey was yet to come and charity was a luxury no family could afford. There were two offers for the oldest girl if she came with the mules, but the twin boys were just eight and not much use. The baby needed milk and should obviously go to a nursing mother or a family with a cow, but no offers were made. Greta stood up and walked down the hill to her husband. She put her arms around his waist and he bent his ear to her upturned face. She finished saying her piece and they stood looking into each other's faces until he at last nodded and pressed his lips to her forehead. Toot looked up the hill to where eleven children sat, seven of his own and four McNabbs. He raised his hands high above his head, fingers splayed, then clenched his fists, and opened one hand again, holding three fingers high.

"Thirteen," breathed his oldest daughter, holding the McNabb baby tight. "Papa means us to be thirteen."

Heidi nodded. She had meant to ask Ruth why the white cabins on the outskirts of Comfrey were called 'Toot's Lucky Thirteen.'

Four days after Faolan and Cora McNabb were buried by the waters of the North Platte River, the wagon train halted at a massive monolith rising up from the dry, lonely prairie scrub. Named Independence Rock by fur traders celebrating the Fourth of July at the site in 1830, the rounded granite leviathan offered a chance at immortality to those who carved their names upon its surface. There would be plenty of opportunity for Death to cull the travellers in the increasingly difficult path ahead, but here they could claim they had made it this far.

Greta handed sleepy little Tobias McNabb to her husband. She held out her hand to Eliza, the baby's fifteen-year-old sister, and the two walked toward the rock with a hammer and a chisel. Toot tucked the baby inside his coat and the baby's black curly hair tufted out the coat's open neck and mingled with Toot's sandy-red beard. Captain Hardy came to stand by them and they watched as families swarmed the rock, running fingers over names, reading them out loud, shouting with delight when they recognized a friend or relative. From the top of the rock children spun in circles pointing to where they had been and to where they were going. Adults who made the climb surveyed the desolate path that disappeared over the horizon ahead and fell silent, refusing to meet each other's eyes.

The Captain pulled off his hat and ran his fingers through his shock of white hair, standing it on end. "Looks like that wife of yours is intending to scribe the Magroot name in that rock," he remarked.

"No, she is going to scribe 'Faolan and Cora, 1852' . . . for the children."

The Captain considered this, then turned to Toot, "You got a plan here, son?"

Toot watched his wife and the McNabb's oldest child examine potential sites for their epitaph, then he rubbed a hand over his face and sighed.

"Say what you need to say, Captain . . . I will listen, sir."

Captain Hardy reached over and gently pulled one of the sleeping baby's black curls and watched it bounce back. He smiled and shook his head. He watched the younger man cradle the baby and remembered holding his own son within his coat in that same way many years ago. He chose his words carefully and prayed his counsel would not fall upon a deaf ear.

"What you did, taking in all four of those children, will get you reward someday son, but not now. Now you have a mighty burden. And that red ox of yours? The one with the white mark like a heart," the Captain tapped his forehead to indicate the ox's blaze, "gets lamer day by day. May make it to South Pass, but I can't see him going further than that. Not with what's to come. What did you name that animal? You name him Sweetheart?"

"He's called Sweetheart, yes sir. Got his hoof caught in some metal scrap, old wheel rim laying just to the side, week or so ago. Swollen at the cleft now, favors it some. Greta's treating the lameness but says it's getting away from her. He's a good animal."

"He is that and your wife's medicine box is surely a thing to behold. I know your Greta is good with the herbs and salves, but you may be looking at butchering that animal. Can't have him suffer much longer. You got those four mules now, but they will not work with oxen."

"I know it. Greta thinks we should look to get off the trail somewhere, but I'm not ready. Not here and not yet."

"May not be up to you son. May be up to Sweetheart and Greta and that brood of eleven young ones you're bound up with now."

The wind picked up suddenly and eddies of dirt, dry leaves and twigs danced around the wagons and in the shallow dry gully between the men and the rock. Toot turned tired eyes to the Captain and searched his face.

"Sir, do you see beauty here? Greta says there is beauty here, in this land." Toot stretched an arm out and shook his head. "I surely do not see it. My wife, she sees things I cannot. I know that. But here is a barren land, not a kind one."

The baby opened his brown eyes and looked from Toot to the Captain. He gave a yawn and pursed his lips, stuck out a pink tongue and sampled the air. Toot put his finger in his mouth to clean it and offered it to the baby who sucked on it contentedly and closed his eyes.

The Captain watched, amused. He had done that same thing to soothe his own child when his wife took sick. He considered Toot's question. He had made his peace with this land, although it was not kind and the beauty was not apparent, but he was not surprised Greta Magroot had seen it. As a matter of course, he would not suggest a family leave the trail but he had a sense that those brown-skinned children would allay some of the fear and suspicion that was brewing in a few of the Indian tribes. This family was different and Greta Magroot and her potions . . . well, he was not a fanciful man, but she had a powerful peace about her.

"She's a woman of hope, your wife," Captain Hardy continued. "Not a tall woman, but she sees further than most. I tell you, Toot . . . soon after the Rockies, there is travel so harsh, so forlorn, each step takes you closer to Oregon or closer to the right hand of God. If I was in your circumstance, I tell you what I would do. As we descend from South Pass there is a trail well used by Indians and trappers. It leads northeast to the base of a range of mountains with snow peaks. That snow *melts into rivers that course here and there. As I was heading back to Missouri from my last journey west, I took this trail for half the day. Just curious I was, due to the well-travelled nature of the path and the beauty of those mountain peaks. It led to a place, just before the mountains, with springs of good water surrounded by cottonwood trees, pasture, some shelter from the wind. If you make it over South Pass with us, I will show you the path. It's at least eight days from where we stand now, so you have some time to consider. You talk to your wife.*

"This is where we learn how Greta saves the day," Heidi told Gering, who had woken himself up with a sneeze. "Listen, I will read it to you."

"Sweetheart set the pace as the Magroot's wagon labored over South Pass, dropping further and further behind the rest of the wagon train. Captain Hardy circled back twice to check on their progress and give words of encouragement, but a look at the suffering red ox confirmed his belief that Toot must lead his family off the trail. Sweetheart strained, favoring his swollen leg by leaning to the side, chafing his neck against his yoke. His head sunk low and dried saliva coated his muzzle like a meringue, despite the rag soaked in precious water Greta repeatedly pressed to his mouth and nose. The air was soured by his pain. His huge muscles bunched under his sweat-darkened hide and his breathing was pitiful to hear. Greta walked alongside the beast, stroking his neck with a small hand caked with dirt from dust mixed with the ox's sweat. Sweetheart's ear moved ever so slightly as Greta continued her soft murmuring. The Captain rode next to them for as long as he could, providing some relief from the sun. When she turned her face up to him to offer her thanks, he did not see Toot's despair in her eyes. He saw empathy, courage and great resolution.

He leaned from his saddle to hear her say, her voice husky with exhaustion, "We will stop at that place you suggested Captain Hardy, and we thank you much. You have taken good care of us, and we wish you well on the journey ahead."

Heidi lifted the orange blanket and said to Gering, "See, I tell you that Greta will save them." He opened a sleepy eye, blinked and curled into a tighter ball. "I do not want to disturb your doggy sleep, so I will read the rest to myself," she dropped the blanket and patted his little form under it, "but I tell you, the woman is usually the stronger one. We know that. And we pray Sweetheart will be alright now."

The McNabb mules, now pack animals and not consigned to pulling a wagon, led the way over South Pass. Four of the older children walked with the mules. Toot, and his oldest son, Caleb, rode the horses. Greta continued walking next to Sweetheart. Hiram Magroot, a sturdy young man of sixteen with the red-gold coloring of his father had developed a particular affinity for baby Tobias and he held the infant in a makeshift sling around his neck. He also kept an eye on the younger children who, relieved at learning their journey was coming to a premature close, quickened their steps and marched with grim determination.

The other wagons in the train could barely be seen now, so far ahead were they, their dust a faint cloud on the horizon. As Captain Hardy had promised, the path to the snowcapped mountains intersected the trail at a small swale about a thousand feet down the western side of South Pass. From the trail, the red dirt path could be seen to disappear and reappear as it snaked its way over and around low hills through tough silver-grey scrub. The mountains, dark as a bruise, pressed themselves against a pale blue, windswept sky. The only sounds to be heard were the creak of the wagon, always the creak of the wagon, and the effort of Sweetheart's deep sonorous breathing that seemed to consume his great barrel of a body from nostrils to tail.

The path was barely the width of the wagon. The red clay-like dirt was less dusty than the trail. A narrow stream bordered the path on one side and some taller vegetation and the occasional tree took root here and there. The stream close to the trail intersection was muddied and foul, but the Captain had vowed that if they continued along the path about a quarter mile, they would come to the shelter of a small canyon where a pool of water gathered, hemmed in by boulders. The water was clear and without strong odor and he and his horse had drunk it with no ill effect. Here, the Captain said, he and two others would leave items that members of the wagon train felt they could no longer transport, but that might perhaps be of use to a homesteading family in this remote countryside.

Sweetheart collapsed before reaching the pool of clean water. His swollen leg failed and he descended with a groan across the path, pulling his yoke mate's neck down with him at a tortured angle. Toot and Caleb, managed to rapidly release both oxen from their yoke. Caleb handed the healthy ox over to the eight-year-old McNabb twins who put a rope through its halter and went to stand in the meager shade of a scrubby pine, their large brown eyes filled with awe at their new responsibility.

When Sweetheart buckled, the path was at its narrowest, winding its way between two rock shelves. He effectively blocked the way for the wagon and second pair of oxen. Greta agreed that she should take the children ahead and they would wait at the pool, leaving Toot, Caleb and Hiram to put a merciful end to Sweetheart's suffering. They would endeavor to move him out of the way and bring the wagon and other two oxen through.

From down the path, Greta heard the shot and gasped. She pressed her hand to her heart and closed her eyes. Eliza McNabb turned and took Greta's hand, which trembled like a baby bird. The mules shook their heads impatiently, their large *ears moving forward and back. The children gathered around Greta, quiet, unaccustomed to her silent tears. She drew a deep breath, opened her eyes and gave them a tentative smile.*

"Such a good animal," she said. "Such a friend."

"Greta, I am so, so sorry," whispered Heidi. She lifted her head and looked blindly at the ceiling, letting her own tears fall for the ox named Sweetheart. And she wept for the orphaned McNabb children and for Nara and for Amadeus because he couldn't let Nara go, and for Marcela's hurt . . . and for Peter, always for Peter.

After a while, drained, she got up, put Gering on the floor and went into the kitchen to splash some cold water on her face. As she blotted her face dry with a paper towel and blew her nose, she became conscious that the house had filled with an expectant stillness, as if telling her it had been a very long day, to finish this little book and go to bed. Heidi heaved a sigh and returned to her chair. Surely in Ruth's story it was time for Death to retreat for just a little while. She resettled Gering on her lap—seven more pages, it seemed like a lot. She opened the book, smoothed the pages and blinked her tired eyes to read more from the voices that had spoken to Ruth.

Toot watched his wife round the bend before he pressed the gun to the ox's white heart-shaped blaze, closed his eyes and pulled the trigger. Hiram knelt by the animal and placed his hand on its neck, waiting for the last contraction of that mighty heart, the last attempt to push blood to the lungs. He looked up, nodded, and stood to join his father and brother. They removed their hats and bowed their heads, humbled by the stillness that consumes the loss of life.

"Papa, we've got to take the meat and do it now. He'll be easier to move if we cut him up some, take what we can, pull the rest of him aside," Caleb said.

"Right," Toot agreed. "We take what meat we can in an

hour and leave the rest to the night. He'll not go to waste. Spread a sheet in the wagon and we'll lay the meat there. Remove your shirts. We wash in the creek before we leave. Can't have the children see or smell so much blood."

The butchering was swift; they took only what they thought they could preserve. Flies gathered from nowhere and the red earth claimed the ox's blood. Within days the ox's white bones would attest to his journey. The remaining two oxen were unperturbed as they passed what was left of Sweetheart. Toot and his sons rotated turns hefting the empty yoke and the going was slow, but they reached Greta and the children before dark.

The wagon train families had contributed two bibles, two chamber pots, a butter churn, eleven children's books, an ornate mirror, a cage of four half grown kittens, three dogs, one lame, one deaf, one just a puppy and Mrs. Bly had donated one of her two cows.

A note written in the Captain's hand said:

"A cow has been known to tolerate being yoked to an ox for a short while.
We wish you well and God bless you all,
William Hardy.

For sixty-three days, the closing of each day had been accompanied by the sounds of parents comforting children and each other, expletives quickly shushed, gentle laughter, a call, a reply, songs and prayers. For sixty-three nights, the Magroots circled their wagon with the others and Toot, Caleb and Hiram took their turns as part of the night watch. Missing now was the ring of tools hammering metal wheel rims. Missing was a neighbor offering a cup of hot black coffee strong enough to mask the foul taste of water. Missing was the pooled light of a dozen campfires.

Sweetheart's right loin sizzled in the fire as Greta took

buckets of water from the pool, filled a washbasin and scrubbed each of the younger children with strong lye soap. Dirty water was tipped onto the earth and a fresh bucket was added as needed. They used the last of their buffalo chips and gathered sage, scrub, and whatever scraps of wood they could find to keep the fire burning through the night. The horses and mules were hobbled, the oxen were left free as they habitually stayed close and the cow was tied to the wagon and seemed to be unperturbed by the strips of Sweetheart's meat that hung from a line stretched between a wagon roof bow and a cotton wood tree. The kittens and dogs crept about for a while and then settled next to the warmth of human bodies. As the sky darkened, the Magroots, including baby Tobias, lowered their voices and gathered close.

Sweetheart sustained them that evening and children, adults, cats and dogs ate their fill, but after providing their supper, Sweetheart beckoned to the night creatures and Toot and Hiram, Greta and Caleb, took turns until dawn keeping watch, conscious of a waiting presence that settled just beyond the light of their campfire. When it was Hiram's turn to sleep, he sought Eliza who slept on her side, curled around her baby brother. When Hiram saw she had moved his bedroll next to hers, his heart swelled and he paused a moment to watch the firelight flicker across the curve of her cheek and disappear into her coal black hair. He moved his bedding so Tobias lay between them and stretched his arm over the baby's sleeping form to rest his hand protectively on Eliza. He fell asleep quickly, feeling very much a man at sixteen.

It wasn't until the sky began to lighten in the east that Toot felt he could relax his guard and allow his exhaustion to pull him down into sleep. In less than two hours, he awoke to Greta's gentle hand offering him a cup of tea. He sat up and pulled his blanket tightly around him in the morning chill.

"The water is sweet, my love. I have made tea," she said as she brushed his hair from his forehead. "I scraped the jar and managed to get a last spoon of honey."

He looked up at her with eyes so dry he could only open them slightly until he became accustomed to the pain.

Greta reached into her pocket for a pot of comfrey ointment and crouched down beside him, using her index finger to apply a thin coating to his cracked lips. She pulled his left hand from the cup he was clutching and examined the nails. They were grey, dry, several split to the quick. The nail of his second finger was just beginning to reform after being torn off the week before as he hobbled the mules for the night. She applied more precious ointment to the nails and a wound that lay open on his palm.

Greta had married this man when she was a girl of nineteen, two years older than he. When Toot was a child, his parents and brother and sister died of cholera. He had no papers to verify his existence, and when asked the origin of his name, he searched for an answer. His family had called him 'The Little Toot' until at age six, he requested they call him just plain 'Toot.' For several days, he had to endure 'Just Plain Toot' until they tired of the joke, and after that he was merely 'Toot.'

When the cholera epidemic that claimed his family joined forces with diphtheria and scarlet fever, so many died that no one paid attention to a child alone. A child of eleven, hungry, so numb that he barely felt afraid, Toot wandered into a blacksmith's shop where he found work and shelter and what passed for friendship from the taciturn blacksmith. He slept in the shop, warm in the winter, too hot in the summer. He fueled the forge, held horses to be shod, fetched tools, swept coals and ran errands. He learned the art of shoeing a horse and an ox and of forming weapons, tools, and kitchenware. For his fifteenth birthday, the blacksmith gave him his own set of farrier tools and a musket.

On a hot summer day in his sixteenth year, Toot heard a sound like a puff of the bellows tempered with a groan and turned to find the blacksmith deflated upon the floor between the forge and the anvil. Toot knelt by his side, offering to get the doctor but the blacksmith begged him to stay and held his arm so tightly, Toot sat on the floor and waited until the great meaty hand relaxed its grip and his only friend passed from life.

Since the blacksmith had no family and few friends beyond Toot, and not knowing what else to do, the boy kept the shop open. One Saturday morning, Greta arrived with a horse for re-shoeing and stayed through the afternoon, sharing her lunch. Her interest in his craft surprised and gratified him and he enjoyed her questions. She looked him directly in the eye as she spoke, not bold but assured, confident. He watched her as she moved about the shop examining a series of ornamental hooks and knobs he worked on in his spare time. She was as slender as a young boy but the mass of light brown hair gathered loosely at her nape with a ribbon, the gold rings through her ear lobes and the smile that played across her lips reminded him of dreams he had some nights when he hungered for a woman and a life beyond the small town where his family died and a blacksmith saved him.

He showed her how to heat a slender iron rod, how to draw out a small length to bend into a shape that would hold a candle. Before she made her leave, they shared a pot of tea and she told him of her family, the distant cousin she was supposed to marry but wouldn't and he told her of the family he once had but could hardly remember. She reached for his hand before she left and brought it briefly to her lips then grabbed her horse's reins and a fistful of mane and swung herself effortlessly into the saddle. Smiling down at him, she took the candleholder he held up to her and tucked it in her bag. She trotted away down the path, leaving him far lonelier than she had found him.

When the following morning, she knocked on his door with a picnic basket in one hand and a canvas sack for collecting *herbs slung across her shoulder, and for the first time in his life, Sunday became more than a day of rest. Three weeks later, after a lunch of bread, cheese and apples, they wandered through a wood collecting comfrey, peppermint and blue cohosh. In a sunlit clearing, Toot caught Greta's hand and pulled her down on top of him. Caleb was conceived in a heat more consuming, more intense than any Toot had experienced at the blacksmith's forge.*

As he lay spent inside her for the third time within the hour, Greta asked. "If I am with child, will you marry me?"

"Of course, he will," whispered Heidi. "He knows he owes you his life."

Toot appeared to consider her question as she watched him gravely, then he laughed, "I will do more than marry you, with child or without. When you open your eyes each morning, I will be there. You will close your eyes each night with me by your side." He felt a great weight had lifted and he buried his face in her hair so she would not see his tears.

In truth, it was Greta who usually arose first to prepare for the day, and she would answer his call with the reassurance that she was near.

Now, nineteen years to the very day after their marriage, and almost two thousand miles away from where they first met, Toot and Greta sat together in the cold light of dawn, by a red dirt path that led way from the Oregon Trail.

"The children?" Toot asked hoarsely, his throat beginning to relax from the heat of the tea.

"They are sleeping still. Hiram lies with Eliza, baby Tobias in between."

Toot considered this. "They are very young."

"Not much younger than we were. My father gave his blessing."

Toot chuckled. "We can thank Caleb for that."

"And I do. Without Caleb, you may have wandered away."

"Never. I belonged to you from the moment you knocked on my door and laid claim to me," Toot said and he opened his blanket to pull her in. Greta nestled in her husband's lap. She gathered his beard in her hands and twisted it into a brush, which she played over her cheeks, her forehead, her lips. He wrapped his arms around her, enjoying her warmth, her smell of herbs and ointments, lye soap and dust. He ran his hands over her breasts, his calluses catching in the wool of her blouse, and rested his lips on her neck. He was too tired for more, weary to his very core. He held her close and drew comfort from the familiar, strong little body that had borne him seven children who lived and two who had not.

Greta leaned back and sighed, "Talk to Hiram. He will wait I think, but not long. Life is hard in this land and they care for and desire each other. I have talked to Eliza to be sure. They will be together. You have seen it too."

"I have."

They watched one of the dogs, the lame one, sit up from where she had settled between the twins. She stretched, yawned and staggered slightly. She regarded the mist clinging to the surface of the pool and limped to the shore. Her soft, rapid lapping made a tender, cupping sound. She emerged from the mist and walked toward the wagon. Sweetheart's remains shifted uneasily on the line as the wind gusted from the south. The dog raised her head and sniffed the air hopefully, wagging her tail. Greta called and held out her hand. The dog lowered her head and came to join them, her uneven gait giving her a graceful rocking motion. She had been lame a long time, perhaps since birth.

"She will have puppies soon," said Greta. "Many dogs fought over her on the trail. Look from the side how her teats begin to swell. "

"And life continues . . ." murmured Toot.

Greta turned her face up to him. "We will find our home

today. This will be a good place for us."

He grinned at her. "Do you feel it in your bones? In these tiny little bird bones of yours?" he teased, his hand circling her delicate wrist.

"In my very bones, I do. In my heart, in my fibers, in my toes I feel it." She smiled, enjoying his hand around her wrist, his teasing.

The Oregon Trail was a night behind them, the dream of the Willamette Valley fading. They would settle by Captain Hardy's fresh water springs at the foot of the snowcapped mountains, perhaps six hours hence. They would build a home in a high prairie meadow, so very unlike the green, lush meadows of Pennsylvania.

Captain Hardy had spoken of a narrow canyon a mile from the springs. Trappers named it Wild Horse Valley and it was rumored that a Palomino Ghost Horse emerged from the valley on the night of a full moon, sometimes alone, sometimes with several mares and young. When the night held no moon, smaller animals came to sit at the mouth of the canyon and regard the prairie with their red eyes.

"Trappers have been known to spin tales," the Captain had mused. "Probably haunted by the spirits of the animals they have skinned."

The canyon offered trees that would provide wood for building, and rocks. A narrow trail led up the canyon to a lake.

"Don't settle by the lake," the Captain cautioned. "Trails on the northeast side lead to land occupied by Arapaho and Shoshone people. A granite peak on that side of the lake is considered sacred ground. I have heard there's a small rattlesnake, smaller than the Prairie Rattler, but with a poison much stronger. It is a peaceful animal but hard to see as its color fades with time. It lives at the base of the peak and there's probably a legend about it, but I don't know it."

The Captain had given Toot a knowing look and said, "Your Greta will come to learn it." And Toot nodded. He had no doubt.

"Make your peace with the Arapaho and Shoshone if you choose to settle on this side of their mountains," the Captain had advised. *"If you can gain their trust, they may help you. They are wise in the ways of this land and they know how to live a good life here. Show them you can learn, share what you have and you will gain their respect. You will need it."*

***

Heidi closed the little book and released a long breath of air. She believed every word. The ghosts of those who had abandoned the Oregon Trail to find refuge at the base of the Wind River Mountains had used Ruth to bring them to life. Toot's Lucky Thirteen, they had passed those cabins today. The little rattlesnake had been on the bulletin board in Lake Cheynook's parking lot, and Wild Horse Valley—Booker McNabb, who had arrived on a motorcycle from Pennsylvania, now lived there.

She looked at her watch, an hour past midnight. She got up and walked outside with Gering into a blustery night. She had forgotten to turn off the fountain when she got home and it was still running. Ray would have to insist his next tenant take care of the fountain because the birds had come to depend on it. She held out her hands to capture some of the water as it fell and bent down to offer Gering a drink. He took a polite lick before trotting off for a short sniff around.

"You leave that killdeer nest alone," Heidi called, smiling as Gering smoothly changed course, as if he'd had no intention of alarming the little bird.

Above the stars shone as brilliant points of light in a cold, clear blue-black sky. She would miss this backyard and the plants she had tended for seven years. She would miss Saint Gemma's and its mission, the McKees and the kitchen crew, but she and the twins had found their home today. She faced the direction she knew Comfrey to lie and held her arms wide to embrace a wind that swept down from the Wind River Range. Her name whispered behind her, a light touch on her back . . . she knew if she turned, she would see no one.

"Hello, Feather Friend," she said softly.

Someday she would tell Amadeus, Nara spoke to her too.

ACKNOWLEDGMENTS

I am grateful for the support and encouragement of family and friends in writing this novel.

In particular:

Marilyn Negip, who tirelessly reviewed my chapters and believed in my characters.

Ana Manwaring, author and teacher, who helped me to find in my voice—and others in her class, especially Dana, Dina, Guy, Nick, Julie and Barbra.

Janet Wallace, who dropped everything to accompany me to Wyoming and walked Independence Rock with me.

Frank No Runner and his colleagues on the Wind River Reservation, who shared their time and insights.

And my wonderful, inspiring students—those who came to love Biology as much as I, and those who did not. You will always have a place in my heart. A special thanks to Anke Hamsen, who kindly checked my German. Any errors are mine.

I am not acknowledging, my husband, Chuck Granata, because he told me not to. For most of my life he has been my fellow adventurer and he truly is a mighty good man.

ABOUT ATMOSPHERE PRESS

Atmosphere Press is an independent, full-service publisher for excellent books in all genres and for all audiences. Learn more about what we do at atmospherepress.com.

We encourage you to check out some of Atmosphere's latest releases, which are available at Amazon.com and via order from your local bookstore:

Tales of Little Egypt, a historical novel by James Gilbert

An Ambiguous Grief, a memoir by Dominique Hunter

For a Better Life, a novel by Julia Reid Galosy

The Hidden Life, a novel by Robert Castle

Nothing to Get Nostalgic About, a novel by Eddie Brophy

Whose Mary Kate, a novel by Jane Leclere Doyle

Stuck and Drunk in Shadyside, a novel by M. Byerly

These Things Happen, a novel by Chris Caldwell

Geometry of Fire, nonfiction by Paul Warmbier

The Dark Secrets of Barth and Williams College: A Comedy in Two Semesters, a novel by Glen Weissenberger

Lucid_Malware.zip, poetry by Dylan Sonderman

The Glorious Between, a novel by Doug Reid*

ABOUT THE AUTHOR

Daphne Birkmyer was born overseas and travelled extensively before settling in California. Her degrees in Biology and Education led to a career in teaching and continue to exert their influence in her written work. She lives in the Napa Valley with her family, dogs and tortoises. She is currently working on book two of the COMFREY, WYOMING series.

Visit her at www.daphnebirkmyer.com

CPSIA information can be obtained
at www.ICGtesting.com
Printed in the USA
BVHW031148091220
595277BV00008B/136

9 781636 495408